INTO THE REALM

To Maryellen

Thank you

Todd Forres

INTO THE REALM

TODD FORREST

Todd Forrest
INTO THE REALM

All rights reserved
Copyright © 2022 by Todd Forrest

Published by BooxAi
ISBN: 978-965-578-015-4

CONTENTS

BOOK I

BOOK II

BOOK III

BOOK 1

"Sunset and evening star
and one clear call for me.
And may there be
no moaning of the bar
when I put out to sea."

sailor shanty

THE BLUFF

From out of a deep blue haze of time, I come awake on a patch of lumpy crabgrass, looking up at the worn tread of a tractor tire swaying above me like a clock weight. The tire is attached to a knotted tangle of frayed hemp running up to a deep grove notched in the former hitching limb of our South Seas pagoda tree. I reach for the tire and hook my right arm through its center. Pushing with my heel-ends against the mossy ground, I rise upwards and back, then swing out over an arching bluff. My body extends above a distant tidal wash littered with barrier rocks and the decayed remnants of a long-ago wharf. The fingers on my right hand stretch the tire's lower lip, forming a drooping scream within its gaping maw, and for that one instant I am flying, attached to neither sea nor landmass, and there is no sound, like being inside a vacuum.

The world beneath me has rotated another thousand feet on its axis with the Earth itself having raced another twelve miles around its ellipse of the sun. Yet I have not moved. I am floating, Godlike, held aloft by a combination of velocity and something else that I'm about to put my finger on when the ever-reliable tug of crumbling rubber slings me back across the bluff and onto the lumpy sod.

"I hope to be at least sixty before that rickety old tire finally gives out," I say to myself.

Tall beach grass whips about my knees as I walk out onto our bluff and stand on its precipice. Fresh sea air abounds as I caress my whiskery gullet. Raking back my rust-colored topknot with my nicked and battered hands, I look down at our small harbor that sparkles as if strewn with Christmas tinsel. It's a view I never tire of: the swollen girth of the bay spreading to the horizon with its many small islands encapsulated within a thin strip of barrier beach. Beyond that, the frothing North Atlantic, or whom I like to call Second Mother, whose booming surf plays eternally in my mind. I've listened to Her flirt with Her landlocked lover since birth. I even hear Her when I'm pulling crab pots north of the Aleutians. She's rhythmic, never-ending, with an almost percussionist-like cadence.

There's a thunderous bass that sounds when She comes crashing to shore. Followed by a thrumming of cymbals as She carries up the beach. And it is the tinkling of wind chimes that I hear when She finally lifts Her creamy skirt and bashfully recedes, knowing that one day She'll bury Her landlocked lover within Her kelp-laced smock only to have His future landmass rise up and toss Her back into Her depths, forever and ever repeating.

I feel lucky to have grown up on this bluff. The view from its precipice always strikes the back of my eyes. It is the same seascape eight generations of Forrest men and women have looked out at, and yet it remains new to me with each viewing. The bluff itself rises some sixty feet above our small harbor beach, where the now half-sunken wharf once fastened many a great schooner and whaling ship to its pilings. I continue to look out over the bay, watching the morning sun rise in the East to pull out the tide and make a frothy chop to call in the gulls.

"Good time to let out," I mutter.

I turn my back on the azure splendor aswirl beneath me and start up the sloping hillside, the sorry bones in my feet cracking and popping from standing too many hours on steel decks, and yet I have just turned twenty-two, though my years working in the world of men having aged me. My head feels groggy, not knowing if I slept for a minute, a month, or a millennium. I must have jumped ship the night before, or was it the night before that? I cannot seem to recall, other than it is possible that I tied one on with the captain and crew, no doubt at the Chatham Squire, before passing out at the base of our pagoda tree. But it is of no importance as I mount a slight rise and come upon the ship's bell mounted atop a fieldstone marker.

There's no inscription on the bell, inside or out, and nobody knows how old it is or what ship it came from, not even my grandfather, and he knows everything, or at least I used to believe that he did. Taking a knee, I tip the bell sideways, and grab hold of its copper clapper; then, releasing the bell, I let go of the clapper and send deep-bellied tolls reverberating across the bay. I do this to let Gramp know I'm in port, so he can tidy up some before my arrival.

Coming over the first knoll, I catch sight of our dueling weather-vanes turning listlessly in the light, hilltop breeze. Mimicking an in-flight harpoon angling downward at a breaching sperm whale. The vanes, made from hammered tin, are positioned at each end of the house with a widow's walk conjoining the two. The 'perch' was put up so the women of the house could look out over the marine layer to see the tall ships as they sailed for port and thus get a head start to the taverns to drag their men home lest any debauchery be committed on their long-awaited return from the sea.

Not that my forefathers went unawares. Those seadogs knew their women as well as their woman knew them. So, whenever a long voyage deemed a reward of village grog, Captains Forrest would tie up in Wellfleet Harbor on the Cape Cod Bay side or, if they really wanted a scurrilous night ashore, they'd lash their lines to the fish-littered piers of Provincetown, or Hell town as it was known in those days, a place where the crew could gamble away their wages and hopefully get in a knife fight or two. Mostly though, Captains Forrest would sail in and tie up at the Chatham Fish Pier, where they would unload their catch, get paid, and return home, choosing the comfort of their women over any vile-tasting village grog.

I summit the last knoll and the house proper comes into view. With its storm shutters hanging at odd angles and roof and sides cloaked in silvery, weathered shingles with patches missing, the house appears to be abandoned, and it is in a way with only me and Gramp residing. I would fix it up if I had the time, but I'm mostly at sea these days. Truth be told, I would rather raze it all and start anew, only the house has been around a while, and I'd no doubt need an Act of Congress to replace the gutters, the Chatham Historical Society being who they are.

To Gramp, the house is a living mausoleum dedicated to those who went before, but to me, it's a place where hallways dip and roll under your feet like a carnival fun house, with doors that won't close properly and windows that let in drafts that chill to the bone come winter. And yet, with its sad and crooked smile, I am always heartened when come upon her, as I am on this day, in the Year of Our Lord 1988.

Approaching the house, I am again reminded of how every board, beam, and brick has a story to tell. It's a known fact that the side of the house facing the bay once served in the British Royal Navy. The story goes that, during the War of 1812, an English gunboat dropped anchor in Nauset Harbor with captain and crew going ashore to drink grog in what they believed to be a Tory-friendly tavern in Eastham, and it was on that same night that my long-ago relations rowed out to the ship and cut its anchor line.

Upon their return in the early, predawn light, the brigade found their ship listing on her beam-ends, run aground on Barley Neck. Realizing their plight, they marched through the streets of Chatham with their muskets cocked and loaded, listening to the townspeople snicker at them from behind closed curtains. Walking along the darkened edges of the King's Highway, now Route 6A, the brigade finally met up with a band of truly sympathetic Tories and boarded another British warship anchored safely off Blish Point in Barnstable Harbor. The Eastham tavern boys took the masts and sails with the men of the Forrest clan taking the rest, leaving only the ship's bones to bleach in the sun and salt. In other words, it was business as usual on Cape Cod's Outer Reach.

Fact was, much of the wood used for building houses in Chatham in those days came from the various schooners and frigates that would break apart on the ever-shifting shoals along the Cape's 'Backside' whenever a hurricane or nor'easter hit, the timber and cargo carried by the wind and waves to the shore where area Mooncussers, like my forefathers, would hitch up their wagon teams and drag the booty across the moonlit dunes, never exchanging a word.

"The Dark Work" is how Gramp refers to it, saying to me once, "And if any of 'em poor scullions washed up on our harbor beach, you can bet their graves would'a been dug deep. This I know because every Forrest would want the same for his remains should he go over the side one day. Ain't no sin to take what the sea offers, Caleb. Sin is not to take it. That don't mean you should light a bonfire and dance around a-hoopin' and a-hollerin'. No! You take what you need and make use of it! That-a-way the circle continues as it will when your day comes, many, many sunups from now."

Brick, blood, and bone is how Gramp sees the house, and as I hike up the last knoll, I quicken my pace, fighting back the gnawing memory of a murder I committed on this very soil one year ago to the day, only I don't see it as 'murder,' per se, but rather 'survival of the fittest,' and I believe Darwin would agree.

VALHALLA

I jaunt up to our back porch and pole-vault over its two missing steps by way of a whaler's gaff, then pull myself up with the help of an overhanging, deadeye block. The porch has seen better days, or it hasn't. The same two steps have been missing as long as I've been alive. The porch itself sits about four feet off the ground on salvaged railroad ties, as does the rest of the house, and there is no cellar. A Wash-A-Shore might believe the house was built this way to let the King tides that we get from time-to-time flow underneath. But given the fact the house sits on an elevated bluff and is protected by a nine-mile barrier beach, this simply is not the case. Essentially, the stilts provide a way for the massive dune creeping across our front lawn to blow into the bay without taking the house with it. Not many building codes existed when the house was first raised. "Back then," as Gramp likes to say, "folks just improvised."

The primary structure was once a stately manor anchored to the cobblestoned streets of Nantucket; the island our family's patriarch called home when not hunting the elusive leviathans east of the Azores. Around the time the mighty humpback and sperm were dipping into near extinction, whaleboat captain Nehemiah Forrest, or Captain Nehi, as he was known in ports the world over, shipped every board, brick, and nail across Nantucket Sound to Chatham's grassy hillocks, with his many descendants adding rooms here, stairs there, and carpentered scrollwork everywhere.

My long-ago grandfather had foreseen the demise of whaling and moved his growing family to Cape Cod, where he'd purchased six-hundred-plus acres of rolling swath land for next to nothing. As a child I had a hard time understanding the reason behind such an epic move and would ask Gramp why the good captain didn't just build another home here.

"Where'd him and his brood suppose ta' live? In a thatch hut under a maypole? 'Tweren't no trees back in those days. Most of 'em cut down for buildin' the shipyards and salt works and such. Captain Nehi had his'self a vision to farm this land, which he done, till the last of his kin turned their backs on 'im and went to sea. And what good it do 'cept get us all killed with not a body to bury 'cept for our women, the poor darlin's all dead from broken hearts."

As a small boy, I always loved it when Gramp talked like a pirate, but what he said back then was mostly true. Those buried in our family plot are mostly women, along with the occasional infant who wouldn't even garner a holystone, only a Plus One when mother and child died together in the birthing chamber. The real reason, however, that the men of the Forrest clan went to work behind the ship's wheel, wasn't so much the Call of the Sea, it was because the land purchased by Captain Nehi sat atop a shell midden created by generations of Monomoyick Indians dating back five thousand years. So, wherever an ancestor chose to sink his plow, a river of broken oyster and clamshell was sure to see the light of day, thus making the soil all but impossible to till.

The good captain was not one to give up easily, however. Instead of planting cash crops like corn and potato, which needed a foot or more soil to grow, he spread about sunflower seeds that could grow in any type of soil, shallow or otherwise. Once planted, however, the rest was deemed woman's work.

In those days, the men living on the Outer Cape who remained on dry land either tended sheep, dried and cured fish, made bricks, or blew glass. Being the proud descendants of a Nantucket whaleboat captain, this simply would not do. So, my many great-uncles and cousins eventually all shipped out, only to freeze in the riggings high above the Hudson, get dragged down by giant sperms in the Pacific, become enslaved by the din of Algiers off the coast of Madeira or, if they did survive the rigors of a nomadic life at sea, they plain never came back.

There are tales of Forrest men staking gold claims in the Yukon and of one relation becoming a tribal king in the Solomon Islands. The latter eventually butchered when he failed to meet the tribe's daily catch expectations. His barely legible marker still exists on an outlying atoll, or so says Gramp, the tombstone reading:

Her'n Lays Jaab Forrest

A True Pagan!
With No Hope of Redemption!
Beware!

The tombstone was carved by a Spanish missionary who had landed on the atoll in the winter of 1822 and is said to lie next to my great-uncle in an unmarked grave topped with empty coconut husks.

Some might believe these lives wasted, but I do not, and I can prove it. There aren't many families on this sandy spit who can boast of having a collection of shrunken heads once attached to Māori tribesmen, or that ours was the first and only family to land a kangaroo ashore. For weeks the large marsupial terrified every dog in town, until the local constable came to our front stoop and shot the roo dead for biting off the nose of a Quaker bishop.

"Damnable bishop showed up at our front stoop one morn demanding your great-grandpap, Jeb Forrest, pay his town-ordered church tax, and when the clergyman wouldn't leave our parlor door, after Jeb tellin' him to 'go smoke a pipe,' Old Jeb sicked Roo on 'im! Now that Roo was a mean son-of-a-gopher, and if it were not for the bishop's gold crucifix getting caught up in its maw, Roo would have bitten his head clean off! I only wish I was there to see his expression. I bet that stiff-necked, hymn-bellowin' Come-Outer thought it was the devil his'self let loose from the Netherworld! Old

Jeb never did pay that town-ordered church tax," Gramp likes to reminisce.

Setting aside the hinge-less screen door, I call out, "Hey, Gramp! It's me! I'm home!" Getting no answer, I call out again. "Hey, Gramp! Are you here or what?" Giving up, I hurry through the kitchen and head for the pantry, kicking away empty cans of Narragansett beer as I go. With walls constructed of horsehair and oyster shell plaster, the pantry is the oldest room in the house, dating back to when it was a sheepherder's cabin. Captain Nehi liked what he saw when he first walked the land and put his Nantucket house down around it, preserving this room and the beehive ovens in the kitchen. Upon entering the pantry, I run my right hand over our long, beach-wood cutting table, stained red from past family feasts. I have a hard time remembering the last one.

There aren't many of us left these days. It's just Gramp and me, far as I know. I would like to have had siblings, only my parents never got around to it. They didn't have time; both having died at a relatively young age. Gramp likes to talk about me one day filling the house with screeching rug rats, but all I ever wanted was to strike out on my own. Only I can't. Not yet. I have to take care of Gramp and keep paying down our delinquent town property tax. Either that or get another Roo.

Before entering the house proper, I pass under a plank of worm-eaten driftwood brought back from a long-ago marooning, on which our family motto is written:

'MAN PRAYS ON HIS KNEES WHILST HIS SALVATION LIES IN HIS HANDS'

I can only imagine what it must have been like sitting on that lonely atoll whittling away and dreaming of rescue. But why the good captain wrote what he did, I haven't a clue. The motto has always been a yoke around my neck, like Captain Nehi wrote it for me, a disenfranchised fisherman whose wealth surrounds him and yet whose belongings he can neither sell nor take a profit from.

Sliding the pantry doors apart, I enter a labyrinth of interconnecting hallways that thread through the house like ruptured arteries: doors ajar, bleeding dust-covered relics, old newspaper piled high for some future avalanche, along with other doors that are locked shut, the rusted hinges providing afterlife storage for their long-ago tenants. I step under an archway of seaman's gear left behind by past boat crews that, were it to collapse on me, I'd be completely buried, and it would take pirate captain William Kidd himself to dig me out. Only the mice would know me, intimately I'm sure.

Many a day have I had our International Harvester lashed and loaded with musty rugs, blistered and battered furniture, broken appliances, and empty parrot cages, only to have Gramp lean from his bedroom window and shout down, "That's our history you're mucking with! Let it be and I'll let you be!" Cursing under my breath, I'd drive the IH coughing and stalling back into the barn.

Continuing down a Z-shaped hallway, I pass a decades-old lobster trap encased in petrified sea lettuce and smelling of rotten fish. I intend to take the trap outside and burn it after I get back from my visit with the ranger, Gramp's protestations be damned! I haven't seen the ranger since my hasty exit on a misty night over a year ago. He lives in a cabin on the southernmost tip of the Monomoy Island Wildlife Sanctuary. We have some unfinished business to discuss, and I want it to be a surprise. I have my reasons.

Looking down, I spot a coiled loop of braided hemp lying under a moth-eaten spool of sailcloth. I pick it up and check the line for tension, finding the line to be salt-encrusted and stiff, so much so that it would take a mule team pulling from both ends to straighten it. Having no use for it aboard my boat, I drop the line and let it sit for another century, then continue onward through the clutter.

I round a tight corner and our Grand Hall comes into view. I named the hall "Valhalla" after our Viking ancestry, though I'm not sure we go back that far, but I like to think that we do. Taking up the center of the house, the hall rises three stories to where chunks of coral taken from the world's great oceans gather dust amid the crisscrossed rafters. It's a massive assemblage of board and beam resembling what Noah's ark must have looked like belowdecks, only without the animals. Though we do have a few cats whom Gramp calls his 'familiars' that prowl about the house without need of attention or feeding. The cats are a special breed of Siamese that have a diamond-shaped spot on their foreheads with litters going back to the Grand Palace of Siam.

I look above me to where a narrow gangplank runs along the second story in a boxlike formation past small, single bedrooms the size and shape of shipboard saloons. The rooms are uninhabited now, but that wasn't always the case. In the past they were let out to foreign-born fishermen and those hired on to help with the harvest when the house was part of a working farm. Closing my eyes, I can almost picture how it was: the constant clamoring up and down the gangplank, the tall tales told in foreign tongues, the exotic spices of which to salivate over wafting from the beehive ovens. What rouses there must have been and revelry after a bountiful harvest or a successful trip at sea! I was lucky to have caught the tail end of it when I was a boy.

My father, Captain 'Mad' Jack Forrest, would quarter his crew when dragging the bay for scallops, and I recall how it was when we had a full house: the manly jousting and jawing, getting passed from one strong hand to the next, then set atop a butcher's block and fed raw scallops by the grimy handful. I'd often thought of letting out the rooms to tourists and summer workers, but that would only invite building inspectors, fire marshals, and such, and we don't need that.

It's as quiet as a graveside funeral as I cross the cedar floorboards scarred with aged patina. Approaching our two-sided hearth, built of staggered brickwork in which a man can stand, I reach onto the rose-wood mantle and take down a sepia-tinted photograph of my mother, framed in sterling silver. I never knew her, my mother, she having passed from viral pneumonia soon after I was born, except for the stories my father would tell of how a Charlestown girl of southern aristocracy ignored her parents' pleas and married a long liner from the Cape, even going to sea with him on occasion.

"That woman could gut and clean a fish faster than any man I had on board, including me," my father would say before falling silent.

"Seems all of us Forrest men are good for is putting our women in the ground before their time," Gramp would glumly add.

Having no way of knowing my mother, I rarely give her much thought except when I look at her picture. Dressed in all white, as she will always be in my mind, with long black hair pulled back in a fashionable braid of the times. The woman in the picture is small-boned with a pretty face which is unrecognizable to me, but for her eyes, which are sloping and deep-set as are mine, though I don't know their true color.

Replacing the picture, I recross Valhalla breathing in the musty odor of Persian rugs in need of a good beating. An octagonal table, once used for spreading maps, sits on top of the rugs like some kind of sacrificial altar. Broad in circumference, the table takes up the center of the hall, surrounded by a circular bookcase holding the great works of their day. Most are first editions and written in their native tongue. I've read the majority, but there's always a literary treasure waiting to be dusted off and discovered. I let my right hand run over the back of our Spanish leather couch, bruised with age yet heavy in its austerity. While doing so, I pass under a ship's figurehead jutting out from the north wall.

The 'Sea Witch' is cloaked in a short chemise accentuating a swollen bosom. She was rescued by Captain Nehi after the taking an English gunboat while privateering for the colonies. And though she belonged to a British warship, the beguiler looks more like a Native American princess than she does a London pub maiden, which is why I'd taken to calling her 'Poca,' after John Smith's Pocahontas. Whenever I'd pass beneath her, she'd always return my smile. Passing beneath her on this day, however, Poca appears strangely aloof and fails to give me her blessing.

Whaleboat captains of yesteryear are thought of today as daring and adventurous, but in their time, they were considered a scurrilous sort along with their crews. "Bottom of the Barrel" was how the Admiralty referred to them, but I've been told Captain Nehi was different. He was an explorer before he changed his sails over to whaling, so he knew the value of a fast, clean ship, and he had a brother. That's where my family tree gets a bit cloudy. According to Gramp, rumor had it the brother sailed with Captain Cook when he rounded the Horn, and he had mapped his own charts in the South Seas before returning to the Cape and becoming a pirate, buccaneering many a Dutch, Moorish, French, and English vessel.

He supposedly ended his days languishing on the shores of the Ile Sainte-Marie, also known as the 'Island of Wanted Men,' located off the coast of Madagascar, and his name has been banished from the family's history ever since. I don't know it and neither has Gramp ever been told, though tales of him have sifted down through the generations even though the subject has always been taboo. One of these days I plan on taking a trip to the island and making a search of the cemeteries. Someone should say a few words over the poor sod. Hopefully, I'll find my great-uncle and spill some rum over his grave and perhaps toss down a Spanish doubloon or two.

I start up the spiral metal staircase, itself salvaged from a captured WWI German U-boat stowed at Groton's Naval Shipyards, where Gramp worked as a welder. Once a Mooncusser, always a Mooncusser! Stepping onto the narrow gangplank, I head for my room and am about to enter when an oblong object catches my eye. Placing both hands on the railing, I peer across the hall at a large oil painting hanging askew on the far wall, and although there are many such paintings adorning the house, I've never had the inclination to study this particular painting. It's like I'm seeing it for the first time. Although I do recall Gramp saying to me the painting was completed in the early 1800s by an artist who may have been a relation, but we'll never know because it went unsigned.

The painting appears larger than I remember it, more lifelike and grandiose. From my vantage point on the gangplank, I make the sailor to be a young man, perhaps my age, though his back is to the viewer with his face obscured, looking up at his wind-bent mast. Standing atop the stern, the sailor appears to be pushing the tiller to port using his left foot, with the mainsheet wrapped tightly around his right forearm. A sudden flash of lightning illuminates the sailor's profile, and I can now make out the beginnings of a right eye socket along with the outline of a pronounced Roman nose. I notice the mains'l flutter near the masthead and I believe that I see a plume of sea spray break over the bow. More chain lightning flashes within the painting, followed by a delayed thunderclap. I tighten my grip on the railing and watch in denial as the sailor's lone eyeball sweeps across the hall before locking its gaze on me.

I step away from the railing and pinch the bridge of my nose to clear my vision. Reopening my eyes, I see the painting how it actually is, only smaller and completely inanimate, with the sailor's identity remaining obscured. It's a neat trick and I'll have to remember it when I have more time, but to be honest, the reality of it leaves me a little seasick, and I never get seasick.

Any and all nausea leaves me as I step into my bedroom and draw open the curtains. It's not much of a room, and I wouldn't call it grand, but it's the only bedroom I've ever known except for the numberless pits I've bunked in whenever I'm at sea. I catch my reflection on my dresser's attached mirror and stare at the ghostlike apparition looking back at me from within the foggy glass. I see that I'm not so tall, but rather on the short side, with a ruddy, sunbaked complexion from working long hours abovedecks. My hair has grown long and now balls about my shoulders from my year at sea, and I have a high bridge that I wouldn't call Roman.

I'm not hard to look at, or at least I'm unique in appearance, and you wouldn't know it by my wiry frame, but I'm as strong as a Flemish coil. The blood coursing through my veins seems to want to shoot from my fingertips, and I've often thought that if I were to grab a fistful of topknot, I could lift myself in the air and hold myself suspended indefinitely. It's the kind of strength my father had, and Gramp has still and he's pushing eighty. A family trait, you might say. It helps when I'm hauling hundred-pound gill net over the sides, but other than fishing, I've never had much use for it until a year ago. Only it wasn't my strength that failed me, it was my conscience, and it's been eating away at me every day since. What's done is done, I keep telling myself and hopefully, after my meeting with the ranger, I'll start to believe it.

I go to the sea chest at the foot of my bed and open it. I expected to find my oilskins folded neatly inside, only the chest was empty. I must have left them behind when I jumped ship last night, or was it the night before? Again, I don't remember. No matter as the sun is up, the air balmy, and the July seas warm enough to take a plunge. What I will need on this day is my speargun that I find under my bed where I put it the night I hastily shipped out. Using great care, I bring the loaded gun up to sight and, cautiously unhooking the titanium-tipped spear from its aluminum housing, pull the trigger and release the vulcanized rubber slingshot, letting it slap harmlessly at the dusty air. Sheathing the spear in its webbed carryall with its five siblings, I grab my spare seabag and leave the room, closing the bedroom door as I found it.

Running down the spiral staircase, I recross Valhalla and take a sharp turn into Gramp's storied Chart Room. Slipping around a large, standing globe, showing how the world once looked to seventeenth-century navigators, I sneak up to Gramp's rolltop desk and take down his antique spyglass from its top slot. I'm not really sneaking per se, but I always feel that I am, and if I were to call the spyglass an antique in front of Gramp, he'd likely rap me over the head with it. I loop the brass chain over my head and let the spyglass dangle from my neck as I leave the room, making sure to close the door lest any of Gramp's familiars gets inside and spray his precious charts. It's the only room in the house they're not allowed.

Reentering the kitchen, I am again struck by the squalor in which we bachelors allow ourselves to live: dirty dishes stacked in the sink to the point of overflowing, tiles stained brown, cupboards chipped and peeling, etc. Gramp tries to tidy up some, but it's just not in him. He was a well-respected ship's captain after all, and he's getting on in years. What the house needs is a woman's touch. Not that there hasn't been a woman in the house, there have been plenty, but none recently.

Gramp's wife, Flossy, was the last, and I'd heard from him and others that she ran a tight ship. It was Flossy who mostly raised my father when Gramp was away at sea, and it was my "Nana," as I called her, who changed my diapers and fed me from the bottle when my father shipped out. But it was after Flossy passed from the 'the cancer' that Gramp began pulling at the cork. He's no doubt at the Chatham Squire right now, drinking away the 'grocery money' I send him at the end of every month. If I were to fall into a bottomless pit, it wouldn't matter much to him as long as he got his grocery money. I don't believe this, of course, but I sometimes wonder.

I go to our refrigerator and open it. There's not much there in terms of freshness so I close the door. Finding an empty milk jug in the trash can, I rinse it out and fill it with tap water, then, stepping up to our cupboard, I take out a round loaf of sourdough bread. Checking the bread for mold and finding none, I stuff the loaf into my seabag. Happening upon a bowl of apples, I take three. "Least he's buying fresh fruit," I say to myself, then toss the apples on top of the bread and leave by way of the hinge-less screen door, carefully replacing it, so as not to invite flies inside.

SECRET MEADOW

I stand on our back porch, itself a nautical waste heap of chocks, blocks, buoys, gaffs, and empty nail kegs, and whatever else has washed up on our harbor beach, and pluck my slime knife from its tackle block housing. Slipping the thin blade behind my belt, I step over a more recent culling, a Mercury outboard with a bent prop. I recall the day I carried the engine on my shoulder from the town landing, where it had been abandoned, or so I believed, to our back porch, where it now sits. I did this three years ago and I still don't know what I'm going to do with it, other than it's all mine. This addiction to salvage obviously runs in my blood. Spotting a coil of rope lying in the mire, I sling it over my right shoulder, for, as Gramp always warns, "No amount of preparation is uncalled for when sailing into the Realm."

I exit the back porch by way of the whaler's gaff. Passing the pagoda tree, I hike through an unkempt field of sunflowers, the bushy blond halos craning in unison toward the early morning sun. Fat bumblebees zip about my head, oblivious to my presence, as I wind my way through the eight-foot stalks in search of the deer run that will bring me to our landing in the Cedar Swamp. Only I can't find it. I am lost, the spring rains and summer sun having transformed the sparse Cape Cod moraine into a Congolese jungle.

With our landholdings spread over three townships, to this day there are hollows and thickets that I have yet to explore and who knows, behind every tree and rock cropping might be the remnants of an ancient Indian village or a smuggler's hideaway or, if I'm lucky, a Viking Cromlech jutting from the ground, buried under a bushel of poison ivy.

An army of paratrooping grasshoppers takes wing as I scramble over an ancient stake and rider, and I am on the lookout for lowland gorillas when a ruffed grouse breaks from the heath and sprints down a matted rabbit run. I give chase, making a path an elephant could follow but lose sight of the small bird as it flees over a fieldstone fence. I seem to recall trying to keep my balance on a similar stone wall as a youth, and if memory of a badly sprained ankle serves, the fence eventually peters out onto a secret meadow abloom in Oriental poppies. It was the ancestral women of the family who tended this crop, partaking of the Asiatic herb to get them through the harsh winters and their husbands' long absences at sea.

I recall the day I came upon a graze of raccoons sprawled about the meadow, lying on their backs and scratching their bellies like a bunch of winos in a hobo jungle. I had my new rifle slung across my shoulders, gifted to me by my father on my tenth birthday. With the rifle came responsibility, my father had told me, only he didn't elaborate, and I never asked. The coons languished under scarlet bulbs and did not stir at my approach. I was sure these were the same swamp cats who had raided our tomato garden and tipped over our trash bins the night before. Could it be the responsibility my father spoke of meant protecting our crops? Standing in the meadow that day, I had a decision to make.

Sliding my red Keds over the wet grass, I creep up on a slumbering raccoon. Slipping the rifle's strap from my right shoulder, I lower the barrel at the coon's face as it continues smiling blissfully up at the midday sun. Cocking back the hammer, I take a breath, I hold it, then exhale and pull the trigger. The bullet impacts the animal's right cheek, blowing back its fur. The coon makes a gurgling sound deep in its throat while holding out its childlike hands as if to blot out the sun. I look on in ghastly horror as the coon's mouth fills with blood, and it begins to choke. Lifting the coon with the toe of my right sneaker, I turn the animal onto its belly, where it dies in a series of raspy gasps. Wiping away hot tears, I push onward through the meadow, reloading my rifle and repeating the process until the whole graze lay dead. Raccoons don't play possum. Gathering the dead coons, I pile them into a rusted, red wheelbarrow, then slog it through the wood and up the sloping hillside to our back porch, where my father sits in his favorite rattan chair, smoking a cheroot.

"That our suppa' you bringin'?" he asks, smiling handsomely down at me. I set the barrow next to our splitting stump and saunter up to the back porch aglow with pride.

"Did what you told me. Took aim, held my breath, and shot!"

"Attaboy!" exclaims my father, slapping his knees and hopping from his chair, and he is beside me in a single stride. Wrapping his strong arms around my slender shoulders, he pulls me close. "Remember to clear the chamber?" he asks. I proudly hand him my new rifle. Ratcheting back the action, he eyeballs the empty chamber approvingly and hands it back. Nodding at the barrow, he asks, "Whatcha' got in there? Tom turkey? Peter Cottontail?"

I shake my head. "Bigger!"

"What's bigger than a tom?" he asks ponderingly.

"Swamp cats," I tell him.

"Coons?" he asks, clarifying.

"Yup," I happily reply. "I got 'em all!"

"What *all* you talkin'?" asks my father, his brow sagging slightly.

"The lot." I beam. "They were lying in the grass like they were asleep or something."

"Where exactly were you shootin'?" asks my father, his mouth drawing into a frown.

"In a meadow…near where the old fence lets out…had these red bulbs all over."

My father hurries down the slope. I chase after him. Falling in at his flailing boots, I shout, "Thieves in the night steeling our food! That's what you and Gramp called them!"

Coming to a stop at our splitting stump, my father reaches into the barrow and takes out a dead raccoon. Examining the pelt, he asks, "All 'em shot up close like this?"

"They wouldn't run!" I mewl, tears streaming down my cheeks. "Why wouldn't they run?"

"Kil't the whole graze by the looks of it," my father grumbles. "Now how 'em babies spose' to eat back in their dens?"

"But they stole our tomatoes," I whimper.

Holding me roughly by my shoulders, my father replies harshly, "'Them coons got a right to live unda' the same trees we do. So what if a few red-toms go missin'? We can afford it!"

"I thought that's what you wanted?" I say, openly weeping.

My father's grip on me softens. Placing me atop the splitting stump, he cups my quivering chin in his strong hand and says to me, "Fishermen take from nature what She gives to him in plentiful supply. We feed the world, Caleb, not just ourselves. It's wrong what you did."

Struggling to speak, I say to my father between sniffles, "I only wanted...to be like you."

"You're a good boy, Caleb. Never do ya' have to prove ya'self to me," says my father. "That's my job to you. Killin' don't make a man. I fill the hold, sure, but I ain't out there sportfishin', and if it's not on my catch list, I throw it back. I figure the more I let live today, the more they'll be in the future, your future."

"Are you going to take away my rifle?"

Looking at the 10 gauge leaning against the porch steps, my father considers it for a moment, then turns to me, saying, "Always take what you need, and not what you can take, and I'll leave it at that." Nodding at the wheelbarrow, he adds, "The two of us will bury the coons before I leave in the morn."

"I wish you didn't have to go," I reply, pulling at the grass at my feet. "I wish that stupid boat of yours would sink."

Standing abruptly, my father walks onto the bluff, where he

remains for some time, looking out across the bay. With his back to the splitting stump, he finally speaks. "Me being away is hard on you. That I know. Hard on me, more than you realize, but it's what we do. What we've always done. Doesn't make it right, just makes it so. Reason I keep bringing you 'em books and tellin' ya' to pay attention in school is so you'll have a choice when the ship's whistle blows."

"Didn't mean it," I say to my father, running the back of my hand across my runny nose. "About your boat sinking."

Turning to me, my father smiles. Walking back to the splitting stump, he ruffles my shaggy hair with his large hand, saying, "Hell, I know that. Never figured any different." Lifting me high in the air, he swings me onto his back, and together we gallop down the sloping hillside. Cutting through the sunflower field, my father easily knocks down the sturdy stalks, and I am in the throes of uncontrollable laughter when he runs the length of our harbor beach with my feet sailing from his back like a windsock. Clamoring up the bluff on all fours without breaking stride, he then sprints the two of us up the sloping hillside and throws our pairing onto the back porch, where we disappear into Gramp's prepared galley. My father never needed no whaler's gaff!

I awoke early the next morn and ran to my father's room, where I found his door ajar and his sea chest open. Leaping down the spiral staircase in my PJs, I stepped onto the back porch and ran to where the red wheelbarrow sat empty next to a patch of freshly upturned earth. My father didn't leave a marker. He didn't have to. Captain 'Mad Jack' Forrest went missing two months later when the fishing boat he captained sank mysteriously somewhere on the Grand Banks. No distress call was sent and there were no survivors. And neither was the boat or any wreckage of it ever found, as if the boat and crew were sucked from the top-water to join Atlantis. I never shot my rifle after that day.

For the rest of that summer, I searched for the raccoon dens, dragging a backpack filled with table scraps down every warren and rabbit run that I came across, then scattering the spoils wherever I believed the dens might be. I never saw a single raccoon during that time, baby or adult. I continued my quest well into the fall, rubbing baking soda on the poison ivy and picking brambles from my clothes and topknot long after the sun went down. Before going to bed each night, I'd place a tomato on my windowsill and lie awake watching it until the Sandman came to call. Crows would usually find the tomato in the early morn and, after punching holes in the skin with their sharp beaks, carry it away, leaving only a scattering of silky black feathers in their wake.

Thanksgiving of that year was a particularly sad one inside the Forrest house. Instead of the usual three plates, there were now only two. Gramp put out a big spread anyway: twenty-pound bird crammed with oyster stuffing, creamed onions with pan-dripped gravy topping lumpy mashed potatoes, along with homemade cranberry sauce with big, juicy cranberries. It felt like we were eating at the table of some Viking king! After supper, I took a plate of leftovers up the spiral staircase and to my room. Holding the plate one-handed, I crawled from my bedroom window and onto a gabled awning. Light snow had begun to fall when I placed the plate under a low-hanging bough.

That night I lay awake thinking of my father and the many lessons he taught me, but more importantly, of the time we spent together fishing the Powder Hole and sailing the inner harbor. But my favorite pastime with him was watching the Chatham Athletics play semipro summer baseball from our perch behind the home run fence. There wasn't a ball hit that my father couldn't run down and catch, no matter how far over the home run fence they went. He was good enough in high school that he could have played college ball and who knows, he might have even gone pro. But when the ship's whistle blew, he was on it, leaving the baseball and hockey scholarships sealed in their envelopes on the kitchen table. Mostly though, he sits on his haunches watching me miss more home run balls than I caught, but always offering encouragement. He never found fault with the obvious, that I wasn't inclined to team sports, that I wasn't fast enough or coordinated like he was. That I was born short and stocky, like my mother, and not long-limbed and fleet of foot like he and Gramp.

That night I went to sleep with hot tears in my eyes. It was the first time I cried since my father was officially declared lost at sea. The following morn, I got up and took a bath, then returned to my room to dress for school. I'd forgotten about the plate I left out until I saw the curtains stirring. Going to the window, I expected to see a tangle of beaks and wings fighting over the scraps, but to my wonder, I found the plate licked clean with not a single black feather littering the freshly laid snow. Examining the plate, I noticed a set of humanlike hand prints leading to and away from the plate and onto the low-hanging pine bough. I stared at the plate for longer than I can remember. Crawling onto the awning, I brought the plate inside and placed it under my bed, choosing not to wash it. Returning from school later that afternoon, I loaded the plate with more table scraps and placed it on the same spot under the low-hanging pine bough, only to find the plate again licked clean the following morn. I continued to load the plate through the fall, never quite sure if I was feeding the entire forest or a single dweller.

Christmas of that year brought some cheer back to the Forrest house as one of Gramp's familiars had a litter. He invited the town elders over along with their grandchildren to pick out a kitten, and as the eggnog flowed, the old stories were told. I was sitting alone in our parlor, staring aimlessly out the frosted windows, when I noticed the many firelit eyes staring back at me from the tree line in eager anticipation. I laughed out loud for the first time in months, causing Gramp to cut short his reminiscing and walk over to me.

"Thought ya' had some lass stashed up in yar' room there for a while. Truth is, I been leavin' a plate out m'self from time to time. 'Em coons will sleep good this winter. Your dad would be proud of ya', Caleb. Real proud. Now, why don't ya' see if 'em thievin' rascals like sweets." Patting my arm, Gramp left a platter of Christmas cookies at my elbow before leaving my side to rejoin his pals.

I reach the end of the fieldstone fence. The sunflowers here are shorter, more spread out, with their wilting blond halos tilted not at the sun but at the ground, seemingly devoid of happiness. I walk onto the gently lolling meadow long ago culled of the scarlet poppies. My

31

ankles are damp with early morning dew as I slink along with my head down and come to the spot where I shot the first raccoon. I take a knee and run my hand over the wet grass, checking for any lingering sign of the crime, but of course, there's no blood. There wasn't that much to begin with. Another crime occurred not far from where I'm kneeling, only I consider it more a matter of conscience than I do murder, and though I don't believe in ghosts, that's where you'll find one, roaming the deep woods near the biggest of our three kettle ponds.

I walk to the edge of the meadow and find myself facing a thicket of bearberry and wild rambling rose. A landscape artist's dream, to be sure, and I am awed by its beauty, but I also know that I must pass through it to get to my boat. Somewhere along the way I took a wrong turn. But to retrace my steps now would take precious time away from my planned day on the water, so I continue into the bramble, carefully picking my way past the thorny stems.

CEDAR SWAMP

A sharp-tailed sparrow trills its strange torch song as I come tumbling out of the prickly rubbish, bleeding from a slew of shallow cuts and a handful of deeper ones. The ground swath here has changed from a footing of grass and stick to that of cone and needle as I step into a pine grove, where a massive granite boulder blocks my way. I begin climbing the rock, no doubt left behind from the retreating Wisconsin glacier that helped form the Cape ten thousand years ago, along with the wind and the waves.

Reaching the summit, I squat on my haunches and survey the grove that responds like a cathedral, the boughs of the trees acting as arches with the quietness within recalling that of a church's nave. I try to imagine an Indian brave doing the same hundreds of years ago. Would his problems be similar to mine, and if so, what would he do? Only I can't think for him. Whatever insights he may have had, he took with him when he went to where the native Wampanoag Nation call the "Cummaquid" or "The Other Side."

The early morning silence is shattered by the screeching of a red-tailed hawk as it comes crashing through the tree limbs to pluck an errant baby squirrel, jumping from limb to limb, in its cruel talons. The hawk alights on a similar altar of rock to enjoy its breakfast. I look away naturally revolted, and yet I am struck by the simplicity of it all. Life begets death and death becomes life as it has since life as we know it began. These and other reflections are cut short, however, as I spy my prized Cat boat through the trees, sitting high and dry on blocks atop slurry 'crick' mud. I smile to myself, feeling that I've just spotted an old friend in some faraway port.

Sliding feetfirst down the boulder, I hit the ground, running like a just-flushed deer. I make it to the landing and kick off my boat shoes. Stepping onto the slurry sand, my feet make sucking sounds as I approach my boat. Reaching down, I scoop up a handful of the warm, wet earth and smooth it over my many cuts to use as a sort of antiseptic balm. I'm not sure that it works, but it feels good.

I arrive at my boat and stand before the bow. Peeling off the protective tarp that I covered her in before I shipped out, I see that she is as I left her, immaculate, with her un-stepped mast and boom laid out bow to stern with her mains'l and jib folded crisply inside her cuddy. I named her *Sea Gypsy* because that's how I see her, without any permanent mooring, drifting with the currents and sailing against the tides with no particular fixed heading as I like to do.

She's all of 14'4", half-decked with a large oval cockpit and decked-over forepeaks. Her stubby mast is steeved well forward above a sharp, plumb-stemmed hull. Carrying 315 feet of crosscut, machine-woven sailcloth sporting five sets of reef points makes her a fast, shoal-drafting craft that I can work with in-harbor and out. I've sailed on her since I was a boy, and she's always sailed true. Bottom, sailcloth, and tiller is all I need to take me into the Realm. The wind is free. All I have to do is find it, and I'm good at that.

I stroke her teak coming rails and hand-kiss the sexy cat eyes I painted on each side of her bow just above her bootstraps for good luck. I got the idea from seeing a Foochow junk in a *National Geographic* that my father subscribed to for me when I was around six. Jumping aboard, I stow my seabag and speargun high in her cuddy, or what I like to call her fo'c'sle. Dropping back over the side, I slap the bowline over my right shoulder and begin the arduous task of dragging my boat off the blocks and into the tea-colored swamp water.

Upon entering the brine, a squadron of dragonflies lands on

Gypsy's improvised pulpit before banking off into a tall cropping of sand reed and puffy pussy willow. Cool bottom muck oozes between my toes as I trudge along waist-deep, creating a swirling cloud of rust-colored sediment in my wake. Darting schools of silver alewives race about my knees, maturing in the inlet before venturing into the food chain that is the Atlantic. Somewhere in the sorrel a raven barks its hunting call, flushing a great blue heron from its camouflaged isle of lily pads and back to its nest. Off to my right sits a box turtle, its black shell brightly marked in yellow stripes. The turtle clocks my progress from its sunny perch atop a cedar stump. I know this turtle, and it does not fear me, having seen this rehearsal time and time replayed. Somewhere a ground robin calls out, "Drink your tea! Drink your tea!"

"I will! I will!" I answer it.

Towing *Sea Gypsy* deeper into the slough, the harsh bite of a horsefly brings a tinge of reality to my day. I try splashing water over my shoulders, hoping to drown the fly, but the stinging pain lingers. It's still early morn, so I thought they'd be asleep, but where there's one Greenhead buzzing, there are thousands. I place the bowline between my teeth and sink up to my chin. Treading water, I prepare my body to swim my boast across the lagoon. To a landlubber, this would be akin to entering Dante's Ninth Circle of Hell, but there was a time my two best friends and me hunted snapping turtles in these same swampy marshlands. This we did without fear or trepidation, until we happened on the giant snapper.

Jimmy moved to the Cape when he was around twelve. His family was well off, only you'd never know it by the way he acted, which was down-to-earth and quick to laugh. His father, Dale Hallet, was an Off-Cape builder turned town politico. After making his mark on the mainland, Mr. Hallet chose the town of Chatham as his next paving project, only what he failed to realize was that most folks around here are against paving of any sort, Gramp being his loudest critic, their antagonistic debates at the town hall meetings rivaling those of

Lincoln and Douglas! He even offered to pave the dirt road leading to his family's newly built home high on Fox Hill for free but was voted down.

The divisions between the two families never bothered Jimmy and me, each vowing to the other that we'd stay out of it, and we had until recently. I never thought of Jimmy's dad as a bad person. He only wanted the freedom to build like he'd had in Scituate, a rich town along the South Shore, only around here that meant dealing with town curmudgeons, like Gramp, who've remained steadfastly against growth of any kind, but also the reason the town has kept its charm for five centuries and counting.

Chumley, my other best friend growing up, couldn't have cared less about the fracas. Being a two-thirds Wampanoag Indian, he believed the land was all his anyway. I never knew him to take a surface road. He'd cut across people's yards, patios, and driveways wherever and whenever it suited him. His justification was that the land was all part and parcel of his tribe's ancestral hunting grounds, and he's probably right. He was a year younger than Jimmy and me, and yet he was as big as the two of us combined. He was always a heavyset kid whom I'd given the nickname of Chumley, after a walrus character on the Saturday morning cartoons. He didn't seem to mind and answered Chumley as quickly as he did Jonathan, his birth name.

His mother, Junebug, made her own shell and bead jewelry that she sold at area craft shows and farmer's markets. She raised her son by herself, and she was not one to be messed with, as I was to discover on one memorable childhood sleepover. Stepping inside Junebug's house was like stepping inside a Navajo hogan, the way she had the place laid out. Intricately patterned tribal tapestries tacked to the walls, webbed spirit catchers in every window with deer antlers hung upside down above every doorway. There was never a curfew. We could come and go as we pleased, and we did. The atmosphere was artistic, bohemian even. I always felt at home there, and yet there was always the threat of impending violence hanging in the air like an unfinished sentence, emanating mostly from Junebug. That woman can be hell on wheels when she gets her dander up!

Usually, around suppertime, one of Chumley's many 'uncles'

would show up at the door with hat in hand. I was never sure if these men were his real uncles or just suitors seeking Junebug's affection. Chumley was blissfully ignorant on the subject. And though there were some in the Wampanoag Nation who claimed to be his father, there was no one Junebug would ever put a name to. I never faulted her for it. She was only playing the angles and trying to raise her son as best she knew how.

On this particular night it was his Uncle Joseph coming to call. He was somewhat of a regular. I had my suspicions, as did Jimmy. Not that he looked anything like Chumley. He looked anything but: tall and lean with a thin nose, Uncle Joseph resembled a young Paul Newman more than he did your typical Wild West Indian from the movies. I was alone in the house with Junebug when he began knocking at the door. Junebug was in the kitchen preparing dinner and wouldn't answer it, so I did.

"You have rescued me from the cold outdoors yet again, Caleb," says Uncle Joseph. "How are you and how is your grandfather?"

"Same," I answer.

"Does he remember me?"

"Calls you the last true Injun."

"Spoken like a true White Devil," laughs Uncle Joseph, stepping around me and over the threshold. "The captain and my father spent many hours together leaning over the wooden drawbridge fishing Mitchell's river together as I did with your father. I am glad that you and my Jonathan are friends. Continues the circle. Where is the boy? Not hiding from his Uncle Joseph, I hope."

"Chumley's outside cording wood with Jimmy," I answer.

"I do not like this name," says Uncle Joseph sternly. "His name is Jonathan. Always Jonathan while in my presence."

"Okay, Uncle Joseph. Staying for supper?"

"Depends on the woman."

"Junebug…I mean, Mrs. Repoza's fixing her quahog pies."

"I can see that," replies Uncle Joseph, looking past me into the kitchen, where Junebug minces onion and garlic on a cutting board while applying eyeliner at the same time.

"It'll be a while!" shouts Junebug. "Hope you brought your own!"

"Got me confused, woman!" shouts back Uncle Joseph, holding aloft a canned six-pack of Budweiser beer. "I always bring my own!"

Chumley and Jimmy enter the house by way of the sliding glass back door, each carrying an armload of firewood. Uncle Joseph's gaze locks onto his 'supposed' nephew.

"That all you could muster, boy?"

"More than you," replies Chumley in defiance. Uncle Joseph stiffens.

"Spread 'em around!" hollers Junebug from the kitchen, age meaning nothing to the Wampanoag. Uncle Joseph does just that and hands each of us a beer.

Jimmy drops his armful of wood into the woven basket beside the fireplace and sips from his Budweiser most greedily. Forming a circle on the floor, in what had become a ritual of sorts for us braves, Uncle Joseph awaits our rapt attention before clearing his throat and reciting one of his many stories that were always filled with Indian magic and tribal lore.

"King Maushop was a giant Indian king who lived long ago. It is said that when he slept, he would lay his head on the dunes of Provincetown with his feet stretching to what is now the Cape Cod canal. During the night, mosquitos would rise from the swamps and bite the giant king, causing him to toss and turn, digging the Cape's ponds, lakes, and hollows with his elbows and knees. It is said that when King Maushop woke the next morn, he took the sand from his moccasins and emptied them into the sea, forming the islands of Nantucket and Martha's Vineyard. But there was another island where he lived. The Isle of Nanoho, a faraway island long ago buried by the wind and the waves. It is told that the First Corn came from the island, flown by a crow across the water as a gift to his people."

"Whatever happened to King Maushop, Uncle Joseph?" I ask, taking a pull of my Budweiser.

"He lived for a thousand years, and when he heard the Europeans were coming, he turned himself into a white whale and passed over the horizon."

"Like in *Moby Dick*," adds Jimmy, draining his beer.

"No," replies Uncle Joseph. "*Moby Dick* is a made-up story told by a white man. But there was a white whale. Two of our people saw it. The ship they sailed was named the *Essex*, out of Nantucket, and she was captained by a man named Pollard, also out of Nantucket. Our people knew the whale to be King Maushop, and they told the captain he should leave it alone, but Pollard had blood in his teeth, and he threw his harpoon, only to have the whale turn on him and break his boat into many pieces. Only our people survived, along with the captain and his first mate. For many weeks and many months, they lived on a small ketch until a passing ship picked them up."

"What were their names?" Chumley giggles. "I might be related."

"We'll never know their true names," says Uncle Joseph sadly. "Ship's log had them listed only as Narragansetts. Both were long dead when the ship picked them up."

"I thought you said they survived?" questions Jimmy.

"They did survive, the boat going down, but not from the captain and his first mate. The sailors returned to Nantucket the following year, where they lived the rest of their lives in shame, the blood of our people coursing through their veins. Bad medicine, that."

The three of us braves sit in reverent silence, reflecting on Uncle Joseph's twice-told tale. Junebug enters from the kitchen carrying plates of her renowned delicacy and hands the plates down to us; we balance them on our knees as we eat. Short of stature but ample in both breast and hip, there's nothing particularly frightening about Junebug, except for when the tips of her ears turn red, like that of a Tasmanian devil, as they were now.

"Talk! Talk! Talk! That's all you're good for, Joseph Pena! Why don't you fix my roof like I asked you to do last summer?" Crushing his empty Budweiser can in his hand, Uncle Joseph laughingly tosses it over his shoulder. Junebug gives him a stern look before calmly retreating into her kitchen.

"If it were me on that ship," says Uncle Joseph, looking at Chumley as if to study him, "I'd have killed those sailors and rode

King Maushop's tail all the way to Hawaii, where I would'a married me one of those island girls they got there. I hear they're good baby-makers and don't talk back like the ones we got 'round here."

Returning from the kitchen in quick, short steps, Junebug rewards her suitor for his candor with a sharp slap to the back of his neck with a hot, greasy spatula. Jumping about the living room like a cat with its tail on fire, Uncle Joseph shouts, "You' crazy, woman!" then runs from the house with Junebug fast on his heels, waving the hot spatula above her head like a war tomahawk. The three of us braves take the remaining beers and retreat into Chumley's room, where we remain, not wanting to test Junebug's mood as she storms about her house-breaking dishes and slamming doors.

It was the summer of my near drowning when my two friends and I came upon the giant snapping turtle. Our raft consisted of wooden pallets nailed end to end under a thin sheet of warped plywood. For flotation, we liberated a pair of Styrofoam packing beams from the dumpster behind the Benjamin Franklin store on Main Street. Fastening the beams to port and to starboard like a pair of pontoons, we pushed off from our landing in the cedar swamp. All we cared was that the raft floated, and it did, as long as Jimmy and I stood at opposite ends, with Chumley in the middle sitting atop Junebug's mop bucket, ready to capture a ferocious terrapin predating even that of the dinosaur.

The July humidity hung in the air like a woolen blanket. Jimmy was astern, pushing the raft forward with a weathered fencepost, with Chumley stationed amidships, attempting to stuff an Italian grinder down his all-consuming gullet. I was on my hands and knees at the bow, spotting. We were pretty far down a winding slough when I saw a snapper resting on the mud-rich bottom with a good two-foot shell on its back.

"I see one, and man, is it a monster! Hard to port!" I command.

"Must be a hundred years old," says Chumley, peeking over my shoulder with a half-chewed slice of salami jutting from his mouth.

"Older," I say, pointing down at the turtle. "Got three bullet holes in its shell that looks like they came from a musket."

"Where's he at?" asks Jimmy excitedly, continuing to push the raft forward.

"Straight ahead," I reply. "Better slow us down, or we'll sail right over him."

"How do you know it's a *him*?" asks Jimmy, jamming the fencepost into the side of a high marsh and halting our progress.

"Tail's longer," I answer, lying flat on the raft with my bare chest pressed against the warped wood. Hefting Gramp's hickory walking stick, borrowed without his knowledge, I let it sink naturally in the still water.

"Trick is to get the snapper mad enough to bite the stick," I say, for Jimmy's benefit, him being a newbie in the sport of snapping turtle hunting. "But not mad enough to spook it." I tap the giant snapper lightly on its shell, but it doesn't respond.

"Maybe it's dead?" offers Chumley.

"Why don't you jump over the side and find out?" Jimmy proposes.

"Not me!" exclaims Chumley. "Snapper's big enough to take my foot off at the ankle. Gonna be a ball-buster getting it in this mop bucket."

I try lodging the walking stick under the turtle's belly and flipping it over, but the snapper takes off running along the murky bottom instead.

"Snapper's on the move! Hard to starboard!" I shout. Jimmy does so, keeping pace with the beast by mimicking an Olympic pole-vaulter, nearly sinking the fencepost along with the raft.

"See it?" Chumley asks, holding Junebug's mop bucket at the ready.

"Too mucked up," I reply, sinking the hickory stick into the swirling silt.

"Keep poking!" says Jimmy excitedly. "Snapper's got to be down there somewhere."

I plunge the stick into the mud twice before hitting something solid on the third try. "Found him!"

Breaking into the clear, the snapper continues its flight along the bottom and heads for a cluster of eel grass, the long black strands shifting in the current like a woman's hair. Jimmy leans heavily on the fencepost, saying, "Fifty bucks, right? The cook at the Double Dragon will pay us fifty bucks if we bring him a snapper?"

"That's what he told me, but we won't get squat if I don't get it to bite this stick."

"Hell, for fifty bucks, I'll bite the stick, and you can bring me to the Double Dragon," giggles Chumley.

"If that happens, I'll never eat there again," laughs Jimmy.

We are gaining on the giant snapper when the raft passes over a ridge of submerged marsh grass lying just under the surface, the quill-tipped stalks scraping against the bottom like a sonic chalkboard.

"What was that sound?" Jimmy asks. Chumley points to the stern, where the Styrofoam packing beams float untethered behind us. "That's bad, right?"

"Not good," answers Chumley. The raft pitches forward as it passes over the sunken marsh, sliding me face-first into the muddy water. The last image I see before going under is the giant snapper making a U-turn.

I thrash about blindly, swallowing what feels like sinkfuls of the salty brine. I finally gain a footing on a patch of sandy bottom and start to run, heaving my knees to my chest and sending up a rooster tail behind my flailing feet.

"Look, everybody! It's Daffy Duck!" guffaws Chumley, pulling himself up a marsh wall ribbed with bluish mussels.

"Where's the snapper?" I ask.

"After you!" shouts Jimmy, himself marooned on a sand-wash Island and laughing so hard that his head appears to be in danger of exploding.

I slow to a slog and join in the laughter, realizing how ridiculous I must look running away from a turtle who, no doubt, wants to be further away from me than I do it. I continue laughing until my right foot lands in one of the many sinkholes Gramp always warns me about but that I'd never found until this day, and I am up to my chin in the silty water within seconds. I tried tugging at my leg, but the sinkhole wouldn't let me go.

"Foot's stuck," I say nervously. "Can't get it out."

Chumley looks at the rising water. "Tide's coming in!"

Jimmy isn't laughing as he leaves his sand-wash island and steps into the slough, carefully picking his spots. Chumley does the same from his position, leaping from the marsh and splashing down without regard. I try again to lift my leg, but my actions cause my foot to sink deeper. Thick mud bubbles up my pant leg and something else that feels like a rope or a hose, maybe or…an eel! I scream.

Careful not to find his own sinkhole, Jimmy leans forward and holds out the fencepost. "Grab the end and I'll pull you out."

I do as instructed and grip the post, half delirious from having a live eel in my pants. Jimmy pulls from his end, giving his all, but the sinkhole won't let go of my leg. By now, the rising tide is up to my chin, and I have to tilt my head back in order to breathe.

"Try twisting your leg like Elvis in *Viva Las Vegas*," offers Chumley, his mother a big fan.

Joining Jimmy, Chumley takes hold of the post as I try twisting my leg. Together, my two friends turn their backs to me and begin to pull. I regrip the post, the tips of my fingers making indentions in the soft-wood, and I believe it is a sucking sound that I hear as my right sneaker pulls free, forever part of the marsh now. With a final tug, my leg slips from the sinkhole like meat from a lobster claw, pitching my two friends face-first into the drink.

I throw my body onto a nearby marsh and rip off my jeans. Shivering on the spiked grass, I watch in revulsion as thick mud bubbles from my pant leg, and then comes the eel, a foot-long blackish thing with long, black whiskers, slithering past the cuff before disappearing back into the marsh. I am at the point of passing out when I hear Chumley's jubilant shouting.

"He bit it! Almost had your balls for breakfast! Must have really pissed him off, Cal!" bellows Chumley, standing in the now chest-deep water struggling to hold the giant snapper aloft, its neck outstretched with its hooked beak locked on the end of Gramp's walking stick.

We brought the giant snapper to the Double Dragon restaurant, where Mr. Liu paid us, not fifty, but ten dollars each. It still seemed a fair price for a day's adventure. But it was when Mr. Liu invited the three of us into his kitchen to show us how he would prepare the turtle that our spirits sank. Setting a large, flat-bottomed pot to boil, Mr. Liu, without fear or hesitation, plucked the giant snapper from Junebug's bucket and dropped it into the pot. I don't know what we were expecting, perhaps that he would do battle with the turtle using one of the long-tasseled swords that hung, blades crossed, above his cash register.

"Now this real Oriental cooking!" says Mr. Lui. "Sea turtle stew! Not on menu. For family. No tell no one!"

We promised not to tell, though we weren't exactly sure why, and nobody talked on the long walk home, only saying to each other that if we did catch another giant snapper, we wouldn't bring it to Mr. Liu. I don't remember what I did with the money. Probably gave it to Gramp for groceries. It just felt dirty to me after that.

The muck under my feet turns sandy and firm as I touch down on the far side of the lagoon, where the nightmarish trappings of swamp stump and tidal marl are replaced by standing pine and a rock-and-shell-strewn beach. I continue walking with my boat, gently guiding her from the stern down a winding watercourse that leads to a greater body of water beyond, occasionally glancing behind my heels to check for any giant snapper following.

ROUND COVE

I t is low tide as I enter the cove so I can stand with my boat as I ready her for our day on the water. I start by splashing her bright work clean and washing the muddy drag marks off her hull. If there's one thing I can't abide, it's a dirty sailboat. While it's true that I keep her in a swamp, that's a luxury compared to leaving her on grass, which would stain her bottom, or putting her on sand, which microscopically scrapes her paint, and I beach her enough as it is. I'd give *Sea Gypsy* a mooring, but for fear, she'd be stolen. Doesn't take much to cut a mooring line. My forefathers taught me that, so I keep her in the swamp. There aren't many who'd dare swim that muck except for us swamp rats.

Sea Gypsy's a classy lady, a working Chatham cat boat fastened together at the famous Crosby Boat Yard circa 1929. Legend has it (ours) that Old Joe Kennedy gifted the boat to Gramp in lieu of payment for stowing twenty barrels of his Canadian Scotch whisky in our barn during Prohibition. Gramp hid the barrels behind bales of hay cut from the salt marshes, that in itself considered 'found money' in those days. Awaiting a full moon, the bootleggers would drop the barrels at the mouth of the bay, where they'd join with the incoming tide to wash up on our harbor beach the following morn. This one time the bootleggers weren't so lucky, and a storm moved in that sank the bootleggers and blew the barrels out to sea, only to wash up on the shores of the Emerald Isle the following winter.

"'Em Micks always get their booze," Gramp likes to say, even though he's part Irish himself. "But far as you taking a nip, not a drop 'til ya' can fight back, and then it's only a matter of time before ya' ship over the side." Only Gramp isn't one to take his own advice, believing himself to be a reverse mirror.

"Look to me and do the opposite 'cept when it comes to the sea. I've sailed this kettle thrice over and don't eva' believe She's your friend. When you're on Her, keep a close watch and save the sunsets for the camera-slingers. And if you're in doubt, look to Her bottom 'cause that's where you'll be if ya' don't give Her the proper respect."

I'd always hear Gramp out and listen attentively, but would continue to stay out well past sundown and in bad weather. On my return, shivering and soaked to the bone, Gramp would wrap me in heavy blankets and sit me in front of our blazing hearth stuffed with driftwood. He'd wait until my teeth stopped chattering before starting in on one of his blustery sermons.

"Never test Her moods! And remember, She's got a lot more behind Her than you and yer tiny boat got. Don't matter if you're the *Titanic* or the *Queen Mary*! When She carries over the side, you'll be swimmin', fancy deck chairs or not. That don't mean ya' can't sail on Her and make a livin'. The Timekeeper wouldn't have made the world three parts water if He didn't want man riding on Her powdery bosom!"

Gramp's a good teacher when it comes to seafaring, but I wish he'd turn that reverse mirror on himself. There are times I'll find him slumped in his copper-studded captain's chair with an empty bottle of Jamaican rum at his elbow and love letters from his Flossy spread out on his lap. The pain he suffers from her loss, I will never know. I've heard it said around town that there was a time Captain Lester Forrest could swing an anchor as easily as he could his pocket watch. These days, however, when I carry him up to his bedroom and put him to bed, it's hard for me to imagine how his withered and weathered frame once stood as if it was cast in cement and it would have taken a wrecking ball to move him.

I should have left him a note telling him I'm in port, but it's best I didn't. What lies ahead for me on this day remains uncertain, but what is certain is that upon my return, should I return, there are going to be some changes made. My first act will be putting a stop to the 'grocery money' I send him at the end of every month. If he wants to continue drinking, he can go out and collect bottles and cans for their deposit money, like the other glassy-eyed inebriates I see walking along the roadsides. Of course, it would never come to that. If Gramp really needed the money, all he'd have to do is sell off an acre of land, and around here, that goes for about half a million. Truth be told, my grandfather, or Captain Let, as he is known in the annals of maritime fishing, is the richest man in town. And right behind him is me, though you'd never know it by how we dress or the state in which we allow ourselves to live.

Our family's landholdings alone cover three townships, with our prime, bay view acreage amounting to some hundred or more acres, depending on the sculpting tide. And with the Cape losing thirty-three acres of upland erosion every year, the value keeps going up! The town has been jealous of our land ever since Captain Nehi first put down stakes, and they've been after it every day since. I look to the sky to check the weather but know that it's too early to tell, Gramp's parable ringing in my ears, "Tween one and two and we'll see what She'll do." I have to smile at that one.

I pull myself aboard at the port rail. Standing in the ribbed cockpit, I unbridle the mainsail and re-step the mast. Hoisting the halyard, I extend the Marconi rig high above her telltale windsock, then thread the mainsheet down the boom and run it through the traveler, making sure to pay out plenty of line before clamping down. I take hold of the mainstay and step out onto the improvised pulpit at the bow, below which lies a Spanish Burton. I took it off an old tug that never left its mooring, to my knowledge anyway. It's a nifty hoisting winch if

I'm ever lucky enough to land a Double Marker aboard (a swordfish weighing two hundred pounds or more). Mostly, I use the winch to bring up lost anchors and wayward moorings when I'm home between trips. The pay isn't much, but it puts me on the water and helps some with the bills.

Dropping from the pulpit, I make my way down my boat to bolt the barn door rudder to the stern and affix its extended tiller, screwing down the flywheels. Walking *Sea Gypsy* further into the cove, I soon find that my supple feet are no match for the razor clams and sea urchins marring the cove's bottom; the hardened soles of my Huck Finn youth now tenderized from spending eighteen-hour days inside rubberized hip boots. Serves me right for forgetting my boat shoes back at our landing. Pushing off the bottom, I hop atop the stern and quickly haul in the mainsheet, but *Sea Gypsy* remains becalmed within the windless cove.

For the moment, I am content to let the ebb tide carry me out, so I dip inside the cuddy and rummage in my seabag, bringing out a juicy apple. Returning to the stern, I lean along the starboard gunwale and chomp away at the fruit, hoping for a gust of wind to kick up and blow me from the cove. I could scull her out, using the shortened oar I keep high in her fo'c'sle, but that would be like putting out on a kayak or canoe, and I'd never disrespect her like that, so I remain seated at the stern with the mainsheet held loosely in my right hand, ready to harness *Sea Gypsy* to the wind at the first blustery blow.

In some ways the cove reminds me of the Deep South, Alabama specifically, with its moss-draped trees and the smoky, early morning fog hovering above the still water like frozen breath. I worked there one summer as a deckhand on a shrimp boat. The work was relatively easy compared to what I was used to, but how I got there? That's another story.

Standing in the rain with my thumb in the air, I was somewhere on the outskirts of Dodge City when a Red Devil semi blew past, drenching me with storm runoff. The eighteen-wheeler got halfway up a highway on-ramp when it screeched to a halt and nearly jack-knifed. The rig's passenger door kicked open and a hand shot out, waving me over. I remained motionless, thinking it might be some kind of demented joke, but the hand kept waving, so I went, running across the tarmac with my jacket over my head to where a man resembling a young Gene Vincent leaned from the cab.

"Like the rain so much?"

"Could do without it."

"Where you headin'?"

"East."

"I'm running south. Sorry, kid."

"South sounds good," I reply, soaked from head to toe.

"South sounds good," repeats the man. "I'll bet it does. Well, don't stand there getting more wet. Hop in, for Christ sake!"

Malcolm was his name, and he was on his way to "Nawlins" to drop off a load of car parts and pick up another. Cutting across the Grass Sea, and the endless hours therein, we naturally got to talking. I told Malcolm of my adventures hitchhiking across the country, and he was particularly keen on hearing of my fishing the Bering Strait. He mentioned that he'd once worked as a shrimper steaming out of Brunswick, Georgia, but it was the way Malcolm described his days shrimping the balmy waters of the Gulf of Mexico that hooked me. With scallop season still three months off, I decided I'd give it a try. Dropping me off at Spanish Fort, deep inside Mobile Bay, Malcolm told me that if I stuck around long enough and made a proper nuisance of myself, I should find work. First on the docks unloading catches and later as a shrimper. The heat was stifling as I climbed down from the air-conditioned cab, hitting me like a blow-torch and soaking my clothes with sweat before I could take a single step.

"Keep fillin' 'em nets, Caleb," Malcolm offered, tossing down my seabag.

"I will. And watch out for 'em 'Smokies,' Malcolm. Way you drive, you're about due."

"Don't I know it," he said, combing a handful of pomade into his jet-black hair, ever the ladies' man. "I'll be hauling back in two weeks.

Tractors to Chicago. You're welcome to ride along if you can stomach my clutch work."

"Hopefully, I won't have to," I replied, grinning.

"Wiseass!" Malcolm cracked. Inspecting his pompadour in his rig's extended mirror, he said in a serious tone, "Now remember what I told you. Crackers they got down here don't like strangers, and they especially don't like strangers who talk like you! I'm a born and bred redneck m'self, so I know of which I speak. Raised more hell than Satan! So much, the judge gave me a choice, four years slinging tar on a chain gang or a hitch in the Corps. I chose the Marines, and let me tell you, the DIs they got on the Island gave me an 'edjication' real quick. Black as the Ace of Spades he was, and the meanest sumbitch who ever lived! I'd be dead and gone if it wasn't for that black devil. Made me high and tight and ready to fight! That don't mean every white boy in the South gets the same kind of schoolin' I did, so watch your back and never let 'em see you flinch."

Not knowing what else to say, I shouted, "Semper Fidelis!"

"Hoo-rah!" howled Malcolm in return.

Shutting the cab's passenger door, Malcolm sounded his dual air horns and pulled his rig back onto the wavy tarmac. Running the first red light he came to, he pushed his bucking beast on down the road like a Horseman of the Apocalypse coming to collect souls. I slung my seabag over my right shoulder and headed for the docks in search of work and something to eat. I followed my nose and in no time, the smell of diesel and rotting fish brought me to a working pier.

I walk down a wide expanse of wharf where off-loaders filled with shrimp, each the size and shape of a dump truck, travel two abreast along the tar-dappled railroad ties. I noticed right away how spare the boats were tied off on the pilings, the majority having open decks with not much tackle except for giant spools of finely woven net hanging above their prams like heaps of shredded lettuce. Most boats I passed flew not the Stars and Stripes but the Stars and Bars above their wheelhouses, and the crews were all white, except for a few of the Cuban outfits who didn't know English or forgot how to speak it when I inquired about a job.

I climbed down onto a narrow pier, whose many missing planks made it resemble a mouthful of broken teeth, and hopscotched my way past the empty berths. Nearing the end of the pier, I came upon a battered trawler checkerboarded in soldered iron patches, like playing cards in a game of 52 Pick-Up. I spotted a man of undetermined old age swabbing the back deck with a whisk broom blackened at the bristles. Balding, with a sloping, reptilian forehead, the man's spine curved so that he resembled a question mark. I approached the vessel, hoping the man to be a grandfatherly type who'd take pity on a young fisherman.

"Excuse me, sir, but would you happen to know of any captain in need of an experienced deckhand?"

"Where you from, boy," asked the man, spitting a long line of tobacco juice where he'd just swept. "Don't sound like anywhere 'round here."

"Fresh off a factory ship in Alaska," I replied, hoping to impress him.

"Sounds north to me," he said, spitting again.

"'Bout as north as north gets," I agreed, nodding my head.

"Where ya' from originally?"

"Mostly, I put out from Cape Cod. Stage Harbor specifically, but I've fished the Carib and Florida plenty."

"Ain't that where that Paul Revere fella rode his horsey?" he asked through cracked and yellowed teeth.

"Close enough."

"Well, I ain't hirin' no Yankee sissies today so you'd best skip it on home, boy, before some other cappy decides he might like you better as his anchor."

The hairs on the back of my neck spiked like a just-kicked mule, and I felt my temper coming on. I expected to get the runaround. That's how it is when you're a newbie on the docks. You're told "No!" and given directions to the next boat, most times leading you back to the first boat. And if you're not hired on the first day, you sleep it off in a motel room and try again the next. Normally, if you hang around long enough, you'll get work because the captains are sick of looking at you. That's how it is on every dock I've ever shipped from.

And I've been yelled at plenty. That's what captains do; they yell but never have I been threatened. I think back to another of Malcolm's warnings in which he said, "Down here you never know who it is messing with you. Could be a nobody, could be a somebody. Might be his daddy is the sheriff, and his uncle the local hanging judge. And once you're in, you're in, and believe me, they'll find a way to keep you in."

As was my nature, though, I ignored Malcolm's warning and stood my ground, leaning against a fiberglass-covered piling and folding my arms across my chest. Three crewmen emerged from the engine room, greasy Neanderthals all, and all with a strong family resemblance. Surrounded by his gangly sons, the old man eyed me comically, spitting another long line of tobacco juice at his feet.

"What'll it be, Yank? Want to join our ranks? More'n happy to let ya' come aboard and finish the swabbing."

The comment stung me like an angry wasp, but I ignored it, letting the cavemen guffaw, slapping each other on the back and punching one another hard on their arms and shoulders. I smiled down at the three idiots like I was watching an episode of the Three Stooges.

"Can I play with him, Daddy?" asked the biggest of the cavemen.

Eyeing me dully under a thatch of long, stringy blond hair, the eldest son had a boyish face devoid of expression, masking what I took to be malevolence within. 'He's a big one, all right,' I thought to myself. Heavy at the shoulders with a thick, round neck. Defeat him and the rest would be like slapping hens at a petting zoo. The old man I didn't even consider.

If it's one thing I learned in the dockside bars of Dutch Harbor, it's to never turn your back on a mob. It only invites chase. The best medicine is to face your aggressors head-on and let them know that you're not going easy. Most times you'll be left alone with the culprits finding someone else to pick on. But there have been other times where I've had to stand my ground, as it appeared I'd have to do here.

The blond giant came forward, a trail of spastic drool escaping his thick, red lips. Taking an eight-inch pigsticker from a sorting table ladened with dead and dying shrimp, he began tossing the knife from hand to hand. I glanced at his pudgy mitts and then at his dazed expression, and I hardly had time to react as the pigsticker left his right palm, rotating end over end before plunging into the piling a mere three inches from my right cheek. I nodded in appreciation of his skills, though I wasn't sure he meant to miss.

Going against my own judgment, I turned my back on the blond giant and positioned my feet on either side of the piling, shoulder width apart. I focused my attention on the impaled knife. Inhaling deeply, I held my breath and exhaled, then swept my right hand across my chest and struck the knife with my palm-heel. The boar's-tooth handle snapped from the blade, leaving three inches of cheap steel shivering within the piling. I picked up the handle and tossed it on deck. Grinning handsomely at me, the blond giant stepped forward. I advanced to the end of the slip to meet him, but the old man held him back.

"Check with the big nigger down the end there," said the old man, pointing further down the wharf. "Hear he's got a man sick. He might'en hire ya' on. Run along now and we'll take this no further. My word on that."

"But Daddy, I want to play with him," whined the man-child.

"I need you workin', boy! Not broke in two!"

"I'll play nice! I promise!"

The old man landed a hard blow to his eldest son's exposed kidney, doubling him over, then followed that with an overhand right to the back of his head, planting the giant face-first onto the steel deck.

"Talkin' back to me? Is that what I'm hearin'?" the old man hollered, his fists clenched at his sides. I broke another rule and ran down the pier, jumping over the missing planks without looking back. I was wrong about the old man. I should have considered him first and foremost!

I hurried down the wharf, thinking this 'New South' I'd landed in was something from medieval times. I'd have hated to have landed in the 'Old South.' What was wrong with these people? Every boat I've ever sailed has been mixed. How could they not be? My father never set a table with white and black plates. Growing up on the Cape, people got along for the most part. We have to in order to survive the long winters. Black, white, English, Irish, Wampanoag, Chinese, Brazilian, Portuguese, Jamaican, Cape Verdean, to name a few, all of us left ashore from one boat or another, and all of us mixing it up and helping each other, not all the time but when it counted. 'The Endless Tide' is how my father described it, "One big wave sweeping the world." Why this wave never reached these southern shores, I do not know.

I came to the end of the wharf and found the shrimp boat, *La Batre*, in the process of tying up. Dropping my seabag, I helped fasten her lines to the pier. The all-black crew viewed me with contained amusement as their captain came out of his wheelhouse. He was a big man, black as ink, with a round, pumpkin-sized head and bulging, white-rimmed eyeballs that looked like wet chicken eggs. He saw me standing with his bowline in my hand. Popping his damaged knuckles against his sweat-soaked chest, he called up to me, "What'ju want wd' us, boy?"

"Work, if you're turning around soon."

Under the captain's stern glare, the crew stopped their gawking and went about the business of unloading the catch.

"Who you wid'?" asked the captain, surveying the wharf for accomplices. Picking up my seabag, I replied, "Just me and my grip."

"Eva' shrimp before?"

"No, but I've fished plenty."

"Ya' come all the way ta' 'Bama to shrimp my boat?"

I shrugged. "Thought I'd give it a try."

Looking down the long line of shrimp boats crowding the wharf, the captain asked, "And none of 'dem other cappies will hire ya' on 'cause ja' gotz' da' Yankee blood?"

"Atta'bout describes it."

"Dem inbred crackers git' more predictable ever'day! Ain't eva' shrimp'd but ya' want ta' learn. Well, I ain't no racist and I could use an extra hand. So happens I gotz' me a man sick wid' da' flu. Long as ya' tow da' line, you'll do all right by me."

"When do we leave?"

"Soon as I getz dis here catch weighed and paid."

"And after?"

"We'll be on the Grounds before sunup ahead of da' rest of 'dese fools."

"What are you expecting?"

"A full hold. Don't come back 'til it iz. Got a problem wid' dat'?"

"Not-a-one."

"Glad ta' hear," said the captain, showcasing a row of straighter than straight gold-capped teeth. "We push off 'round midnight when da' moon is at her fullest. Shrimpies love it. Leaves me a trail as bright as the Yellar' Brick Road! Like following paydirt! Until then, stay outta the bars and find someplace ta' rest up. You gonna' need it."

"What do I call you besides captain?" I asked, hoping to get a surname so I can find out what reputation he has as a shrimper. It's a habit I started when I first arrived in Alaska, and it's saved me from going to sea with captains who no longer sail amongst the living.

"You don't, but you I'm callin' Tecumseh! That should give 'em crackers a real kick in 'da pants!" Tilting back his large head, the captain let out a loud, throaty laugh.

I came off the docks feeling good about my hire. The captain had a sense of humor, which was important because it meant he was making money, and if he was making money, so would his crew. A captain not willing to laugh at life's foibles is unlucky, or he's so tight with his wages that he's no doubt stealing from his crew and doesn't care if a man signs back on or not, his motto being 'Run 'em up and run 'em out!'

I started down a dirt road, passing abandoned cotton markets and tired-looking gas stations on my way. Putting heel to toe under a bluer than blue Alabama skyline, I felt the True Tramp, that I could walk forever, drink ditch water if I got thirsty and eat dirt from my bootheel if I get hungry. Bed down on the side of the road if I was ever tired enough to sleep, and use the stars overhead as my only blanket, free to pursue whatever I felt like pursuing, with no job too big or too small.

Over the past year, I'd sheared sheep in Montana, volunteered as a smoke jumper fighting wildfires in the High Sierras, and rode the rails from Sacramento to Juneau, where I ended up on the floor of a factory ship cutting salmon. And here I am, with eighteen trips around the sun, about to ship out as an Alabama shrimper working the flat calm of the Gulf of Mexico. 'One foot in front of the other' is my only mantra and as I tramp it on down the road, that's just what I do.

Walking five or so miles outside of town, I came to a cleared field with a giant beech tree growing mightily in its center. Stepping under the tree's cooling shade, I felt the temperature drop by ten degrees, the leaves on the hanging boughs acting as natural air conditioner. Taking out my bedroll, I unfurled it on a cropping of brittle grass and lay down at the base of the tree. Placing my hands behind my head, I closed my eyes, listening to the light wind rustling through the leaves with visions of the South dancing in my head. And though I wasn't at all tired, I soon fell fast asleep, undoubtedly due to my long walk and being unaccustomed to the wavy heat.

After a time, or no time at all, I found myself dreaming of a dark-haired debutante trailing a long, tapered white dress across a broad plantation porch. Walking between fluted Roman columns, the girl's head was tilted downwards with her hands clasped under her chin as if in prayer. A male voice called to her from somewhere near, a beau perhaps, but the girl took no notice. I watched the drama unfold from atop my bedroll, knowing that I was dreaming but unable to distinguish it from reality. The male voice called out for a second time, only I couldn't make out what he was saying, like I was hearing him underwater. The girl kept walking, never looking up. I wanted to call out to her, but I couldn't because my mouth was sewn shut, so there I lay, my body motionless as if trapped in ice.

Wringing her small, delicate hands, the debutante hastened her pace along the porch's rim. With her head still held low, I had no way of knowing her facial features and yet there was a familiar aura about her, as if I and I alone knew of her every sin and saintly act. Details of her life strobed before my eyes in a myriad of flashing images. I saw her as a young girl sitting at her father's knee, listening to him recite from a leather-bound tome within a gracious library. I saw her as a teenager, slipping out of a tightly bound corset before diving into a moonlit bog, her skin as luminous as the moon's reflection. Next, I saw her tending to a just-birthed calf, cleaning placenta from its nose and mouth and helping it to stand. I saw many things, but for her eyes that remained a mystery to me. Hoisting her dress, the debutante came off the porch and onto the lush green lawn before taking a knee and screaming through her fingers, "Wake up, Caleb! Wake up and swim!"

Ripping the stitches from my mouth, I broke through my frozen skin and took off running, with the debutante chasing after me. I saw the dirt road ahead, but no matter how fast or far I ran, I couldn't seem to escape the tree's shadow, the hanging boughs extending outward from the trunk to keep me in darkness. I was almost to the dirt road when I felt the girl's hot breath on the back of my neck, her voice continuing to call out, "Wake up and swim!" Lifting my knees to my chest, I escaped the girl's clutches and leapt into the light of the road. Shooting awake on my bedroll beaded in sweat, I expected the debutante to come leaping after me, only when I looked to where the plantation house had stood in my dream, there was nothing there.

The dream didn't make sense. Swim? Where would I swim? I'm in the middle of a grassy field far away from any standing water. Besides, I'm a great swimmer. I once swam from our harbor beach in Harwich all the way to Cahoon Hollow in Wellfleet, just to see if I could. Took me the better part of the day, but I did it. And weren't those surfers surprised when I swam in from the blue horizon to pass them before making my way up the National Sea Shore cliffs and enjoying a cheeseburger at the Beachcomber Grill.

The girl was real all right, only not from my time. I tried picturing her face, but I couldn't. It wasn't allowed. Rubbing the back of my blistered neck, I rolled up my bedroll and stuffed it inside my seabag, then took to the dusty crossroads which, in a few hours' time, I was to begin my tutelage as an Alabama shrimper.

Peering up the mast, my thoughts return to the present, where the wind has yet to show itself, so I remain in the cockpit spitting out apple seeds. My attention falls on a group of toddlers splashing about in the light surf of Community Beach. This is the beach where young mothers come to introduce their children to the sea. Though I have the not-so-pleasant memory of my father taking me by my ankles and tossing me into the face of an oncoming roller, telling me simply, "Swim!"

I watch an older boy catch hell from his mother further down the shoreline. Apparently for not keeping an eye on his baby brother at play in the tide pools. The boy nods in silent obedience, but I can tell he's pissed. He no doubt would rather be off exploring for wrecks and chumming for sand sharks with his friends rather than hanging on the kiddy beach babysitting his kid brother. I am about to turn away when the young mother, visibly frustrated, lifts the boy's chin with one hand and slaps him sharply across the face with the other. I sit up in the cockpit, but the boy takes the abuse like he's used to it. Slumping to his knees, he reluctantly helps baby brother build his sandcastle while their young mother rejoins the other young mothers reclining on beach chairs, sipping their Diet Pepsis through straws and chitchatting between quick drags of their long-stemmed cigarettes. It is a picture so grotesque that I laugh out loud, the sound carrying across the open water and onto the beach.

Standing abruptly, the boy knocks down the walls of the sand-castle with the sides of his feet. Baby brother bawls amid the ruins while big brother sprints along the water's edge. Spitting out the remainder of the apple, I climb on deck and onto the pulpit. Taking hold of the mainstay, I shout, "Sorry, kid, but your mom shouldn't do that!" The boy scans the cove, looking in my direction. I expect a vengeful tirade when his attention turns to a group of mastless sail-boats attached to a single mooring off to my port. And though the cove is cluttered with many moored boats, I am without doubt the only sailor within earshot.

"Name's Caleb!" I yell through cupped hands. "Live in the big house on the bluff! Stop by sometime! If I'm in port, I'll take you sailing!"

"Sailing?" asks the boy, a look of confusion on his face. "Sailing in what?"

Does he think I'm a merman treading water?

"The kid must be nearsighted," I say to myself, so I don't answer him. Instead, I let go of the mainstay and drop back into the cockpit.

Taking hold of the mainsheet, I mutter, "What self-respecting sailor lets an ebb tide take him out anyway? It's time I got up and got after it." With the wind remaining at a standstill, I take the boom in hand and carry it to port and then to starboard, creating my own wind, the brass jaws of the boom clanking against the mast as I begin to make way. The boy runs along the shoreline, following my progress. Near the cove's mouth, a stiff wind slips in and billows the mains'l. I climb atop the stern and kick the tiller to port. Hauling in the mainsheet, I take a starboard tack away from shore, leaving the boy at the end of a jetty breakwater scratching his head.

SQUALL

L ow-lying ground cover of heath and bayberry seemingly rewind along the far shoreline as I sail from the cove and into the bay. Off to my port, a bevy of black-hooded terns hovers in the updraft created by a red and white lobster boat as it bounds out from Namequoit Point. To my starboard, trap fishermen work the outwash plain, bringing up scores of blue crab in their crippled, outdated nets. I ride the wind a while before setting the bow chuck over the Chatham Yacht Club, standing bleach white behind a rippling sea of beach grass. I spot workers erecting catering tents on the crochet lawn and festooning them in red, white, and blue bunting.

"Bit late, ain't they?"

According to my calculations, it should be the 7th or possibly the 8th of July, but no way can it be the 4th. We pushed off from the docks in New Bedford on the 15th of June, hoping to fish both sides of the full moon by the end of the month, and we would have if a squall hadn't kicked up, flooded the engine room, and forced the captain to steam back early for repairs, at least that's how I remember it. It took us two weeks to get to our last fixed position on Georges Bank, and it would have taken us at least that long to limp into Stage Harbor for repairs. The only problem with keeping dates aboard a commercial fishing boat is that they have no meaning when you're working eighteen-hour shifts every day for a month. I was on the back deck repairing a leader cart that had been hauled in too tightly the night before, when a fierce wind whistled through the stray wires sounding like Jimi Hendrix playing "The Star-Spangled Banner" at Woodstock.

We were trolling ninety miles east of Block Island with limited success when Captain Jenkins got it into his head to steam for the Banks. The vessel I had signed on was a rusted heap named *Sea Pearl*, of all things, and at the helm was a captain who drank warm Budweiser the day long and wouldn't employ a Doppler Fish Finder or an Ocean Temperature Gauge. What with the overregulation and the already weak catches these days, that's like leaving your bait and tackle back on the dock.

"Captain Jenkins has the Fish Sense," his equally inebriated crew told me. Fish Sense, hell! Most times I'd find the captain asleep in his wheelhouse steaming for Spain, and it would take half the day to locate our sets. Not that it mattered. The tub trawls themselves were so filled with junk that the fish would have had to be blind to swim into them. It was like we were dragging pieces of the Berlin Wall down there, and when we did catch something, like the time I gaffed a giant sunfish swimming too close to the surface, it didn't do anyone any good because the compressor for the boat's salt water ice machine had broken down the day before. I had no idea why we were still steaming for the Banks. I tried to voice my concerns, but the captain wouldn't hear it, saying to me, "Not to worry, newbie. I'll fool 'em with a fresh catch sandwich. Now stop standing around askin' stupid questions and get that line wet!"

I watched the giant Mola Mola rot in the iceless fish hold for three days until the crew couldn't stand the stench, at which time the captain ordered me to "Bait her up!" Which I did, and for the next set the only fish we dragged through the back door were eight blue dogs. "Hole 'em and I'll sell 'em for cat food. I know a buyer," promised the captain, only there was no price on blue sharks, not even as bait. Couple that with the damage they did to our nets, and I knew I was on a broker.

I've sailed on a trawler like this before, and when the time came to settle up, the captain and boat were nowhere to be found, no doubt three states away shanghaiing another bunch of inebriates at some other dockside bar with tall tales of hungry fish and overflowing fish holds. It always amazes me how these clowns get put inside a wheelhouse, but when you're an owner, you're an owner, and Captain Jenkins was the sole owner of the *Sea Pearl*.

I came aboard after fishing a slammer trip on a Caribbean swordfisher out of San Juan. After landing on the New Bedford docks, I decided I'd sign with a local trawler rather than hitchhike back to the Cape, generally an easy gig compared to swinging a meat saw on a sword boat. Four weeks and I'd be dropped off at the Chatham Fish Pier with a few extra sawbucks in my pocket, or so I was promised. From sunup to sundown we set and hauled against the tide, reeling in miles of fish-free gill net seemingly for the fun of it. The boat should have been named *Calamity* because that's what happened not soon after.

Sinking the forked-end of a crowbar into a tangle of net, I pull back, hoping to draw some slack, but the tension remains as tight as when the spool was last hauled in. I spit on my hands and try again, but to no avail. Running my grimy sleeve across my sweaty brow, I look to the sky and notice the anvil top of a thunderhead forming above the southern horizon. Right then, a flock of low-flying geese comes over the cart house heading for dry land, that in itself is a sure sign of bad weather to follow. "Shit," I say to myself, with my emaciated shipmate standing beside me staring vacantly at the growing seas.

I return my attention to the port spool and re-sink the crowbar, thinking that surely Captain Jenkins is on his SSB radio by now checking with the captains of the southern fleet to get a fix on what's in store for us. How could he not be? If he's awake and sees his barometer dropping, he'll know we're in for a rough patch, and yet the boat keeps steaming south. The realization that I'm at the mercy of 'Captain Grog' and his equally inept crew sends a shiver up my spine.

I look past the port gunwale and see that the wind is now blowing off the tops of the waves. Freeing the crowbar from the spool, I stow it in the toolbox as the leading edge of the storm comes over the boat, blotting out the midday sun and casting the surrounding seas in silvery darkness. A sudden microburst rains on deck in a slanting fashion. I take my shipmate by his spindly arm and drag him under the cart house to get him out of the weather, the old shellback mumbling, "Cape Cod girls have no combs. They comb their hair with codfish bones." It's all for naught, however, as *Sea Pearl* takes a windward roll to port that sends the two of us sliding across the back-deck and slamming into the starboard gunwale. I help the old fisherman to his feet and point at the strewn deck.

"We'd better stow those flag buoys, or we'll be the ones fishing them out after this dirty wind blows."

I'd hoped the threat of extra work would get the fisherman up and going, but the man remains a heap in my arms, slurring the words, "Emperors own empires and as Man owns the seas," quoting Melville, I think. How I wished I was back on the teak wood piers of San Juan unloading Double Markers under a blazing Caribbean sun, but wishing doesn't make it so. With the howling wind building a confused sea around us, I wrestle the fisherman into a Mae West (life jacket) and leave him gripping the starboard rail, then forge my way to the belowdecks hatch, where the rest of the crew are sleeping one-off.

Lifting open the hatch, I call down, "All hands on deck! We got a blower coming on!" Getting no response, I am about to call down for a second time when Captain Jenkins shows himself on the gangplank, appearing untucked and rueful.

"Leave 'em alone, newbie!" bellows the captain. "They been hauling in all night!"

"But I've seen this before, Captain!" I shout back to him. "Where She comes up like She's been there from the beginning!"

"This ain't nothin' but a pissin' contest!" replies Captain Jenkins, looking about him as if seeing the weather for the first time. I leave the belowdecks hatch open and launch myself up the gangplank.

Pointing at the growing waves building beyond the bow, I say to the captain, "*Sea Pearl*'s listing. Shouldn't we transfer some of the ballast and snug down? Or at least drop the outriggers?" Seizing me by my rubberized bib overalls, the captain hauls off and clips me on the chin. The blow sends me cartwheeling over the gangplank and onto the deck, where I land spread-eagle on my back.

"Been fishing these waters before ya' eva' sucked on your momma's teat! Now get to un-fouling that port spool before I throw ya' into the World my damn self! This is what we do, boy, or didn't you say you'd been to sea?"

"Year...round," I moan, turning onto my elbows and breathing haltingly. "Summer...I drag for scallops...Fall...cut salmon on a factory ship...Winter...pull crab pots on the Straits...Spring...work on a sword boat in the Carib..."

"This should be a walk in the park for ya' then," laughs the captain, but I can tell he's impressed. Not many fishermen work year-round these days and even fewer will chance fishing the Bering Strait come winter.

"Tell ya' what I'll do," offers the captain. "Forget mending the net. I want you to get the starboard spool ready. Mackerel love this foamy chop! Brings 'em up from the bottom to feed! We'll get our catch on this set and I'll have 'em back on the docks before they start to stink." Massaging the knuckles of his right hand, the captain takes another look at the roiling seas before ducking back inside his wheelhouse.

I touch at my swollen jaw, grateful that it's not broken, then pick myself up and zigzag my way across the back deck. Upon reaching cart house, I find my shipmate bent at the waist in the throes of the rum horrors, tossing up colorful batches of liquid courage over the side. Unlocking the starboard spool, I ready the net for its three-mile trek out *Sea Pearl*'s back door.

Blind Rage is the term commonly employed, and I've suffered from it since I was a small boy. I've had episodes in the past where I got so mad that I blacked out, never remembering the incident that triggered the rage until days and sometimes weeks later. As Gramp tells it, he would have to submerge my beet-red body in a tub of cold water just to calm me down, jokingly adding that steam would rise when he lowered me in. And it's not physical pain that triggers it. I could be beaten with a lead pipe, and my blood pressure wouldn't rise a notch, not that I'd ever let it come to that. Whatever anger issues, I have run deeper, and yet there have been other times when the slightest of slights have set me off.

I am reminded of the day I was invited to a classmate's birthday party. The girl's name was Layla and her family had recently relocated to the Cape from Brockton, a tough town outside of Boston. Her father had moved his plumbing business to Chatham and invited the entire fifth-grade class to his daughter's party being held at the Cape Bowl in Hyannis. I didn't know the girl very well, but she seemed nice, and she was pretty, so I went. Gramp drove me in the IH with the engine, choking and coughing the whole way, so needless to say, I was late.

Dropping me off in front of Cape Bowl, Gramp handed me a ten spot, but I told him that it was a birthday party, and that I didn't need money. I also told Gramp that I could get a ride back with my new friend Jimmy, another recent wash-ashore, so he wouldn't have to pick me up, not knowing at the time that Jimmy was at home with a cold. I ran inside the bowling alley and rushed up to the counter to get my bowling shoes.

"Five dollars," says the pimple-faced clerk, holding up a pair of black and white bowling shoes.

"I'm with the birthday party," I tell him, pointing to my fellow classmates stuffing their faces with cake.

Shaking his head, the clerk points to a thin man with a thinner than thin mustache standing amid whirling dervishes aswirl around him. "Talk to that guy," says the clerk, replacing the shoes on the rack. The thin man sees me approach and takes out a clipboard.

"Name?" he asks, looking down at me with a plumber's smell about him.

"Caleb Forrest."

"You're late."

"I'm here now."

"I can see that," says the thin man begrudgingly. Nodding his bird-shaped head at my classmates, he continues, "Go on and grab a piece of cake before it runs out."

"I need to rent bowling shoes."

"Why are you telling me for?"

"I need five dollars and I don't have it."

"You come late to my daughter's party and now you want me to pay for your bowling shoes?" he asks incredulously. "I suppose you need a ride home too?"

"I might," I answer truthfully, looking around for Jimmy.

"If you leave now, you should make the Chatham line before sundown," says the thin man, with an even thinner smile before turning his back on me and rejoining the party. I sit around for a while, until I can't take the clerk's dirty looks anymore and head for the side exit.

Once outside, I decide to take the plumber up on his challenge. I start walking west to where Main Street Hyannis connects with Route 28 in the town of Yarmouth. I keep walking, passing through the towns of South Yarmouth, Dennis, Dennisport, and Harwich before entering Chatham proper, only I don't stop there. Passing through the towns of Orleans, Eastham, and Wellfleet, I am almost to the Truro Headlands when my mental fog finally lifts and I realize where I am.

Gramp is awake and sober when I drag my sore and exhausted body into our kitchen. He doesn't ask me what happened or my bowling score. Propping me on our kitchen counter, he gently unties my threadbare sneakers and peels off my sweat-soaked, bloody socks. And when he does ask me what happened, I'm too tired to lie and tell him the truth. Emptying the sink of dishes, Gramp runs cold water over my swollen and blistered feet before wrapping them in thick gauze and carrying me up to my room, where I sleep until noon the next day. It was during this *time out* that the town elders began showing up at the house, the ringing of the ship's call bell attached to the salon door wreaking havoc with my dreams with each visit.

It wasn't more than two months later that Layla's father withdrew her from school. He'd decided to move the family yet again, this time to the town of Lynn, which, at the time, was also the stolen car capital of the East Coast. Turns out my 'walkabout' had traveled from mouth to ear, and no one in town would give Layla's father any business. The Cape's a small place and when you go up against someone of Gramp's good name and stature, you're writing your own ticket back across the canal. Nobody will deal with you. It's like you're invisible. As it should be. Too bad for Layla. Like I said, she seemed nice, but to hell with her father! Who doesn't give a kid five bucks to rent bowling shoes?

I recall being at Jimmy's house months later when his dad called me into his private study for a chat. I didn't know what his intentions were until he brought up my walkabout, which I had since forgotten.

"I mapped it," he said, without explanation or expression. "You walked for forty miles and more on the day you left the Cape Bowl in Hyannis."

"Could be," I replied.

"Trust me, Cal, you did. I know the captain has a difficult time getting around these days, so I want to give you this." Reaching onto his blotter, Mr. Hallet took out one of his Hallet Paving and Construction business cards and handed it to me. "If you ever get into another situation like that, I want you to call this number, and I want you to call collect, any time, day or night, and I'll come to pick you up. And don't think twice about it, do you understand?" I took the card and nodded before asking, "Were you one of the ones who ran him out of town?"

"Never mind about that," replied Mr. Hallet. "Just know that me and others, along with your grandfather, are making sure that something like this never happens again. It could have been any of you kids, even Jimmy. I believe he would have made it, not all the way to Truro like you did perhaps, but that doesn't matter. What matters is that one of ours was put in danger, and that's not going to happen on my watch. Jimmy carries the same card and he knows the drill. I'm glad you're all okay. Keep watching each other's back, like I know you do. Now, why don't the two of you go outside and throw the ball around? I've got some work to catch up on. Oh, and you're welcome to dinner."

"Thanks, Mr. Hallet. Another time, maybe. Gramp's got fried chicken on the grill tonight. Can Jimmy come over?" Mr. Hallet smiled for the first time during our conversation, saying, "Of course. Bon appetit!"

For some reason, I can't seem to remember cutting the trip short and steaming back. The punch to the jaw didn't do it. If I were the captain, I would have punched me. Experienced or not, I was still a newbie aboard his boat. I should have kept my mouth shut and done the job he was paying me to do or not paying me to do. There must have been another incident aboard *Sea Pearl* where I got so mad that I blacked out because, according to the raised tents on the Chatham Yacht Club lawn, today is definitely the Fourth of July.

THE HORSE SHORE

The boom whips above my head as I come about to take a port tack for the Horse Shore. Riding the outgoing tide, I pass the dilapidated oyster shanties on the beach that appear to be clinging to one another in desperation, along with the remnants of an old bottle dump, the many shards of colored glass shining like wet fish scales on the collapsing hillside. Rounding the bluish dune at the Point, I sail into the lee of a crescent cove, where a long-billed dowitcher scoots across the white sand before disappearing under a tangle of poverty grass. I put the bow into the wind and render the mainsheet, then tie off on a tilted piling capped in slippery strands of blue-green algae, what Gramp calls "Mermaids' Hair."

I feel guilty for not leaving him a note saying I was in port. I could be pushing eighty, like Gramp, and he'd still want to know my where-abouts when I'm out sailing the Realm. It's a pact we've had since I first set out on a box dory.

"How'm I supposed ta' know where ta' find ya' if'n I don't know where ta' look? I don't want to know your bidness or what purdy lass ya' got on the High Seas. Just how far out and what time back. That'a way if'n ya' do get into trouble, I'll know the whereabouts ta' get you out!"

From this angle, our bluff reminds me of the face of some unknown mariner jutting from the cliff, waving his whiskery chin down at me in silence and defiance. I stand before the mast and take hold of the mainstay, shouting up to the bluff, "Gramp! Hey, Gramp! Are you there?" I wait a full minute and call again. If he's at the house and he hears me at all, it will take him a while to show himself on the bluff, so I dip back into the cuddy and take out a second apple. Returning to the stern, I bite off a chunk of the tasty red flesh, and it feels like I've wadded cotton in my mouth, like my tongue forgot how a Red Delicious is supposed to taste. I eat the apple down to its core anyway, spitting out the seeds.

"Hey, Gramp! Are you there up there or what?" I wait for another full minute before cursing his name. But I can never get too mad at the 'Old Man,' though. After all, it was him who raised me. Not that we haven't argued on occasion, we have plenty, but never to the point of raising our voices. As a younger man, whenever I had a problem that I deemed worthy of discussion, Gramp would lead me into his chart room and sit me on his copper-studded captain's chair. Listening to my grievances, he always gave them the attention I thought they deserved.

These discussions stemmed mostly from our self-imposed impoverishment, like why we couldn't afford new clothes or why we never went anywhere, not to restaurants, not even to the movies. I'd argue that, if he were to sell off an acre or two, we could live like kings, and he wouldn't have to push a broom at the Orleans Court House anymore, and that, with the extra money, I could one day go off to college and try to make something out of myself. I'd given the speech more than once, and it always left me out of breath and mentally exhausted. Gramp's rote answer to me then is the same as it is today.

"Can't tell ya' what for, Caleb. You'll have to figure that out for y'self. 'Bout me not workin', that's not why the Timekeeper put me here. I've done my share and you'll do yours. A boy your age should work hard. Far as your schooling goes, all ya' need to know is up there on 'em bookshelves. Doesn't take a college degree to make a man. Most the authors ya' see on 'em shelves neva' had a degree and yet that's who they're all studying afta'! Somethin' interests ya', let me know, and we'll find the answers together." Then, in a serious tone, he'd continue, "True knowledge comes from experience and the effort it takes to overcome our failures firsthand. Mental will and desire is what forces our outcomes, as it has since the day we first crawled from the mud." He'd always pin me to the mat on that one.

Debating Gramp was like debating Moses on the Mount. It would be a blight on my character to say that I needed the money, me being so young and strong and him an old man. And yet here we were, each as well read as any Rhodes Scholar yet living well below the poverty line. A man of Gramp's age and stature pushing a broom! I feel ashamed whenever I think of it, that I let him down, but at least it gives him pocket money and keeps him out of the Squire three days a week.

Gramp's all the family I have, and me him, my mother's side of the family having disowned her after she married my father. And Gramp's worked plenty — from the time he was eight, unloading catches and mending nets down at the Fish Pier, until now. And he'd just turned sixteen when he first joined the Army, taking part in the Battle of Ypres and helping to drive back the Germans for the first time in the Great War. WWII found Gramp in the Pacific serving aboard the USS *Pennsylvania*, where he manned an anti-aircraft gun, fighting off Japanese fighter pilots at the Battle of Leyte: the gunners of the mighty *Penn* blasting four Japanese Zeroes from the sky in less than five minutes! His fireside tales of adventure read better than that of Conrad or London!

Gramp was in command of his own sword boat when my father was born, and he had long since hung up his captain's hat when my father donned his. Whenever my father was at sea, it was Gramp's job to look after me, which he did, for the most part, even taking me with him to the Fish Pier to bend the ear of a captain or two. Other times he'd leave me alone in the rambling house, which was fine by me, only to stagger through the door upon his return smelling of Jamaican rum. At least he kept his drinking out of the house in those days. He doesn't anymore, and why should he, with my long absences at sea.

It was the spring after my father's boat went missing that Gramp climbed the spiral staircase to his room and took out his oilskins.

Most of the insurance money paid out on the *Debra Ann*; also the name of my mother, went to the families of the drowned seamen, as per my father's instructions, with the remainder going to some made-up town tax, according to Gramp. Taking down his crinkled sou'wester from the hat rack in our parlor, he read me the riot act before shipping out on an oyster boat, and he was pushing seventy at the time.

The boat's owner knew Gramp from his time harpooning swordfish off Cape Hatteras. The story goes that a young fisherman nicknamed "Skip" was standing watch one night when a rogue wave shipped over the foredeck and carried him over the side. No one knew of the fisherman's plight until his relief came on deck an hour later. That's when the 'Man Overboard' call went out, suspending all fishing on the Grand Banks. The twelve-vessel sword fleet made up of mostly Gloucester, Nantucket, and Chatham fishermen, along with the Coast Guard and a crew of seal hunters from Newfoundland, began crisscrossing a five-hundred-square-mile patch of near-freezing water in the vain hope of finding the lost fisherman.

The *Florence* was long-lining fifty miles to the northeast when the call came over the ship-to-shore radio. Captain Let jotted down the coordinates to where the fisherman was thought to have gone over and took out his charts. These weren't the charts given to sea captains by the NOAA (National Oceanic and Atmospheric Administration). No, these were his own charts passed down and updated by eight generations of Forrest sea captains who'd plied these same waters in pursuit of the various catches of their day.

Wetting the tip of a freshly shaved #2 pencil, Captain Let lightly traces a line between the coordinates given on the lost fisherman and his own position. He asks his first mate, Mr. Rondike, to drop a lead over the side and check the speed of the current. "Six knots and pulling east," reports Mr. Rondike, returning to the wheelhouse. The captain jots down the numbers and returns to his charts while the *Florence* ghosts in the water. After an hour or so the crew begins to hem and haw, for when a man goes overboard, which could be anyone of them at any time, they expect a quick response.

Mr. Rondike, a rather tall Dinka tribesman from Sudan, guards the gangplank with his imposing forearms folded across his muscular chest. And when the call comes for the captain to show himself, Mr. Rondike steps out onto the gangplank and smiles down at the crew.

"Capt'n's workin' izz magic and ain't none of ya' mackerel-snappa's gettin' past me no how. So stow ya'selves and maybe ya'll learn sumpton."

Captain Let continues to study his charts. Most were drawn on linen, frayed around the edges and yellowed with time. Coming back inside the wheelhouse, Mr. Rondike peers over the captain's shoulder, saying, "What'ja' got, Capt'n? Da' natives are getting' restless."

"If'n this is where he leaped," says Captain Let, pointing to a nautical degree on his chart. "He's either dead from hypothermia by now and food for the sharkies. But, if he went over 'bout here," he says, pointing to another spot, "and he's got some type of floatation, then he's got himself a chance. Not much, but some."

"Where's 'here,' Cappy?" asks Mr. Rondike, staring at the nautical hieroglyphics. "All's I's see'n is dem little wiggles disappearin' into dem small circles."

"An offshoot of the Gulf Stream. Fifty-eight, maybe sixty-two degrees this time of year. Right whales once followed this break to get to their breeding grounds in the Hudson. Might still. No wider than a mile and no longer than twenty. Get the birds up and cut the set. Let's get steaming."

And Mr. Rondike does just that, severing the four-mile line of dragnet with his razor-sharp machete. He told me once that he used that very machete to shoo away lions when he was a boy herding sheep on the arid plains of Sudan.

"Ta' us, dem lions ain't nothin' but a bunch of kittens, like dem sharkies ain't nothin' but worthless sea dogs, chewing up our nets and stealing our catch. No lion will attack a man if he has a stick with 'im.

But if he ain't walking wid' purpose, dem cats will drag 'im off inta' the bushes and eat 'im up. So it izz' with 'dem sharkies. And if ya' eva' find yo'self over the side and one comes up and starts nosin' at ya', swim strong and they'll usually let ya' alone. But sometimes ya' might get a big bossy fella, maybe wants to use your leg for a tooth-pick. If that happens, hit 'im on the nose and let 'im know ya' ain't goin' easy. It's when ya' scared and start kickin' and a-screamin' that they come for ya'. Like it is on dry land, only da' lions and da' sharkies is us! What'cha Uncle Rondike izz' tryin' ta' tell ya', Caleb, izz' ta' neva' show weakness. Do so and ya'll likely end up in a cage. And where would ya' rather be, in the maw of some great beast or in a cage?"

"I'd rather be somewhere I can fight back," I answered Mr. Rondike, in my pajama'd youth.

"Good!" exclaimed a wrinkled and aged Mr. Rondike, sitting on our back porch. "'Cause ya' ain't a man 'less ya' can fight back! Goin' unda' when ya' made yer' best effort ain't no sin, it's just nature come callin' is all. There's a sayin' where I come from and it goes like 'dis, 'Somewhere da' Sky touches da' Earth and da' name of that place izz' da' End.' Long ways off for you, little man, but for me, I ain't there yet, but I sure can see it."

Mr. Rondike passed not long after our conversation. I found him on the back porch sitting in my father's rattan chair with a freshly lit Winston smoldering betwixt his knuckles. His eyes were wide open as if in surprise, looking out across the bay like he'd just been slapped. Gramp and I were the only family Mr. Rondike had, as he'd chosen to take from the ample sea rather than farm his sandy, drought-ridden birthplace.

And he'd long since outlived his three wives and thirteen children, all dead from his country's never-ending civil wars. Though he never mentioned it, I could tell that it pained him, and he was hard measured to spend a dime on himself, sending all of his earnings to his kinfolk, not that it did any good in the end. He slept aboard ship and ate aboard ship, and when he wasn't at sea, he slept and ate here at the house, and he was the only man living or dead who Gramp would let take the wheel, besides for my father of course.

Gramp selected the finest cedar planking and fashioned a casket in our barn. Using square-headed nails, salvaged from the decking of a long-forgotten shipwreck, he worked the planks into a fitted prow and stern, then spent the rest of the week caulking and varnishing the small boat until it proved seaworthy enough to carry his friend into the Realm.

Aboard *Sea Gypsy*, I ferried the three of us across the Bar and past Pollock Rip to where we awaited a brilliant sunrise. Using his own slim knife, Gramp cut the towline and, without sermon or prayer, sent off his longtime friend with his bootheel; the casket drifted with the outgoing tide to where the Sun meets the Sea, and I was glad for that.

Steaming into the North Atlantic chop, Captain Let remains at the helm with Mr. Rondike manning the port spotlight. The crew keeps a lookout along the gunwales fore, aft, port, and starboard. Nobody takes a mess this night and nobody sleeps. The *Florence* is some thirty miles east of where the Coast Guard and the sword fleet are grid searching when Mr. Rondike spots the lost fisherman floating on his back, tied inside a horseshoe life preserver. Hearing the news, Captain Let emerges from his wheelhouse to the cheers of the crew.

Mr. Rondike takes control of the boat from the remote helm and gently brings the *Florence* abaft beam of the lost fisherman. Bounding down the ladder, the crew parts before the captain as he reaches over the side and plucks the fisherman from the pitch-black sea. He then hands the unconscious fisherman to Mr. Rondike, who cradles the body like he's cradling a football while hitting the man repeatedly on the small of his back, releasing a torrent of seawater from his mouth.

Shaking violently, the fisherman groans, and that's when the crew takes over. Stripping him of his wet clothes and dressing him in flannels soaked in hot oil, the fisherman is carried belowdecks, where he's placed in the glory hole and wrapped in warm blankets. Tied inside a swinging hammock with a slop bucket positioned underneath, Mr. Rondike stays with the fisherman, clearing mucus from his nose and mouth and turning his face toward the bucket whenever the need arises.

The fisherman, known as Henry "Skip" Warren, regained consciousness aboard the *Florence* midway into her rendezvous with the Coast Guard cutter *Reliance*. The first question Skip asked was, "Who was it fished me out?"

To which Mr. Rondike replied, "'Twas Capt'n Let who snatched ya' from the dark trenches. Ya' have 'im ta' thank, but he ain't havin' none of it."

Skip smiled before saying, "I've heard of him. Never lets a man drown less he knows how to swim. How'd he find me in all that blue?"

"Same way he finds da' fish," answered Mr. Rondike. "Wid' his magic charts. Dat'mon could bring Poseidon his'self though da' back door long as he thought he'd fetch a good price!"

Though Gramp had piloted many a vessel in his day, he was far too old for deck work, so Skip made him his tongman. Scavenging the bottom of Wellfleet Harbor in his motorized dredge, Skip would drop Gramp off at low tide on Billingsgate Island, where he'd walk the shallows culling oysters with a long-handled, wooden tong. Gramp had a few good weeks, even out-hauling the dredge on one occasion, but on his last fateful day he unknowingly stepped on a drab, grey skate lying on the bottom. The fish took off and he lost his balance. Falling backwards, he landed on a partially submerged rock, fracturing three vertebrae in his lower spine.

There was nothing like workman's comp back then for fishermen. Skip helped out as best he could, paying for Gramp's initial hospital visits and continuing with his tongman pay. But Skip had a business to run and his own family to provide for. Truth be told, Skip was having a hard go of it. Between the already small hauls from the over-dragged oyster beds along with the escalating cost of diesel, he eventually had to sell his dredge and relocate his family to Marathon Key, where he opened a bait shop that he continues to run to this day.

With Gramp laid up, I started a strawberry patch on what I like to call our back forty. At first, I had only a few scraggly rows of struggling seedlings, but by harvest time, I had over fifty rows tilled, sown, and growing, and boy did they grow! I must have planted on an old Indian latrine! Unlike Captain Nehi and the rest of my forefathers, turns out it was me who had the green thumb. I put up a fruit stand along Stoney Hill Road that runs along our property.

The summer tourists loved the overflowing strawberries I'd place in woven baskets wrapped in wax paper, thinking it homespun and quaint, not realizing that we were eating on the money I took in. And while it might be homespun, nothing people do on the Outer Cape to support themselves should ever be considered 'quaint.' We do it to survive the long winters. My most profitable customers were the wives of the Portuguese fishermen, who bought my strawberries by the bushel to use in their summer jams and preserves, and also because their husbands gave them the money knowing of our hardship.

The time came when Gramp's doctors told him that if he were ever to walk again, he'd need an operation. Gramp put it off as long as he could, sometimes spending a week or more lying atop the kitchen table so he could be in arm's reach of the fridge when I was out working the fields. Upon the realization that his back wasn't going to heal itself, Gramp reluctantly submitted, only it wasn't the operation that almost killed him. It was the selling of a quarter acre of land to cover the cost.

"Never did I believe it would come to this. Our land is our blood, Caleb. She is our sister. Let 'em cut up their own. Not a hemline would I take from her but for this foolish accident. An old fisherman too long on the beach. I should have swallowed the anchor and stayed ashore!" Waiting for the orderlies to wheel him into the operating chamber, Gramp grabbed my wrist with his liver-spotted hand. "If I go on the table, I want ya' ta' do one thing for me."

"Name it and I'll do it," I told him, my eyes beginning to well.

"Promise me you'll have plenty of young'uns so they can enjoy the land and pass it down to theirs. Children need a place where they can play and explore. A wild place and to hell with trimmed hedges and white picket fences! What I done is a sin, Caleb! If I were a braver man, I'd have rolled myself into the drink, but I have you to care for, don't I? Captain Nehi would understand. I had to sell!" As the order-lies wheeled him away, Gramp called out to me for what I feared would be the last time. "Promise me you'll keep her intact! Let 'em hoot and holler at the town meetings! Who are they anyway but a bunch of wash-ashore Coofs! Wherever ya' go and whatever ya' do, keep paying down her tax. If ya' do that, they can't take her away from us!"

I look again to the bluff, but no Gramp. Untying the bowline from the tilted piling, I coil the slack and toss it on deck. Pushing the tiller to port, I shove off and haul in. I am gaining way when I chance a quick glance over my right shoulder and spot a sticklike figure standing on the bluff. I wave my arms and shout, "Gramp! Hey, Gramp!" but the figure doesn't appear to hear or see me, Gramp's eyes and ears being what they are. Bringing the spyglass up to sight, I align the crosshairs to where stands my grandfather with his fists balled at his sides, staring blankly over the barrier beach. His face appears ashen and his cheeks look damp, like he's been crying. Perhaps he's taking to drink and is out searching for his Flossy.

Sea spray kicks up and wets the lens. I wipe the lens clean with the tail of my T-shirt and bring the spyglass back up to see that Gramp has left the bluff. In his place stands a large, black dog with pointed ears and quilted fur, like a husky. I have never seen this dog and have no idea what it's doing on our bluff. What strikes me most about the animal isn't its great size but its eyes — clear, like glass marbles, appearing to be looking out at nothing and everything at the same time, as if it were blind. I spit on the lens and look again, but the black dog has vanished too.

Approaching the Narrows, I consider coming about, but I'm in stays with no place to tack, so I continue onward, deciding then and there to continue sending Gramp his grocery money when I'm away, as if I had a choice. If he wants to drink rum the day long and spin his bygone tales of yore, so be it. If there's a man alive who's earned the right, it's my grandfather, sword boat captain Lester J. Forrest.

THE NARROWS

I pass the channel buoy marking the racing waters between Sipson's and Little Sipson's Island and haul in. I notice a blitz of blues churning the water ten yards off to my port in a feeding frenzy, the piranhas of the sea having found their way into the bay. They were a favorite of my father's, especially batter-fried. Not that he was much of a fish eater, he wasn't, my father saying to me once, "Living with 'em a month or more at sea, the last thing you want is to be snackin' on 'em when ya' get back!" I'm a lot like him in that regard. I'll take a charbroiled hamburger over a lobster roll any day of the week, but if it's freshly dug clams you're talking about, stand back and watch me eat!

Many a summer day did Jimmy, Chumley, and I walk the flats digging up clams with our feet, usually in beds of ten or more. Opening the thick, rounded shells with our shucking knives, we'd slide the slippery meat into our mouths, feet and all, then toss the empty husks over our shoulders as we went along. I miss those days and my heart stings with the memory, but I keep telling myself what's done is done, and yet no matter how far I travel, my conscience is always there waiting for me, ready to pounce. I hope to rid myself of this burden when I visit with the ranger later today, only "visit" isn't the right word. More like "confront." Until that happens, I have to stay focused, and the best way to do that is by commanding my boat.

Taking hold of the tiller, I angle the bow chuck between the islands' competing shorelines and join with the current. Not many sailors take this shortcut to the inner harbor due to its shallow draft and racing current, but I've done so since I was a small boy. To me, it's like getting a free ride on a roller coaster. Sailing along the outer edge, I come about and head into the fold where waves within waves undulate beneath the hull, propelling *Sea Gypsy* forward as if on rollers. I am now in the Narrows with no need for any artificial conveyance, so I lower the mains'l and reef it to the boom, then take up the centerboard to let *Sea Gypsy* spin on her bottom like a carnival teacup.

My sudden appearance causes a flock of black-backed gulls to take wing. Lifting from the flats like a squadron of B-52 bombers, the gulls glide inches above the roiling water before rounding a smallish sandbar and circling back to base. I look to Sipson's Island and chance spotting a coyote sticking its pointy head above the growth to watch me carry along. The canine stretches wide its glistening jaws before ducking back beneath the heath to continue in its pursuit of Peter Cottontail.

I smile at the simplicity of it all. It doesn't take much to enjoy oneself, and lately, I've been forgetting that. For some time now I've had the feeling that life was passing me by, that I wasn't doing what I should be doing. To be a commercial fisherman is a way for me to make a living and nothing more. While it's true that working aboard a scallop boat pays a lot more than manning a cash register at Snows Hardware store, I never saw it as carrying on the *family tradition*. My forced profession is due purely to economics. With Gramp laid up and strawberries out of season, I hit the docks. First mending nets and unloading catches, like Gramp and my father had done, then climbing aboard and shipping out. I had no idea how dire our family finances were. Whatever I brought in, I gave to Gramp. I never asked him what he did with the money. What did I care? There was food in the fridge, and I was working. It wasn't until my nineteenth birthday that Gramp invited me into his chart room and creaked open the family ledger to show me the books.

Sitting at his chart table, Gramp took down a broad ledger from his rolltop desk and placed the book in front of me before leaving the room without saying a word. Leaning over the table, I began peeling back the delicate pages. I noticed right away that the ledger's pages weren't paper but vellum, known also as calfskin, with slotted columns running down the page filled with numbers and dates, each page accounting for one calendar year going back generations. These pages showed every keg of nails bought, sails replaced, seed purchased, piano gifted, wooly monkey sold, cases of rum stored, doxy lady quieted, ship pirated, and booty claimed. My eyes ached from the dull light, reading the figures written like they were stacked Chinese characters. What finally caught my attention, after hours of reading, was the net profit against the sum owed double-underlined at the bottom of the last page and written in Gramp's chicken scratch. I rechecked the numbers against his tried-and-true Victor adding machine, and they proved out to be true.

As if on cue, Gramp walked in with two steaming cups of hot chocolate. I took my cup and put it down, and when I confronted him, all he could say was, "Captain Nehi bought the land from an old Indian fella. Paid 'im his price. It was afterwards that then-governor John Hancock threw in the rest for the captain's service to free the States. Truth is, nobody 'round here wanted the land 'cause they knew it to be a rocky mess. Though no one in town stood up to tell the captain, being who they were and are still. For whatever reason the bloody town's been after it ever' day since! We've been payin' the scoundrels back for generations. What makes us so poor. It's me who's failed ya', Caleb, not expectin' your dad to leave us so soon. They got no right!"

Working sunup to sundown, practically the year-round, I barely make enough to keep the two of us afloat. It's the reason I can't ever save enough to fix up the house. And what I make on the High Seas isn't chicken feed. I make more fishing in one month, but not every month, than the realtors and stockbrokers I see strutting around town dressed in their expensive clothes and driving their BMWs, and it's still not enough. If I were to stop working, we would last a month, maybe two, before the taxman came to collect and toss us out on our ears.

I realize that Gramp wants to keep the land intact, but when I get my chance, and it could be any day given Gramp's advanced age, I'll sell every square acre, go to college, and head west like I've always wanted to do. Only, deep down I don't want that to happen. I love my grandfather and to go on living my life without him would be dull at best. And that's the crux of my problem. And yet it's not so much the land tax bringing us down, but the State's accruing interest that has been growing since the early to mid-1800s. How is one supposed to get ahead of that? Meaning that I have become the snake-head eating its own tail.

I'd thought by now I'd have accomplished more, done more, seen more. My father had his own boat by the time he was my age, and yet here I am vagabonding on the High Seas with no intention of ever becoming a captain. I've never sailed on the same boat twice, which is the reason I've never made first mate, as if I believed the work was beneath me, that I was holding out for something better to come along. But there was a time when I thought the world was my oyster and I the champion shucker. Only the world keeps spinning, and I find myself at the point where I first began, except with the shadow of a noose hanging around my neck. Not so long ago I had a chance to escape my bondage, and I blew it by letting a silly thing like pride get in the way.

Standing in the hallway of Chatham High School, I prepare myself to knock on my guidance counselor's door, and even though I am well into my junior year, I have yet to meet the man. Truth be told, I hadn't given his office much thought until I decided that I might want to try for college, and at the end of every college application was a space reserved for a guidance counselor's recommendation. It has always been rumored that Mr. Vick gravitated toward the more well-to-do students, the sons and daughters of prestigious university alumni, and not the kids of the working stiffs, but I decided I'd give it a shot anyway. What do I have to lose? I am about to knock when the office door opens abruptly. Filling the frame with his enormous girth, my guidance counselor looks down at me like I'm a Jehovah's Witness about to hand him a copy of the *Watchtower*.

"Can I help you?"

"I have an appointment."

"An appointment with whom?" he asks, looking past me down the hall.

"With you. You're Mr. Vick, right?"

"When and with whom did you make this appointment?" he clarifies in a tired manner.

"Yesterday. With your secretary."

"Ah, yes! I was away attending a graduation party. A student I helped get into university. Invited, you understand."

"That's why I'm here, to talk to you, about college."

Checking his watch, Mr. Vick quickly ushers me into his office and shuts the door. "Let's keep this short. I have a teachers' meeting scheduled, and we have a number of important issues to discuss."

"Teachers' meeting, huh?" I mumble to myself. I once peeked in on one such meeting and all I saw were teachers sitting around smoking their brains out and stuffing fistfuls of potluck into their greasy mouths. It was like a scene from a Roman orgy. It's a wonder they kept their clothes on!

"Your name again?" he asks.

"Caleb. Caleb Forrest."

Aiming his extended belly at the far wall, Mr. Vick follows it across his office to a filing cabinet and opens a drawer marked C-F. Rifling through the manila folders, he stops on the one stamped FORREST J CALEB and pulls it out.

"Here we are!" he exclaims, with his back to me. "Caleb Forrest," he continues, appearing to read from a single page. "You wouldn't happen to be a relation of the elderly gentleman I sometimes see at the town hall meetings, would you?"

I nod. "Gramp. I mean, my grandfather."

"A real malcontent, is he not?" asks Mr. Vick, turning to look at me.

"He's content," I answer. "To keep his land."

"Always arguing against progress of any sort, is that the man?"

"One man's progress usually leads to another man's loss is what he'd argue, but I'm not here to talk about my grandfather, I'm here to see what it takes to get into college."

"Let's not get ahead of ourselves," says Mr. Vick, holding up his hands like he's about to be robbed. "One should realize that the university system only accepts those students who've achieved a high measure of academic merit."

"My grades are good," I reply, grimacing at my word choice.

"I'm sure your grades are satisfactory. However, excelling at shop class is not the kind of academic merit I am considering."

"Why should I take shop class when I live it?"

"My point exactly!" beams Mr. Vick. "I should think that, with your family's heritage, you would have no problem finding your way aboard a working fishing boat. Gainful employment also has its merits."

"Have you seen them?"

"Seen what?"

"My grades."

"Of course! Though I do admit, your file is in need of some updating."

"I've got them right here," I say, patting my shirt pocket. Mr. Vick motions impatiently. I take out a folded sheet of computer paper and hand it to him. Mr. Vick makes a show of smoothing out the folds before reading.

"This is highly irregular," he says, frowning.

"How so?" I ask.

"It appears that you've taken a number of college preparatory classes and, according to what I'm reading, have done quite well. Of course, I'll have to check this with your teachers. Not to worry. I'll get to the bottom of it."

"But those *are* my grades," I say, struggling to keep my voice from cracking. "It's printed on the school's computer paper."

"I see that. However, you must understand, students these days are capable of the most elaborate forgeries. I'll have to get back to you on this," replies Mr. Vick, nodding at the door. "Now, if you don't mind…"

I start toward the door, but before I open it, I turn to Mr. Vick and tell him, "No matter how many cookouts you're invited to, or how many graduation ceremonies you attend, they'll never really let you in."

"And just what exactly are you implying?" says Mr. Vick, bristling.

"They're rich and you're not. Simple as that."

"Careful," warns Mr. Vick, wagging a chubby finger at me. "Let's not overstep ourselves."

"Those kids don't need your help," I continue, standing my ground. "You're just the icing on the cake. This university system you speak of, they probably don't even read your recommendations. It's all a rubber stamp with that lot. Not that I begrudge them, I don't, but your job isn't only to help them, your job is also to help us, the ones who really need it."

"Congratulations, young man! You've just earned yourself a three-day suspension!"

I point to the computer paper crumpled in his fat fist and say to him, "Keep reading. You'll see at the bottom that I've completed all my graduation requirements."

"Rubbish!" bellows Mr. Vick. "I'll have you expelled!"

"See you at the reunions!" I say with a backwards wave before stepping into the hallway and closing his office door behind me.

I never did send out those college applications. They sit where I left them, stacked on top of my bedroom dresser. I couldn't afford college anyway. I never took to sports like my father, so there were no athletic scholarships waiting for me. Truth be told, Mr. Vick was right. Gainful employment does have its merits, and you'd think by now that I'd have a PhD in the subject. My only wish is to one day prove Mr. Vick wrong, not because I care what he thinks of me, but for my own personal benefit.

I tried to alleviate my situation a year ago only to have it result in a murderous act of betrayal. Now it's up to me to reverse the trend. I only hope that what occurred between the ranger and myself was a miscommunication and not an outright theft. I don't think I can take any added remorse, but if it comes to that, I'll take action, or I'll die trying and none of this will have mattered. I can see the goal line, but the yards between will be hard-fought and treacherous. I take a moment to reposition myself at the stern when the ever-rushing flow of eddy unceremoniously spits *Sea Gypsy* from the Narrows.

LANDLESS GULL

I angle the bow chuck three points to the weather and re-sink the centerboard, intentionally leaving out the brass pin. I do this to let the centerboard bounce off the shoals that echo outward from the Narrows mouth like intermittent sound waves. Most boats *Gypsy*'s size won't let you skirt the shallows because they draft too deep, but the hull of a working Chatham cat boat was built for skimming across sandbars in pursuit of a school of bluefish. The boats were originally designed to hunt the bays and inlets and yet be seaworthy enough to ply the open ocean. There's nothing fancy about her and most day sailors stay away due to her costly and time-consuming upkeep. And they're always stubbing their toes on her ribbed hull.

My toes have become impervious to her insults, though I wouldn't want to bed down on her. That would be like sleeping on a pile of baseball bats and is also the reason I keep a sleeping bag stuffed into a rucksack high in her fo'c'sle. I do this in the event I want to camp in the dunes, the best spot being Bean Hill on Monomoy Island. The sand there is soft and level with berms on both sides to buffer the wind. The area was once used as an amphibious training station for the Army during WWII, and if you dig deep enough, you'll unearth rusted can after rusted can of Army issue beans, hence the name, Bean Hill.

Any flatulence has long since blown away, but the stars remain. There's nothing like lying in the dunes at night. Humanity's progression doesn't seem so pronounced. Centuries can come and go and it wouldn't make much difference there. If you were a caveman or some future version of man, you'd be staring up at the same celestial bodies. It's a spot I've always kept a secret. Not even Chumley and Jimmy know of it, though I've brought my fair share of female companions there.

I'm thinking of a particular girl presently at sea. If I remember correctly, she's residing somewhere near the equator, studying algae plumes and what effect they may or may not have on something called atmospheric warming. I haven't seen her since she shipped out from the Woods Hole Oceanographic Institute a year ago. I took her sailing the day before she left. We pushed off from her family's beach house in Harwich, where we plied the waters of Nantucket Sound before landing on Monomoy's South Beach and making camp in the dunes.

After laying out our sleeping bags, the girl busies herself building a small mess while I walk the beach gathering driftwood. For supper this late afternoon we enjoy fresh-caught sea bass topped with grilled zucchini, along with thick slices of beefsteak tomatoes plucked from my personal garden that I keep behind our ever-creeping dune. For drink, I empty a cheap bottle of red table wine into a deep-bellied frying pan and, after adding a small jar of fermented honey and a fistful of cinnamon, I set the pan atop a makeshift grill to simmer, recalling Gramp's recipe for mead.

After supper, we walk to a cleft in the dunes and sit on the soft white sand, watching the roiling whitecaps travel to shore in a myriad of aqua colors. And it is after the last of the sun puts down on the western sky, bursting the watery horizon in a carroty orange and casting the clouds in a diffused magenta, that I take the girl in my arms and await the Evening Star to show in the East. As the Roman

Goddess of Love (Venus) pokes through the velvety curtain above, I reach into the front pocket of my khaki cutoffs and bring out a small, cube-shaped box. I place the box on the girl's exposed kneecap, feeling a shiver run through her body as she hesitantly unties the bowed ribbon. Slowly lifting the fitted top, a gold ring is revealed, made more brilliant by the twinkling stars. Spinning the ring betwixt her thumb and forefinger, she wonders at the aquatic life engraved throughout.

"Dolphins," I say. "Swimming against the tide like the two of us."

"It's beautiful," she replies, the light from her serpentine eyes outshining even that of the ring.

"A way for you to remember me by when you're a thousand miles out."

"Is that what this is, a remembrance ring?" she asks, frowning slightly.

I nod, afraid to call it an engagement ring. Instead of trying it on, the girl loops the ring through her Saint Christopher necklace, saying with a thin smile that she didn't want to lose a finger to a barracuda while she was taking an algae sample.

That night we slept under the stars but in separate sleeping bags. After a mostly silent breakfast, I dismantled the firepit and kicked the campsite clean, and there wasn't much in the way of conversation on the trip back, what with me at the stern manning the tiller and the girl sitting on the bow with her back to me, fingering the ring on her necklace. I cut across the Sound with little fanfare before hauling in and setting the bow chuck over her family's long pier.

Approaching the pier, the girl suddenly drops over the side. Standing in the waist-deep water, she takes the bowline in hand and spins *Sea Gypsy* around, saying to me, "You're a stupid, stupid man, Caleb Forrest! And if you're not at the docks in Woods Hole when I get back, I'll be very upset!" Pushing off, she turns her back on me and wades through the surf. I wait for her to laugh and invite me inside, but she doesn't. Instead, she heads for her family's private beach and into her house. Hauling in, I set sail for home, feeling as dumb as I was first born.

I realize now that I should have told the girl how I felt, but like most of the men in my clan, I let my feelings go unsaid, and it pains me when I think of her. We planned to write to one another, but not long after she left, I left, in the middle of the night, stepping from one deck to another and never in the same port twice lest my crimes come to light. Truth be told, I was too ashamed to write, and if she wrote me, I wouldn't know. My only outside contact was when I'd deposit Gramp's grocery money at the end of every month, and even then, I never used the same paymaster.

Plausible deniability is the term for it. There are some actions you take that are best kept secret. Gramp taught me that when he was running booze behind his wife Flossy's back. My business is my business, and as far as the girl is concerned, the ring is our bond. If she's wearing it on her return, I'll know we were meant to be together. If not, then all my efforts will have been in vain, and I'll go on as I always have, that is, if I last the day.

Re-knotting the halyard, I cleat it to the deck and look up the mast to where a large gull has alighted itself on the masthead. It's a big gull, full-throated and wide at the shoulders, and I'd be right to call it an albatross but for its short, ring-tipped bill. I rap my knuckles on the mast, but the gull ignores me. Not that I mind the company, only I know what it's got in its hold and that I'm the bullseye.

The gull's splayed tail feathers are a bit disconcerting, so I haul in and put *Sea Gypsy* heeling on her beam-ends. The gull rides the masthead like a giant metronome, all the while looking down at me in what can best be described as contempt, as if saying, "That all you got?" Paying out plenty of line, I let the mains'l flutter and sail onward at an even keel.

"If I get an eyeful, I'll hunt you down in every landfill from Barnstable to Boston!" I shout up at the gull with my fists raised.

Balancing one-footed on the masthead, the gull shakes its tail feathers at me and returns its attention to the channel, where the shadow of a marsh hawk plays across the water. Surprisingly, the gull doesn't take wing and seek cover. Instead, it lets out a guttural bark that sends the hawk diving into the tall pines of Eastward Point.

"That kind of bravery deserves a reward, big fella!" Ducking inside the cuddy, I bring out the round loaf of sourdough bread and rip off a chunk. Wadding the bread in my fist, I toss it skyward. "Soup's on! Come and get it!"

I watch the bread-ball sail past the gull's beak and land unceremoniously behind the stern. I rip off another chunk and repeat the process and get the same result. I'm about to rip off the third chunk when it occurs to me that this is no ordinary seagull. This gull doesn't spend its days wheeling over dumpsites or hanging around clam shacks looking for handouts. No, this gull is a true seabird, a landless gull, the kind that likes to ride the deep troughs of the North Atlantic with a good-sized grouper bleeding in its beak. Then, as if on cue, the gull spreads its great expanse of wing and lifts from the masthead. Rising in a headwind, it barks down at me, as if thanking me for the ride before soaring over the Nauset dunes and back out to sea.

INNER HARBOR

S*ea Gypsy*'s rust-marked mains'l billows with wind as I head for the tideway east of the channel marker. I stretch out in the cockpit and let my free hand drag in the temperate water, watching a group of kayakers round the tip of Money Head before disappearing behind the grassy hedges of Hog Island Creek as if they were never there. A sleek cigarette boat races past on my starboard, towing a bikini-clad girl on water skis and leaving *Gypsy* rocking in its wake. I feel a part of it all, like being in a painting some artist might be sketching from the beach. It's a feeling that I rarely have on land these days.

Most of the townsfolk I grew up with are either dead or they've moved on, no longer able to afford the town's high property taxes, the Year-Rounders' having been replaced by the Summer People who arrive in May complaining of the rainy weather only to leave in late August complaining about the stifling heat. Rarely do I exchange a hearty "hello" or "good afternoon" with anyone, and when I'm strolling Main Street these days, it's like I'm a stranger. The latest batch of teenagers manning the cash registers couldn't care less about those, not in their age group, and why should they? We're not of their world. Even the old-timers who like to sit on the well-worn benches in front of Eldredge Library and chat up people as they walk by are no more, choosing instead to remain shuttered behind closed doors, or they just plain died without so much as a placard in their place.

Even the shops I knew growing up have changed. Gone are the mom-and-pop stores that catered to us townsfolk, selling everything from toothpaste to model airplanes. The five-and-dimes of my youth, along with the bait and tackle shops, shipwrights, and sail-making lofts, are no more, replaced by overpriced restaurants, real estate offices, and tacky T-shirt vendors filling every third storefront. These days I can't find a decent pair of socks without "Cape Cod" stamped all over them or a simple T-shirt without that silly Black Dog silhouetted on the front of it.

In an effort to bring in more tourist dollars, the town selectmen, in their infinite wisdom, zoned out many of the homegrown businesses in favor of the tacky tourist traps. But what these checkered-pant-wearing nobles failed to realize was that tourists go home at the end of the summer and the rest of us live here the year round. Walk Main Street fall, winter, or spring, and you'd think you were in a western ghost town.

Jimmy's dad is one. He's not a bad guy to meet on the street, and I've always liked him. Whenever I was at the house, he always seemed genuinely glad to see me. Sitting around the kitchen table, the three of us would discuss the issues of the day like real grown-ups. He'd let us voice our concerns and opinions, whatever the subject, and would only interrupt when a misrepresented fact merited comment. Those were some great talks, and I always left Jimmy's house feeling that I'd learned something.

Gramp has a different opinion of Jimmy's father, not that he's ever come right out and said it. As acrimonious as the verbal sparring between the two men at the town meetings might have been, Gramp never brought it home with him, saying, "Every man got a right to wag his tongue. Every man including me!" But it was after Gramp's snubbing of Dale's proposed town purchase of thirty-three of our bayside acres that tensions between the two families began to rise. I was at the meeting the night it all went down, and it wasn't pretty, at least for Jimmy and his father.

I arrived late, after spending an extra hour at the Fish Pier helping to unload a catch of pesky dogfish that were wreaking havoc with the fleet. According to Tracy Hopkins, captain of the trawler *Clementine*, the packs were grouping together and feeding on the netted haddock. Weighed and paid, the sand sharks barely covered the cost of the diesel, but Captain Hopkins couldn't have been more pleased. She was happy just to land the predators and hopefully thin out the pack, even if that meant she was in violation of fishing a federally protected species. Shows you how much "they" know.

The hall is overflowing with townspeople as I enter, and I am forced to take a seat in the back pew. Constructed in the Greek Revival style that was all the rage in the 1830s, Chatham's Town Hall, while ornate in structure, is also the place where the men of the Outer Cape came to enlist for every American conflict dating back to the Civil War. I don't see Jimmy anywhere, but I know he's here, no doubt sitting front and center to hear his father speak in what can best be described as rapture. I do see Mr. Vick, however, hovering around the free coffee table, attempting to stuff a custard-filled Danish into his all-consuming maw. I laugh to myself, quoting from the Good Book, "Swine cheweth not the cud is unclean to you," then adding my own "Friggin' grissy."

Peeking above the bobbing heads, I see Gramp sitting on the elevated stage alongside Mr. Hallet, with the fire and police chiefs, along with other town officials, lined up behind the two men. A call to order is asked for, after which Mr. Hallet stands from his chair and brushes at his navy blue blazer. From my point of view in the crowd, it appears Mr. Hallet is as tall standing as Gramp is sitting. Approaching the lectern, he tugs at his collar and clears his throat before beginning his oration.

"Given the town's finite amount of land on which to build, how can one man sit on so much of it, the vast majority of which is undeveloped, and not believe he isn't hurting the working men and woman of Chatham? Does he not realize that, with controlled development and ecologically sensitive planning, we can better house and feed our growing populace? How can he not feel empathy for the town's skilled tradesmen who've lost their jobs in this trying economy? And how can we, the duly elected, remain idle while our good neighbors suffer?"

I watch Gramp. Not a grumble does he utter nor facial tic show during his opponent's allotted time before the people. He remains stoic, like a ship's figurehead looking out over a watery waste.

"I'm not up here trying to steal this man's land," continues Mr. Hallet, frowning slightly at his choice of words. "But facts are facts. One fact being that should we pass this resolution tonight, which I'm sure we will, the good captain stands to be the richest man in town!" Pausing for effect, Mr. Hallet expects a loud round of applause but is refused, except for Jimmy's staccato hand clapping from the front pew. Reshuffling his notes, he begins anew.

"I have the utmost respect for the man sitting here beside me, and I view his family's long heritage as a cornerstone of this community. His grandson Caleb and my son Jimmy are the best of friends and have been since grade school. This isn't a disagreement over personalities, it's a disagreement of priorities. On the one hand, the captain's belief in wild, open space as our saving grace. An Eden, if you will. And on the other, my notion for the town's purchase of thirty-three of the six-hundred-plus acres that the captain and his family have held over the town like the Sword of Damocles for more than two hundred years. An offer, I should add, at twice the land's current market value. Not only is this resolution in the best interest of the town, but it's also in the best interest of Captain Let himself. We've all heard that his back taxes are in arrears and have been for some time, and that is why it is my sincere desire that the good captain takes this offer rather than chance having this conversation become moot in the coming months."

I watch my fellow townspeople squirm in their pews, uncomfortable with the airing of another's financial troubles. Jimmy's dad picks up on this and reshuffles his notes again.

"The town doesn't want that and surely I do not, and yet, at the same time, we have to be realistic. With this allotment, the town can build more affordable housing so that our summer workers won't have to commute from towns like Hyannis and Plymouth. Housing that will employ carpenters, painters, plumbers, housing that will need furniture, drapes, bedding, appliances, artwork, and all the other intangibles that go into making a house a home. Lest I forget, in its subsequent finality, the proposed land purchase will benefit our tax base as well, leading to the hiring of more firefighters and police so that we can better protect and serve the good people of Chatham. In closing, should Captain Let choose to ignore the town's generous offer, I believe the issue of eminent domain should be invoked, not only for the benefit of the townspeople of Chatham but for the benefit of the good captain and his grandson as well. I thank you for your time."

Rising from their pew, Mr. Hallet's building buddies cheer heartily, as do Jimmy and a few others, including Mr. Vick, clapping loudly from the back of the hall. I remain seated, and while I mostly agree with Gramp over the kitchen table, what Mr. Hallet said rings true to me, not to mention that it would also make us rich. But being that Dale's a wash-ashore, and not a Cape Cod born and bred Pineknot, he's remained blissfully ignorant of the town's unwritten code of conduct. And though many in the town have vested interest in the land's development, it's still courtesy and procedure holding sway with that lot. And when the selectman walks in front of Gramp, and not behind him, while returning to his seat, it becomes clear to me, by the looks on the old salts' twisted faces, that he has made an injurious slight. Brushing at his wrinkled trousers, Gramp stands from his chair. Forgoing the lectern, he chooses instead to address the crowd from the lip of the stage.

"Let me start in by say'n, I agree with Dale. Makes a lot of sense." The crowd responds with a bustle of noisy confusion, including Mr. Hallet, who views Gramp from his chair on stage with a look of mild amusement. "Makes a lot of sense if we were a growin' town. We ain't. Haven't been for some time. That land you're all hung'rin' afta', if it were to be developed, we wouldn't be a small town. We'd be a big town with big town problems, like Hyannis, like Plymouth, and we'd need more police and fire people. Far as me not carin' 'bout the workin' man, I've been a workin' man my whole life. Wrote my own paycheck 'til recent. Now, if these plumbers and electricians and such can't make ends meet without cuttin' up my land, then I say, let 'em suffer!"

A loud ruckus sweeps through the hall. I square my shoulders and get ready to run the gauntlet if the crowd turns ugly. Though, even at Gramp's advanced age, there aren't many in the town who would be brave enough to challenge him.

"Do we go build crazy every time a red tide washes up or a nor'easter hits? Do we pave our way to prosperity whenever the government takes away half our catch with their newfangled rules? No, we do not. We adapt like we've always done. No different today than it was when my great-great-grandpappy, Captain Nehemiah Forrest, first broke ground fixin' to raise crops in soil better suited for growin' rocks. I say, if ya' can't adapt like the rest of us, then ya' got no business livin' here in the first place."

I watch Mr. Hallet squirm in his seat, knowing that with every word Gramp speaks, another nail is hammered into his argument for eminent domain. Thumbs tucked behind his belt, Gramp moseys along the lip of the stage like he's checking it for wood rot.

"City folk been comin' here for some time now. Might be they like the view of the bay from their back deck. I don't begrudge 'em. Got the same view m'self. Might be they like the clean sea air. Been breathin' the same air since I was a babe. They like ta' tell us how we can eat betta', dress betta', talk betta'," says Gramp, with the crowd chuckling at his good-natured ribbing. "Do we take their advice?"

"Hell no!" shouts Martha Stall, a longtime waitress at the Captain's Table restaurant, standing in her pew and shaking her fist.

"Course not. We put up with 'em like we do every summer. Now, if these city folk want ta' live amongst us and stay the year round, then they'll have to adjust like we do. This spit of sand might be paradise ta' some, but ta' the rest of us, it's the place we live, work, and die. My land's my business. You're all free to traipse about it anytime ya' please. I neva' put up a fence and I neva' will. Just don't tell me how good it'll look with telephone poles and streets runnin' through with a Dunkin' Donuts on every corner." And with that last utterance, Gramp struck down any arguments against him.

The old-timers know that it's not talk gets you through the long winters, it's action. And with that single action, Gramp proved there are two types of people on Cape Cod: those who wash-ashore and those who stay-ashore. The majority of the townspeople rise from their pews and cheer. I cheer along with them, only not so loudly.

Later, after Mr. Hallet's motion for eminent domain is voted down, and the speakers have left the elevated stage, I walk down the center aisle and slide in next to Jimmy, sitting in the first pew with his head in his hands.

"How goes it, Jimbo?" I ask my friend.

"He's ruined us. I'll never be able to show my face in this town again."

"Oh, I don't know. I thought your dad made some good points."

Jimmy turns to me, his face beet red. "My dad? I'm talking about your grandfather! Why'd he have to paint us like we were a bunch of robber barons?"

It's my turn to look at Jimmy with mild amusement. What had always been a distant rumble between us has turned to thunder. Jimmy has taken sides, and it's like I'm looking at him for the first time.

"If the shoe fits" is my reply.

Sliding from the pew, I walk up to the stage and knock twice on the hardwood in appreciation of the wizened master. Giving Jimmy my back, I leave him stewing in his own juices before pivoting on my heels and pushing through the exit doors. Outside, I come bounding down the granite steps to where Mr. Hallet stands, leaning against a diseased poplar tree, smoking a cigarette.

"How are you, Cal?" he asks, putting out his cigarette with the toe of his expensive Italian loafer.

"Same ol'," I answer.

"And Jimmy? Have you seen him?"

"He's inside."

"How's he taking it?"

"Not well."

Putting his arm around my shoulder, Mr. Hallet says, "One should never take personally what is strictly a business matter, and I've told

Jimmy that. Promise me that you won't let this disagreement between your grandfather and myself upset you too much. Promise me that, and I'll promise to get Jimmy to do the same."

"Okay," I say, nodding my head in doltish obedience.

"Glad to hear it," replies Mr. Hallet, slapping my back. "You know, Cal, it won't be long before the two of you will be running this town, and I can't think of a better friend and ally for Jimmy. Sure, you've had your differences lately, but this too shall pass. What matters most is friendship." Pointing to a stand of unspoiled greenery just beyond the Hall's newly paved parking lot, courtesy of Hallet Paving and Construction, he asks, "Any idea who owns that quarter-acre parcel?"

I shrug.

"You and your grandfather. That very spot is where your property line ends. I sometimes take my lunch there. My own personal sanctuary where I can get away from the pressures of the office. With this job of mine, I sometimes have to play both sides of the coin. That doesn't mean I don't appreciate your grandfather and the sacrifices he's made. Imagine all that land going undisturbed in this day and age. But the town needs it, Cal. People grow old and die and the tax base dries up. We need to find a way to keep our young people from leaving, and to do that, we need to attract good-paying, year-round jobs. Did you know that by the end of this decade, the median age of this town will be fifty-seven?"

"I did not know that."

"Listen to me. I'm giving the speech I should have made tonight! Do me a favor, Cal. Mary, our youngest, has been after me for a kitten, and I'm no match for those baby blues of hers. Will you let me know when one of Captain Let's 'familiars' has a litter? Those cats are more a symbol of this town than the town seal itself. Will you do that for me? It would mean a lot to Mary."

"I'll keep an eye out."

"Great!"

Mr. Hallet shakes my hand long and hard like he's grooming me for future handshakes. I take it as nothing more than politicking. He knows that when he speaks at these town meetings, his message of growth falls on mostly deaf ears. The majority of townspeople are like Gramp. They don't want change. It scares them. They want everything to remain the same, and it has for the most part. It's what gives the town its charm, only Mr. Hallet doesn't care much for what the townspeople think. He takes their cheers as he takes their jeers with ambivalence.

It dawns on me then what he is after. He knows that he'll never turn the town against Gramp, so he's chosen me as his point man in negotiations. I'm the key. It makes me question my friendship with Jimmy, only I know that what the two of us have is real. We've been through too much together. Jimmy will swim out of it eventually and after a while, we'll be back sailing the Realm. At least, I hope so.

"Don't be such a stranger, Cal," says Mr. Hallet, walking me to the curb. "Stop by the house sometime. I miss our talks." Leaving my side, the Chatham selectman and CEO of Hallet Paving and Construction walks off to glad-hand with his builder buddies.

With the ranger's cabin still hours away, I let *Sea Gypsy* relax in the outgoing tide and duck inside the cuddy to bring out the speargun. Taking a seat on the port rail, I inspect the weapon. There's not much to it, really. Just a stock trigger grip with a vulcanized rubber bowstring running up a three-foot aluminum shaft. I check the trigger for tension and find it. Even without an actual spear housed, the gun makes me nervous.

Off to my starboard, a horsehead seal pokes its blackened snout above the waterline behind the stern, so named by early mariners who mistook the fin-footed marine mammal's elongated snout for that of a horse when they were first seen plying the bay. This particular seal has a silken coat resembling marbled Roquefort as it barks at me in search of food. But unlike the landless gull, I'm in no mood to give this scavenger of the bay any handouts. Many a day have I had a fish hooked only to land it on deck with nothing showing but the head and gills, with the fish thief resurfacing soon after to lick its whiskery chops.

Puppy-dog eyes and pouting mouth notwithstanding, whatever sailors believed these animals mermaids must have been drunk on seawater. I take aim with the speargun and pull the trigger. The seal duck-dives under the boat as the rubberized bowstring slaps harmlessly at the air. I wonder if it will be that easy, shooting a man instead of a seal with a real spear? At this juncture of my journey, I don't see the difference.

STRONG ISLAND

S witching the tiller from hand to hand, I change seats in the cockpit and come about. Fresh wind fills the mains'l as I take hold of the mainsheet and hike out over the water to keep my boat at an even keel. *Sea Gypsy*'s lap-straked hull glides over the slight chop, sailing effortlessly onward with her bow pointed due south as I head for the channel marker. We are one, *Sea Gypsy* and me. I feel her pull before the mainsheet tightens in my grip, and I always know when she's bored and wants to run, just as I know when she's tired and wants to list. I plant my feet on her floorboards, and it's as if I've grown a mast and boom, her tightened sailcloth serving as my skin with her guiding tiller, my conscience.

Her sweet lines fold around me, and though I've never afforded her a cushioned seat, I always find comfort wherever I repose. While it's true, she's only an assemblage of brass, sailcloth, wood, and paint, albeit lovingly fastened together by a master craftsman, there's always been a fleshy element about her. To climb aboard is, for me, like falling into a woman's heaving bosom and to sail another would be like cheating.

I am alone with my thoughts as I close in on a forty-foot Newporter anchored in the lee of Strong Island. Taking up the spyglass, I sight it on the top deck and see that it's an older crowd onboard, and they appear to be enjoying themselves. I can almost hear the ice clinking in their gin gimlets. I look to the vessel's unmarked prow and seriously wonder if she ever tasted a rough sea in her life. From this angle, I can't make out the boat's name or port of call, but I do notice that she's flying a burgee from an Antigua yacht club.

I envision the skipper daring to cross the Bermuda Triangle, then steaming up the Intercoastal Waterway from Fort Lauderdale to Norfolk. After a night of party-hopping on the D.C. cocktail circuit, the skipper would await a fair-weather report to take his party up the coast and across Nantucket Sound before finding safe harbor here in Pleasant Bay. Though you never can tell. Some of these rich old buggers really know their way around a ship's wheel.

I got picked to crew for such a skipper a few years back. It was by chance. He was trying for the America's Cup Challenge and I'd just finished a three-month stint cutting fish on a factory ship in Alaska, where it was so cold on the factory floor that I'd have to stomp my feet to keep them from freezing, and whenever I pricked myself, which was often, I wouldn't bleed. After picking up my pay, I decided then and there that I needed a vacation. Somewhere warm, I was thinking, the Mexican Baja or Costa Rica, maybe. Sitting in a dockside diner, slopping up runny eggs with a fork, I read in the *Fairbanks Gazette* of the America's Cup Challenge taking place in San Diego. Grabbing my grip, I hitched a ride to the airport and boarded the next plane for California.

Touching down on Lindbergh Field, I had the Guatemalan cabdriver take me to the San Diego Yacht Club, where the boats were said to be moored. I was hoping to see the Cup up close, but I had no intention of stepping aboard a vessel or crewing for anyone. All I wanted was to get a peek at the boats and maybe talk with a crewmate or two. Arriving at the docks, I found the slips to be ten people deep at the pilings, so I wandered into an upscale restaurant called the Chart House. Upon entering the main dining room, where waiters, waitresses, and busboys darted around me like I wasn't there, I grabbed a menu and took a seat, only before I could order, I was hustled from the dining room by an overbearing hostess who didn't even take my name down, believing that I'd be better suited standing in line for the men's room.

Aimlessly awaiting my turn, I give up my place in line and stroll over to the restaurant's overhanging picture window, where the racing fleet is lined up bow to stern below. Now, these are truly magnificent yachts, sparkling in brighter than bright candy colors with sails glowing like fresh-cut whalebone and prows as sharp as a barber's razor. Vikings wouldn't have stood a chance against these sloops. Their keels would have knifed through their longboats like an ax splitting a pear. And the lines! Never have I seen so many halyards, lazy sheets, prevangs, jabs, and different measures of spar pole. And the boats were all so clean, as if soiled deckhands never touched them. Neither smudge nor rust plume do I see on a single cleat or grommet! Standing within sight of all that glistening cleanliness, it's hard for me to imagine that less than forty-eight hours before, I was swinging a meat cleaver in a grimy fish hold. I suddenly feel dirty and back away from the window. And I am turning to leave when I bump into a robust woman of about fifty.

"Watch where you're going!" the woman chastises me, brushing at her brightly patterned blouse like she'd just rubbed against a beached blackfish. "What are you doing out here anyway? Shouldn't you be in the kitchen washing dishes?"

I am about to return the compliment when I catch my reflection on a heavily polished brass pole sticking up from the floor like a submarine conning tower. Within its golden sheen shows a scruffy young man dressed in jeans ripped at the knees along with a ragged T-shirt. But it's not so much my outfit that shocks me, as it is the gas station motto printed on the front of the T-shirt: *ORLEANS PUMP AND GO – WE DO THE PUMPING!* Not the best match for these Izod- and Nautica-clad yachtsmen. The woman about leaps over a bus cart to get away from me.

I leave the restaurant proper and stumble into its adjoining Rough

Seas Lounge, where the bawdy and boisterous crowd appear affluent day sailors, but there's enough old salts spread about to give the bar a dash of color, so I stick around. This is where the action is. I can feel it. Dodging elbows and sliding around bulging bellies, I push my way into the lounge and up to the bar, where I order a Harpoon lager specifically. The weary barkeep pours the beer and places it on the bamboo bar top.

"Ten bucks, and we don't take food stamps," he snaps.

I take out my billfold and peel off a twenty and toss it at him. "Keep the change," I say. The barkeep takes the twenty without looking at me and walks to the other end of the bar. I drain the lager in a series of thirsty gulps, and I am turning to leave when a heavy hand thumps me between my shoulder blades.

I come around slowly, my fists clenched at my sides, expecting the offended lady's husband to make a charge, or perhaps one of the bouncers has spotted my shoddy duds and thinks me an easy mark to toss.

"From the Cape, hey?" asks a man of about sixty. He's got a stocky build and a thick mane of wild, red hair, and though we are the same height, the man's shoulders are twice as wide, and he has the kind of fire in the eyes that you never turn your back on. I can tell right away he won't be easy.

"Who wants to know?"

"Pumped some pain there m'self!" says the man, pointing at my T-shirt. "Hot damn! A fellow bogger! What part the Cape ya' from?"

"Chatham."

"I'm a Harwich 'Hair Legger' m'self. How 'em cranberries doin'?"

"They're ripe," I intone. If this guy was looking for a fight, he found one. Spending three months inside a freezing fish hold makes one a bit ornery and quick to temper.

"No meaning to it," says the man, sensing my discomfort. "Was 'em red berries that got me an ed'jication. Not that you'd ever know by how I talk. Family's Ocean Spray, 'Straight Out of the Bog!'"

"We get ours wild."

"Tastes best that-a-way. What's your name, son? Bet I know your family."

"Caleb Forrest."

"Of the same Forrest clan owns all that land on the bay?"

"We've got a few acres. What of it?"

"Nothing, 'cept the millionaires ya' see floating 'round here can't hold a stick to ya'!"

"I'm no millionaire, mister, if that's what you're thinking. Far as the land goes, all that makes me is a poor fisherman paying his debt in back taxes."

"What that makes you, m'boy, is my guest, so sit!" Pulling out a barstool, the burly man extends his hand, saying, "Name's Skipper Mack, and it's a pleasure to meet you, Caleb Forrest. What'cha' drinkin'?"

"I'm not. I'm just leaving."

I give the man my back and stride toward the swinging saloon doors that lead out to the street. "I knew your father," I hear the man say, forcing me to stop in my tracks. There aren't many in his own hometown who knew my father. He was always away fishing. Those who did, I'd glom every tidbit of information to the point of annoyance. My father rarely dallied ashore, but those he came into contact with would always tell their stories in vivid detail, like it happened earlier in the day. Turning on my heels, I walk the length of the bar and stand in front of the man calling himself Skipper Mack.

"You knew my father?"

"Never actually met the man, but I knew of him. He was four, maybe five years ahead of me. And he was a hell of a ballplayer. Hockey too. Skate like the wind he could! Cape's a small place when you're growing up. You know that."

"But you never actually met him."

"I'd see Jack sometimes fishing the Powder Hole. I was a kid, but I remember the way he'd stand on deck twirling a baited hook over his head like he was a cowboy on the Texas plains!" This man knew my father all right. I motion for him to continue.

"In those days, the unwritten rule was whoever got to the Hole first had it for his'self to fish. I'd head out from Andrews River well before sunup and ahead of everyone else, or so I thought. And I'd be skirting out of Cockle Cove when I'd see Jack rounding Amos Point in his Wianno Senior. By all rights, I should have made it to the Hole first, but that man always knew where to find the fast water. Jack would lip in well ahead of me and my knockabout. Dropping anchor, he'd sit on deck cutting bait and never give a backwards glance in my direction. So, I stuck to the flats and practiced my tacking and jibbing. And it was always right as the morning sun peaked over the Monomoy dunes that he'd cut his line and doff his baseball cap to wave me in, leaving the better part of the morn for me to fish. I'll always remember him for that, and I was sure sorry to hear about his last trip."

"Back at ya'," I say, lost in the memory.

"How ya' fixed for work?" asks Skipper Mack.

"I'm not. I'm on vacation."

"No such thing! I'm talkin' real work, aboard my boat."

"You got a boat in the race?" I ask incredulously.

"*Hard Charger*, and she is. Sweet lines all around."

"I'm no barnacle scrapper if that's what you're asking."

"I'd never insult a fellow bogger with scrub work! I have a man down and could use a knowledgeable hand on the lines. I'm sure you've hoisted a sail or two?"

"More than two, but nothing like what you've got out there. I'd hang myself in all that rope."

"There's no lyin' in ya', Caleb, and I respect that. Far as hanging ya'self in the lines, I know that to be a false modesty. Given your family's history, I'll bet dollars to donuts you've had the tiller in your hand since you were a babe. Whatever else I have to teach ya', you'll pick up real quick."

"Another time, maybe."

"There ain't no other time. This is it. The Big Race! And I'm givin' ya' a chance to be a part of it."

"Think I'll sit this one out, but thanks just the same," I say to the skipper, then head toward the swinging saloon doors for a second time

"Been fishin' the Strait, I'll bet."

I stop in my tracks and turn around. "How'd you guess that?"

"Did the same m'self when I was your age. And where ya' gonna' go afta' that freeze? Not back to the Cape in February. So, you come here, or Mexico maybe. Besides, ya' got a fisherman's build on ya', so I just figured."

"Figured right," I say, re-walking the length of the bar to stand in front of the skipper. "I'm still not sure what you're offering."

"What I'm offerin' ya', Caleb, is the chance go up against the best sailors in the world. And with the boat I got, crew, and you maybe, I'd say we got a chance to win this thing. Not much, but some. You won't be fighting crab pots, you'll be fighting the wind! Stretching and pulling Her to your convenience, running off Her sides and yoking Her mighty strength to your purpose! I've sailed the world over and no time have I taken Her for granted."

"Let me get this straight," I say, hoping to deflate the situation. "You want me to crew for you even though I've no experience."

"Best way to get experience is to get experience."

"What's the pay?"

"Paltry."

"Hours?"

"Long and arduous."

"When would I start?"

"Tomorrow, the next day, and the day after that."

"How long do I have to decide?"

"I'll know you're on board when I see ya' at the slip in the morn."

"And that's all there is?"

"Not exactly," says Skipper Mack, grinning secretively. "First, there's a contest of sorts. A tradition, ya' might say."

"What kind of contest?"

"A contest ta' see that you can tow the line and you're not just some rich kid slumming it on the docks."

"Mister, you've got some imagination," I say, flushing red I'm sure.

"Good! Keep that anger! You're gonna need it," warns Skipper Mack. Turning to his group of back-slappers, he continues, "Someone get Boondocks!"

I square my stance in the event some drunken sailor breaks from the crowd and tries to rush me. Skipper Mack sees this and comments,

"No fightin' now, just arm wrestlin'. Billy's been braggin' he can hoist a sail faster than any man's eva' been born. I told him that he ain't met a true bogger before, one who can hoist a sail with one hand and pull up a net of fish with the other. I'd challenge the braggart m'self, but it ain't dignified, me being the skipper and all."

Of all the clichés!, I think to myself. Arm wrestling in some dockside bar! I try to rescue the confused skipper from any future embarrassment by saying, "You're a real character, but I'm nobody's paperboy. Find yourself another arm or use your own." I leave the man on his barstool and I am on my third trip to the swinging saloon doors when the slightest touch grazes the back of my neck, accompanied by the most pleasant aroma of wet cloves.

"Don't tell me you've lassoed another challenger for Billy," says a woman, a girl really, as she steps around me.

"This'un's different, honey. A true bogger like your old man! I think he can take the Boondocks."

The girl steps back and eyeballs me from toe to topknot. "He's a little small, isn't he, Pop? Too small for Billy, I mean."

"He's not so tall, that I admit, but he's got a pair of shoulders on 'im and just look at the forearms he's carryin' and them ropes he's got for veins!"

I never felt so helpless in my life, like I was some desperado in a Spaghetti Western about to be shot. I stand there speechless, hypnotized by the girl's serpentine eyes that are greener than any ocean I've ever sailed. Greener still than any hue ever mixed on a painter's palette. She is of an olive complexion, speckled with freckles as if the Timekeeper blew them on with a straw. Sun-lightened hair streams past her shoulders in twisted tendrils along with a curious brow stationed above high cheekbones and a sensuous, full mouth, with it all sitting atop an athletic frame struggling to break free of its hourglass figure. Nothing seems to fit and yet it works wondrously as a whole. She reminds me of the mysterious sea creatures from the deep that get hauled up in the net from time to time that I marvel at not knowing the name for.

"Someone get Billy!" commands Skipper Mack. "Oh hell! I'll get him m'self. Probably out back having a smoke." He leaves his barstool and pushes his way through the crowd.

The girl continues to circle, as if sizing me up like I'm a prized tuna about to be auctioned. Stepping behind me, she whispers in my ear, "It will be easier on you if you let Billy win. He doesn't like it when he has to work too hard. Makes him mad. That's why Pop wants you to pin him. Take him down a notch or two. But watch out. The last guy who challenged Billy, he threw in the harbor."

"Sound advice," I mutter like a robot.

"It speaks!" exclaims the girl, clapping her hands. "Now, does *it* have a name?"

"Ca…" I stammer, looking past her right shoulder at the biggest brute I have ever seen. Veins on top of veins bulge from his neck, and he has a pair of arms on him that look to have once belonged to Atlas himself.

Dragging the behemoth through the lounge, Skipper Mack brings him over to me. "Caleb, this here's Billy Boondocks. Four-time Pro Bowler and Super Bowl champ. And Billy, I want ya' to meet Caleb Forrest. Comes from a proud family of fisherfolk. Whalers they once were, seafaring men they are to this day."

Looking out from under half-closed eyelids, the brute they call Billy Boondocks replies, "I'll snap his arm like a twig. What's the point?"

"There's a day off in it for ya', Billy. If ya' beat 'im, that is," clarifies Skipper Mack.

Billy points at me. "He knows he can't win. Look at him. He's shaking like a leaf." While it's true, I am shaking like a leaf, but not from the brute standing before me. It's the girl who's weakened my stance and turned my knees to jelly. And yet, as I look about the bar, the girl is nowhere to be seen. She's disappeared.

"Why do you keep throwing these lowlife fishermen at me, Mack?" asks Billy. "Nobody's quicker on the turn than me, and you know it. Besides, you wouldn't even be in the race if it weren't for me."

"What'cha' talkin', Billy? Just because you got that ring on your finger, you think everybody owes you a livin'?"

"It's all about sponsorship, Mack. And the sponsors want me. That's what you signed up for and that's the way it is."

"Way it is, hey," snaps Skipper Mack, with his dander up. "Maybe I want to win! Did'ja' eva' think of that? And I can't do it with a two-hundred-pound slab of beef who don't know his jib from his spinnaker!"

"Tell me what line to pull and I'll pull it," booms Boondocks. "Other than that, you've no say in the matter. The deal's inked, and I'm along for the ride, whether you like it or not. Far as me talking the day off, that's what I was planning to do anyway. Besides, even if this gull-bait pins me, which he won't, what'll it prove?" The bar becomes very quiet, listening to the two men argue. A few of the other skippers, including Bill Kock and Dennis Conner, leave their tables to stand behind Mack.

"What it'll prove, Billy, is that I can have a man strong as you on the lines but twice as quick and more seaworthy to boot. Nothing personal, Boondocks, but I want to give the Auld Mug my best shot. Pin this man and I'll let it rest. Far as your sponsors go, like you said, the race is set, so they can pull out anytime they want. Ya' see, Billy, whatcha' got here is bigger than any Super Bowl. It's how we first got from This Place to That Place. It's like the Super Bowl of the human race!" A rousing applause erupts from the Chart House crowd, along with vigorous slaps on the back from his fellow skippers.

"Have it your way, Mack," glowers Billy. "Somebody better call an ambulance 'cause I'm about to tear this fisherman's arm off."

"Quit that talk, Billy," says Skipper Mack, coming between us. "They'll be no ambulance calling today." Turning to me, he asks, "You ready, son?"

All eyes are on me. What can I do? If I refuse, it will be like Ali walking out on Joe Frazier at Madison Square Garden. I'd never be able to show my face around this crowd again, not that I was likely to ever see any of these people again. Then there's the girl to think of. Letting her father down would be the same as letting her down. She warned me not to put up a fight, but did she really mean it?

"I'll probably get my wrist broke because of you," I say to the skipper.

"I'll pay all medical expenses out of pocket," Mack replies.

"That's encouraging," I deadpan.

"Where'd you get this guy, Mack?" asks Billy, looking at my shabby clothes. "The Salvation Army? Send him back to Skid Row before he gets his arm broke. I'll pay for the cab."

"I have to warn you, Billy," I pipe up. "I arm wrestle my grandfather every morning."

"So, you can beat an old man," laughs Boondocks. "That supposed to scare me?"

"Pin Gramp? I wish! No, he still pins me on a regular basis."

The crowd gets a kick out of that one. I can tell that most of the people gathered around are with me, not that it matters.

"You're a funny fisherman," says Billy, smiling thinly between pressed lips. "I'll remember that after I pin you. Later on, we'll have us a little talk, you and me."

"No one's talkin' to no one! Okay, boys! Grip up!" commands Skipper Mack.

Billy steps forward, snorting like a bull. I fit my childlike mitt into his inflated fist, and it's like Bugs Bunny shaking hands with King Kong. I have to come up with a strategy fast, or the brute is sure to bury my knuckles into the heavily varnished bamboo bar top on the first throw.

I see my chance as Skipper Mack cups our two hands in his one. Slipping my index finger betwixt Billy's middle and third finger, I split his grip and thus give my wrist more elasticity on the thunderous throw down that's sure to follow. Billy is about to complain when Skipper Mack releases our hands and shouts, "Go!"

Boondocks grunts as he drives down my wrist in a rush of strength. I hold him off at the last millisecond, the hairs on my right hand tickling the bar's raised lip. Eye-level with the bar, Skipper Mack is ready to call it if he has to. The crowd presses in, the lady with the brightly patterned blouse breathing clam breath down my neck while shouting her support for Billy.

"It's over for you, fisherman," Boondocks snarls. "Time you went back to your skates and flounders."

My wrist bends backwards like a rubberized broom handle and is in danger of fracturing. I pay it no mind as I glance about the lounge, searching for the green-eyed sea creature who has yet to resurface.

"You're done, fisherman," Boondocks hisses at me, bent over my wrist. "Give up now, and I won't take your arm for a trophy."

"Biggest boat doesn't always win," I hiss back at Billy through clenched teeth. Bunching my shoulders, I slam my knees into the bar and start to pull.

Some in the crowd cheer as I come off the railing, but not Billy, who looks on with flushed amazement. Like others who have gone before, he's failed to take into account that years of pulling net over the side has hardened my slender frame from within and made me used to fatigue. Only Billy isn't done. Re-cupping his grip, he arches his broad chest and falls on his fist. Putting my thumb over his, I turn my arm into a steel bar to hold him off. Billy brings all of his great strength to bear, but it's to no avail. The sweat from our working hands pools on the bar, and I can almost smell flesh burning inside our fused fists. I test a throw, but it doesn't take. I need more time to wear down his bulk.

"Starting...to...piss me...off," Billy spits. Letting out a primal scream, he surges anew.

I reward his effort by putting his wrist four points past his right shoulder. I feel a slight tremor in the palm of Billy's right hand. I wait. His cannonball-sized bicep begins to quake and spasm. I wait. A thin rivulet of blood leaks from the corner of Billy's mouth where he's bitten his cheek. I start to pull.

I meet Billy's eyes halfway. They appear scared and confused, like some intelligent animal that's about to be gaffed. Bulking up, Billy tries a throw of his own, only it's too late as his engorged bicep finally gives out, deflating like a truck tire running over a railroad spike. Billy's eyes flutter and blink as I align my right shoulder with his and drive down his wrist, where his knuckles land on the bamboo bar top with a loud "RAP!" A wavelike cheer circles the lounge as Billy rests his sweat-soaked head on his throbbing bicep while I massage my right wrist and wipe back my soggy topknot.

"Don't take it too hard, Billy," I say to him. "Gramp once pinned Arnold Schwarzenegger when we were over at the Compound for a fish fry. He was pushing sixty, and Arnold had just won Mr. Olympia for the sixth time."

Lifting his head, Billy looks at me and says, "You're staying and you're drinking. And nobody's buying 'cept me. Welcome aboard, fisherman!"

The crowd cheers. Reaching across the bar, I go to shake Billy's hand, but he waves me off. "Had enough of your patty-cake tricks for one day." Calling over the barkeep, Billy takes out a C-note and places it on the bar. "Whatever he wants." Standing, he turns to the crowd. "I'm going back to the hotel. Got me an early rise in the morning. Ain't that right, Mack?"

"That you do, Billy! We all do, including our newest hire!"

Giving a backwards wave, Billy Boondocks easily shoves his way through the crowd and exits the bar through the swinging saloon doors.

"What'll it be, fisherman?" says the now smiling barkeep, eyeing the C-note on the bar. "Hope you're thirsty!"

"I'm not." Plucking the bill from the bar top, I stuff it in my back pocket and say, "I'll make sure Billy gets this back." The barkeep bristles. Skipper Mack sidles up next to me and claps me hard on my back again.

"Thought Boondocks had ya' there for a minute, but I can see now you've been in a few of these scrums before."

"Billy would have beat me easy, if he knew how to arm wrestle," I admit.

"Can't take a compliment. Same way m'self. What good's it do?"

"Do you truly have a boat in the race?" I ask, seriously mulling his offer.

"I truly do."

"And what's up with that daughter of yours? Is she nuts or somethin'?"

"She's the devil herself let loose on the men of the world." The skipper shudders.

"She's the one who got me into this mess, along with you. Where'd she go anyway?"

"Out laying a trap for you, I suppose."

"What happens now?"

"We leave the slip at 7 AM sharp. If you're there, I'll know you're on board. If not, have a safe trip back to the Cape." Shaking my hand, Skipper Mack leaves my side to go collect on his bets. I make my way through the swinging saloon door and finally leave the Rough Seas Lounge with the barkeep hurling insults at my back.

I join the main drag and bounce like a pinball amid the drunken party people crowding the docks. Cutting through a narrow alley, I head for my cheap hotel room by way of the beach road, where I walk for some time before actually seeing a beach. Not liking the sidewalk so much, I jump the abutting seawall and land on hard-packed white sand. Psychedelic surf music drifts from the bars along the boardwalk as I pull off my boat shoes and walk slipshod through the retreating surf. I try picturing the girl, but all I can remember are her eyes, the greenish gemstones of alternating brilliance bouncing off the back of my skull. I notice a cloaked figure huddled against the seawall further along the beach, dimly lit by the burning tip of a cigarette and the slow exhalation of white smoke. I am about to hop back over the seawall when the most pleasant smell of wet clove enters my nostrils.

"How was your swim?" the girl asks.

"Invigorating," I answer, plunking down next to her and rooting my feet in the sand.

"You don't feel wet," she says, running her hand over the front of my shirt.

"This full moon will dry you out fast. Should have stuck around."

"I don't go for that male macho stuff," says the girl, flicking her clove cigarette into the foam. "I'm only here because of my father."

"Daddy's little girl come to help him win the big race. Is that it?"

"I've been in the riggings since I was six, and I've sailed competitively since I was around ten," she replies sternly. "I'm first mate because I've earned it, but winning the Cup? I'm not so sure. That's why I'm here. To be with him. When he loses. Does that sound horrible to you?"

"No. But it might to him. Mack must be doing something right. I mean, he got this far."

"Pop won the Luis Vuitton Cup in December only because two of the faster boats got disqualified. That's when I took a semester off and came aboard. Don't get me wrong, I love my father and he's a hell of a sailor. Did he mention that he won the Velux 5 race, twice?"

"That's the race where sailors sail solo around the world, right?"

"One boat. One sailor. No help. Only when Pop won it, it was called the B.O.C. Challenge."

"Boats Off Course?"

"Worse. British Oxygen Corporation. Catchy, huh?"

"He hasn't."

"Hasn't what?"

"Mentioned to me that he was in the race, or that he won it twice."

"That's just like him. Believes a skipper's got to earn his crew's respect every time out."

"Sounds about right. But wouldn't experience like that give your dad an advantage?"

"Normally it would, but these skippers only go from marker to marker. They don't care about oceanic currents or changing trade winds. All they want is crowed sails and the arms to hoist them, and Dad doesn't understand that."

"He must have understood some of it," I say, defending the old man. "You're all here."

"Yeah, by the skin of our teeth."

"What's Billy's involvement in all this?"

"The win in December got us the invite, but we still needed money. You have no idea what it costs to compete for the Cup. Billy did some competitive sailing in college, but in reality, he's just another quasi-celebrity trying to keep his name in the papers. That's his muscle drink you'll see splashed all across the boat."

"Why should a man owning Ocean Spray be in want of money?"

"Family's Ocean Spray. We're what you might call black sheep. Pop's not much of a businessman. More of a wanderer. Married a girl from the islands: part Dominican, part something else. That's why I look the way I do. The brothers never took to my mother, or to me for that matter. She passed when I was little and it's been me and Pop against the world ever since."

"I know the feeling," I say, reaching across the sand and giving her hand a squeeze. I continue to hold her hand. She lets me.

"Anyway, the brothers got tired of my father's vision quests and bought him out. We got the house in Harwich along with ten bogs and not much else. The price on cranberries isn't much these days, and with the cost of my tuition at BU, it sure as shit doesn't leave much left to vie for the Cup."

"I always wanted to be a true Corinthian sailor," I joke.

"Line forms behind me," says the girl with a giggle.

"I haven't any experience on a boat like this. None, in fact, and I told Mack."

"I'm sure he has his reasons."

"What reasons can he have?"

"Let's just say you stood out."

"Stood out how?" I ask, feeling a little miffed. "Wasn't wearing the right cologne?"

"Are you kidding? Look at what you're wearing! Pop spotted you right off."

"I'm glad that I amuse you," I say, starting to stand. Grabbing my belt, the girl pulls me back down.

"I'll take honest sweat over cologne any day of the week! Do you have any idea what it's like sailing with a bunch of Biffs and Martys? God forbid anyone takes a wave in the face and gets their hair messed!"

"I don't know your name," I say.

"Toby, with a Y," the girl answers.

"So, Skipper Mack wanted a boy?" I joke, prompting her to hit me hard on my left arm, raising a welt.

"But I know yours; it's Ca…"

"Close enough."

Slipping my right arm around the girl's shapely waistline, I draw her close. Stars flutter and dance in her eyes as our lips touch, quivering and hesitant at first, then we kiss, and the rest I'll leave on the beach that night.

A strong tailwind builds behind the stern and I am glad for it. The wind gives me something to do and clears my mind of Toby. I have work ahead that she's not a part of. To share my burden would no doubt lessen the crushing weight on my shoulders, but what if she doesn't see my side of it, that I had no choice? I might as well turn myself in, only I have to keep looking out for Gramp. Without me, he'd starve to death, and the town would take the land. A loss of innocence happens to all men, but I don't want that for her. Whatever burden I have to bear, I'll bear it alone. Compounding this problem is my perceived belief in a double-cross at the hands of the ranger. I kept waiting for the money to hit my bank account, but it never did, and nor was it placed into Gramp's account, and yet when I made an anonymous phone call to the National Seashore and asked to speak Monomoy Ranger Watson, I was told that he was out on patrol and couldn't be reached at the moment, so I hung up. But it told me that Tiger was still employed and hadn't been arrested. So what happened to the money? And though it would never hold up in a court of law, being that our endeavor was illegal, to begin with, I feel that I've been wronged.

Either the ranger will have my money when I see him, or he won't, and if he doesn't have the money, I'll go down swinging. Honor amongst thieves is the way I see it, with me as the blood simple mule with blinders on, drawing a carriage of revenge up a steep hill with only one way forward and no way back.

BOOK II

"White waves heaving high my boys,
the good ship right and free.
The world of waters is our home,
the merry men are we."

sailor shanty

PLEASANT BAY

I see the kids are out today splashing about in their dories and capsizing them, sometimes for the fun of it and sometimes not, while their older siblings race about the bay in their Boston Whalers, trying to look cool and succeeding. It's the same body of water where my father taught me to sail. We'd start the day gunkholing the bay's many coves and inlets before venturing into deeper water where I could practice my tacking and jibbing. He'd tell me of the many currents aswirl beneath the boat and always warn me of staying within the barrier beach.

"She's real ocean out there," he'd say, pointing a crooked finger at the frothing North Atlantic trying to fight its way into the bay. "And She don't care how young or old ya' are. She just wants her ante. If you're ever in the 'smoke,' look to where She's breakin' and follow Her in. And remember your tides or you'll be sailin' for Spain. She don't breathe like you and me, so if ya' do go over the side, keep your chin up and swim, not too fast, like you're swimmin' for a tennis ball I tossed over ya' head. I know I taught ya' how to swim, so I don't want to hear any excuses."

I'd sit at the stern, taking in my father's every word as if they were coming from the Timekeeper Himself. After which, he'd have me capsize the boat, and there I'd be, in the middle of the bay, with my ninety-eight-pound frame trying to flip the boat up with my father treading water beside the boat, shouting orders like "Face the bow into the wind!" or "Dive down and untie the mains'l!" But it was afterwards that our day together really began. Munching on ham and cheese sandwiches packed by Gramp, we'd stroll the flats talking about everything and nothing while looking for interesting pieces of driftwood to put up in the rafters.

Abaft beam, I watch the Yacht Club boys jockey for position for the start of their annual Fourth of July Regatta. Secured in the cockpits of their sleek, white Lasers, the sailors draw in their mainsheets and come about. I recognize Jimmy's kid brother Sam's boat from its red boot markings and sky-blue jib. The starting horn sounds and the sailors tack to the east, passing the green marker. Sam is three boat lengths from leader and tacks west, away from the group. I take up the spyglass and look past Sam's bow, where I notice a cat's paw building in the water off to his port.

I smile, knowing the reason for Sam's tack, and sure enough, as the other racers round the yellow marker, their sails luff and fall limp against a headwind. Approaching the ruffled water, Sam's sails fill and begin pulling him along at a decent chop. The other sailors try to paddle their way out of the dead spot, but they're too late as Sam passes the yellow marker alone with crowded sails clear for running. I let go of the tiller and jump on deck. Taking hold of the mainstay, I shout, "Attaboy, Sam! Keelhaul the bastards!"

I can remember teaching Jimmy and Sam that tack back when the only thing separating the families was the wind and the waves. It's funny how life draws those invisible boundary lines. You can't see them when you're younger, but as you get older, they turn into long driveways lined by tall hedges with NO TRESPASSING signs posted on them.

I recall a time Jimmy came by for a visit. It was an unusually warm day in April. I hadn't seen Jimmy since the town hall meeting. Most of that year I was away fishing somewhere for pay while he was at Dartmouth finishing up his studies. I was on the back porch, soaking the brains of an outboard motor in a chum bucket filled with gasoline, when Jimmy appeared on the back lawn like a mirage. Clad in white linens and holding a leather satchel, he reminded me of a young Colonel Sanders, only without the mustache and black bow tie.

"Cal, we need to talk."

"So, talk. Nobody's stopping you."

"Concerns your land."

"Gramp's land. He's in the kitchen. I'll get him."

Jimmy waves me off. "I'm here to talk to you. Not your grandfather. Can I come up?"

"You know the way."

Taking the whaling gaff in hand, Jimmy vaults over the two missing steps and lands at my side. Placing his satchel at his feet, he collapses in my father's now frayed rattan chair.

"What gives, Jimbo? Shouldn't you be on spring break getting drunk and chasing girls on San Padre Island?"

"That was last year. This year I was in a ditch in Haiti, digging wells for UNICEF."

"Noble," I say, meaning it.

"My father got through to me, and it was about the land. I flew out of Port-au-Prince this morning."

"Gramp's department. Talk to him. I don't want any part of it."

"Oh, I'd say you're part of it, all right. Captain Let hasn't told you?"

"Told me what?"

"That he turned the land over to you. Three days ago."

"Bullshit," I say, rubbing my gassy hands on my gassy overalls.

"I have the property deed transfer right here," says Jimmy, reaching into his satchel. Taking out a single sheet of waxy paper, he hands it to me.

I look at the paper and shake my head. "Why would I read from a photostat?"

"Because the original's locked in a safe down at the town clerk's office. Shall I read it for you?"

"Sure, not that it matters," I say, handing him back the photostat.

Jimmy smirks. "You always were a hardheaded bastard." He continues, "On this date, as witnessed by Town Clerk Michael Jermyn. Remember him? Skinny kid used to walk around the high school in a tank top thinking he was Bruce Lee?"

"I remember him. Keep reading," I say.

Jimmy scowls and continues. "The deed in question has hereby been bequeathed to Caleb Jeremiah Forrest by Captain Lester Joshua Forrest, totaling 648 acres in the townships of Chatham, Harwich, and Orleans. The rest is archaic mumbo jumbo. Want me to read it?"

I shake my head, saying to him, "Another one of your father's dirty tricks."

"I'll pretend I didn't hear that," replies Jimmy. "Saves the two of us from knocking each other's teeth out."

"Fair enough. Where's the original?"

"I told you, clerk's got it locked up in his safe."

"Original land deed."

"If there is one, it's lost somewhere in bowels of the State House in Boston. But this will do for now," says Jimmy, eyeing me sternly. "You still don't believe me?"

"I've always believed in you, Jimbo, but this is ridiculous. Let me get Gramp."

"With all due respect to the Captain, he's out and you're in."

"I thought we agreed to let the grown-ups work it out."

"We're the grown-ups now, Cal. You and me. And we have to move fast on this. The fax machine in my office is giving me a migraine."

"You have an office?"

"Dad made me president and CEO of Hallet Construction."

"When did this happen?"

"An early graduation present, you might say."

"This is a joke, right?" I ask, hoping for a punch line.

"Sure, Cal, I flew all the way from Port-au-Prince to play a joke on you. Some joke!"

"What are these bids you're talking about?"

"Construction bids for the thirty-three-acre parcel my father first proposed."

My back stiffens. Jimmy sees this and shakes his head. "Dad's retired. Cut all lines financially, so there won't be any conflicts of interest. He's strictly a town selectman these days. It's just you and me on this one, watching each other's backs like we did when we were kids. You always told me the land was a yoke around your neck. Now here's your chance to break free."

"It's not about me, Jimmy. It's about Gramp. It'll break him if I sell. I know it will."

"Could be the reason he turned it over to you, so it won't break him."

I turn away from Jimmy and grip the porch rail. Looking out across the bay, where the refracted sunlight spreads across the water like a broken mirror, I feel the weight of eight generations on my shoulders. The clerk's office must have made a mistake. Gramp would have told me. Why should I be the one to decide? Gramp should give in. He fought the good fight and now he's old. The people, our people, would understand if it came from him.

"Listen to me, Cal," says Jimmy, interrupting my thoughts. "You're never going to pay down those town taxes no matter how many trips you make. I've done the math. The monthly interest alone is enough to bury you. And if you get injured out there, what then? You're not exactly employed as a school crossing guard. That shit you do is dangerous. Either way, they'll take it from you. They'll take it and you'll still owe. This land where your house sits is valued only slightly behind Nantucket, and that's saying something. We could wait you out, like my father's willing to do, but I'd rather pay you the money now while there's still time. I want to. You're a stubborn bastard, but you're still my best friend."

"What's your overall plan?" I ask, continuing to give him my back.

"Twenty premium lots on 1.3 acres each. Separate road, sewer, electric, etc. And not one lot with an ocean view. I put them all out by the power lines, the northernmost sector of your property, and they're still tugging at the leash. You won't even know they're there. It's a win-win!"

"Gramp will know."

"What doesn't Captain Let know?" says Jimmy, sighing in frustration. "You can't hide behind your grandfather. Not this time. We're the ones in charge. Now it's your turn to give it to me straight."

"What's in it for Gramp and me if I make this deal you're all so hot for?"

Jimmy reaches into his satchel and brings out a glossy brochure along with a contract embossed with Hallet Paving and Construction letterhead and hands it to me. I wave him off. Jimmy scowls and reads it instead.

"Thirty-eight percent over current market value, that's what. You'll be able to take care of the Captain if he lives another eighty years. And what about you, Cal? Fishermen are a dying breed, you said so yourself. With this money I'm offering, you can go to college like you've always talked about. You've got the grades. Hell, you scored better than me on the SATs!"

"I met with Mr. Vick, but I…"

"Screw Mr. Vick! Guy's a joke! My father's the one with the real pull. He'll get you in whatever college you set your eyes on, and he'll be happy to do it. He always did like you better than he does me."

"That's not true, Jimmy."

"Doesn't matter. Forget I said it. Yes or no, Cal."

I cross the back deck, kicking at the scattered marine flotsam lying about. It wouldn't surprise me if Dale was behind this. He's a tricky SOB. Jimmy might not even know. The clerk's office might have gotten it wrong, or maybe they're in on it too. And why wouldn't they be? They've been trying to take the land long before Jimmy and his family ever moved to town. I want to believe Jimmy, I do, for my own sake and Gramp's.

Facing the bay, I lean on the railing again and follow the land upward, and what has always been a yoke around my neck suddenly transforms itself into that of a babe in its crib. I see the land bright-eyed and full of wonder. Giddy with life and breathing each breath as if it were the first. Every warren and nest comes into view, as do the land's many streams, creeks, lagoons, ponds, and eddies that speak to me in gibberish, whilst its many inhabitants call to me from the treetops, swamps, ponds, and hovels. Looking up at the house proper, I imagine that I see them, the long-ago residents watching me from the many windows in translucent silhouette, awaiting my decision. And then it dawns on me... *What does money know anyway?* Nothing, that's what. It's inert. Money doesn't burrow in the soil or nest in trees. Money doesn't feed its young and protect them from predators. Money doesn't swim upstream to spawn. What's more, money has no friends. Its only allegiance is to those who possess it. Even then money will leave you standing on the curb shirtless and broke at the first opportunity.

"No" is what I tell Jimmy.

"Cal, you can't keep this up."

"I'll think of something."

"They'll take it from you."

"My problem. Not yours."

"Is it the number? We can work on that."

"Not the number."

Jimmy shakes his head. Refolding the brochure, he slips the contract inside and thrusts it at me. I wave him off, but Jimmy continues to hold out the brochure.

"Goddamn it, Cal, take it! I didn't come all the way out here for nothing! My offer still stands. Who knows, you might even change your mind."

"I won't."

"Keep it anyway."

Folding the photostat, brochure, and the offer sheet, I slide them into my back pocket. Jimmy lifts himself from the rattan chair and looks inside the chum bucket. "You're soaking it too long." Picking up his leather satchel, he leaves the back porch by way of the whaler's gaff and rounds the corner of the house without so much as a backwards wave.

Gramp comes out of the kitchen and stands at my side. "Smart boy, that friend of yours. Lot like his Pap. Can't hold it against 'im, no matter how hard I try."

"Is it true?"

"Always said the land would be yours one day. I've done my share of the heavy lifting and now it's your turn. Precious thing, this land of ours. Carries with it a great deal of responsibility. I hope I've instilled that in ya', Caleb, but I'll abide by whatever decision ya' make."

Gramp leaves my side and walks back into the kitchen. Lifting the circuit board from the chum bucket, I wrap it in old newspaper and place it on the porch railing to dry in the sun before joining Gramp in the kitchen while carefully replacing the hingeless screen door.

———

I return to the cockpit and take my seat at the stern. Watching the sailors draw in their sails for the final leg, the finishing horn sounds with Sam crossing the red marker alone. I take up the spyglass and focus it on Sam as he sails for the Yacht Club pier where his family awaits, cheering him on. I don't see Jimmy anywhere, and I don't expect to. I have a sudden urge to come about and join them in congratulating Sam, only it would be awkward if I did. The gap between our two families has grown, and I am sad for it. Mr. Hallet was right when he said to me, "If you don't grow, you die," only he forgot that you also have to adapt. He lost his business because of it and, more importantly, his eldest son.

A wave of heartfelt sorrow grips my chest. It's a pain fraught with loneliness and a tinge of despair. "Time heals all wounds," the grown-ups tell us when we're young, but I don't see that happening. Jimmy's gone with no real hope of ever returning, and I might not make it past sundown. A shadow has been cast, and whatever hopes I have are fast-fading on diminishing winds. I collapse the spyglass and haul in the mainsheet to carry me past Fox Hill and out of sight of the Yacht Club pier.

MINISTER'S POINT

S *ea Gypsy* shivers in the outgoing tide as I haul in and cleat down. Passing over a series of shallow shoals, I slip into the channel where the tall spars of the many vessels in port come into view. To quote Melville, "The sea is a broad highway of nations," and if that's true, then Chatham is its parking lot. I have to pay attention to the water and to the other skippers who may or may not know the channel's rights of way. There's always the skipper who will sail straight at you, believing that he has the right of way because he has the bigger boat. But that rule only applies if you're in a narrow channel where the bigger boat can't navigate safely. Otherwise, the boat underway has the go-ahead. But try telling that to the day sailor standing atop a fifty-foot flying bridge with a double shot of Cutty Sark in his glass.

It's the reason I'm always more attentive in-harbor than out, and yet many sailors I see these days choose to remain within the barrier beach and chance running into each other rather than venturing offshore where they have all the space they'll ever need. These "yachtsmen" don't seem to realize that a single fathom can drown a man as fast as a hundred. I guess it's all about familiarity. If I hadn't grown up with the sea at my back, I might feel the same way.

But the boat I will always give way to is the *Mystic Yankee*, and I do as the seventy-foot tri-decker steams past my port, taking a boatload of tourists out past the Truro shoals in the hope of spotting a gam of humpbacks. I've come across plenty of grumpas when fishing the Banks. In my opinion, they're Earth's most majestic creatures. There's something solemn about them when you're running alongside, rising and sounding like breath and leaving placid footprints in their wake. It's like they're from another planet, only one much larger than our own.

Had I lived in Captain Nehi's day, I no doubt would have hunted these magnificent creatures, rowing out in heavily planked whaleboats with a barbed harpoon held at the ready. What a sight it must have been! The torrents of blood gushing in the roiling water with great plumes of sooty black smoke wafting from the tryworks. It took thirty men to crew a whaling ship and the captain would be lucky to return three years later with half that. As much as I admire my family heritage, I'm glad I was born in a more humane century. How much more humane, I can't say.

I notice a young couple leaning over *Yankee*'s top rail, attempting to feed a hot dog bun to a hovering gull. Our eyes lock and for that one instant, we are but three sentient beings enjoying the air and the sea with only the naked reality of space separating. I wonder what their lives are like, what hopes and dreams they have, and if theirs will come true. The gull veers off, refusing the bun, as I knew it would. Not enough trust, and why should there be? The great bird lover Audubon himself shotgunned as many species of fowl flew within range of his twelve-gauge, only to then paint and catalog the birds.

I pilot *Sea Gypsy* behind the boat's stern and enjoy the calmness of her wake. Jellyfish bob in the slop, emitting fluorescent blots of pink and blue while flocks of stormy petrels, or what Gramp calls "Mother Mary's chickens," dart and dive in the misty updraft. I wave up at the couple, but they ignore the ritual and turn away. "Canadians," I say to myself, shaking my head. I grow tired of the smell of diesel and come about, sweeping the bow chuck across the sail-dotted horizon before settling on the bulwark of dunes spilling down from Minister's Point.

The history books claim that this was the spot of the first Indian resistance. While it's entirely possible, this was the spot, but given the similarities between the two, I like to think it happened on our bluff.

According to the ship's log of French navigator Samuel de Champlain, circa 1605, the vessel he captained, *La Bonne Renommée*, 'the good name' was mapping the Outer Cape when its rudder broke while crossing Pollock Rip. This was Champlain's second voyage to the New World when he entered this as-yet-named bay for repairs. A contingent of Nauset braves paddled out with fresh provisions to greet Champlain, having known the captain from when he ran aground at the harbor's mouth the year before. This first meeting between the two tribes was relatively uneventful; the Nauset braves helping to pull the French flagship off the sandbar and back into deeper water for repairs. As a reward, Champlain promised any brave willing to sail with him a paid adventure on the High Seas. Two of the Nausets volunteered, only to be sold into slavery when the ship made port in France. It was during this second incursion, however, that bows were drawn and arrows took flight.

For ten days the Nausets and the seafarers exchanged bracelets for fish and beads for grapes, as work on the damaged rudder progressed. During this downtime, Champlain thought it a good notion to send a dozen or so harquebusiers ashore to walk amongst the natives, spying for hidden booty and hopefully gold. Little if any gold was found. However, the French mercenaries did notice the women of the village taking down their huts and moving them deeper into the wood.

Learning of this, Champlain ordered his mercenaries onto the ship, only the company had already begun drinking their daily allotment of grog and were in no mood to return to the squalid confines of the "hole." Instead, they erected a wooden cross on a small beach and began parading around it, shouting religious gibberish. The Nausets kept their distance during the night, even burning their crop fields. The following morn, with the ship's rudder repaired, Champlain threatened desertion charges if the men did not return to the ship. The mercenaries steadfastly refused, believing themselves New World Vikings. Shortly thereafter, the company found themselves surrounded by four hundred Nauset warriors looking down at them from the bluff.

"From atop the highest precipice," wrote Champlain in his ship's log, "there was sent such a volley of arrows that to rise up was death!" Four of the company were killed outright, leaving the rest swimming for their lives back to the ship. Champlain watched the debacle unfold "with great displeasure...the savages coming onto the beach and beating down the Cross in mockery...scattering the corpses in the high dunes." In a final gesture before hoisting anchor, the French navigator loaded his flintlock pistol and aimed for shore. "Sighting a large buck standing defiantly on the tall hill, I took aim and fired my pistol. It was my luck the volley exploded in-chamber and blackened my nose."

I find it ironic that the very bluff where the Nauset braves supposedly fought off the first papal invasion also happened to be the spot where the Big Sunday Camp Meetings took place three centuries later. Large groups of Methodists, or "Baby Dunkers," as they were more commonly referred to, would flock to the Outer Cape during the summer months. Congregation after congregation from every state in the Union came to Chatham's North Shore, sometimes even setting up in our wood.

Once tented, these preachers would evangelize from sunup to sundown for weeks on end. My long-ago relation was a follower. She was a teenager when she arrived with her family from Ohio. Isis was her name, and she was walking our harbor beach one day when she ran into Old Joe, as Gramp tells it.

"Old Joe, being the wolf he was, chased young Isis into the wood where he set upon her with great fury and done nature's callin'. Now, there's another version that goes, it was Isis who set upon Old Joe.

Nobody's sure who set upon whom that day, but I can tell you this, it was my pap and your great grandpap Joachim who poked his head into the world not nine months afta'!'"

Whichever the true version, Isis set up house with Old Joe, much to her preacher father's disdain. "Problem lay in that, to get her pap's approval, Old Joe would have to be baptized Methodist, but Old Joe weren't havin' none of it. He told that preacher fella that if he were good enough for his daughter, and she was good enough for him, what business was it to anybody? He'd make his peace with the Timekeeper when he sees 'im." Joe's refusal only added fuel to the fire. The preacher returned to the house day after day to shout blasphemes, even holding a prayer meeting on our front stoop next to the ever-creeping dune.

"Old Joe sat inside the house pullin' at his ears, but no matter how hard he tried, he couldn't drown out that preacher fella. What could he do? They were people of the Cross! Fanatics! So it was his Isis who picked up the scattergun, standin' on our front stoop and yellin', 'Don't you ever come back here, Daddy! Don't you ever come back! What we got, you can't ever know! What we got was made right here on this earth! That book you been waving at me since I was a little girl says you ain't supposed to bite the apple! Well, I bit the apple, and I'm gonna have a young'in because of it! You done your share of biting on me, Daddy, and don't think I forgot! I ain't! So'd you'd best git before I commit another mortal sin and blow out your stinkin' guts!' And with his Isis holding sight with Joe's shotgun, you can bet that every one of 'em hymn-singers packed their tents and went! One thing's for sure, Isis had herself an appetite and Old Joe was high on the menu!"

Gramp's wife Flossy, or Florence, was another firebrand, and according to the story he tells, she'd been chasing after him since they were both in grade school together. But what finally landed the crusty long-liner wasn't Flossy's chasing, but her whisky barrel-splitting ax. She was a Prohibitionist, and when word got out the captain was hiding booze in his barn, it was Florence O'Sullivan first at his front stoop.

"If I know this man, and I believe that I do," she is thought to have said to her fellow Prohibitionists who were with her that night. "I've had my eye on him since he was in short pants, and I'll know if he's hiding something." Turning to the towering oaken doors that let into our parlor, she began banging on them with her gloved hand. "Get to this door, Lester Forrest, and be quick about it!" She was about bang a second time when the heavy doors creaked open, and Gramp stepped out onto the stoop. Looking down at the diminutive Flossy, he is supposed to have said, "What took you so long, woman?"

A stunned Florence could only crane her neck, looking up at the tall captain. Reaching down, the bootlegger lifted his future wife high in the air and kissed her. The length of the kiss varies depending on the townspeople who were witnesses that night. Placing Florence inside the foyer, the captain gestured to the house, saying, "If it's the barrels you're afta', have at 'em. I won't stand in your way." Shooing her fellow Prohibitionists from the stoop, Flossy stepped inside the house and quickly closed the heavy doors behind her. Nobody knows if any barrels were split that night, but one thing's certain, there wasn't a drop of liquor to be had in the Forrest house as long as Florence O'Sullivan held roost, barn not included.

When the fire is low, and the cold seeps under the doorjambs, Gramp will sometimes reminisce, "I'd've split the barrels with her 'cept we were in a Depression and the price on fish weren't much. So, I ran the booze, hiding it in the swamp and mostly when she was away doin' the good work. Neva' felt so ashamed, but we had to eat and afford her travels. Imagine today a woman with nothing to do 'cept for the cookin'? Your Nana helped change that." But it was after Flossy got the cancer, and later died from it, that Gramp began pulling at the cork. At first, he'd only take a couple of slugs, just so he could talk to her. I'd listen from my perch on the spiral staircase, and I'd hear her talk back, but in his voice, mostly to scold him for his drinking.

For reasons unknown, the men of my family attract women of the strongest will and put them under the sod long before their time. I fear for Toby, I do. I want to break the cycle, smash it. If I were to go back and undo what I did, I would. Not out of any sense of remorse, but for the girl's sake. What's buried is buried, but in my case, submerged. Ghosts I can deal with, but to have Toby out of my life, I fear, would break me. I am a pity party for sure, only tears are for the angels, and I'm no angel.

TERN ISLAND
SANCTUARY

The falling tide is a smelly one as I navigate the surrounding shoals of Tern Island. The sanctuary itself is abuzz with nesting terns, darting and diving about *Sea Gypsy* in defense of their eggs. The island is small and will probably disappear in my lifetime, be it tomorrow or fifty years from tomorrow. At one time, the island housed a community of summer cabins now lost to the wind and the waves.

I pass the osprey nest set high atop an abandoned telephone pole stationed midway on the island. Made of large branches and blackened twigs, the nest gives the impression of a deep-bellied bowl sculpted by Edgar Allan Poe. As kids, we used to sail out and crawl along our bellies on the hot sand to see which of us could get close enough to touch the pole. The sea eagle would always spot us and, rising in a headwind, dive-bomb us back to our boats. On this occasion, the raptor remains in its nest, calling me names, no doubt remembering me from when it was a chick.

I skip into Aunt Lydia's cove and the Chatham Bar Inn comes into view, its red brick stairway spilling down from an open-air portico, forming an impressive amphitheater from which to view the bay. The Inn is palatial, to say the least, the kind of place where Henry Ford and William Rockefeller Jr. stayed when they were visiting the Cape, as did the Dutch royal family, who used the Inn as a retreat during WWII. I've never been, except to deliver my own fresh catches to the kitchen's rear entrance, where master chef Sam Ricker would then put them on his "Specials Board" and charge the equivalent of a car payment.

Sailing past the Fish Pier, I don't see *Sea Pearl* tied off anywhere. Captain Jenkins must have off-loaded his stinking catch and up-anchored. I didn't expect to get paid anyway. I'm just happy to be off that floating landfill. I'm still not sure why we steamed back early, and when I try to recall, all I remember is the squall hitting. After that, it's like I'm watching a movie frame by frame by frame.

Unhooking the stopper latch, I kick open the back door and throw out the first buoy. Four miles of gill net shoot through the gap with me attaching a buoy marker every hundred feet. It's a two-man job, but I let my emaciated shipmate slack off under the cover of the cart house, bent at the waist in a furious bout of the dry heaves. Waves kick up and slap against the gunwales. I widen my stance, careful not to get my boot tangled in the line lest I be taken overboard along with the bait.

Sea Pearl takes a sudden plunge that sends me airborne. Weight-lessly suspended, the deck flips up like a springboard, popping my knees and causing the bones in my feet to sing out. I roll onto my side and crab-crawl my way over to the belowdecks hatch. I open it and I am about to call down when a giant roller plows into the bow and arches the boat skyward. I slide down the deck and am about to shoot through the back door when another giant wave crashes against the stern, righting the ship. I regain my footing and look to the cart house only to find it empty of fishermen. The old shellback has left his puking post.

I search amid the foul-weather gear strewn on deck and quickly come to the conclusion that my sickened shipmate may have shipped over the side. I do a quick check along the gunwales, and nowhere in that roiling expanse of sea do I spot the bearded fisherman. He's thin enough that he could have slipped through a scupper, but that would have taken the blunt end of a drub stick. The only other explanation is that he got washed into the pit. I look again over the gunwale and realize that if he did carry over, he would have sunk like a stone; without an ounce of body fat to keep him afloat, his rubber hip boots alone would be enough to pull him under.

I stop the starboard spool's controlled release and head for the open belowdecks hatch. Water aplenty ships over the sides and takes me out at the hips. On elbows and knees, I crab-crawl my way across the back deck. Reaching the hatch, I grip the elevated rim and call down into the pit. "Hey! Mooney! Are you down there?" Getting no response, I take hold of the handrails and descend the steep ladder, landing just outside the engine room in a foot of sloshing water. I try opening the bunkhouse door, but find that it's locked from the inside. Using the sleeve of my grimy sweatshirt, I swab the condensation from the portal window and peer inside to where four ghost-white faces stare back at me from their bunks, the feared lost fisherman shivering amongst them.

I pound on the door, but my shipmates won't leave their bunks, like they're nailed to their beds. I start back up the ladder. Nearing the top, I am greeted with a bathtubful of near-freezing North Atlantic, the weight of which knocks me from the ladder and back into the pit. Reaching through the deluge, I grab the rails and, rung by rung, start back up with an endless sea pouring over me. I resurface and close the hatch to save the engine room from any further swamping. I sit squatting on the hatch, watching the skies darken further, and it feels that I am there forever when a cresting wave lips over the side and spits in my face.

Awaking from my self-imposed funk, I cross the deck and climb the gangplank. Kicking open the wheelhouse door, I find Captain Jenkins at the helm, fully awake, spinning the wheel to port and then to starboard, struggling to keep *Sea Pearl* pointed into the wind as the mountainous waves rise, crest, and crash against the ship's high-impact plexiglass windows.

"Why ain't ya' out there manning the starboard spool like I ordered?" asks the captain, without looking at me.

"Thought we had a man overboard, so I stopped it. False alarm, turns out."

"Stopped it!" shouts Captain Jenkins. "Christ, boy! Can't you see we're backing up!"

Not waiting for the order, I turn and run from the wheelhouse. Hurdling the gangplank, I land on all fours, then race across the back deck with waves from both sides of the ship lashing at my body. I reach the cart house and pry a rusted machete from the tool rack. Raising the machete above my head, I begin hacking at the net, only the dull blade won't cut. I try again, but to no avail. The stern buckles from below, sinking my stomach into my bowels. I take hold of the net and feel it snap from below, sending up a mostly harmless marker buoy that shoots through the back door and slams against the right side of my face.

The force of the blow could have easily caused a concussion, which would explain my memory loss, but when I touch the right side of my face, there's no swelling or bruising. I was knocked out for sure, and if there was a seaman amongst the crew, I would have been wrapped in warm blankets and placed in the glory hole. Truth is, I screwed up. I should have kept my eye on the starboard spool. What was I thinking? We would have sunk for sure if it wasn't for the line breaking. Thinking back, I have new respect for captain and crew. They took care of me when they could have easily rolled me overboard, and nobody would have been the wiser. As far as Captain Jenkins is concerned, maybe he's not such a bad captain. He did get us back to dry land, after all; I mean, I'm here, aren't I?

THE SALEM WITCH

I sail from the cove, having to tack around a half-sunken mussel dragger long run aground on a sandbar. You'd think by now someone would have towed the rusted hulk out to sea and scuttled her, but I guess she's no more a threat to navigation than the sandbar itself. To me, the dragger is a reminder of how feeble we humans are when we put out to sea. If such an impressive assemblage of steel and iron can find itself ruined here amid the calms, what's to guarantee any vessel making it past the Bar, where the real ocean boils and spits, coughing up the chance of destruction with each impending roller? Looking at the dragger now, with its bow pointing skyward and speckled in black and white egret droppings, it's a view only a painter of Jackson Pollock's talents could appreciate.

I switch seats and tack back to starboard to follow the narrow yet swift current running along the shoreline. The water here is surprisingly deep and I've fished my fair share of swimmers from its racing waters. Though it doesn't appear dangerous when you first wade in, just a quick swim out to the sandbar and back, but when an ebb tide is running, as it is now, that quick swim can turn into a trip out to the breakers. The only reason it doesn't happen every day is that it's a heavily trafficked area.

Most swimmers are pulled aboard well before they reach Lighthouse Beach, breathing in gulps, eyeballs inflated with their exhausted limbs of no use. There are others, however, who get swept from the bay's mouth sight unseen, the poor wretches ending up in the net three miles out only to be brought in deader than the catch, and still, others who are never brought up, but for the occasional hand, foot, arm, or toe found in the belly of a tuna, bluefish, or shark. Scanning the shoreline, I see that nobody is in danger of drowning today, so I haul in and sail out of the current, seeking calmer waters.

With the sun beating down and the wind at its noontime retreat, I set *Sea Gypsy* over a shallow shoal and drop anchor. Peeling off my sweaty tee, I step out onto the improvised pulpit and try to balance myself on the two-by-six-foot girder made of heavily varnished teak. I soon find that I'm no match for *Gypsy*'s tricks as she tosses me into the July waters, warm enough that I don't bite off my tongue, yet still cold enough to give my heart a jolt. Taking a breath, I dive beneath my boat.

Cast in *Gypsy*'s shadow, I open my eyes and pull at the water, my blurred vision becoming sharper the deeper I descend. The water itself is as clear as I've ever seen it. I've never thought of using a mask and snorkel. Why would I? Once adjusted, my eyes are like that of a fish, and it is only when I remember to breathe that I resurface.

Swimming the day long, as I used to do, my skin takes on a slippery fishlike coating, allowing me to scoot through the water like a giant minnow, my khaki cutoffs the only impediment from maturing into a true bonefish. And I'd go bare-ass if it wasn't a misdemeanor, though I have, plenty, but mostly after the sun goes down. The sea is more buoyant at night and feels almost electrified when the moon is full, my favorite pastime being imagining myself a shark chasing game fish into the shallows, trailing oily bits of pinkish-white meat in my wake.

Skirting along the bottom, a fishery of full-bellied schoolies swim with me, picking at the dead skin on my elbows, knees, and feet. They're somewhat bigger than their swamp cousins and will make a tasty treat for the stripers when they run in August. Touching down on the bottom, I fall in behind an armada of horseshoe crabs marching across the rippled, white sand like they're playing a game of leapfrog, but in actuality are only mating.

I part the water before me, following a pair of underwater dust devils, unsure of which bottom current to follow. Each its own miniature tornado, the reverse whirlpools stir up a cloud of cockle and clamshell along with an occasional sea urchin that has no choice but to enjoy the ride. I feel that I could stay down forever but remember that I'm not of Her, that I don't have gills and that to breathe, I must resurface.

I come aboard at the stern and shake myself dry. I see that *Sea Gypsy* has drifted some, with Watch Hill now looming over the channel, the wind-stunted pines leading up the hillside holding out their twisted branches like the arthritic mitts of an old crone. And it's a favorite haunt of ravens, the silky black birds exploding from the limbs every morn like a cave full of blood bats, the small pines appearing to lift from the ground when the birds take wing.

I'll be on the bow cutting bait, hoping for a run of sea bass to swim by, when I hear the first "caw" from the tree line. The boughs of the trees will start to shiver and shake, and then I'll see them, hundreds of ravens in flight, enough to blot out the sun as it rises in the east.

The Round House, set high atop the hill, only adds to the scare factor. Made entirely of poured cement, the walls are fissured with settlement cracks partially hidden behind a thick web of climbing ivy. Cubist windows descend like steps along the home's outer shell, seeming to peer out over the channel from behind slanted Bahama storm shutters, and thus giving the appearance that the house is in deep slumber, albeit a malevolent one.

Built in the late 1850s, it was put up by a woman who hailed from Salem and was said to be a known occultist — according to local legend, the reason she made the house round was so evil spirits couldn't hide in the corners. Whatever else I know about the Salem Witch, I got from Gramp.

"Claire Burlingame was her name, and she done most the work herself. Money for the land came from her dead husband. Ship's captain he was. Fought for the North in the War of the Rebellion and got his'self dead and sunk somewhere off the Carolinas. She started with the land and used what she had, which was plenty of sand. Brick by brick she built up the walls until the house rose above the bay like a Scottish castle. It was later that Old Joe helped build her galley, at least that's what he told his young son Joachim, my dad and your great-great-grandpap!"

"Old Joe would come home in the wee hours of the morn," Gramp would go on. "Covered in red dirt, and his Isis weren't the least bit put out about it, which was strange because word around town was that Old Joe had the bit so far back in his mouth that he'd forgotten about it. Fact was, Claire and Isis were friends. Took long walks in our wood together, talkin' politics, philosophy, and such. The other ladies in town thought 'emselves too proper to have anything to do with the witch lady and the preacher's daughter. Not that the two of 'em gave a damn. Isis kept counsel with Old Joe, but Claire had her own friends, mostly city folk and people from the arts, like that writer fellow, Thoreau, who walked himself ragged around the Cape. Harriet Beecher Stowe and Freddy Douglass were others that young Joachim would see at the house from time to time when he was a-helpin' his pap build her galley."

"Folks 'round here thought it odd a woman puttin' up a house by herself with no man around, but she had her friends and your not-too-distant relations were high on the list! I'll tell you this, Caleb, neva' judge a person by what others say. Get to know 'em first and always give 'em a second chance, even if they spit in your eye the first time out. Cause ya' neva' know, they might'en be the ones ta' pull ya' from the darken' trenches when the time comes."

The woman known as the 'Salem Witch' passed in the early 1900s, though town records show no funeral announcement nor any church-affiliated interment. It's rumored that she roams the house to this day, and there are those who claim to have seen her sitting at her bedroom window looking out across the breakers for her dead husband's return from the sea. And that is why six of us teenagers broke into the Round House one All Hallows Eve.

The plan was to meet up after school at the village bandstand. There were six of us, three boys and three girls, sophomores all. It was the time when the testosterone was pumping and the training bras were busting! To start things off, I got the town drunk to buy me a six-pack of beer. Rufus Perry was a well-thought-of fisherman when he was working aboard a boat, but when he was ashore between trips, he'd hang around the back of Martin's Liquors and buy beer for teenagers, sating his own alcoholic needs with the change. A beer apiece was enough to catch a good buzz, and a good buzz was just what we needed on this night.

Furtively cradling a brown paper bag, like I'm carrying a ticking bomb, I cut across Gould Field, where Hailey spots my shadowy figure and calls from the bandstand steps. "Didja' get the beer, Cal?" Hailey was always a full-figured gal in the style of Dolly Parton sort of way, and she was also Chumley's girlfriend at the time, though you'd never know it by the way they bicker, or it could be the reason they do.

"I'm carrying a brown paper bag, Hail! Do the math!" I shout back.

"Math can kiss my ass!" exclaims Sue 'The Jew' Elkins, slapping her backside. With hair the color of black ink to match her eyes, Sue looks more Arab than she does Jewish, not that I'd know the difference, or if there is one.

"Hurry, Cal! These two are starting to get the shakes," comments Jen Crosby, of the famous boatyard Crosbys and also the head cheerleader for Chatham High's football team.

"What took you so long?" Jimmy asks, always finding fault.

"Knowing Cal, he probably drank 'em all and filled 'em up with Dr. Pepper," guffaws Chumley, coming out from behind the bandstand after stealing away for a smoke.

Jimmy peers into the paper bag. "I only count six."

"That's right, Jimmy," I say. "Six, as in six-pack?"

"One beer each?" asks Hailey, rolling her eyes. "Takes a lot more than that to get me drunk."

"You were born drunk. What's the difference?" chuckles Chumley.

"Screw you, Tubbo!" Hailey fires back.

"I'm not fat," replies her boyfriend in a high-pitched voice. "I'm Rubenesque is all."

"Well?" Jen asks me.

"Yeah, Cal," says Sue. "Break 'em out!"

"Gimme," says Jen, motioning for the bag.

I hand Jen the bag. Handing me a beer, she takes one for herself and passes out the rest. I bite off the cap with my back molars and spit it on the grass. A trick I learned by watching Mr. Rondike drink bottle after bottle of Red Stripe on our back porch and spitting the caps at his feet.

"How gauche," moans Jen, frowning slightly before smiling seductively and saying, "But I like it."

Five of us waste little time in gulping down our beers, followed by a cacophony of belching and spitting. Jimmy, for whatever reason, makes a show of pouring his beer out on the grass. We all look at him. Jimmy hunches his shoulders, saying, "Somebody's got to be sober," as if in victory.

"Typical Jimmy," says Sue, shaking her head.

"Hailey would have drunk it," adds Chumley.

"Yeah, ya' stinge!" his girlfriend agrees.

Borrowing a cigarette from Chumley, Jen places it coolly between her sultry lips, lights the tip, and inhales deeply. Holding the smoke in her lungs, she exhales a white plume through her nostrils like some 1930s movie vamp. "So, Cal, what do you have in store for us tonight?" she asks.

"You and me?" I reply.

Jen smiles as she stubs the cigarette out on the bandstand steps. "No, Cal. All of us."

"Well, it's like I told everybody at lunch. We find the old girl's house and break-in."

"Some plan," says Jimmy, throwing up his hands like he had a better one.

"We're talking about the Salem Witch, right?" asks Sue.

"And people call me dumb," says Hailey.

"Sit on it and spin, Hail," retorts Sue, holding out her middle finger.

"How do we find this so-called Salem Witch?" Jimmy wants to know. "Put on scary masks and go around knocking on doors until she answers?"

"Might have to walk down a few driveways," I admit. "I only know the house from the water."

"I know where it's at," says Chumley casually.

"How would you know?" I ask incredulously.

"The house was on my paper route when I was a kid."

"She still gets the paper?" asks a confused Sue.

Chumley nods. "*Boston Globe*, Sunday edition. Paid by check, but every Christmas, there was a ten-spot in the mailbox."

"You do realize that we're talking about a woman who's been dead for like a hundred years?" asks Jimmy.

"What about on Hannukah?"

"That's like eight days, right, Sue?" asks Chumley, tabulating with his fingers. "I wish!"

"Think you can find it again, Jonathan?" Jen inquires.

"Follow me," Chumley replies, taking his beer bottle and throwing it at the bandstand, where it smashes on the steps. The five of us follow suit, smashing our empty beer bottles on the bandstand and running after Chumley laughing like loons.

Not using the sidewalks so much, we stay away from the over-hanging streetlights and take to the paths we knew as kids: into and out of seemingly impenetrable hedges, jumping over picket fences, and tiptoeing across driveways as quiet as a team of ants. Dashing from shadow to shadow, the six of us reach Shore Road, where we slink along a storm-rut. Raising his right hand, Chumley brings the group to a stop in front of a wrought-iron gate affixed to a towering pair of brick-and-mortar pillars.

"Is this the place?" asks Sue.

"Last house on my route," Chumley says, nodding.

I strain my neck, looking up at the twisted bars that are so tall they appear to meld into the nighttime air.

"Are you sure this is the place?" asks Jimmy. "I'd hate to climb this gate and find it's the wrong house."

Scraping away a clump of lumpy moss on the left pillar, Chumley then points to a number painted on the pillar. "Twenty-three. This is the place, all right."

"How can you be so sure?" asks Hailey.

"My mother made me memorize the number."

"Why would Junebug do that?" asks Jen.

"Because the house sits on a Nauset Indian burial ground."

"You could say that about any house on the Cape," says Jimmy. "There's dead Indians buried all over the place."

Ignoring Jimmy, Jen asks, "What else did Junebug say about the house?"

"That there's evil spirits inside and for me to stay away."

"How would she know that?" Sue presses.

"She had a vision."

The six of us fall suddenly silent. Those in town who know Junebug, which is everybody, tend to listen to her when she has one of her visions, but not to humor her. They listen to Junebug because they're apt to turn out to be true.

"Sounds like a bunch of mumbo jumbo to me," says Jimmy.

"Everything isn't always about you, Jimmy," snaps Hailey. "We're not all rich!"

"Me, rich? I'd be at a private school if we were rich, not some crumbling building where the toilets don't flush and the pipes leak."

"Try holding down the handle next time," chirps Sue.

"Children, behave!" Jen snaps. Turning to Chumley, she asks, "This vision of Junebug's, what else did she say?"

"That whoever goes inside would be cursed for life."

"Are you making this up?" I ask.

"Could be," Chumley admits with a snicker.

"You're a ripe bastard!" says Jimmy.

"It's Halloween for Christ's sake! What'ja' expect?"

"Dirty red savage!" spits his girlfriend with a snort.

Taking hold of the wrought-iron bars, slick with mist, I begin my ascent using the soles of my boat shoes for traction. I reach the top, where the bars have morphed into African spearheads, and clamor over the flared points. Having succeeded without impalement, I slip down the other side. Jimmy and Jen take to the bars like a pair of

Olympic gymnasts and easily clear the points before setting down next to me. Hailey sets herself to begin her ascent, but her boyfriend pulls her back and ushers Sue forward. Sue scrambles up the bars in a mad dash only to catch a cuff of her tight-fitting jeans on a spear tip. Pitching forward, she hangs upside down flailing her arms.

"My new Jordaches! I bought them with my own money!"

The cuff tears free of the spear and Sue falls. Jimmy and I step forward and catch her. Standing Sue right-side-up, she admonishes Jimmy and me by pounding on our chests and yelling, "Those jeans cost me $27.50! You both owe me, especially you, Cal!"

"Why me?" I ask.

"This was all your idea, that's why," she retorts.

"I'll get my sewing needle," I say, smiling.

"Nice catch, by the way," replies Sue, smiling back.

Hailey takes hold of the bars and turns to her boyfriend. "If I fall, you'd better catch me!"

"Why would I do that when there's a perfectly open gate to walk through?" Pushing the wrought-iron gate, Chumley and Hailey walk through hand in hand like newlyweds leaving church under a hail of invisible rice.

"Could have broken my friggin' neck!" Sue complains.

"Never said the gate was locked," says Chumley with a laugh.

"You're a ripe bastard, Chum," Jimmy growls, fighting back a guffaw.

"Good one, Jonathan," says Jen. "At least we know the gate's open if we have to make a run for it."

"Not me," I say. "I'm heading for the beach."

"Why the beach?" asks Hailey.

"I'm faster swimming than I am running."

"What are you, Aquaman or something?" jokes Sue.

"Cal's a natural born sea otter," Jimmy affirms.

Stepping in front of the group, Jen sweeps her slender arm before the rest of us like a theater usher showing us to our seats and asks, "Shall we?" Nodding as one, we follow Jen down a ghostly trail lined with crushed seashells. The pathway twists and turns through an ominous wood where bowed limbs poke at us like silent centurions, ready to run us through should any prisoner try to escape.

"You sure can pick 'em, Cal," says Sue, hugging herself and shivering.

"It's like he's leading us to our graves," adds Hailey.

"We can still catch the second feature at the Wellfleet Drive-In if we hurry," Jimmy offers.

"Not me," says Hailey, holding hands with Chumley. "Once I start, there's no backing me up."

"And when she does, she goes BEEP BEEP BEEP!"

"Indians," replies Hailey. "Give 'em a beer and they think they're the next Richard Pryor."

"That doesn't even make sense," I say, laughing.

"Welcome to my world," says Chumley.

Passing under an archway of fallow grapevines, we descend into a garden of sculpted hedge work, clipped and trimmed to emulate various religious symbols: Magen David, Maltese Cross, and Archepiscopal Cross, to name a few that I know.

"Where are we, Easter Island?" asks Jimmy.

"More like Stonehenge," Jen replies.

"What's that doing here?" says Sue, pointing to a tall hedge pruned in the shape of a swastika. "Nobody told me the Salem Witch was a Nazi!"

"Not sure that's what it means," I say.

"What else could it mean?" presses Hailey.

"Symbol itself goes back three thousand years to the Egyptians. Hitler only adopted the symbol and reversed the arms for his corrupt cause."

"Hopi drew the same shape on the walls of their pueblos five thousand years before that," Chumley adds.

"Interesting," says Jen.

"The ancient Greeks had a name for it. Tetraskelion or Gammadion, I forget which. Supposed to mean Sun-Power-Strength."

"Thanks for the history lesson, Professor Forrest, but I thought we were here to find the Salem Witch?" Jimmy scoffs.

"Typical Jimmy," mutters Sue. "Always puts down what he doesn't understand."

"If it weren't for me, we wouldn't even be here," Jimmy retorts.

"Cal came up with the plan, Jimmy. Not you," Hailey points out.

"Cal came up with the plan, all right, but he wouldn't have gone through with it if I didn't get Jen to join the party."

"Thanks a lot, Jimmy," I say, blushing visibly, I'm sure.

"Very interesting," says Jen, flashing her long eyelashes at the both of us.

"Give me a friggin' break," Sue cuts in.

"Are we doing this or what?" asks Hailey, taking the attention away from Jen.

"Sieg Heil, Mein Führer!" says Chumley. Raising his right arm with his palm held flat in true Nazi fashion, he turns on the heels of his new Herman Survivor boots and marches up a slight berm, goose-stepping the whole way. Needless to say, the rest of us follow.

TIGER

I am in the busiest part of the channel now, so I have to stop my reminiscing and keep my head on a swivel. Running close to the lee, I sail with the wind keeping my eyes focused fore, aft, starboard, and port. It's the place where boats leaving and entering have less than a quarter-mile in which to navigate between the pincerlike bluffs that guard the inlet like a pair of bearded sphinxes. I hold tight to the weather mark and out-point a forty-foot scow only to be overtaken by an out-bounding catamaran, its port pontoon careening off the water, nearly running afoul of my hull and skull. Our three boats must make for quite a sight from shore, like we're all part and parcel of a single, fractured hull flying a sheet of multicolored sailcloth.

Over the years this inlet has widened and closed like a retractable gate, sometimes filling with sand taken as far away as Provincetown's Race Point. Other times it's blasted wide open by thirty-foot parabolic rollers that work like giant bulldozers whenever a hurricane or nor'easter hits. The channel itself can literally change overnight. You could steam a tanker through it one day and drive your truck across it the next. And that's just what the old-timers did, steering their Puffing Devils and Tin Lizzies over the sand and marshes to the very tip of Monomoy, where they'd picnic for the day. And if a breach occurred during their repast, they'd leave their flivvers where they parked them and row back to the mainland on skiffs, the rusted relics long ago buried under the dunes and marsh grass.

Chatham Light passes on my starboard. It's one of the few still relevant light beacons on the Cape, what with the advent of radar and other navigational equipment. But when the fog rolls in, or what uncle Joseph calls "King Maushop's Pipe Smoke," that cutting beam may be the only way to dry land. They say the seas off Chatham make fog for the rest of the country, and with balmy summer air mixing with the cold North Atlantic, it does make for a potent fog factory. Sometimes, however, the fog arrives without warning, and when that happens, it's like having a wet towel thrown over your shoulders. And it's eerie, like you're floating inside a cloud bank. But the fog has had its advantages.

It was during the American Revolution that a distant cousin of mine, Captain Marek Forrest, sailing out of Brewster, used the fog to get around the British blockades in order to deliver food and supplies to the Cape's half-starved populace. He knew these waters by their depths alone, and whenever a British warship pursued his schooner, they'd either find themselves aground on a sandbar or lost for a day or more in the "smoke." However, it was the pirates of the day who used the fog best.

These masters of the sweet trade would skulk into the bay under the cover of the mist, but not necessarily to plunder. No, they drank their fill in the taverns and left good tips. Pirates of that era weren't the murderous scullions the books and films depict. The majority of their robberies took place on the High Seas, and they thought of themselves as seafaring versions of Robin Hood, sacking the merchant vessels that were considered the corrupt bankers of their day. What booty they took would be divided equally amongst the captain and crew, with the spoils finding their way to dockside taverns from New York to New Delhi, but, more often than not, followed them down to the murky bottom.

Prohibition brought the fog full circle when town stalwarts, like my grandfather and Joseph P. Kennedy, used its cover to run booze by the boatload into the Cape's many coves, harbors, and inlets. Like the Minutemen who went before, they too were protesting a law they felt was unjustly imposed, not that Gramp and JPK, or "Block Head," as he was known, didn't enjoy the spoils. They did. Gramp's role in the lawbreaking was to hide the barrels amid his six-hundred-plus acres.

The money he earned helped stave off the land's back taxes and also helped his neighbors and fellow fishermen get through the Great Depression. I've heard the town elders say that Gramp "supported half the town with that lawless gambit of his." Gramp having once run the liquor is no secret. Most of the year-rounders know. Part of his legend, I suppose, but he never told me any details and I never asked.

What I did learn about his bootlegging days I got from a ledger I found wedged in a thin crack in the wall behind his headboard while I was cleaning his room. Gramp was out, most likely at the Squire, so I had the house to myself. Sliding out the ledger, I climbed down the spiral staircase and entered Gramp's chart room to study it. Opening the ledger on his rolltop desk, I added up the figures penciled in the columns, be they whiskey barrels, spent fuel, rifle stocks, bribes, or collections, etc. and quickly came to the realization that there was a lot of money to be made hiding Old Joe's booze in our wood, and it got me to thinking about my situation.

Prohibition has long since been stricken from the lawbooks, but there's a similar prohibition that many people feel is equally unjust. And while I'll never be the seaman of Gramp's or my father's caliber, I know for a fact that I'm a better farmer. I was around ten when I grew out of my Buster Browns and first met the ranger, only he wasn't a ranger then; he was a troubled Vietnam vet living in our wood.

The mid-1970s was a vastly different time on Cape Cod. What remained of the Summer of Love had finally washed up on our shore – hippies, free love, drug culture, etc. Volkswagen vans painted in Day-Glo colors now toured the countryside in search of their own private Woodstocks, and our great expanse of land was an ideal setting. "Sex, drugs, and rock 'n' roll" was the mantra of the day, and the groups communing in our wood continued the love fest unfettered.

Gramp knew of these visitors, as he knew of everything that happened on his property, but he never seemed to mind the extra guests, saying to me, "People need trees and trees we got. So what if they go 'round bare-assed? That's what the Timekeeper intended in the first place!"

This strange new lifestyle intrigued me so that many a day would I slink down my secret pathways to spy on our guests, wondering how they got their psychedelic school buses and converted ice cream trucks so deep into our wood. Gramp's only concern was the mess these visitors would sometimes leave behind: empty jugs of cheap wine, soggy issues of *Zap Comix*, split bedrolls inside torn tents with bent poles. These were mostly weekend gatherings, and on the Monday following, the two of us would get up early to go inspect the damage. With a long-handled rake slapped across my shoulders and Gramp carrying his red gas can, we'd hike through the wood until we spotted a camp, upon which I'd rake the debris into a pile, and Gramp would set fire to it.

Some of these piles were so high that the fires would last until late into the day. If it upset Gramp, he never said, feeling, I suppose, that it was his burden for owning so much land, and there was always a gleam in his eye when the fires reached their highest zenith. Rather than fume over the mess, he seemed to actually enjoy it, realizing the true relevance of it all and the freedom that it meant.

I took my rod and tackle box with me on one such excursion figuring, after the burn, I'd hike out to one of three kettle ponds dispersed on our property like holes on a bowling ball. The ponds themselves are small in circumference, each no bigger than a swollen storm puddle, but they are deep, the result of long-ago glacial deposits, and they hold fish, mostly redfin pickerel and smallmouth bass.

Before the advent of refrigeration, my forefathers used the ponds during the long winter months to cut ice that they would then sell to the neighboring townsfolk, even setting up an icehouse along Shore Road. Nobody thought about fishing in the winter in those days, the fish being too deep and the weather most foul, so they improvised. The kettle pond I was planning to fish that day was the largest of the three and also the furthest from the house. No trails led to it, only deer runs and the occasional Indian path, long overgrown to the point of invisibility to those standing five feet or taller.

The hike itself is long and arduous and I am panting like a Saint Bernard as I come upon the crater-shaped pond. The surrounding growth is thick with brier and I am reminded of Christ's crown of thorns from my brief catechism days as I step into it. Fighting my way through the tangle, I edge down a steep slope to arrive at a razor-thin beach where a felled pine has been judiciously placed to serve as my workbench. I take up my tackle box and begin a search for my favorite feathery lure within. Rifling through the lures, I look to the pond and notice a white bob afloat on the surface.

Squinting, I see that the bob is attached to a wisp of monofilament running across the pond and up the slope before disappearing into the brush. I place the tackle box on the tree and walk the length of the beach to where the line lifts from the water. Taking hold of the line, I follow it up the slope and feel it tug in my hand. Instinctively, I give the line a quick jerk and as I glance over my right shoulder, I see the bob bobbing in the water.

"Fish on!" I shout to no one.

Hand over hand, I reel in the line, and it isn't long before a rainbow trout appears flapping in the still water, hooked through the gills. I lift the trout from the pond and bring it to me, dragging it up the rocky slope and over the thorny thicket. Holding the trout by its bottom jaw, I examine the lure as I attempt to free it. A homemade job for sure, I think to myself. Straight out of a sewing kit: worked-over bobby pin twined around a single lug nut for weight, with a blue jay's tail feather serving as its lure. It could have come from a long-ago tramp, but that doesn't explain the live fish I have flopping in my hand. I free the trout and stuff it headfirst into the front pocket of my cutoff jeans, then continue up the slope.

Mounting the rim, I follow the test and find it tied to the branch of a small, rubbery elm, as if the tree had taken up fishing of its own volition. I take the trout out of my pocket and flip open my buck knife. Slitting the fish chin to slop-shoot, I clear away the nuts and guts and impale the fish on the jagged limb of a defoliated spruce. I figure it will keep until I find the furtive fisherman.

With my buck knife held low at my waist, I creep into the wood toes first, Indian style, and what appears an impenetrable thicket shows itself on second viewing to have the slightest shading of a foot-path running through it. I step lightly onto the path and after ten yards or so, the dampened rut turns into an actual trail with waxy skunk cabbage on both sides.

I plug along, not paying much attention to where I'm going, when I notice a series of elongated shadows that are so pronounced in size and shape that I look up. And there, in the treetops, stretched from limb to limb, are these green and blue tarps, their bulging bellies swaying above me filled with rain, no doubt from the night before's drenching.

Looking up at the tarps, I am reminded of a clipper ship under full sail, only upside down and reversed. But who put them there and why? Not to get fresh water. The kettle ponds we have on our property are the freshest water on the cape, siphoned through ten-thousand-year-old bedrock and beyond. Nobody really knows where the water comes from, but it's always tested pure whenever the scientists come around to take samples.

I fight my way through the stinky stalks and come stumbling onto a campsite freshly raked of any leaf, rock, or stick. The camp looks to span a quarter acre with recycled furniture spread about here and there. This is no hippy camp. This appears to be a permanent installation belonging to one man and not a weekend affair.

Canned vegetables — carrots, corn, peas, tomatoes, spinach, etc. — line a cedar shelf nailed between two trees. Pots and pans hang from sawed-off nubs, the polished bottoms reflecting the sun in diamond-shaped patterns like a disco ball set a-twirl amid the wood. Missing from the camp are empty wine jugs, nor do I see any split mattresses or collapsed tents, but I do notice an Army hammock slung above a foldout card table with a high-backed metal chair tucked underneath.

Keeping an eye out for its inhabitant, I step silently into the camp and go to the card table, where stands a framed picture of a girl of about my age, in a white dress with flowing blond hair, forever kicking her feet up on a tire swing. Next to the girl is another picture housed in a cheaper frame of stamped tin. This picture shows four hardened soldiers linking arms in front of a stand of banana trees, their faces dour and painted in jungle camo. Along the bottom, in a felt-tipped pen, is written

TIGER SQUAD

DIEN BIEN PHU

'73

Whether it's my land or not, what I have stumbled upon is private. I back away from the card table and am turning to leave when my gaze falls on a freshly oiled M16 combat rifle leaning against an exposed boulder. I stare at the rifle transfixed, then walk hesitantly to it. Reaching with my right hand, I trace the eight-inch bayonet attached to the muzzle with the tip of my index finger. Yelping, I stick the bleeding tip in my mouth.

"Always go 'round touchin' what's not yours to touch?" booms a husky voice behind me. I spin around quickly, and there in the pathway stands a mammoth of a man, tanned down to his eyelids. A long, red scar runs down the right side of his hairy body and he is completely naked, but for the kiddy beach towel he has wrapped around his waist.

"Can't even go for a swim in the bay without someone monkeying about. What were you plannin' on doin' next, pull the trigger?"

The mammoth storms past me and takes up the rifle. Holding the rifle at arms, he clears a brass round from the firing chamber, then replaces it against the boulder, careful not to scrape its maple stock.

"Whatcha doin' out here botherin' me for?" asks the mammoth, stepping into a pair of cutoff jeans.

"I 'wiv' here," I say, chewing on my finger.

"That give ya' the right to go 'round touchin' my property?"

I hunch my shoulders indifferently. Looking at the picture of the girl, I point and ask, "Who's shwe?" The big man follows my gaze and I notice his shoulders losing their tension.

"Lizbeth. My daughter."

"She's p'witty."

"Too old for you, little dude," laughs the big man. "Picture was taken the day I signed up for my third tour. Dumbest move I ever made."

"Where's shwe now?"

"Lives with her momma down in Mississip. Likes cheeseburgers and Coca-Colas."

"I wike cheeseburgers and Coka-A-Cowla's," I mewl.

"I'll bet you do. Always go 'round talkin' with your hand in your mouth?"

I take my bleeding fingertip out of my mouth and hold it up to him.

"Sweet Christ!" booms the mammoth. Stepping past me, he reaches into a hollowed burl and extracts an aluminum tube stamped with Chinese characters. Tugging off the cap with his long white teeth, he grabs me by my arm and pulls me to him. "Hold still," he growls. Roughly splaying my fingers, he then rubs my forearm down to my hand and squeezes my injured finger, forcing fresh blood to ooze from my wound. He then applies a yellowish substance to the cut, and I have to clench my teeth to keep from crying out, not that it would do much good so far from the house.

"Supposed to hurt," says the man. "Means it works." Letting go of my finger, he tells me, "Keep it above your heart and no Band-Aids! Let the air get at it. I told the Old Man you'd find me out sooner or later. Got too much Injun blood in ya'."

"Gramp?"

"What other old man you got 'round here?"

"He knows about you?" I ask, feeling slighted.

"That old cougar could spot a prairie dog pissin' on an anthill a hundred yards out. Could've used him in Nam. Woulda' made a hell of a sniper."

"He never told me," I say, hanging my head.

"Why would he? I'm none of your business."

"You're on our land," I say, the burning in my index finger subsiding somewhat.

"As much my land as yours, way I see it."

"How's that?" I ask.

"I was there, little dude. I walked the walk."

"Vietnam?"

"Just Nam. Forget the Viet. Weren't nowhere to be found unless you count the Cong. Couldn't see 'em, but they were *there* alright."

"You're Tiger?" I ask, pointing at the picture of the soldiers. "The tall guy in the middle?"

The big man nods, the dual emotions of pride and sorrow showing on his face.

"Pistol Pete's on my left. His call name. Not because he could shoot straight, because he couldn't. Pissed all over hisself every time he took a leak. Didn't make it. PFC Eddy Everett is the red-haired guy on my right, and it's because of him I'm here talkin' with you."

"Everett," I say out loud, thinking. "I know the family. His father runs the lumber mill in Brewster. He and Gramp were in the merchant marines together. Three boys. Stevie's my age. Billy's in the middle and Eddy's the oldest. I thought he died over there?"

"Was me who brought him back, what was left of him. Carrot Top was his call name. Red hair and freckles. Fought so hard he'd dig hisself a hole manning his 50 cal. The two of us would be out on patrol, squatting in the mud with fat raindrops coming down. That's when he'd start in with his stories about growing up 'round here. Clamming, sailing, and whatnot. Always liked his stories. Felt I was there with him, breathing the sea air and not stuck in a sweaty jungle picking leeches off my neck. Knowing my situation, 'Old Bones' Everett came up to me after the funeral and told me about Captain Let's place. Had nowhere to go, so I set up camp here."

"And Gramp said it was okay?"

"Three summers running. Only he had one rule, and he wasn't negotiable about it. That was to leave you and your friends alone. And that's just what I done till you come up here splittin' your finger and damn near blowin' your fool head off to boot! And I'll tell you this, little dude, I ain't no freeloader, like the others you see around here. I pay my way. Always have."

"With money?" I ask.

"Don't believe in it."

"What then?"

"Who you think been cording all that wood out behind your barn these past three summers? Bunch of happy woodchucks?"

"I always wondered about that," I reply. "But I didn't have to do it, so I never asked questions."

"Good man," says Tiger, putting on a denim shirt. "Never volunteer. Always leads to more work, and it'll likely get you killed."

"You caught a fish," I tell him. "It was on your bob. I cleaned it and stuck it on a tree."

"Lotta good it do anybody now."

"Did it go bad?"

"Ants. Never gut a fish until you're ready to eat it. Didn't your dad teach you that?"

"He's dead," I say, running my left wrist across my nose.

"Oh," says Tiger, looking down at his bare feet. "The captain told me he was away fishin'."

"He was away fishing. He never came back because his boat sank."

Taking hold of my trembling shoulders, Tiger looks me square in the eyes and says, "Where we all end up one day. Hopefully, your dad got a chance to stare it down and appreciate it. Getting blown to pieces by a trip wire sure as shit ain't any way to go." I look at the sun setting below the treetops and know that I should start heading back or risk losing the path once the sun sets.

"Would it be okay if I came around and visited?"

"Can't stop ya', but only you. Not your friends and not all the time. Meeting you is like meeting Peter at the Pearly Gates. No man should suffer so many questions! And not here. Go to the pond, and

I'll come to you. If you don't see me, means I'm busy. And let your grandfather know. If he don't mind you comin' 'round from time to time, then I got no problem with it, from time to time, just not every day."

I clap my heels together and give Tiger my best salute.

"Save it for the generals," says Tiger. "Another part of me I left in the jungle. Better head on back. The captain finds you late for suppa', he's liable to come stomping out here and hang me by my thumbs, and he's strong enough that he just might to do it!"

Entering our kitchen, I find Gramp at the stove frying chicken in a blackened skillet. Looking at the clock on the wall and then at me, he is about to comment when he notices the beet-red tip of my still-throbbing index finger.

"Where'dja git' that? Not some rabid fox, I hope."

I shake my head and reply proudly, "Nope! A bayonet!" Turning off the stove, Gramp turns to me and inspects my index finger, paying particular attention to the flap of healed skin.

"I see you've met our summer boarder."

"Tiger," I say. "Why didn't you tell me about him?"

"Mr. Watson is his name, and you are to refer to him as such. Far as you knowin' or not knowin', fact is, I didn't want you out thar' botherin' the man with your endless questions. Not that it's a bad thing, your questions. Just your nature is all."

"He's got a daughter!" I say excitedly. "Lizbeth. Lives with her mom down in Mississip. She likes cheeseburgers and Coca-Colas just like me. And he said I can visit him from time to time."

"Don't mean ya's should be out thar' every minute of every day!" barks Gramp.

"He seems so lonely."

"That's a different kind of lonely, the kind that's self-imposed. A man can go sideways in the world comin' out of a bad war like that. If Mr. Watson wants our company, he'll seek us out."

For the remainder of that summer, I hiked out to the kettle pond against Gramp's wishes. I never told Jimmy and Chumley about Tiger. He was like an imaginary friend, only he was real. And I'd go straight to the pond and never to Tiger's camp. I'd see him sometimes, standing on the rim watching me fish. If he wasn't in the mood for company, he'd disappear into the wood, where I'd imagine him returning to his camp and tucking himself inside his hammock with his two fists pushed into his eye sockets, fighting off nightmarish visions of war. Other times, Tiger would come thrashing down the slope to join me at the felled pine and we'd sit, casting his homemade lures into the still water shooting the bull. We'd talk about all kinds of stuff, but mostly he'd talk about his Lizbeth and growing up along the banks of the mighty Mississip', where he had similar adventures as me, only with real alligators!

It was late September when I broke Tiger's first and only rule. I was back to school and hadn't seen him since Labor Day. With the nights turning cooler and October around the corner, I gathered some blankets and hiked out to see him. Not finding Tiger at the kettle pond, I hiked on to his camp. Keeping to the well-worn path, I knocked back the now-withered skunk cabbage and stood at the entrance. I placed the blankets on a large flat rock and crossed over the threshold, and it was like his camp was never there. Hammock and foodstuffs, along with the pots and pans, including Tiger's moldy paperbacks, were gone. Card table, chair, pictures, everything. He'd even dismantled the ring of stones that served as his firepit.

I remained at the ghost camp, kicking away pinecones and uprooting small trees, mad at Tiger for not having said goodbye. I stumbled about in a fugue and meandered away from the camp without meaning to. And when I finally did look up, I found myself surrounded by a dense woodland with a cardboard sign nailed to a white birch reading: DANGER! UNEXPLODED ORDNANCE! KEEP OUT!

I stared at the sign knowing full well there weren't any exploded or unexploded ordnances on our land. The reason I knew this was that Gramp would never allow it. No hunting, only fishing, and no fire-works of any kind. I don't know why Gramp let Tiger keep his M16 at his camp, except maybe for their shared military experience. I pulled the cardboard sign from the tree and tore it into squares, then continued deeper through the wood.

Descending onto a steep-sided ravine, I walked its length and found it to be floored in perfectly aligned, bisecting rows of recently disturbed earth. I took a knee and picked through a dirt pile, hoping to find what plant or plants Tiger had planted. Picking up a strange leaf, I examined it between my thumb and forefinger, finding it to be unlike any leaf I had ever seen on our property: sparkling green and sticky to the touch, with five distinct points leading out from the center. It suddenly dawned on me where I'd seen this leaf before.

Clearing a campsite with Gramp one summer morn, I'd spotted a brightly patterned tie-dyed T-shirt and pulled it from the pile for no other reason other than it looked cool. On the front of the tee was an enlarged silkscreened replica of the very leaf I was holding, with the words LEGALIZE – DON'T CRIMINALIZE! underneath. Holding the shirt up to Gramp, I asked him what he thought it meant. He just shrugged, saying to me, "Our government. If it feels good, they don't want us havin' none of it."

THE BAR

With the surrounding landmass shrinking behind me and the endless seascape expanding before the bow, I haul in and come about to take an easterly tack, away from shore. A hatchery of silver darbies leaps before the pulpit as I sail from the bay, either for the fun of it or to escape the game fish pursuing beneath. I point the bow into the wind and walk the length of my boat to check the lines, Gramp's mantra forever ringing in my ears, "No amount of preparation is uncalled for when sailing into the Realm," and many have gone to the '*Locker*' for doing less. Testing the lines, I find them as tight and taut as when I first set out. Sailing over the emerald green waters of the inlet, I push the tiller to port and set the bow chuck over the deeper and darker waters of the North Atlantic.

It's a funky, irregular wind that causes *Sea Gypsy* to fan along, but I'm not complaining. I'm just glad to be on the water and in command of my boat. I am less than three miles from my house and yet the air smells cleaner here; there's a freshness to it that you can't experience on land. It clears the senses and makes one feel more alive, smarter even. It's no wonder man has been seabound for centuries.

Drafting two fathoms, with no shoals in sight, I bear up to the weather as a caravan of sportfishing boats overtakes me on my port, their flying bridges stationed high above the decks as they head out to sea. Doffing my imaginary cap, I bid them, "Good fishing!" I expect the captains to blow their foghorns, but I am denied. I don't fault them. Why would I, when they have fuel to burn and game fish to hook?

I fetch past the windward mark without having to tack, but before I get to the passage that will take me across Monomoy and into the Sound, I first have to get past the storied Chatham Bar, where rollers with ten-foot faces crash and burst against each other like miniature tsunamis. I let *Sea Gypsy*'s lap-straked hull slap against the oncoming rush of waves, thinking I have been too long standing on steel decks above Her natural pitch and roll. It feels good to be on a shallow drafting craft again, sensing the force of wave underfoot, for it's a false wind that blows when you're on a motorized craft. And while it might feel like you're going fast, you're really not because you're not part of it. A sensory illusion is what it is, like being a rook on a chessboard inside a jet fighter traveling at Mach 2. But to be hiking off the side under crowded sails with the mainsheet straining in your grip, now that's going fast!

I suddenly feel the need to take *Sea Gypsy* out to where Second Mother plays Her games with sudsy frolic. I sail further onward and the Bar appears at dead reckoning. Switching seats at the stern, I pass the tiller from hand to hand and come about to take a northeasterly tack where I can meet the rollers head-on. Most day sailors avoid the Bar, and with good cause; She's taken Her fair share of them to the bottom. Mostly, they switch to a southerly tack and stay close to shore, trying to outrun Her. But I've never held with that notion. I like to take Her as She is, head-on, because you never know what She's got in Her back pocket further down the line.

Skipper and boat spank along at a good clip as I pass the barrel day marker at the head of the channel. I snug down and stow away any loose items I have on board — water jug, speargun, seabag, coiled rope, etc. — and toss it all high in the fo'c'sle. Running the mainsheet through the traveler, I clamp down and take hold of the mast and step on deck to watch a series of ghostly shoals reappear, reaching up from the depths like the outstretched fingers of a dead man. This is the spot where the faint of the heart normally check their pulse and come about, only I know there's no real danger here, it's still too deep. This is only the first set of shoals before reaching the true Bar. Even so, I take out the brass pin and lift the centerboard, letting it bob. I do this in the event a cresting wave rears its ugly head and plunges *Sea Gypsy* into a shallow trough. That's where the real danger lies, coming to a dead stop atop a sandbar and leaving *Sea Gypsy* rife for swamping.

I push the boom to port and catch all the backwind as the rising swells tip the boat fore and then aft. This is the kind of adrenaline rush that puts a smile on my face, and I'm not alone, as a junior shark, three feet long and purplish black, leaps from wave to wave, putting on a show of its compact power. These aerial acrobatics aren't finished, however, as a sooty shearwater crashes into the face of an oncoming wave only to come out the other side with a silvery fish flapping in its bill.

I drop the mainsheet and let the mains'l luff, then step out onto the pulpit to look ahead to where a wave set builds beyond the Bar, the towering whitecaps marbled in dissolving foam, rising and crashing as they carry toward shore. A covey of larks hovers in the misty vapor lunching on sand eels brought up in the froth as the first wave of the set rushes under the hull, sinking *Sea Gypsy* to her bootstraps. I wedge the centerboard in its box and hold tight to the halyard, looking beyond the second wave of the set as it breaks harmlessly over the bow. And it's not the third wave that concerns me, as it too carries over the foredeck before dividing on the coaming rails and shipping over the sides, but the fourth, trochoidal wave.

To me, there is nothing so boring as a flat, calm sea, but Her playfulness can sometimes turn into violent bashing when She doesn't get her way. I've always found it wise to never complain of Her many moods, and I've known captains that will put a man ashore for cursing Her name. Whenever She rises up from Her depths to do battle with the angry sky, the best thing to do is clamp down and try to enjoy the ride, only this ride I'm about to take doesn't appear it will be too joyful as the fourth wave comes into view, and She's a monster.

Taking up the mainsheet, I tie the line around my waist and hunker down behind the cuddy. I watch the wave's crest rise up and draw a great swath of sea that leaves *Sea Gypsy* a mere half fathom from the bottom. Running back to the stern, I take the tiller in hand and haul in the mainsheet, deliberately pointing the bow into the belly of the wave as twenty feet of sea wall builds before the boat. Picking up speed as She carries over the Bar, I look for the wave's lowest point, only there isn't one, She's all one wave of equal height. I lay crosswise over the stern and pull taut the mainsheet, ready to ride *Sea Gypsy* like a surfboard. She's feeling frisky today and wants to dance. "Okay then, let's dance!" I shout.

Sea Gypsy's six-foot pulpit spears the belly of the wave, releasing an onslaught of water that planes my body. I grit my teeth and close my eyes. The roar of the wave reverberates in my eardrums and I know it to be from Second Mother. She's calling out my name, screaming it. The maelstrom thunders past me, lifting me from the stern and hurling me overboard. I try catching a breath before going under, but all I get is a mouthful of seawater, except that the fisherman's knot holds, jerking me forward and nearly snapping me in two. I feel that the line might drown me, so I slip the knot from around my waist and continue with the current, bouncing along the bottom of the Bar.

I am underwater and I am numb. My throat aches and my body feels like it just went fifteen rounds with Marvelous Marvin Hagler. Kicking off the sandy bottom, I pull at the water and breach the surface, gulping air. I look to where *Sea Gypsy* flounders like a swollen log in the lingering wave set. I've put my beloved boat in harm's way yet again, and again she has survived. Had she capsized and sunk, I would have had to swim to shore fighting an outgoing tide with my boat no doubt washing up on the shores of Nantucket a day or a week later, battered and mastless. I don't know why I take these chances, except that I do.

I try swimming to my boat but sense that I am being taken in the opposite direction and out to sea. Observing the whitecaps rolling under me, I notice rivulets of spidery foam slipping down their muscular backs, a sure sign that I am caught in a riptide. I try swimming sideways to get out of it, but I'm not sure that'll work this far out. I am taken further and further from my boat, away from the shoals, and into deeper, darker water. Nervously treading water, I look back at the thin strip of beach still visible and slow my breathing, trying to remain calm.

I've seen plenty of blue dogs while fishing this area over the years, and while they're not the most aggressive shark, they can be if there are enough of them circling, and they're plenty tough. The worst is when they get tangled in our nets. It takes an entire crew wielding baseball bats to stop just one blue shark from thrashing about. I think of the time a former captain had a blue shark hoisted on the ship's yardarm. He slit open the fish's belly to see if it was stealing our bait; it was, and the twelve-foot shark was so ravenous that it bent forward and began eating its own stomach. Not the best memory to have when you're treading water this far out.

I look about me to see if any dorsal fins are circling and don't see any, but that doesn't mean they're not there. I am about to start swimming when a blunt object rams into my upper thigh and turns me sideways. I reach down to inspect the damage, hoping that my leg is still attached, and it is, but for a sore area that is tender to the touch. With my teeth chattering, I summon whatever courage I have and dip below the surface. I look past my dangling feet, and there, to my astonishment, is a glowing orb so brilliant in its aura that my eyes actually squint from it. Rising to my depth, I blink my eyes twice and see what the glowing orb truly is: a large dolphin with skin as blond as butter.

The size of a pilot whale, with a bent dorsal fin, the blond dolphin circles me as if I were a school of mackerel. I turn with it, noticing the many scars running along its flanks, no doubt caused by numerous shark encounters. To have its steely camouflage genetically taken away must have made for a difficult childhood, glowing so brightly in an ocean filled with so many teeth. Though, given the dolphin's great size, there aren't many that would challenge it now.

Slipping its rubbery snout under my right armpit, the dolphin rockets me to the surface and races me to my boat. Holding on to the dolphin's snout with all my might, I soon realize that I am no match for the fish's power and have to let go. The good news is that I am closer to my boat. The bad news? *Sea Gypsy* is about to have another bout with the Bar. I start to swim.

I see that the water around me has lightened somewhat, but to make it to my boat in time will take some doing, given my draining strength, and I'm not so sure I can do it. I watch my boat carry toward the Bar, where a culmination of wave against wave bash into one another with unchecked fury. I watch *Sea Gypsy* for what I fear will be the last time. With no one to guide her tiller, she's sure to go over.

I begin swimming anew, and though I have the stamina to continue, I don't have the strength as the cold begins to seep into my bones. Bobbing in the slop, I can barely keep my chin above water when a yellowish blur launches itself over my right shoulder and sounds. I look on in stunned amazement as the boat's trailing bowline suddenly pulls taut and *Gypsy* abruptly changes course, traveling over the arching rollers as if motorized. Finding calmer seas, the bowline slackens and my boat glides gently toward me through the mist and out of harm's way.

I climb aboard on the portside and go to the stern. I make sure the rudder is still attached, and it is, but for its extended tiller that has broken off at the flywheel, which is not bad, considering. And though she is soaked through and through, like she went through a car wash with her windows open, her boom, mains'l, and mast appear no worse for wear.

I take up the bail bucket that I have tied to the bottom of the mast and begin dumping water over the side while letting the sun reheat my brain and body. I am alone in my chore and I've quite forgotten about the blond dolphin when its bulbous head suddenly rears itself along the starboard gunwale, clicking its teeth and squealing in good-natured levity.

I drop the bail bucket and go to the dolphin. Reaching over the coaming rail, the great beast lies immobile in my arms, its conical eyes tightly closed, resembling repressed laughter. I scratch vigorously at the dolphin's beak, clearing away algae spores and crusted plumes of dried blood. It shows me its mouth, and I begin by rubbing its gums, then picking clean any decayed squid and mackerel. Now, these are the teeth of a large, dominant predator: evenly spaced, long, pegged, and strong. I have no idea what I'm doing, only that it feels right, and I'm not afraid of losing a finger.

"You really saved my bacon back there, my friend! I sure wish I had a treat for ya'." As I say this, I hear something flapping around inside the cuddy. "Hold that thought!" Reaching into the cuddy, I bring out a good-sized black sea bass, no doubt picked up during the swamping, and toss it high into the air. "Come and get it!" Rearing backwards on its massive tail, the blond dolphin leaps into the air and snaps up the bass, spinning three hundred and sixty degrees in a grandiose display of its aerial dexterity before diving into the water and returning to the sea. I shake my head in wonder. In all of my time at sea, never have I had an experience like that. Magical is the only word that comes to mind.

MARINE LAYER

With my head down and my back to the horizon, I go about the business of bailing out my boat. I am lost in thought, as I sometimes get, and it isn't until I look up that I find I've drifted to the outer edges of the ever-present marine layer. Many times have I traveled to this ghostly partition, so the distance doesn't concern me. What does concern me is how swiftly the fog can move in, so swift that you wouldn't know until it was too late. By the looks of it, the fog appears to be holding off, waiting for the sun to draw down, so I take a moment to punch dry the mains'l and right the salt-heavy lines.

Gathering the mainsheet in hand, I take a seat at the stern and slide the tiller to port, and I am readying to come about when I notice a towering shadow lurking within the mist. I bring the spyglass, miraculously saved from the swamping, up to sight and focus the crosshairs on the effervescent fog. Puffs of wispy clouds float above the water like balls of cotton. All is peaceful and serene until the prow of a wooden ship rising three stories cuts through the shifting vapor like a Flying Dutchman ghost ship. I catch only glimpses of the tri-masted vessel as it sails along the spotty haze before disappearing back behind the 'smoke.'

I am hard-pressed to believe what I'm seeing but intrigued enough to sail onward into the Realm, hoping for a better look. Heaving the mainsheet taut, I hike off the port rail and hurry *Sea Gypsy* along, knowing just where to hold her without capsizing. The two of us travel above the water as if on a high-speed rail, and I am making way at a good clip when the ship reappears, showing herself to be what I first believed her to be: a Spanish galleon, the scarlet cross-stitched high on her tops'l giving her away.

Being a keen student of naval history, I know the difference between a fifth-rater frigate and a sixth-rater sloop of war, but I can't explain what a fifteenth-century Spanish galleon, with its long beak head for ramming and high poop deck weathercocked to the wind, is doing sailing along the Outer Cape. And while it may be possible that the galleon is part of a contingent of tall ships that normally meets every ten years or so to tour the eastern seaports from Maine to the Carolinas, I seriously doubt it.

Years ago, Gramp and I went to see the tall ships when they were berthed in Boston Harbor. The ships were more than regal with not a speck of seaweed nor barnacle clinging to their freshly painted bowsprits. Hundreds of spectator boats crowded the waterways to watch them sail out, with TV news helicopters hovering overhead. The ship I sight within the crosshairs on this day, however, has no spectator boats following, and nor are there any TV news helicopters hovering. And unlike the vessels I witnessed on that sunny day in Boston, this galleon is dully painted and beaten about the bulwarks with broken spots along her gunwales that only real cannon fire could produce.

Through the viewfinder, I spy tiny figures perched high in the riggings, walking shirtless and barefoot along a fifty-foot yardarm one hundred feet above deck, dropping and hoisting giant reams of patched and yellowed sailcloth. I sail further into the mist and I am about to call out a jaunty "Ahoy!" when another tri-masted vessel creeps from the clouds and into the clear. I follow the mast from deck to top and see that she's flying the Letter of Marque and not the fleur-de-lis, thus making the boat a French sloop of war or a privateer: a government-commissioned vessel allowed to prey on an enemy's commerce for private gain.

Continuing to peer through the spyglass, I watch the galleon out-point the sloop to the wind, but the sloop is faster on water and comes alongside, angling for a broad shot. Aligning itself in a box formation, the galleon surprises the sloop and fires first. The sound of iron-splitting wood fills the air as a series of firelit cannonballs cuts down the sloop's Royal mast at the shrouds, sending it toppling into the sea along with a dozen screaming men. The French "mousses" run amok, jumping from deck to deck, as the galleon comes abeam the sloop. Dressed in seamen's stripes, the Spanish marineros run along the port gunwale, twirling grappling hooks high above their heads.

A pall of black smoke envelops the sloop as the Spaniards toss their hooks from deck to deck and swing out over the water like a bunch of crazed Tarzans to do battle with their French counterparts in close combat: cutlass against buckler shield, dirk against dagger, marlin spike against belaying pin, spilling buckets of each other's blood only to die gruesome deaths in one another's arms. Balancing on the pulpit, I pin my ears to the sound of shouting and screaming men as another peal of cannon fire carries across the water, followed by brilliant bursts of red, yellow, and orange. I watch the supposed reenactment unfold in numbed disbelief as the fog moves in and lowers over the action like a giant stage curtain.

The nausea begins in my stomach and rises to my throat. I collapse at the stern, gagging involuntarily. My body feels like it's turning itself inside out as seawater mixed with bile spews from my mouth. Clutching at my swelling throat, I think that it will never end as still more seawater pours from my cracked lips like a spigot, seemingly gallons of it. I remain a crumpled wreck at the stern, coughing and spitting over the side. Clutching my knees, I tumble forward onto the ribbed cockpit, where I land in the fetal position. Silence surrounds me as I close my puffy eyes, broken only by the occasional screeching of gulls before darkness descends and I am returned to the night of the Salem Witch.

A large, cylindrical shape looms in the distance as the six of us come over the berm. With twilight fast fading and a full moon rising behind it, the Round House resembles a witch's cauldron more than it does an actual house. The only thing missing is a broom. Dropping into a low swale, our group fans out along the house's perimeter in search of a front door or a back door. I notice a darkened recess within the cloaking ivy and go to investigate. Leaning forward, I reach into the darkness and place the palms of both hands on a cold, bumpy surface that feels like pebbled glass. I cup my hands and try peering inside, but it's too dark inside to see.

"Did'ja find a door?" asks Chumley, walking over.

"No, but I found a window, at least, I think it's a window."

"We can make it into a door," says Jen, crossing the lawn to join us.

"Like smash it?" asks Hailey, coming up behind her boyfriend.

"Breaking and entering is a felony, last I heard," cautions Jimmy, rounding the corner of the house without corners.

"What'ja expect, Jimmy? That we were going to ring the friggin' doorbell?" says Sue, bringing up the rear.

Rummaging amid the bushes at his feet, Chumley comes out with a good-sized boulder. "Here, use this," he says, then hands me the rock.

"Why me?"

"It's your party, Cal," says Jen.

"But won't it be loud?" asks Sue.

"Who's gonna hear it way out here?" says Hailey.

Lifting the boulder, I balance it on my right shoulder. The others back away as I rush forward and shot-put the heavy rock that sails through the air like the Goodyear blimp before taking a downward trajectory and hitting the pebbled window dead center. The boulder bounces off the glass like it was a Wiffle ball before returning to the surrounding shrubbery.

"That's one strong window!" exclaims Sue, right as the window abruptly implodes, sending shards of thick-cut glass raining into the house.

Striding past the group, Jen begins delicately removing the

remaining shards from the frame. Sweeping the sill clear with the sleeve of her cheerleader jacket, she turns to the group, saying, "Let's visit a while, shall we?"

Surprisingly, it's Jimmy who's first through the opening. Once inside, he reaches for Jen's hand, but Sue steps forward instead, and I know that it pains him. Jimmy's pined for Jen since we were all in the fifth grade together, as have I, though neither Jimmy nor me had ever mustered the courage to ask her out on a date. Maneuvering Sue over the tricky sill, he lands her safely inside. I feel a tap on my left shoulder and turn.

"Think you can lift me, Cal?" asks Jen.

"To the moon, if that's where you want to go," I reply with a wink. Jen winks back. Placing my hands on her sultry hips, I lift her as easily as lifting a newborn and drop her inside the house. Not waiting for an invite, Chumley plucks Hailey from her feet and tosses her through the window, where she lands with an audible thud.

I take the opportunity and climb Chumley's back like a stepladder. Kneeling on the sill, I grab the collar of his letterman jacket and drag him over and thus return the favor.

"Where are we?" asks Sue, at least I think it's Sue, the cloaking darkness so complete that I can't see my eyelids blinking.

"A sort of antechamber, I think," I hear Jimmy say.

The room is small, empty of furniture, with no noticeable way out but for the broken window we came in through. Pressed shoulder to shoulder, the bumping and nudging get to be contagious, with the laughter getting downright out of control. The sound of sticky kissing fills the chamber. I turn and grab the first soft hand I touch and pull it close. The hand turns out to belong to Jen. He shoots! He scores! After some heavy petting, she turns me around and whispers in my ear, "Lead the way, Cal."

And I do. Taking a few steps, I face-plant into a hard, immovable object with a knob attached. "Found the other door!"

Rubbing my sore nose with my right hand, I turn the knob, and the six of us enter a room that can best be described as a wedge from a pie chart. As my eyes begin to adjust to the dim moonlight streaming in from slanted storm shutters, what appears to be a sitting room begins to take shape, with walls painted floor to ceiling in murals depicting various signs of the Zodiac.

"Nice digs!" says Sue, fingering a standing lamp shaded in opalescent glass that might be Tiffany.

"I could get used to this," adds Hailey, landing her plump tush on a sheet-draped settee that sends a plume of hundred-year-old dust into the air. I spot a latch, hidden within the eyeball of Pisces the Fish, and pull it. A hidden door slides back and another room appears, only bigger.

Coughing and wheezing, the six of us file in. Filling three quarters of the first floor and rising to a second, the room reminds me of our Grand Hall, only our hall doesn't have an impressive chandelier that sparkles and blinks in the gloaming, nor does it have an Arthurian round table topped with Old World bronze and surrounded by six high-backed cherrywood chairs as if the Salem Witch was expecting us.

"Isn't it magnificent, Cal," says Jen, taking my hand. The two of us spin around the room like we're standing on Gramp's self-cranking Victrola. Pinching my left butt cheek, Jen leaves my side to steal away with Chumley for a quick smoke. Hailey and Sue take to the cylindrical outer wall and begin opening the drapes, revealing the checkerboard windows lined up like stepping-stones. Jimmy appears at my side.

"What's going on with you and Jen? She was supposed to be my date."

I shrug. "Ask her."

Jimmy drops the subject and looks about the room. "I helped my father remodel a place like this once. Another round house in Hyannis. It had these hidden passages running through it so the servants wouldn't be seen coming and going. Like a house within a house. Ring the dinner bell, and a butler appears out of nowhere. Push on a wall and a maid pops out."

"What the hell is that?" asks Sue, pointing at the flat wall behind us.

Jimmy and I walk over to investigate. Joining Hailey and Sue, the four of us stand before a giant mural that makes the hidden door we

177

came in through look like a mouse hole. Made hazy by the floating dust, the mural depicts a family of African slaves picking cotton with a surely white overseer on horseback wielding a long black whip over their bowed, subjugated heads.

"Doesn't make sense," I say. "Her husband died fighting for the North during the Civil War."

"Whose husband?" asks Chumley, clomping over in his new Herman Survivor boots. Jen steps around me and rests her head on my right shoulder, causing my knees to quiver.

"Claire Burlingame," I mutter.

"The Salem Witch has a name?" asks Sue. "How do you know all this, Cal?"

"Cal knows everything, or didn't he tell you?" says Jimmy, eyeing Jen and me jealously.

"She was a friend of the family way back," I answer, ignoring Jimmy.

"But why have this here?" asks Jen defensively. "We're not like that. This isn't the South."

"Tell that to the Wampanoags," says Chumley. "What's left of us, that is."

"We're not *all* bad," Hailey replies. "I mean, I'm dating one, aren't I? That should count for something?"

"Depends if we be makin' the wampum tonight," replies Chumley, salaciously making out with his hand.

"Listen to him! He doesn't even know his own language!" snorts Hailey.

"I know some," giggles Chumley.

"My family has never been enslaved," scoffs Jimmy. "We're the ones who've always done the enslaving. Isn't that right, Cal?"

"If you're talking about your father," I reply. "I wouldn't know, but you, Jimmy, he gets for free."

"All in due time, Cal," Jimmy says, leering. "All in due time."

"Both of you are going to get a punch in the mouth if you don't cut the crap!" says Sue, shaking her right fist.

"We should have bought more beer," says Chumley. "Now, what are we supposed to do?"

"Have a séance," says Jen, stepping in front of me.

"A séance?" asks Sue. "To do what?"

"Conjure up the Salem Witch, that's what. My mom's into it," adds Jimmy. "Calls it her *guilty pleasure.* You know us Catholics. We're all basically a bunch of witches and warlocks with the Pope backing us up."

"Let's do this!" says Hailey.

"Yeah, but where?" asks Sue.

Jen points to the brass-topped table. "There."

"Perfect," says Jimmy. "Six chairs. Six of us."

Jimmy takes a seat at the head of the table, if you can call it that, with Jen and Sue sitting on either side of him. Hailey sits on Chumley's right with me sitting opposite Jimmy to complete the circle.

"Okay, I want everyone to join hands and bow your heads," says Jimmy. The rest of us do as commanded. "We are gathered here today…"

"It's not a funeral, Jimmy."

"…that we may call out the Salem Witch," continues Jimmy, shooting Sue a reproachful stare, "so that she may appear before us and…"

"Explain that damn mural!" Jen demands.

Glaring at Jen now, Jimmy clears his throat and clarifies, "That she may come down from the Heavens and…"

"Cook us up a mess of French fries! I'm friggin' starving!" exclaims Hailey. That's the crack in the dam that brings our collective laughter pouring through.

"This is serious!" Jimmy responds.

Chumley pushes his chair back and stands from the table. "There's got to be booze in this place and I'm going to find it."

"I'm going too," says Hailey. "Hopefully, the old girl left behind a bottle of Scope for Lover Boy here."

"Girls blow chunks!" replies Chumley. Taking his girlfriend by her wrist, he drags her, kicking and laughing from the room.

"We'll need candles if we're going to do this right. I think I saw some in the other room," says Sue, fast on the heels of the giggling couple.

"Great!" says Jimmy, throwing up his hands. "There goes our quorum!"

"Why do we need a quorum?" I ask.

"Every séance needs at least five people to conjure up the dead."

"Maybe it's a good thing," says Jen, grinning mischievously.

"How so?" asks Jimmy.

"More for us," Jen replies. Taking her purse from under the table, she empties the contents on the polished brass revealing a tube of red lipstick, a blue Bic lighter, and a clear plastic baggy holding three rolled joints.

"You smoke, Jen?"

"Don't be such a priss, Jimmy." Turning to me, Jen asks, "You've smoked before, haven't you, Cal?"

I clear my throat and say, "Sure. Lots of times."

"When have you ever smoked pot?" asks Jimmy accusingly.

"I've smoked plenty, just not around you."

"Yeah, right!"

There's always been competition between Jimmy and me, be it girls, grades, or sailing. I never took it seriously, and I was always glad when Jimmy lipped in ahead of me, but happier when I did is all. And I never brooded over it, like I know he does whenever he loses at something. I'd just as soon compete for the sake of competing. Gramp's standing in town made him an honorary member of the Chatham Yacht Club. He never had to pay any dues and rarely showed up to any of their events. All he did was to put in a good word for the club every now and then at the town meetings so I could sail in their summer regattas. I never cared about winning. I only wanted to match my skills against the so-called "privileged class." Not always, but usually, I'd be well ahead of the other racers when I'd spot something on the far shore and sail for it. This would always infuriate Jimmy, especially if someone else besides him crossed the green marker first. "Hold it low or Caleb Forrest might sail by and take it back," Jimmy was apt to say to the winner. What do I care about a silly sailing trophy?

Eyeballing the baggy with distrust, Jimmy asks, "Where'dja get it?"

"Steve gave it to me."

"Steve who?" I ask, a bit too defensively.

"Steve Lattimer."

"Never heard of him."

"He's a senior, Jimmy. Starting quarterback? Captain of the football team?"

"Yeah, I've seen him around," I say, trying to sound indifferent about it.

"Steve's a friend, Cal. Don't worry. You're doing just fine." What Jen means by this, I have no Idea, but I am willing to smoke a pound of weed if it impresses her.

"So, are we going to smoke or what?"

Jen shoots Jimmy a look you give to a petulant child. Taking a joint from the baggy, she coolly places it between her full lips. Taking her blue Bic lighter, she sets flame to the tip and inhales. Blowing the smoke out through her nostrils, she hands the joint to Jimmy, who holds the spliff like he's taking a dead rat out to the trash by its tail. Jimmy puffs twice before thrusting the joint at me. I take the joint and suck on it like I'm sucking gas through a garden hose, the spliff burning up to my fingertips before going out. I hold in the smoke, then exhale and proceed to cough my lungs out. Jimmy comes around my chair and pounds me on the back.

"Hey! Jerry Garcia! Save some for the rest of us!"

I push Jimmy away and head for one of the checkerboard windows, in dire need of fresh air, only to find it nailed shut, as are all the rest. I continue to cough uncontrollably, the curved wall spinning before my eyes like a fairway Tilt-A-Whirl. I close my eyes, hoping it will stop, but the wall continues to spin within my brain's bony casing. Jimmy and Jen station themselves at my sides, helping to keep me upright.

"Cal, it's not a contest," says Jen. "You didn't have to smoke the whole joint in one drag!"

"Didja just escape from a carnival freak show or something?" asks Jimmy.

The thought of me escaping from a carnival freak show causes a ball of laughter to rise in my esophagus and explode from my mouth.

Jimmy and Jen join in, collapsing on my back and laughing like a pair of loons. Wiping hot tears from my eyes, I try to focus on the soothing, sloping hillside outside the window, and I am in the beginning stages of regaining my composure when something else alters my already altered psyche: globs of light bouncing across the lawn like flaming tennis balls.

"Fireflies!" I say aloud.

"Those aren't fireflies, dumbass," whispers Chumley, creeping low into the room. "Those are cops with flashlights."

"I am so screwed," moans Jimmy.

"We're all screwed, Jimmy," corrects Jen.

"Maybe not," says Chumley. "I might have found another way out. I don't think they know we're in here yet, or they'd be busting down the doors. Follow me and stay low."

The four of us dip down and tiptoe across the long room like mice, that is until my right foot hooks on a chair leg, and I tumble into Jen, who knocks into Jimmy, causing him to fall on Chumley and thus creating a domino effect of wood crashing against bone. Leaping to his feet, Chumley yells, "Run!" And we do, tripping and crawling over each other, then picking one another up and surging forward as a whole.

Streaking down a narrow hallway bouncing off the walls, Chumley cuts to his left and triggers another sliding door that brings us into a galley of sorts, perhaps even the same galley Old Joe helped build.

"Where's Hail and Sue?" asks Jen.

Chumley points at the floor. Dropping to his knees, he begins slapping at the tile like he's having a heart attack. I am about to stick my hand in his mouth to keep him from swallowing his tongue when a trapdoor springs open.

"Sprang it when I was searching for the booze," says Chumley. "Leads to a basement. Dark as hell down there. I figured out the layout, so I'll go first." From somewhere inside the house, I hear the sound of a lock turning and a door opening.

"Hurry," whispers Jen.

Squeezing his large frame into the trapdoor's small opening,

Chumley descends into the cellar and quickly disappears. I follow Chumley down, not sure if I'm stepping on the ladder's rungs or his hands. Jen follows me, only she doesn't bother with the rungs. Instead, she plants her Chuck Taylors on my shoulders and goes down as I do. Jimmy comes next, stepping down gingerly before closing the trapdoor above him and plunging the cellar into absolute pitch.

The sound of a rung snapping echoes in the darkness, followed by a feeling of weightlessness, then a falling sensation, and ending with a chorus of grunts and groans. Rolling from the pile, Jimmy begins lifting everyone to their feet.

"Over here," whispers a female voice.

Taking out her blue Bic lighter, Jen fires it up and leads the group through the darkened cellar with her hand raised like a modern-day Joan of Arc. Following Jen, the three of us shuffle single file through the dusty pall. I make out shovels and picks laid out on a hardened dirt floor along with an old wheelbarrow and cement mixer. Long discarded clothing is piled high in the corners, along with rows and rows of bedless bunks, giving the impression the cellar was once a dormitory of sorts. Eventually, the crouching figures of Hailey and Sue come into view, huddled in front of a low, wooden corral holding back a sloping hill of sand.

"There you are!" my voice booms, still in my elevated state.

"Shh!" shushes Sue.

"The police already know we're here," says Jen.

"Yeah. Cal took care of that," adds Jimmy.

"They know we're here, but not down here," Chumley clarifies.

"You've trapped us like rats," his girlfriend hisses.

"Rats are always the first to escape a sinking ship," I put in, giggling to myself.

"I thought you said you found a way out?" Jimmy asks.

"I did," says Chumley, pointing at the top of the sandhill.

"I don't see anything," Jimmy replies.

"You will."

And we do. As our eyes adjust to the dark, slits of dim light appear spaced out along the upper rim.

"Hoppers," states Jimmy. "You open them in the spring to let out the damp after a long winter."

"I wouldn't know," I say, giggling again. "My house sits on stilts."

"No way I'm fitting through that," says Hailey.

"You will with me pushing," her boyfriend promises.

I take my cue and hurdle the low corral. Clambering up the sand hill on all fours, the slits become more pronounced the higher I ascend. I reach the summit and lie on my stomach. Squeezing my body under a moldy joist holding up floorboards spiked with carpenter nails, I roll over a raised rim and drop into a shallow trench abutting the foundation. Kneeling in the trench, I take the sleeve of my denim jacket and clean a spot on the window, through which I see clumps of beach grass waving back at me in mock freedom. I feel for a release latch, but the metal frame is rusted over. Picking at the foundation, I find the cement to be soft and crumbling, as footfalls and what sounds like the claws of a large dog clicking and slipping over hardwood echo down from above.

Jimmy peeks his head over the rim. "Try the latch," he says.

"Rusted," I answer. "But if I can get my fingers behind the frame, I might be able to pull it out."

"What's the delay?" asks Chumley, joining Jimmy.

"No delay," I answer. Sweeping away the concrete tailings, I find purchase behind the frame and begin to pull. Pressing my knees against the foundation, I flex my arms and shoulders and the frame slips free of its cement casing, glass and all. Flakes of rusted metal fall from my fingertips as I pass the frame to Jimmy, who hands it back to Chumley. Working fast, I return to the now open slit and, with my fingers, start digging at the softened cement, hoping to enlarge it.

"Send the girls up," I call over my left shoulder.

Sue is the first to the rim. Pushing past Jimmy and Chumley, she tumbles into the trench and throws herself into the slit. Head and shoulders disappear almost instantly, but her hips catch on the sides.

"Try kicking your feet like you're swimming," I say. Sue does, and after some twisting and turning, she breaks free of the foundation and scoots to freedom.

Jimmy maneuvers Jen forward. Kissing me on the cheek, she whispers in my ear, "See you on the other side, Cal," then shoots through the slit like it was a door held open.

"No effing way," says Hailey, eyeballing the narrow passage.

"Yes, effing way," replies her boyfriend. With little or no time to spare, Chumley hauls Hailey over the rim and pushes her headfirst into the slit. Lowering his right shoulder, he rams her plump tush like he's blocking for a halfback, popping Hailey from the foundation like a champagne cork on New Year's Eve, where she rolls about the beach grass rubbing her inflamed hips and silently cursing our names. Jimmy nudges my elbow and whispers, "You and me, maybe, but Chumley? We'll need a bulldozer." Jen kneels down and waves me forward. "Give me your hand, Cal, and I'll pull you out."

"Can't fit," I say, shaking my head.

"Of course, you can," Jen urges.

"Can't fit," I say again, nodding at Chumley.

Understanding my decision, Jen withdraws her hand and whispers, "I'll wait for you at the bandstand if it takes all night." Blowing me a heartfelt kiss, she joins her two best friends hiding behind a stout holly tree. I watch the girls reconnoiter the open ground before running across it like ghostly apparitions trailing frosted breath.

"Who's next?" asks Chumley.

"Can't fit," I say.

"What about you, Jimmy?"

"Can't fit," Jimmy begrudgingly replies.

"Bullshit. Let me through," blusters Chumley.

I reach behind Jimmy and roll the excavated window down the sand hill, where it lands on the hardened dirt floor with a loud crash.

"Are you nuts?" asks Jimmy, gritting his teeth. "Now the cops will know we're down here."

"Right," I say. "Down here and not out there."

"So the girls will have a head start," adds Chumley.

"You're smarter than you look, Cal," says Jimmy.

"A Mooncusser never gives up," I remind him.

"Are we still calling ourselves that?"

"We are, and that's why we're going to hide," I reply.

"Where?" Jimmy asks.

I point at my feet.

"In your boat shoes?" questions Chumley.

"No," I say, shaking my head. "Where I'm kneeling."

"The trench?" Jimmy asks.

I nod.

"Old-timers used to dig them so the damp from the dirt wouldn't run up the walls and bleed into the studs. Probably runs around the entire foundation," adds Jimmy. Reaching over the raised rim, he measures the trench with his forearm before saying to me, "Might work."

"Doubt I'll fit," says Chumley.

"You'll fit even if I have to bury you."

"You'd like that, wouldn't you, Jimmy?" he giggles.

"We spread out and lay down," I continue. "And when the cops shine their flashlights up here, they'll see the smashed window and think we escaped."

"What then?" asks Jimmy.

"Come the morn, we walk out the front door like we own the place. If we can find a front door."

"It's our only play," Chumley agrees.

The beam of a police flashlight cuts through the murk, shining down from the trapdoor above. Jimmy dives into the trench and heads west along the foundation. Chumley and I do the same but heading east. Scurrying on our hands and knees amid the mouse and rat droppings, I slap at Chumley's raised backside to hurry him along. I keep slapping until I miss, which is surprising given the size of the target. I don't see Chumley anywhere. He's disappeared. And when I try to put my hands back on the damp sand, they keep carrying forward. Empty air rushes past my ears as I tumble headfirst into an abyss.

"Ugh!" groans Chumley, as I land on him for a second time. Sliding off, I squat beside him, pawing at the gummy wood of this shaft-like enclosure we've landed in.

"What is this place?" I ask.

"Who knows, but whatever it is, it's got hold of my right boot."

Feeling down Chumley's pant leg, I find that his boot is indeed caught between two broken planks.

"Whatcha do, break into Hades?"

"Feels like," he answers.

I stand in the shaft and peer across the cellar between thin wooden slats. "This is perfect. Cops won't think to look in here." As I say this, more footfalls sound from above, along with unintelligible chatter, before a knotted rope is lowered and an officer in blue descends. With the powerful flashlight sweeping to and fro, I get a good look at the layout. The space is enormous, with many fenced-off rooms and corrals. Scanning along the raised rim, I don't see Jimmy anywhere, and that's a good thing. The beam bounces my way and I am forced to duck back down.

"Won't budge," grunts Chumley, continuing to tug at his leg.

"Worry about that later. Right now, we keep our mouths shut."

"Come out and show me your hands!" bellows the officer.

I chance another peek through the slats and watch the officer as he steps around a roughly constructed baby crib. Continuing his search, he nearly trips over the shattered window casing. I grit my teeth as the officer shines his flashlight along the hardened dirt floor and follows the backwards trajectory of broken glass up the sand hill. Speaking into his radio, he reports, "Four, maybe six perps. Tracks lead up to a broken window on the south wall. Teenagers by the looks of it."

"Roger that, Fred," sputters the radio. "I'll send it along to patrol. Come on up and help secure the house."

I pump my fist in silent jubilation, and I can barely contain my euphoria and find myself choking Chumley to help contain his when the radio sputters again, "Hold on a minute, Fred. I'm sending Rusty down. We don't want to leave any kids trapped inside, especially on Halloween. The parents would hang us by our short hairs."

"Roger that, Sarge. Send down my baby!"

I hear the muffled whining of a police dog being strapped into a harness and lowered into the cellar. Peeking through the slats, I watch the officer catch the German shepherd and lower it to the floor. "This is your last warning. Come out with your hands up!" Not getting a response, he removes his canine partner's muzzle and urges, "Go get 'em, Rusty! Get 'em, girl! Sniff 'em out and bring 'em out!"

Rusty races across the cellar, sniffing at the scattered debris as she goes, and it isn't long before the dog heads for the sandhill. I dip back below the slats to find Chumley still tugging at his boot. I try to help, but I'm of no use. What I really need is the cop's flashlight.

"I'm caught for sure," Chumley says to me in a hushed voice. "If you get the chance, Cal, run."

"Forget it. We're in this together."

"I'm a Wamp. Remember? They catch me, what are they gonna do? Send me back to the rez? We don't even have a rez."

"What about Jimmy?"

"Jimmy's rich. His dad will get him out of it."

The sound of Rusty scampering over the low corral ends our conversation. Crouching deeper in the shaft, we huddle together, listening to the police dog's labored breathing as it lopes along the far side of the sandhill. Rusty begins to whimper, like she's run down a bobcat and now has to tussle with it.

"Good girl, Rusty!" cheers Fred, the cop. "Now, bring 'em out and bring 'em down!"

The police dog's whimpering ceases, replaced by a low, guttural growl. Rising in the shaft, I peer through the slats just in time to see Jimmy getting pulled from the trench by his pant leg. Rusty has him. I squat next to Chumley listening to the metallic clink of Jimmy getting handcuffed.

"Your friends? Where are they?" asks the cop.

"Got away," replies Jimmy.

"Why not you?"

"Couldn't fit."

"What are their names, these friends of yours? It'll go a lot easier on ya, kid, if you tell me their names."

"I don't remember."

"Met 'em all tonight, I suppose?" Jimmy stays mute. "Talked you into it, is that what you're telling me?"

The radio sputters, "What have ya' got, Fred?"

"One lonely teenager with no friends. How he tells it. Basement's clear."

"Okay, send him up. We'll sort it out."

My heart fills with pride; Jimmy stuck to the code. Once a Mooncusser, always a Mooncusser! It was a pact the three of us had since we were kids. One goes down, the other two pick him up. Two go down, then it's up to the third.

My elation is short-lived, however, as the radio sputters, "We have him, Fred. It's Dale Hallet's kid. Shit's gonna hit the fan on this one. Let's give Rusty another sniff around, just to make sure."

I watch Chumley's chin lower to his chest, hopeless, as we squat, listening to the police dog's sniffing getting closer and closer, and then there is silence, as if Rusty fell into a bottomless chasm. All is peaceful and serene within the moldy shaft when a massive, furry head shoots past my left earlobe and bites down on the collar of Chumley's letterman jacket. Rusty lifts Chumley from the shaft as easily as if he was a pup, leaving behind his Herman Survivor still wedged between the broken planks.

Clambering from the shaft, I race across the sand hill on all fours like a crazed ape. Reaching the raised rim, I roll into the trench and throw my body into the slit. And I am halfway to freedom when Rusty's jaws clamp onto my right ankle. Visions of the Hell Hound eating me from the feet up fill my brain, but I'm too close to freedom to give up now. Gripping a fistful of the tall beach grass, I try extracting myself from the hole, only Rusty won't let me go, vigorously shaking my ankle like it's a chew toy.

I turn on my side and kick downward, striking the police dog squarely on its snout. Rusty whimpers and releases my ankle. Extracting my body from the foundation, I spring to my feet and take off, limping across the lawn with no policeman blocking my way. I snatch a quick glance over my right shoulder to see Rusty's massive head wedged within the slit, barking at me like a werewolf.

I continue limping along. Reaching the tree line, I duck and dodge my way past the raven wood and come bursting onto a secluded beach, where I dive into a rushing flow tide. Swimming the channel, I pass into the bay where time feels like it's standing still. Floating into Round Cove, I switch over to a backstroke and have quite forgotten my turmoil as I maneuver through the tidal passage and step out of the marl and onto our landing in the Cedar Swamp. My clothes are all but dry as I ascend the knolls, passing our South Seas pagoda tree along the way.

Sauntering up to our back porch, I notice Gramp lurking behind the hingeless screen door with his face bloodred. So I walk past the porch and around the side of the house to where I know Fred, the cop, will be waiting. And he is, leaning against his black-and-white, dangling a set of handcuffs. Knocking the ash from his victory cigar, he puts his handcuffs away and opens the back door of his Crown Vic. Once I'm inside, a muzzled Rusty lays her massive head across my lap and falls fast asleep.

Jimmy and Chumley had already been released by the time I arrived at the police station. Gramp chose not to come and get me, and for that, I was grateful. Whatever punishment I was to face at the hands of the local constabulary was half of what I expected him to dole out when I showed my face on our front stoop. After spending the night in stir, I was released pending my arraignment.

No one else was charged with the trespass. Only me, with the added charge of striking a police officer, Rusty. Turned out the punishment wasn't much: sixty days community service picking up trash along US 6 from Orleans to Truro. The fact that Mr. Hallet, through his lawyer, had the charges expunged meant nothing to Gramp. He held his own court, electing himself judge, jury, and executioner. I was too big to put across his knee, so he gave me the silent treatment instead, but after about a week, he couldn't take the quiet and finally spoke.

"They're all lookin' for an edge, Caleb. And you'd about gave it to 'em if your pal Jimmy hadn't been caught up in the fracas. At least you three hellions left her fine china alone and didn't disgrace her murals."

"How'd you know about the murals?" I ask. "Police let you in?"

"Why would they when I have a perfectly good key?"

"The sculpted hedges? Grounds cut so fine that you can putt on them? That you?"

"Who else would it be?"

"Since when?"

"Since I was your age. Probably me that left the gate open. I put a chain on it, so don't get any ideas."

"How come you never told me?"

"I don't have ta' tell ya every little thing I do. I gots my secrets. Those walks I take ain't always to the Fish Pier or to the Squire, neither. Time comes when I can't do it, you'll get the job, like my pap gave to me when he got hisself tossed up on Bishops Clerk shoal. The other cappies tried bringing 'im in, but Joakim weren't havin' none of it. Embarrassed, he was. Wouldn't come ashore with anyone 'cept me. So, I drove the IH to Hyannis and rowed out from Baxter's Fish Pier, finding the captain bruised and battered, clinging to a wet rock like a harbor seal. But I'll tell you this, Caleb. If you and Jonathan had dug a bit deeper where the two of you were hiding that night, we wouldn't be havin' this conversation." At the time I didn't know what Gramp meant. I thought maybe he was talking about digging the trench deeper, but he wasn't.

For the rest of that school year, Chumley stopped coming by the house. The arrest had given him a jolt, so he threw himself into football and went on to become one of the top offensive linemen in the state. Jimmy's dad shipped him off to Choate Academy during the winter break, no doubt believing me and Chumley a bad influence. He never said goodbye or that he was going. He just went. No longer were we the Three Merry Mooncussers. The bond between us had broken. But the question remained. Someone had snitched, and it wasn't me. The subject was never brought up, and I never asked. I wanted the guilty party to stew in his own juices, hoping that someday the truth would come out.

I'd see Hailey and Sue from time to time, mostly between classes, smoking Camels behind the gym like they were a pair of Russian supermodels. Jen hung out with the senior crowd more and more, as I knew she would, but she did slip me a note our junior year asking me to our prom and, like an idiot, I declined. I sent her back a note saying that I'd be aboard a scallop boat that weekend and couldn't make it, but I did offer to take her sailing on my return. Jen accepted my offer, but when the time came to push off, Jen couldn't go because she was dead. The car she was riding in on prom night sideswiped a tree on the way to an after-party. Jen was killed instantly, with no one else in the car receiving so much as a scratch. The tree they hit was barely big enough to put a dent in the IH when I drove out to the site and rammed it, uprooting the tree, stump and all. I miss Jen. I wish I could take her in my arms and hold her, tell her that it's going to be all right, that her lungs weren't crushed and that her neck wasn't broken, and that it's all a bad dream, but I can't and my heart hurts whenever I think of her.

THE CUT

My eyelids are puffy with sleep and slow to respond as I regain consciousness, not remembering what I dreamt or if I dreamt at all. Forcing my eyes open, I look up to where the boom sways above me, blotting out the midday sun, then returning it to my face. Squeezing mucus from my eyelashes, I peel my body from the ribbed floorboards with my head feeling like it's filled with cement and my throat like a stretched overinflated inner tube.

Standing at bow, I look to the horizon and see that the marine layer has backed off along with my soul-draining nausea, and for that, I am grateful. I sense that I've drifted south, and I have, as Great Beach rolls by on my starboard. It would appear that, during my downtime, I recrossed the Bar without incident, perhaps even with the help of the blond dolphin, though I wouldn't know. I can only attribute the blackout to my having drunk too much seawater during my trip across the Bar. I've heard tell of this before, where a sailor hallucinates shortly after experiencing a near-drowning, only these hallucinations usually have to do with mermaids and sea monsters and not, as in my case, a fifteenth-century pirate battle. At this point in my journey, I'll take what I can get and not ask questions.

I look about the cockpit and see, to my surprise, that *Sea Gypsy* is relatively dry. Whatever mess I made during my seemingly endless upheavals must have washed over the side or is sloshing around high in the fo'c'sle. To tell the truth, I don't give a damn. Moving unsteadily about the cockpit, I take up the mainsheet and kick the tiller to port. Taking my seat at the stern, I haul in and sweep the bow chuck over the watery horizon, then onto the chalk-white shore, where not a single bather do I see basking on the fluffy white sand. Nor do I see any sail or motorized craft beached or bobbing about. And when I look to the heavens, neither do, I see any jetliners streaming across the sky with their ever-present contrails littering the blue yonder. I have a sense that I am the last man on earth. Where did everybody go?

I experience a shortness of breath, having never felt so alone. A sharp pain stabs at my chest and I feel nausea coming back. I am about to retch over the side when I notice numerous masts-a-try jutting up from behind a wavelike dune. Tacking hard to starboard, I skirt around a Cape-like shoal and whatever nausea I am experiencing quickly leaves me as I come upon a group of high schoolers racing across the hot sand chasing brightly colored Frisbees, the males oiled and buffed with the girls wearing skimpy bikinis to show off their summer tans. I have the urge to sail in and join in the frolic, only I don't want to disturb the image and chance it disappearing. I'm just happy to be back amongst the living. So I sail onward and enter the tidal passage that will take me from the frightful and frigid waters of the North Atlantic and into the warm and placid waters of Nantucket Sound.

Progressive schools of scup swarm along the sides as I sail along the purplish edge of "the Cut," keeping a keen eye so as not to run aground on the shimmering shallows. Peering over the gunwale and it's like I'm looking down at an aquarium. I spot a rarely seen eagle ray, the fish's paisley spots pulsating along its wing-shaped body as it glides under *Sea Gypsy*, swimming in the opposite direction. This passage has always been a magical place for me, one where ruddy turnstones skim across the flats, shifting and turning as one, and gannets of the purest white dip and zip over the dunes, lunching on winged locusts. But it's their grounded cousin, the piping plover, that catches my attention, scooting along the water's edge, sucking up the insect-rich flotsam into their long, fluted beaks, like it's all part of an elaborate crib mobile designed by the Timekeeper himself. I'd just as soon drop anchor and let it play with my senses, but the hour's getting late, as the Bob Dylan song goes.

Deftly handling the tiller, I continue to navigate the watercourse and recall the day I took Toby through the Cut, only it was at night and the moon was floating above the water like a giant, illuminated beach ball. I hadn't seen her since losing in the America's Cup and, given my performance that day, I was surprised she wanted to see me at all. She'd somehow heard that I was in port and tracked me down at the house. Skipper Mack dropped her off at our front stoop before retiring with Gramp to his storied Chart Room while I led Toby to our landing in the cedar swamp, always the romantic.

Sailing out of Round Cove, we started the day by bodysurfing the short waves rushing into the mouth of Nauset Harbor. Afterwards, we swam the inlet and marsh together, Toby with her mask and fins and me with my ugly mug and feet, helping her gather a plethora of specimens for her summer internship at the Woods Hole Oceanographic Institute. She informed me of their Latin names, mating rituals, predator versus prey, estimated population, and such, and I told her of their actual names, known only to the local shell and crab fishermen, and of their real-time mating rituals and how many were expected over the side this season so there would be that many more to bring up the next, but at the end of the day, we agreed to disagree and set sail for Monomoy.

The sun begins to set as I drop anchor over a silver-flecked pool dotted with isles of smooth, white sand. And when I turn toward the bow, Toby's body is again revealed to me. Framed against the rising August moon, I marvel at the firm yet slender lines of her legs, back, and shoulders as they dissolve into the supple curves of her hips, bosom, and neck, like wet clay spinning on a potter's wheel. Trembling in the slight breeze, she nervously motions me forward. I do as I am told, disrobing as I stalk Toby onto the pulpit, where she teeters, holding on to the short jib.

"Don't make me come out there," I warn.

"No fair," she says, pointing at my boat shoes.

"I'm faster with them off," I reply, smiling.

"You'll have to catch me first," says Toby, with a wink.

Letting go of the jib, she dives from the pulpit. I grin to myself in anticipation of her reaction when she hits the water. And sure enough, after breaking the surface, Toby comes up screaming. I kick off my boat shoes and drop over the side. Standing in the chest-high lagoon, Toby leaps into my arms, stammering, "Sh...Sh...Sharks!" I look past her right shoulder at the moonlit eyes looking back at us from the shallows.

"Or what us fisherfolk call the common dogfish, or sand shark," I teach. "They look the part all right, except they don't have teeth, not real teeth. Might gum you some, though. And here I thought you were studying to be a marine biologist?"

"Chodrichthyes," clarifies Toby. "And they do have teeth, small teeth. I know what they are, but why so many, and what are they doing here?"

"Escaping the horrors of the deep, be my guess." Toby makes a face. I continue, "They flood the shallows feeding on baitfish whenever the moon is full. Thought you'd get a kick."

"Some kick! More like a heart attack! How do you know so much, Caleb Forrest?"

"Simple. Because I live it."

"Aren't you forgetting something?"

I look at Toby cradled in my arms and ask, "What did I miss?"

"You haven't caught me yet."

Using my chest as a springboard, she pushes off with her feet and dives backwards into the water. I take a moment to massage my bruised pectorals, then, giving Toby a couple more seconds head start, I follow her under.

Swimming along the sandy, moonlit bottom, I part the water with long, lateral strokes, occasionally slapping away the inquisitive, blunt-nosed sand sharks as I swim. Fleeing baitfish blot my vision and I am forced to the surface, where I switch over to a breaststroke. I don't see Toby anywhere, but I'm not concerned. I know I'm faster in the water than she, faster than most, outside of a pool anyway. What is there to prove swimming in a pool? You're never an arm's length away from safety. But to be on the open ocean with the moon at your back and dry land is a distant memory, now that's competitive swimming!

I quickly close the distance on a pair of smallish feet expertly churning the water twenty yards ahead of me. I match Toby stroke for stroke, and in no time, I am beside her. Toby swims on unawares. I gather my breath and dive. Turning on my back, I admire her form, made more luminous by the moon. Floating naturally upwards, I try for a kiss only to be rewarded with an inadvertent knee to the solar plexus. I sink to the bottom like a liver-punched prizefighter, clutching my gut amid the skates and flounders.

Pushing off the bottom, I breach the surface and spot Toby kicking furiously, heading for the Cut's deeper and darker waters. I try calling her name, but she doesn't hear me, or she pretends not to. And Toby is a good way from shore when she suddenly goes under, disappearing from the black-on-silver horizon with hardly a ripple. Having seen gray seals in the area earlier in the day, I know that where there are warm-blooded mammals swimming about, there could also be large predators, especially at night. Jutting twelve miles into the open ocean, the sandbars off Monomoy are no joke. Whatever is swimming out there could be swimming in here.

I dive forward, the luminosity of the shallows all but forgotten the further out I go. After ten minutes or so, I come to a stop but nowhere do I see Toby. A row of cloud cover drifts across the moon, casting the surrounding sea in a cold, metallic hue. Silvery splashing churns the water off to my left. A tinge of panic grips my chest. It could be Toby, but it could also be a shark. I start swimming, rotating my arms like I'm hitting a speed bag. Looking up, I see the white soles of Toby's feet kicking in the distance and start after her, leaping from the water like a just-hooked sailfish.

I quickly come alongside Toby, but she banks to the right and swims away. Rather than overtake and startle her, I try driving her back to shore in a circular manner, like I've seen dolphins do when corralling schools of haddock. The clouds disperse and the August moon takes shape above the tideway. I slow my stroke and let Toby swim in unmolested, and it is only when she climbs from the water and steps onto the beach that I follow her in. Shaking myself dry, I find Toby lying on her back behind a low dune with a sheet of white sand covering her naked flesh like a lace curtain. I feign exhaustion and collapse beside her. Lying on our backs, the two of us look up at the night sky to where Sagittarius, the Archer, forever aims his bow at Virgo, the Maiden.

"I win," says Toby, panting.

"Too fast. That's what you are," I reply, smiling to myself.

"I've been thinking," murmurs Toby.

"So have I," I say, leaning over, trying to kiss her, but she pushes me back.

"I've learned more in one day with you than I have in my two months at the Institute. What a breath of fresh air it would be to have an actual fisherman take us into the field and not another lab rat."

"A fisherman only knows what he knows so he can fill his hold. The scientific method need not apply. I try not to look at it as a way of life. I do the job, do it well, get paid and go home and, after a while, I ship out again. It's not like we're splitting atoms out there."

"But you're on the front lines, and we need that kind of input if we're going to get this right."

"Here we go," I moan.

"What?"

"You're the one trying to save the ocean and I'm the one who's spent the better part of his life pillaging from it. I hope your side wins, but people have to eat. Someday I'll wash the scales from my hands and use my brain for a change if I still have one."

"Don't you see?" asks Toby, turning on her side and looking me in the eye. "You'd be the perfect spokesman for the fishing industry. You're unbiased, smart, articulate…"

"Not bad to look at?"

"Obviously," Toby admits, squeezing my hand. "It's not like I'm after you for your money," she jokes. I smile at her remark, knowing she doesn't mean it, but it hurts just the same.

"What about joining the CFA?" she asks.

"The who?"

"Commercial Fishermen's Association, duh?"

"Those guys? They'd laugh me out of the room!"

"Why are you being so negative?"

"First of all, to become a member, you have to own your own boat. My father owned his boat, as did Gramp and every other male child in my family. But I do not. And I've no secondary education. I'm not a lawyer, marine biologist, or whatever. I'd be of no use."

"You could volunteer," offers Toby. "Work your way up."

"I can't afford to. I have to make money and take care of Gramp. You're disappointed, I know, but that's the reality of my life."

"I'm not disappointed. I only want to help you succeed. Anyone can change their own destiny."

"I've got a few pokers in the fire."

"Can I help?"

"No!" I reply sternly. "I'd tell you, but I don't want to spoil it. You'll know when I know, okay? But I know this, you're a keeper, and I'm not throwing you back."

"How romantic, comparing me to a fish," laughs Toby. "You really know how to get a girl's heart pumping."

"There are other ways," I hint.

"Shouldn't I get some kind of trophy for winning?"

"Is that what you call it?" I laugh.

"What else would it be?" Toby asks coyly.

I sit up. Turning on my side, I brace my arms and lift my body over Toby's, before saying to her, "Whatever it is you think you've won, you earned it."

"Show me," she says, exhaling, reaching around my waist and pulling me into her. The sweet exhaust of Toby's breath blows back my soggy bangs as I replace the Babylonian gods circling above with Toby's hypnotic, serpentine gaze, and it is then that I realize I have found my own heavenly goddess.

I sit atop the stern with my eyes closed, hoping to revisit the tenderness of that night, only I can't. It's not allowed, but I do feel there's an endgame I can work toward, a renewed sense of purpose where nothing else matters. I have no past and there is only the future, and that future is with Toby. I realize now that I should have walked away and dealt with the consequences of my initial crime. Is it so bad that I would have been accused? I don't think so. A short stint in the gaol and I'd be out, ready to pursue whatever I felt like pursuing. Only now, instead of a couple years of 'soft time,' I've unwittingly signed myself up for some eternal damnation, at least that's what the preachers preach. I am the Archer, gazing down from the stars, watching my folly unfold step by misguided step.

HAMMERHEAD

I sail into a triangular lagoon where the low-slung shorelines of North and South Monomoy compete in a beauty contest of sorts. I have the urge to make landfall and drop a line, but ignore the Sirens Song and haul in instead. What's the point when there's not much to catch? But there was a time when the fish here were so plentiful they'd literally jump into your boat. And that's just what happened when Captain Bartholomew Gosnold first visited in 1602, naming the windswept dune-scape Cape Cod after the great migrating schools that inhabited these very waters.

Originally the land was known simply as "Cape James," after the Spanish king, so named by Captain Estevan Gomez, who was the first to touch shore in the spring of 1552, but it was Gosnold's name that took. Times change and the migrating schools are no more, cut down by overfishing on a scale never imagined by the Portuguese and Dutch fishermen who were some of the original European settlers to call this spit their home. Tromp into the surf in a pair of hip-waders these days, and the best one could hook would be a hake or haddock. Not bad eating, but a poor substitute for the mighty cod.

It's flat-calm as I sail around a small atoll jutting from the water like a baby's first tooth, and it is there that I take a southerly tack, sailing past waving fields of marsh grass interspersed with finger canals. These canals look to offer the wayward sailor a sure way to dry land, but more often than not, they will leave them boxed in, sitting high and dry to await the next high tide. And yet somewhere amid all that grass is a stumpy pier marking the trail to an old gunner's cabin where Monomoy Ranger Tiger Watson calls home. Tucked into a narrow ravine, the cabin has but one room with a small mess built into a corner. Gramp got Tiger the job through his Kennedy connections when then senator Ted Kennedy made Monomoy and its isles part and parcel of the Cape Cod National Seashore.

It's the time of day when Tiger's usually out doing his rounds, kicking sunbathers off the environmentally sensitive dunes and generally making a nuisance of himself. Hopefully, that's the case today. I'd like to have a look around the cabin and see for myself if he's hiding something. I try sailing closer to shore, but the pulling tide makes for a shallowing draft, too shallow even for *Sea Gypsy*, so I push further into the Sound seeking deeper water.

Letting the sail luff, I climb on deck and I take up the spyglass, but nowhere in that marshy muck do I see the short pier. It's been a while since I came out this way, so the pier could be further along than I remember it to be. No matter. I'll spot it when I spot it. I recline on deck and let the rushing ebb tide take me out while the pulsing, overhead sun reheats my soggy bones. The taste of flounder roasting on deck becomes strong in my mouth. A taste sensation that I haven't had since I was a young boy. It's a taste so strong that I roll from the deck and drop into the cockpit. Reaching inside the cuddy, I take out the speargun and load a titanium-tipped spear. Throwing out my bell anchor, I somersault backwards and drop over the side.

Corkscrewing my body through the warm Gulf Stream waters, I reach the bottom, where sand eels power away from me, leaving puffs of fine white dust in their wake. Continuing on, I spot a chub mackerel fanning its fins in the current and staying just out of range. Smart fish. And I have a clear shot at a tomcod as it swims hurriedly past, only tomcod's not on the menu. Today, I'm after a flatfish, and I spot one lying camouflaged on the silty bottom, its beady eyes migrated to one side of its dish-shaped body as if strewn together. The flounder's a hogchoker all right, or what the finer restaurants refer to as fillet of sole, and that's what I'm going to do when I get the flounder on deck.

I swim slowly onward to where I can get a better shot, but the flounder senses my approach and flutters its gill rakers, creating a swirling cloud of disturbed silt before running. Banking off to the right, I avoid the dust cloud and pass over a miniature peach-colored forest of wavy grinnel. I spot the flounder making for the darkened ridge of an outer sandbar. I quicken my kick and twist my body sideways. Taking aim, I release the spear. Traveling at thirty knots, the spear pierces the flounder's flattened body like a bullet through rice paper and yet the fish continues in its escape, taking the spear and the tether with it across the sandbar before dropping over a rocky ridge.

I stand on the sandbar, struggling to control the speargun jumping in my hands. I try reeling it in, but the flounder is determined to stay down. I jerk the line and the line jerks back, only with more force than any flounder could possibly muster. I'm thinking that maybe a wolf shark has taken the bait. Built more like a moray eel than an actual shark, 'congers' are slightly smaller than your average sand shark, but they have sharp teeth. And they're one nasty fish, I can tell you! Haul a wolf shark aboard, and you're in for a fight, and you'd better watch out for their poison-spiked dorsal fins. Step on one and expect a three-day hospital visit with your foot swollen to the size of a basketball, as has happened to me. Whenever I hook one nowadays, I always cut the line. They're not worth the effort. At this point, I don't care about the flounder. All I want is to get my titanium-tipped spear back. They don't come cheap.

A pressure wave rises from the depths and blows back my hair. I reopen my eyes to see not a wolf shark struggling at the end of the tether, but a full-fledged hammerhead with the spear, along with the flounder, lodged in its gums, sending a thin rivulet of dark, red blood spiraling toward the surface. Having the girth of an oil drum, the shark looks to measure some eighteen feet from the tip of its scythe-like tail to the top of its cephalofoil-shaped head, thus making the shark a great hammerhead, the rarest of the rare, seeing that its fins and dorsal are the main ingredient for shark fin soup.

I keep hold of my speargun as man and fish engage in a tug-of-war. The ridgeline begins to crumble under my feet and I feel myself going over when the great shark abruptly turns, snapping the strong tether like a string of dental floss before slipping back over the ridge and vanishing into the deep. I push off the crumbling ridgeline and kick my way to the surface. Breaching the waterline, I spot *Sea Gypsy* anchored twenty yards to my port and swim for her, and it is the longest swim of my life.

I've never seen a hammerhead, let alone a great hammerhead, this far north, though I've spotted plenty while swordfishing in the Carib. I've always held a high degree of respect for the apex predators I've encountered, both below the surface and above. They're as extraordinary as they are perilous. Given their great size, it's easy to fear them, but in reality, we're not on the menu because we're not of their world. They're curious about us is all, as we are of them. Except the hammerhead.

Of the other sharks I've encountered — tiger, mako, reef, bull, and even the massive great white — all seem sluggish when compared to the sleek torpedo that is the hammerhead. It's the one shark that will eat you even if it isn't hungry. I witnessed a school of hammerheads feeding on a whale carcass once, and the memory of it has never left me.

We pushed off the docks of sunny San Juan, hoping for a slammer trip hauling aboard double markers; swordfish weighing over two hundred pounds. The hammerheads met us at the mouth of the harbor and trailed our boat for miles, cruising alongside in packs of thirty or more. Our captain thought he'd finally outrun them when we dropped our sets at sundown only to return the following morn to find the hooked swordfish eaten from the tail up, leaving only the pointed foils as trophies.

A day later, we came abeam a dead humpback a hundred or so miles east of the Leeward Islands. Every man was on deck: cook, cabin boy, crew, and captain with a harpoon held at the ready should a mighty kingfish rise up and take a nibble. Our spirits sank, however, when all aboard saw the many T-shaped shadows circling beneath because wherever there are hammerheads circling, you won't find many game fish swimming about unless they're suicidal. Captain and crew watched in both horror and fascination as the sharks rose from the depths and devoured the dead whale. I felt nauseous watching the bloody feast, and when I thought the sharks had finally had their fill, the hammerheads turned onto their sides, exposing their bulging bellies to the pulsating sun, and ate still more, reducing the giant grampus to mere mandible and fluke sinking slowly to the bottom in the reddening tide. Again, not the best memory to have when you're trying to get away from a great hammerhead.

I close in on *Sea Gypsy* and reach for the barn door rudder. Pulling myself aboard at the stern, I toss the speargun and its webbed carryall into the cuddy, then collapse in the cockpit, counting my toes and muttering, "Damnable fish."

A wave of some magnitude punches the stern and pitches the boat forward. I take hold of the coaming rail to keep from going over. Jumping onto the bow, I grab the mainstay and step out onto the pulpit to watch the unmistakable shadow pass beneath the boat. I try pulling up the anchor, but it, like the spear, appears to have hit a snag. Normally, I'd jump over the side to investigate, but not today. Instead, I take out my slime knife and cut the line. I can always get another anchor. There are about ten of them sitting on our back deck amid the nautical mire.

I sit shivering at the bow, having just come face-to-face with my nightmare nemesis. I'm not so much afraid of the shark as I am shaken by it. What concerns me isn't the terror I felt, but the harm I've done. Plying the world's oceans with a spear wedged in your maw is a fate I wouldn't wish on my worst enemy. Truth be told, I've killed more sharks that could ever kill fishermen, and with all the other sea life I've hauled through the back door over the years, I'm what some might call the Killer Ape run amok! Only, I have to ask, what difference does it make if your "victim" is man or beast?

What makes us so special? Is it because we believe we're closer to God or that our consciousness puts us on a higher plane because we can remember our victims? Does a shark remember its victims? I don't believe so. It's an eating machine, as are we, except that we do it on a much grander scale. There's not a fish, bug, bird, plant, or animal that we humans don't consume in some fashion or another. Where's the separation, and is there one? Does our purity of spirit last only until our adult teeth grow in? Why should I feel guilty for what I've done? Does a dog feel guilty after it bites? Perhaps, but only if it expects to be beaten for its behavior, and maybe that's the point. It is only when we are beaten, physically, mentally, or spiritually that we feel regret. Otherwise, why bother? We're all basically Attila the Hun raiding a village of Goths, then poling their heads on spears. Did Attila feel remorse? I think not.

I've yet to feel it, regret that is. I might struggle with the concept from time to time, but don't we all? Shouldn't there be some type of blood atonement? The Bible says so, but Jesus says no. My onetime friend only knows is that he is dead, if he knows anything. And not knowing might be the best. When I'm six feet under or floating below the top-water, maybe then I'll get my answer, or not.

SAILING THE REACH

The rushing ebb tide takes me out faster than the wind can take me in, so I come about and sail along the shoreline at a beam reach. Heading for the mile marker east of the tideway, I pass the spot where the Chatham Lightship once anchored. Not every lighthouse was land-based in the early to mid-1900s. The Boston shipping magnates, who controlled the lanes from New York to Bangor, grew tired of having their frigates and tankers wash up in pieces along the banks of the Outer Cape, so they thought it prudent to anchor a floating lightship to better warn away vessels from Chatham's ever-shifting shoals.

I try imagining what it must have been like for a crew of three afloat on nothing more than a glorified tugboat held in stays by twin, four-ton mushroom anchors. It would have made for a hell of a ride, especially in the dead of winter with a nor'easter kicking up. I talked with one of the surviving crew members once. He was a friend of Gramp's from his merchant marine days, and he described to me how a typical day went.

"Fog as thick as soup coupled with angry seas. Trapezoidal shoals that could turn us on a dime and face us sideways against the monster waves. I had to tie a coffee can around my neck whenever I worked outside so I'd have someplace to upchuck. Working that lightship was a hell not many could take. Me, I lasted five years before jumping over the side and swimming for shore. Didn't care if made it or not, but I made it, and I never went back."

I shiver at the thought of it, or perhaps I haven't stopped shivering since my encounter with the great hammerhead. And while it's entirely possible the shark traveled up the Gulf Stream and found its way into the Sound, I find it hard to believe, like the other strange encounters I've had on this stranger than strange day. No true seafarer would ever mistake a breaching whale for a sea monster, and yet that's what they wrote in their ship's logs dating back hundreds, if not thousands of years.

The Old Testament mentions sea monsters no less than four times! Spend extended periods on the water, as I have, and you start imagining things. I've never seen a Kraken, the legendary cephalopod-like sea monster of gigantic size in Scandinavian folklore, and I don't believe they ever existed. Although some of the old sailors I've met do believe, including Gramp. Only my tug-of-war wasn't with the fabled Kraken, it was with a great hammerhead and I have the torn tether to prove it.

The surrounding seaway is heavy with traffic. Motorized craft steam in and out of Stage Harbor along with the many day sailors, their whitened sailcloth dotting the horizon with seemingly no fixed heading. The waters on this side of Monomoy are peaceful and the waves lolling. It's the kind of sea day sailors love, and for once I agree with them. A blank space where I can stow away my troubles and just be. Threading the mainsheet through the traveler, I clamp down before collapsing on the bench seat with the broken tiller resting at my elbow. Hiding within the mains'l's shadow, I am dimly aware of my surroundings as I think back to the day Chumley came to call — only he wasn't Chumley anymore, he was Officer Jonathan Repoza of the Chatham Police Department.

I walk alongside a ten-foot work table sprinkling Miracle-Gro over a row of budding clay pots left over from my strawberry patch days, tamping down the nutrient-rich soil with my thumb and forefinger. I'd placed the pots in rows under an equally long fluorescent grow light hanging from the barn's exposed crossbeams. The work is tedious as it is gratifying, with each female plant expected to yield 17.5 ounces of premium buds. There's not much to it, really, except for the planting part. Once these ladies are in the ground, all they will need will be plenty of June sunshine and the occasional downpour, the same as when Tiger was growing, only on a much grander scale.

I look to the exposed bulbs and then to the barn's open carriage door, where I notice a hefty shadow making its way up the shell and cement ramp. I go to the barn's lone window and peer through the thick, wavy glass, watching a heavyset officer in blue ascending the ramp while tugging at his tightly fitting uniform that appears to be strangling him from the waist up. I return to the work table and reach into the Styrofoam cooler at my feet. Stopping under the hayloft's extended beam and tackle, the officer draws his revolver and leaps into the barn.

"Drop your cocks and grab your socks!" yells the officer, right as I whip an ice-cold bottle of Red Stripe at his head. Dropping his police-issued Colt revolver, the officer catches the bottle one-handed a mere inch from his face.

"Fucking hell!" shouts the officer. "What gives, Cal?"

"Looked thirsty struggling up the ramp. Good thing you still have those catlike reflexes."

"Damn near knocked my teeth out!"

"What can I say? I have confidence in your athletic abilities."

"Ripe bastard! Lucky my gun didn't go off."

"Chief's counting your bullets again?"

"Something like that," giggles Chumley, twisting off the top and draining the beer to its last sudsy drop. "If you don't respect me, you can at least respect the uniform."

"Got it backwards, Chum. I always respected you. It's the uniform I can do without. What am I supposed to do, call you Officer Repoza now?"

"It's a start."

"Well, you can forget it. But I promise to not call you Chumley in public. I don't get out much anyway. So, to what do I owe this pleasure?"

"Didn't think I needed a reason."

"You don't, but I'm a little busy. Got to get these pots in the ground before I ship out."

"Saving a bushel for Junebug, I hope."

"First batch, always."

I'd heard Chumley had turned cop, so I wasn't surprised to see him in uniform, just disappointed is all. Blowing out his knee senior year, the college scouts stopped coming around and with his already low grades, he was lucky to have graduated at all. But rather than joining me on the Fish Pier or stomping off into the woods and drinking himself to death, like some other members of his tribe have done over the years, the genetic affliction being what it is, Chumley applied to the police academy and got accepted, going on to become Chatham Police Department's first recruit of Wampanoag descent.

"I know how you and the captain feel about cops," says Chumley. "Same as us Wamps. Can't trust 'em."

"Why'd you join?"

"To change it from the inside."

"Have you?"

"Not yet. Mostly I write parking tickets."

"To your fellow Wamps?"

"Hell no! I'd be scalped!"

"Red savages!"

Chumley giggles into his fist before saying, "Speaking of white devils, remember the night a bunch of us broke into that round house on the beach? What did we call her...the Salem Witch?"

"I remember," I answer, in a flat tone. "What of it?"

"Last week a call came in about a gas leak," says Chumley, sitting on the work table. "And get this, the address was 23 Shore Road."

"No shit," I say, my interest piqued.

"Nobody wanted to take the call, so they sent the *'low man on the totem pole,'* which of course was me."

"How would anyone know about a gas leak way out there?"

"Some groundskeeper called it in. Whoever it was, he was gone by the time I got there. I found the front door, not the window we smashed that night, but the actual door, completely covered in ivy. We never would have found it."

"Did you go inside?"

"I did, but it was daytime when the call came in, so it wasn't as scary."

"Were the murals still there?"

"Where else would they be?"

"Good point."

"Smelled like rotten eggs. I went around prying open windows, then I called the ComElectric guys. What do I know about gas leaks?"

I toss Chumley another beer and take one for myself, before saying, "Please continue."

"After they showed up and fixed the leak, I went back inside to secure the house, only that's not all I did," he says, winking at me.

"You didn't?"

"Went straight for the kitchen or galley or whatever, sprung the trap door and poked my head in. It was dark like before, only darker."

"What'ja do next?"

"I turned on the light, what else?" Chumley giggles.

"Ripe bastard," I say, smiling. "Then what'dja do?"

"I climbed down, but before you ask," says Chumley, holding up his right hand, "someone replaced the broken ladder."

"And?"

"Went straight to the shaft."

"Find your missing boot?"

"No. The shaft had also been replaced. All new wood, and get this, there was another trapdoor at the bottom, also new."

"Weird," I add.

"Yeah, it was weird all right, but that's not all."

"Don't tell me!"

"I went down, and guess what? The trapdoor leads to a tunnel."

"And you went in, I suppose?"

"Protect and serve," says Officer Repoza, proudly pointing at his badge, which is pinned to his chest upside down. "It was a tight fit, obviously. I had to go down on all fours. Once a Mooncusser, always a Mooncusser! Right? Isn't that what we used to call ourselves?"

"Yes, and it meant something," I say, in a flat tone.

"We were kids, Cal. What could it mean?"

"Never mind," I say, kicking the can further down the road. "How's this tall tale of derring-do end?"

"Not so fast," replies Chumley. "The bottom was muddy and the walls had roots sticking out. It was creepy. I expected an opossum to jump on my head any minute. And it was long, football field long. I would've gone back but there wasn't enough room to turn around, so I kept going."

"What happened next, did you finally find Hades?" I ask, feigning boredom as I straighten the pots.

"There was another light."

"Like from a train?" I guffaw.

"No, dumbass. From another shaft, only this one led up to a stable on the other side of Shore Road, all part and parcel of the same property, turns out."

"Great story, Chum," I say. "But I've heard it before. Houses up and down the Cape, old houses, specifically captains' houses, all have hidden passages running through them, along with tunnels. Either to hide food and stores from the British or to hide booze during Prohibition."

"That's what I thought at first. I was born here, remember, like you, and my fam goes back five thousand years. Long before any of yours showed up, Vikings included."

"Got me there," I admit.

"Why aren't you a writer and not a fisherman?"

"Because I read too much and I know I can't compete with the masters, so why should I bother?"

Chumley waves me off, continuing, "Anyway, after word spread about the tunnel, the ladies from the Chatham Historical Society showed up with a professor from Harvard. Black guy teaches something called ethnic studies, whatever that is. He thinks the house was part of the Underground Railroad. You know, helping runaway slaves escape from the South? Remember the mural?"

"I do. He's probably right."

"Maybe, but the old girl wasn't alone."

"What are you saying?" I ask, thinking of my long-ago relations.

"She got the runaway slaves to England using area sea captains, that's what."

Reaching into his back pocket, he takes out a clapboard ship's log fastened together with deer sinew and tosses it to me.

"Ship's logbook?"

Chumley nods. "Found it wedged behind an I beam when I was in the tunnel. Has the escaped slaves listed as chattel. Made eight trips to Bristol, England, before the Civil War broke out. It's yours."

"Why give it to me?" I ask, slowly opening the brittle log.

"Boat's name was the *Lady Isis* and the captain was one Forrest, Joseph J. Thought it belonged more to you and the captain more than with the Chatham Historical Society."

"Old Joe, I'll be damned. Thanks, Chum," I say, humbled. "I mean, Officer Repoza. Helps fill the gaps."

"And get this, now the Society wants to turn the witch's house into a museum, only nobody knows who owns it."

"Have them check who's paying the taxes. They'll find out soon enough."

"Taxes are paid in full until 1999. Part of the mystery. And nobody knows by who. Jimmy's dad is looking into it."

"Good luck with that," I reply dismissively.

"Imagine a bunch of fifth graders standing around the shaft we hid in that night? We could have escaped if we knew what was below us."

"I did escape. It was you and Jimmy who got caught."

"What are you getting at, Cal?"

"How did the cops know my name and where I lived?"

"Why ask me and not Jimmy?"

"You're here. Jimmy's not. I wouldn't have brought it up if you hadn't taken me down memory lane. Don't get me wrong, Chum. It's a hell of a story, but the question remains."

"Police deduce, Cal. That's what we do."

"You're right. Forget I brought it up."

Draining the rest of his beer, Chumley says to me, "Don't be such a stranger, Cal. Give me a shout when you get back and we'll go to the Squire and drag Hail and Sue off their barstools."

"Sounds like a plan. Thanks again for the log."

Nodding, Officer Repoza glances at the potted plants and adds, "Little late in the season for planting strawberries, don't ya' think?" I watch the officer descend the shell and cement ramp, thinking that my childhood chum might not be as dumb as he appears.

With the sailor's adage "Catch a shark, catch a breeze" ringing in my head, I sail close-hauled to the lee and put the Monomoy headlands high above the bow chuck. I stand in the cockpit and slap the boom to starboard. Scanning the surrounding seascape, I look for any scythe-like tail and dorsal fin circling, but none materializes. For all I know the hammerhead could be trolling the Nantucket shoals by now. I wish the fish good hunting and tack to port. Looking toward the head-lands, the topography this far out changes with the seasons, so I'm not exactly sure what I'm looking at. The trick is spotting the blue and white telltale windsock attached to a tall spar pole marking the short pier. But depending on the color of the sky that day, this can some-times be hard to do. Worst-case scenario, I'll have to hump it overland and, having bobbed about the bay the day long, a good hike may be just what I need to clear my head of pirates, blond dolphins, and great hammerheads.

TIGER'S CABIN

A steady offshore wind buffets the mains'l and I have to keep tacking in order to gain way on the outgoing tide. Advancing from the southwest, I skirt around an exposed sandbar that might not make it past sundown and it's not long before I spot the blue and white windsock waving in the breeze. I drop the mains'l and pull up the centerboard, wedging it forward, then drift in to where a smattering of grassy isles steps out to greet me. I stand in the cockpit, wrapping the mains'l around the boom then, un-stepping the mast, I lay it and the boom lengthwise across the cockpit before dropping over the side. Standing waist-high in the shallow water, I sling the bowline over my right shoulder and tow *Sea Gypsy* deep into the wetlands — more specifically, a tall stand of puffy pussy willow.

I use my slime knife to cut down an armful of reeds that I drape over her deck and bow. Not the best camouflage, but it will have to do. I don't see Tiger's weather-beaten skiff knocking about and that's a good thing. Tiger doesn't trust the water. He normally patrols on foot and only uses the skiff when he has to go to the mainland for supplies or to visit one of the lonely widows who trail him around town like a bunch of lost puppies whenever he's ashore, meaning I'll have the cabin to myself until he returns, if he returns and doesn't stay over in Chatham.

I take the speargun, along with its webbed carryall, from the cuddy and slog my way through the retreating waters. My bare feet slosh in the tepid tide pools that are alive with blue crab, the crustaceans' shells skirted with seaweed with their claws held open, ready to fight. I step over and around the crabs and push onward through what is now a mere runnel before coming upon the short, rickety pier whitewashed with sea salt. I spot a dark, oval shape hanging from a piling at the head of the pier and go to it.

Closing in on the object, I am horrified to find a giant snapping turtle nailed to the piling through the neck and covered in black flies. Who could have done such a cruel thing and why? Certainly not Tiger. He's a lover of all creatures, great and small. It's us humans he can do without. He won't so much as swat a mosquito whenever they rise up from the swamp and infest his camp, saying, "These fleas ya' got here ain't nothin' compared to the ones we had in Nam. Come down with a case of dengue fever and you'll know what I'm talkin' about. Besides, I done enough killin' for one life."

The only time I ever saw Tiger kill anything was a morning when I accompanied him on his rounds. We were hiking along Monomoy's backside when we came upon a seal that had washed up in the surf. The seal was bleeding badly, no doubt hit by a shark. Tiger left me on the beach and ran to his cabin. I thought of trying to roll the seal back into the surf, but I knew it wouldn't do any good, so I took off my T-shirt and tied a tourniquet around the wound, but the seal continued to bleed out. Tiger returned carrying his M16. Shoving me aside, he took aim and shot the seal in the head, killing it instantly, then rolled the body into the surf with his boot, saying, "Sharks gotta eat too."

I watch the flies crawl into and out of the snapper's eyes, mouth, and neck to lay their eggs before flying off in a whirling black cloud. Kids probably, no meaner than the three of us back in the day. Only that's not true. We were turtle hunters, not turtle executioners. I examine the snapper's shell and there, amid the thornlike tufts, are three tightly placed musket holes. My inner horror has come full circle. "Can't be," I say to myself. I rub my eyes vigorously, and when I reopen them, the beast has vanished. Another mirage on a day full of mirages.

I leap from the pier and step over a bed of seaweed left over from a previous squall, perhaps even the one that lashed *Sea Pearl* a week ago, or was it two weeks? I still don't remember and don't care. I only want to get to the ranger's cabin. I do so by running across a draining bog of spongy peat and clambering up a medium-sized dune. I notice the wavy belly print of a snake laid across the white sand like a Mexican bullwhip. I follow the print to where it disappears under a tall cropping of club moss.

Knocking back the scaly leaves with the edges of my feet, I see the snake. It's a hognose dressed up to look like an eastern diamondback due to its similar skin pattern and spade-shaped head. It's coiled and hissing, but I do not fear the snake for I know it's not poisonous, as there are no poisonous snakes on Cape Cod, though some, like the hognose, do have fangs, and that is when it strikes, sinking the afore-mentioned fangs into the soft tissue between my thumb and forefinger, drawing blood. Catapulting backwards, I land on my butt and begin sucking on my injured hand. I watch the hognose slither away and vanish into a flaxen field of wavy saw grass. The bite doesn't hurt as much as it surprised me. I hold the snake no ill will. I'm to blame. I shouldn't have spooked it with my tomfoolery.

Swiping my snakebit hand across my mouth, the smeared blood tasting like heated iron, I leave the wetlands behind and continue my trek over the low dunes, careful when stepping over any folded clump of dune grass or swirl of goldenrod. After a short span of steady, over-land hiking, I merge with the actual trail that will bring me to Tiger's cabin. The trail leads through a pine grove covered in yellow pollen. I take cover under in the spotty shade and notice a stubby pine standing off by itself at the edge of the grove. Opening the webbed carryall, I remove a spear and load it into the speargun. Pulling back the vulcan-ized bowstring, I lock the spear in place, take aim, and pull the trigger. The spear impacts the tree dead center, running it through. Not bad for a practice shot, I think to myself. The next shot could be for real.

"No way I'm getting that out," I mutter, and leave the spear shiv-ering in the tree. I'm two spears down and three to go. If I do come upon Tiger, and he's carrying his rifle, I'll only have time for one shot because what will be coming back at me will be traveling a lot faster than any spear has ever gone.

The scent of pine is strong in my nostrils as I step onto an overgrown sheepherders' trail lined with blueberries ripening in the summer sun. I pick a handful of the plump berries and pop them into my mouth, knowing they'll be sour, and they are, but I chew and swallow them anyway. Hiking further, I come to the spot where Jimmy, Chumley, and I used to camp out as kids.

Nestled within a shallow glade, the campsite spills onto a small beach and I remember how scared we used to get telling each other ghost stories and how rabbits, seemingly hundreds of them, hypnotized by the fire, would hop to within inches of us before darting back into the bush. One rabbit wasn't so lucky and we ate it, not because we were hungry, but to justify the kill. Plodding into the glade, I stand over our campfire ring, resetting the rock, clam, and whelk shells with the soles of my now blistered feet. Damn that hot sand! But the truth is, it feels good, blistered feet or not.

I try imagining what my life would have been like if I had just stayed the course and went along. I should have taken Jen to the prom. Maybe she would be alive today and who knows, we might have even eventually married and had kids together. Why did the world have to force its way into our lives? It's so big. Couldn't it have left us alone and spun on by itself? If I were to restart the charred wood within the ring, would the scent of burning driftwood cleanse my spirit or condemn it? I don't have the answer, so I hike on.

Heading back up the wash, I push onward down the trail. Ascending a windswept shelf footed in elderberry and heather, I pull up a fistful of flesh-colored goldenrod and bring the flower to my nose. I breathe in, but the petals have no fragrance like I'm smelling a silk corsage. Thinking that my nose might be clogged with pollen, I expunge my nostrils with a series of loud snorts that prompts a fawn, still in her spots, to rise up in the tall grass upwind of me. I remain on one knee, holding the flowers out to the fawn as if proposing. Picking its way toward me, the fawn stops and starts again before sniffing the flowers in my hand and nibbling on the petals. I look into the deer's round, brown eyeball where I see the surrounding hillside reflected but cannot place myself within the landscape.

Fierce snorting erupts behind me. I turn my head slowly and there, in the heath, stands a majestic five-point buck with its tail flag up. The stag steps onto the trail, its long ears twitching in the slight breeze. If I were to chance running now, I could be gored, so I stay put and let the fawn finish the goldenrod down to the stems. Its hunger sated, the fawn prances past me to bury its wet nose in the stag's muscular chest plate. The stag drops its tail and, as if on cue, the rest of the herd lifts from the grass and passes me one by one, leisurely feeding on the sides of the trail. The stag is the last to move, its flared nostrils expanding and contracting, taking nervous, clipped breaths.

The stag steps hesitantly onto the trail sniffing at the air and grunting. I lower my head and hunker down as it nears. Extending my right arm, I let the tips of my fingers run along the deer's silky flanks. The stag leaps from the ground as if struck by lightning and within seconds the entire herd bounds into the bush, disappearing almost instantly. I look about me and it's as if the herd never existed but for their cloven track marks.

I continue along the onetime sheep rut and the ranger's cabin comes into view, wedged between a pair of arching, wavelike dunes. I stand on the ridge looking down at the saltbox-shaped cabin. Half buried by sand with a sunken roof and a slat-pine door slapping in the wind, the cabin appears abandoned, but I know that's how Tiger wants it to look. Dressing it up and putting a padlock on it would only invite trespassers, not that there would be many this far out. But you never know. Look at me!

I come to a cleft in the ridge and slide down. Skidding to a stop at the back of the cabin, I peek around the corner and reconnoiter the open ground. I see no signs of life but for a single blue jay perched atop a rusted water pump. Ducking, I run along the side of the cabin, making sure to keep below its lone, east-facing window, and while my stealth might seem like overkill, with the amount of money at stake and the quarry, I'd rather have the drop on Tiger than the other way around. A quarter million is enough to put a bounty on any man's head. Including mine.

I lean against the cabin's chipped and weathered shingles, then take a spear from its webbed carryall. Loading the spear, I take a deep breath, round the front of the cabin, and throw open the slat door. Entering the cabin, I sweep the speargun to and fro and quickly come to the conclusion that the cabin is empty. I check behind the door for good measure. No Tiger. I move about the cabin, examining Tiger's meager possessions: a foldout cot topped with a Navajo blanket, a bookshelf crammed with moldy paperbacks penned by his favorite author, Louis L'Amour, with his foldout card table set in front of his high-backed metal chair. Always the Spartan.

I go to the card table and stare at the same two pictures he's kept framed, except the picture of his daughter, Lizabeth, has changed. No longer the *jeune fille* kicking her feet up on a backyard tire swing, this new version has her older, mid-thirties perhaps, and dressed in designer fashions along with two towheaded boys, kneeling in front of a newly placed, manufactured home. Good for her, only where did the money come from? The last I heard from Tiger was that she was divorced and broke. Obviously, Tiger made the delivery and got paid. That's great! But where's my share?

Placing the speargun behind the flapping door, I search for Tiger's M16, knowing that he'd never leave it out in plain sight. Taken apart, Betsy Ross, as he calls his rifle, could fit anywhere, wrapped in a blanket and stuffed under the floorboards or hidden inside a foot-locker that I see stationed at the foot of his cot. Funny that I didn't notice the locker when I first stepped inside. I go to it and creak open the lid. Inside I find his ranger khakis with the US Park Service emblem emblazoned on the right sleeve, neatly folded next to a pair of rolled socks and underwear. Missing, however, is Tiger's BDU, or US Army Ranger Battle Dress Uniform, along with his black beret and the service medals that he only takes out when attending the funeral of one of his fallen bros. I look down at the locker, wondering which of Tiger's former brethren no longer resides on the right side of the grass. There weren't many, as he told it, who came back from that "CIA-inspired mess," and even fewer, if they did get out, survived the war at home, what with the drugs, alcohol, loneliness, and such.

Closing the lid, I walk the length of the cabin, which isn't far, and come to the rust-rimmed sink in the corner holding a day's worth of dirty dishes, which strikes me as odd. I've never known Tiger to leave a single pot, pan, or utensil un-scrubbed. He's anal retentive about it, meaning that if he did leave for the mainland, he left in a hurry. I take a last look around, then exit the cabin, leaving the door slapping in the wind. Standing outside, I consider heading back to my boat and sailing for home, but I'm too close. If I'm ever going to put these events behind me, I'll have to see the body and relive the murder, and that means continuing onward to the decommissioned light station located at the tip of Monomoy, step by blistered step.

THE BARRENS

I start my trek with a hike through the low dunes that are abuzz in winged tiger beetles darting and diving about. I'm about to put my foot down when a dune vole crosses my path, scurrying from dune mat to dune mat. Right then, a fleet-footed fisher-cat leaps through the dunescape and snatches the vole with its pointy teeth, leaving only a blackish blur and pungent stink in its wake.

"Memento mori, carpe diem," I mutter. "Remember that you are mortal and seize the day. Too late for you, my furry friend, but not for me."

A stiff wind builds at my back as I come off the dunes and step onto a sunken valley floor where dust devils rise above the cracked clay, spinning away in the heated air. You wouldn't know it by the looks of the place, but this seemingly lifeless land can turn into a shallow lake during a summer deluge, and I've even seen tadpoles squirting amid the short stalks. Devoid of any human touch, these barrens have always held a special place for me. There's something eternal about it. Stand at its center and it's as if time has come to a standstill, neither progressing nor regressing. However, anyone out here on a day hike better not hike with their heads down or they'll find themselves walking in circles due to the valley's oval shape, with no beginning and no apparent end.

I look at the sun's declination in the late afternoon sky and realize that it hasn't moved from its noontime position. I don't know the mathematics of it, only that perhaps it's due to my viewing the sun from inside a natural depression. I hold out my right arm like a human sundial and try to gauge the time, but for whatever reason, I cast no shadow. In other words, I have become the Invisible Man! Or perhaps it's an optical illusion created by the wavy heat rising from the sunbaked clay. And there is no breeze. I could use a drink of water, but I left the milk jug back in the cuddy.

If I have to, I can always drink from one of the two freshwater ponds that lie somewhere off to the north. The water there is stagnant and brackish, and it would take a desperate man to drink from it. I'm not that desperate, not yet. I have to keep putting one foot in front of the other and I'll get there. I always do. I bide my time by recalling the day Jimmy stopped by the house to give me his final offer, or so I thought, and when he didn't find me on the back porch, he hiked down to our landing in the Cedar Swamp, following the secret path he knew too well.

I had *Sea Gypsy* up on blocks in what I'd dubbed our "Careening Area." I wanted to get my boat sanded, caulked, and painted before my planned absence at sea once the grow is harvested. Better that I'm away when that happens. I was lying on my back, scraping sea lice from *Gypsy*'s underbelly, when I saw Jimmy bounding through the knotty pine. He was attired in his usual linen vestments and running headlong. Approaching the beach, I called out to him, "Don't do it!" but I was too late as he leaped from the wood and onto the beach, where his expensive Italian leather loafers sank in the slurry sand.

"Forgot about the sloppy sand. Been a while," Jimmy murmurs, looking down at his Enzo Bonafe brogues buried in the slurry sand.

"Little soap and water and they'll clean right up," I say, from under my boat.

"Not the smell," Jimmy answers.

"No, not the smell," I admit. Stepping out of his ruined shoes, Jimmy tosses them into the woods and asks, "Hear the news?"

"What news?" I reply, still scraping.

"The Salem Witch wasn't a racist, she was an abolitionist. Turns out she was part of the Underground Railroad."

"Yeah, I heard," I say, crawling out from under *Gypsy*. "Chumley stopped by last week, or should I say, Officer Repoza stopped by last week."

"Screw that! He'll always be Chumley to me, even when he's writing me a parking ticket, which he has."

"Good for him!"

Jimmy smiles. "Got a minute?"

"I've got to get *Gypsy* scraped, caulked, and painted before I ship out, but I'll listen to you talk while I work."

"While *we* work," Jimmy clarifies, rolling up the cuffs of his linen shirt and the legs of his linen pants.

"Might get messy," I warn.

"No shit, Sherlock. Where do you want me?"

I take a scraper soaking in a chum bucket and toss it to Jimmy. "Start at the port bow and make your way to the stern. I'll start at the stern and make my way up the starboard side." Jimmy goes further and removes his linen shirt, hanging it on a pine bough. The work begins and continues uninterrupted, and in no time, we are both at midships.

"God, I miss this," says Jimmy, scraping away.

"Not if you had to do it for a living," I quip.

"How do you know, Cal? Why are you always selling me short?"

"You're right, Jimmy, I don't know. But I know this, you didn't come here to scrape my boat." Inspecting Jimmy's work, I point, saying, "Missed a spot."

"Haven't got there yet. Back off and let me work," Jimmy admonishes. The work continues until we are both covered in flecks of white paint and spongy slivers of worm-eaten wood.

"Okay, let's have it," I say, mopping my brow with my sweaty tee.

"I could never get one past you, Cal," Jimmy admits. "Not on a pond. Not at the rink. I told anyone who'd listen that if we had Caleb Forrest in net, we would have won the State's junior year."

"What can I say? I never took well to grown-ups telling me what to do. Your turn."

Tossing his scraper into the chum bucket, Jimmy takes a seat on an ancient cut of cedar. I toss him a towel and Jimmy begins wiping himself down. "My father's coming for you," says Jimmy. "He found a chink in your armor and he's calling in his markers."

"Why should I care what Dale does or doesn't do? I own the land. Not him."

"He found the original title."

"Where?"

"Stuffed away in the basement of the State House, like we first thought. Paid a mint for it, but he's got it and he's not taking any prisoners."

"What's it say? Not that I care."

"The document isn't a land title, per se, but a land lease."

"So? What's that make us?"

"Sharecroppers, basically."

"Sharecroppers, huh?" I repeat, palming my scraper and coming up behind Jimmy. "What does this supposed lease actually say?"

"I did some research. Turns out the State wanted a large, working farm on the Outer Cape and Captain Nehi's land fit the bill. The lease, signed by Captain Nehi and then governor John Hancock himself, had but one caveat, that the land produces, and for over two hundred years, it hasn't, your strawberry patch being the exception, and when it comes from the State, it comes with strings. I'm surprised they've been so lax about it all these years, this being Taxachusetts and all."

"Is that why your father sent you, to give me a history lesson?"

"*I* sent me," says Jimmy, running his slim fingers through his sandy blond hair. "I'm here to give you a heads-up. Dad took back Hallet Construction. He quit the political game. Wasn't paying off like he thought it would. He's strictly a builder, and you know what that means."

"No. What does it mean?"

"That he's got blood in his teeth."

"Did you get that from Uncle Joseph?"

"Probably."

"So what? Dale's always been after the land."

"Yeah, but this time he means to get it. All out, like he used to do before we moved here. Every dirty trick in the book. He'll be coming after you in the fall after the summer people leave and the year rounders take a much-earned nap."

I watch Jimmy run his towel across the back of his neck, my right hand shaking as I bring out the scraper.

"Old-timers won't let him," I say.

"Old-timers are a dying breed," replies Jimmy, toweling his hair. "Besides, Captain Let turned the land over to you, and you're not your grandfather. It's the captain they fear. Not you." Hot blood pounds in my eardrums as I hold the scraper a mere millimeter from the back of Jimmy's neck. "And I would have went right along with him if I hadn't seen his secret plans."

"Secret plans?" I ask, my stance wavering.

"Stopped by his office this morning," says Jimmy, unfolding his pant cuffs. "I needed to clarify a zoning code and I thought he might have the paperwork on it. He was out, but I got what I needed anyway. I was turning to leave when I saw that he'd left his safe open. He never leaves his safe open, even when I was a kid playing under his desk. And he's never given me the combination and I never asked. Why would I? There were no secrets between us, or so I thought. I wanted to trust him; he's my dad, after all. But I needed proof, so I went to the safe, and there they were. His plans. His real plans for your land."

"Another brochure?" I laugh.

"Worse," Jimmy replies.

"Worse how?" I ask, tightening my grip on the scraper.

"A marina, right where we're standing, for one. Of course, he'll have to get permission to drain the swamp, but he will. He always does. Then there's the PGA-style golf course with the eighteenth hole drilled right on your bluff. Quite spectacular, actually. Makes Pebble

Beach look like a roadside pitch and putt. Not to worry though. There won't be any golf balls sailing through your windows."

"Why's that?"

"House won't be there. Bulldozed. In its place, Whispering Pines Executive Golf Club. Members only. Might help, though, if you bought one of the thirty or more residences set to line the course. And let's not forget the parking lots, service roads, roundabouts, and all the other paving projects that will keep Hallet Construction in the black for decades to come."

"How was all this a secret with you being CEO?" I ask, bringing up the scraper with its warped, metal edge angled downward.

"Turns out it was in name only," says Jimmy, wiping his hands on the towel. "My father used me, Cal. He used me to get to you, and that's why I left him."

"Hallet Construction?"

"No. My father."

I toss the scraper into the chum bucket and stand in front of Jimmy. "That's not what I want. He's your father, Jimmy. Whatever's between Dale and me, I'll handle it."

Jimmy tosses me back his towel. "This mosquito-infested hellhole means as much to me as it does to you. This is where we grew up, and I'll be damned if I'm going to let him destroy it."

"Fall will be too late. Whatever's owed, I'll have it paid off by then."

"What are you going to do, rob a bank?"

"Something like that. What about you? What will you do?"

"Don't be surprised if you see me standing next to you hauling net someday," says Jimmy, standing and taking his shirt from the pine bough.

"I'd be disappointed if I did."

Jimmy shakes his head. "There you go again, selling me short. Whatever shenanigans you're up to, do it quick and don't get caught." Clapping me on the shoulder, Jimmy puts on his shirt and begins buttoning it. "If you do somehow pay off what you owe, it'll make it harder for my father. After all, the land lease was signed by John

Hancock himself, and he'll have a hard time justifying a golf course in lieu of a working farm, but like I said, he's calling in his markers."

"A Mooncusser never gets caught, remember?"

Jimmy looks me in the eyes and says, "It was me that night. I was the one who ratted you out to the cops." I square my stance. Jimmy offers me his chin like a prizefighter on the take. "First one's on the house, Cal. No guarantees after that."

I could punch Jimmy, but that would only leave the two of us rolling around in the slurry sand. And he's no pushover. Like me, he has an unseen anger bubbling inside him, wanting to break out. I unclench my fists.

"Let's hear it," I say.

"Chumley, they released right away. Turned him over to Junebug, who nearly pulled his right ear off, leading him out of the police station. Me, they let wait for my father in the chief's office. When he showed up, the first thing he asked was where you were. He demanded the chief to send a patrol car to your house and have you arrested. He told him that you were the ringleader which, in a way, you were. Only the chief said that he wouldn't go near your place unless I confirmed it. He knew the fury the captain would unleash if it turned out my father was only grasping at political straws. So, he asked me, my father did, in front of the chief. I answered. Like you said, he's my father. That was all the chief needed. On the ride home, I was told how I helped the family business and that with you on the hook, I wasn't the town's only juvenile delinquent, and it's been eating at my guts every day since. I thought I owed you one and this, my friend, is it."

"You don't owe me, Jimmy. Coming out here and telling me what you did took guts, and that's payment enough. And don't worry about your father. These 'markers' he's so keen on — they'll take his money and do his bidding from time to time, but at the end of the day, they're only humoring him, like we do with all wash-ashores. Why do we do this? Because we know that people like your father are not of the Cape mentality, that they'll get frustrated to the point they'll eventually pull up stakes and leave. That's how it is and how it's always been and Dale has yet to understand this. The town elders will wait him out until he's of no more use to them. When that happens, they'll take their lanterns and hike off into the dunes, hoping to call ashore another ship in distress, only to watch it break apart crossing the Bar. We're the descendants of Mooncussers, Jimmy. All of us. The lot."

"I'm going to miss this place," says Jimmy, looking around. "I hope you win, but do me a favor, Cal."

"If I can."

"Promise me that you'll hang up your fishing gear soon. The odds are stacking up and they're not in your favor."

"I'll try, but tell me this before you go. Are you gay? Not that I care either way, but are you?"

"What gave me away?"

"You could have gotten any girl in town, including Jen, but you chose not to."

"Jen knew. She was my 'beard' right up to the day I went away to prep school."

"And your father, does he know? Is that one of the reasons you're leaving?"

"Let's just say good Catholics, like my dad, frown on homosexuality. Not to worry, Cal. You were never on my dance card. See you when I see you," says Jimmy, turning and walking barefoot through the pines.

I want to believe Jimmy, and with what he just told me, it would be a hell of a ruse if he was making it all up. One thing's for sure, the Fates are hard at work. Except that he had lied to me in the past, and if he lied to me once, what's to stop him from lying to me again? Nothing, that's what. If I've learned anything in my dealings with Hallet Paving and Construction, it's to never let my guard down, and that goes for dealing with Jimmy also. I wish him luck with his newfound freedom, knowing that time would tell, as it always does.

I continue hiking due south with sweat seeping from my pores and coating my exposed skin in a thick, milky substance, like my body is producing a sort of sunscreen on its own. I wipe haphazardly at my mouth and it is only then that I remember the snake bite. Swollen to twice its normal size, my hand resembles a catcher's mitt. Could the hognose have been an actual rattlesnake and, more importantly, do I have rattlesnake venom in my veins, on its way to my heart? Who would put a poisonous snake on Monomoy? Certainly not Tiger. He's terrified of snakes, part of his jungle experience, I guess. I am alone, stumbling about a seemingly endless barren without shade, without water, and apparently rattlesnake-bitten to boot!

BLACK DOG

A steady stream of cloud cover moves in from the west, and I am grateful, for it gives my head, back, and shoulders a much-needed reprieve from the pitiless sun that has refused to move from its noontime position. I don't recall these barrens ever taking so long to cross. The valley itself seems to have lengthened since my last visit. And it can happen that fast in this ever-changing landscape. The very light station I am seeking once stood on the east-facing side of Monomoy but now resides on the west-facing side. And yet the station itself has not moved. The wind and the waves are the culprit, taking sand and seed from east Monomoy and depositing it on west Monomoy over the many years, no doubt the reason the light station was finally decommissioned in 1968.

I spot a tall dune standing alone in the distance and go to it. Reaching the summit, I look out across the valley floor. I should be well within sight of the light station's forty-foot iron tower, and while it's possible that it may have blown down during my time away, I don't see that as having happened. The tower and its keeper's quarters have fought off every hurricane and nor'easter since 1848. What's another year? I seriously doubt anybody came out here and knocked down the iron tower. Pockmarked with rust and sand, it would be worthless as scrap, and the birders would have a hissy fit. Where else are you going to see, on the east coast anyway, a bald eagle family nested and feeding their young? Not that I've ever seen a bald eagle on Monomoy, but I've heard tales from those who have.

I am about to continue my journey when I spot a dark shape weaving its way through the dune fields. At first glance, the shape appears to be that of a black dog, perhaps the same black dog I saw earlier standing with Gramp on our bluff. I recognize the animal's clear, marble eyes, only this is no dog, it's a wolf, a timber wolf specifically, tall at the shoulders with long, lean flanks and an elongated snout housing forty-two whiter-than-white teeth, twelve of which are pointed incisors. To the best of my knowledge, the last of its kind to roam these lands was over four hundred years ago. What this wolf is doing on Monomoy, I have not the answer. The wolf doesn't bark, nor does it growl, it just sits at the bottom of the dune looking up at me, transfixed, with its clear, marble eyes appearing to spin in their sockets.

I once crossed paths with such a wolf while hitching Alaska's Alcan Highway. Neither car nor truck had passed me going in either direction in over five hours. I had my subzero sleeping bag with me along with a new flex-pole tent, so I wasn't put out about it, until I came upon a pair of grizzly bears feeding on a caribou on the bank of a river running alongside the highway. Needless to say, it put a hop in my step. I only hoped the bears had had their fill and weren't interested in a skinny fisherman from Cape Cod. Whatever rational fear I had of the grizzlies was quickly washed away as a white wolf emerged from the tree line and crossed onto the road ahead of me.

The wolf appeared to be a lone wolf, with none of its brothers and sisters following. It padded down the middle of the road heading in my direction. Passing each other like a pair of down-on-our-luck hobos, I held my slime knife tightly at my side and kept my eyes focused on the road in front of me. Hiking up a slight rise, I stopped and turned. The white wolf did the same from its position, and for the briefest of moments, our eyes locked. Viewing me as nothing more than a mile marker, the white wolf continued on its way. I did the same, only I couldn't seem to gather enough spit to swallow.

Slowly lifting my right arm to avoid drawing the wolf's attention, I reach behind my back for the speargun but grasp air instead, realizing that I left it leaning behind the cabin's single, slapping door. "Perfect timing," I say to myself. I feel around the inside of my belt for my slime knife, but to show the wolf fear now could bring about a confrontation that I'm not sure I'd win. So, I choose a different tack and hike down the dune with my arms swaying at my sides like I'm going for a walk.

Surprisingly, the black wolf doesn't flatten its ears or bare its teeth as I pass. Instead, it follows me at a respectable distance, stopping and starting as I do, and it is only when I stray too far to the right that it howls or too far to the left that it whimpers. And it is only when I am forging straight ahead, passing through thicket and clambering over dune, that the wolf stays silent, as if guiding me to some final terminus. I stay the course, recalling a proverb once told to me by a Russian berthed fisherman, "Volka nogi kormyat," or "The wolf is kept fed by its feet."

I plod ahead, dimly aware of my surroundings, the swirling wind lifting sand and marl from the valley floor and hurling it at my face, lashing my exposed skin like a beaded whip. So fierce is the wind that I have to bury my chin in the crook of my elbow like some movie vampire stalking a virgin across a stage floor. My knees tremble with effort as I mount what appears to be the last dune. I take what I believe will be my last step. As I do, the wind suddenly ceases with the blustery maelstrom dying out as quickly as it began.

Shaking sand from my shaggy topknot, I rub my eye sockets while snorting like a bull, expelling globs of sandy snot from my nostrils. Bent at the waist, I continue coughing up phlegm, and when I look at my snakebit hand, I see the swelling is gone, the venom having apparently run its course, and when I look behind me, I see that the black wolf also has vanished, like the ghost that I knew it to be.

BOOK III

"Our anchor we'll weigh
and our sails we will set,
the friends we leave today,
we will leave with regret."

sailor shanty

POINT RIP

Dropping onto the declining shoreline, I pivot to the south and walk the water's edge, listening to the rocks along the shore clack and smack against each other in the retreating surf. I look further out to where a new sandbar has formed, new to me anyway, and watch the thundering rollers rear up with vengeful sneers, only to be denied true landfall after traveling all the way from the coast of Africa. At least there's no mythical sea monster lifting its scaly head from the surf.

Hiking further along, I come to the place where the ocean meets the Sound. The French navigator Samuel de Champlain named this outlying bar '*Cap Mallebarre*,' loosely translated to mean "Cape of the Evil Sandbar," and many a doomed sailor has proven Champlain right over the years. The bar is now known as Point Rip, because of the strong currents that exist here, pulling a menagerie of sea creatures into the Sound by day only to reverse course at night when the moon rises to pull the reluctant creatures back into the North Atlantic. And while it might not look impressive on first viewing, just an oval slab of sand forever dissolving into the sea, but beyond that seemingly dull edge, potent currents war with one another, making it the fastest-moving water on the Cape. For a child to stick a toe in would be uneventful, but if an adult were to wade in waist deep, they'd be sucked out with no chance of ever returning, except perhaps bloated and bitten on the incoming tide.

The collapsing waves burst in aqua colors as I continue down the beach. This is the place where the Timekeeper paints his greatest masterpiece, forever wiping his canvas clean and starting anew. A wild place where mankind is reduced to mere spectatorship, not having the higher inclination nor imagination to attempt something so astonished. Further along, the shoreline curves southwest, and I come to the pair of blackened monoliths jutting from the water's edge like the bottom jaw of some long-extinct beast. These "Teeth," as they are referred to, have scared away mariners going back to the pilgrim days and beyond. As kids, however, we'd sail straight through them; the surging tide acting as a watery tongue, lifting each boat like a pill before swallowing us whole and depositing our boats high onto the beach along with a mouthful of foamy slather.

Once beached, we'd divide into teams with the older kids usually choosing to be the guards, leaving Jimmy, me, and Chumley as Vikings storming an English castle. That meant having to scale a perilous cliff rising some fifty feet from the beach to the bluff where the decommissioned Monomoy Light Station served as the castle. There's nothing like a good rock fight. Even though you're not trying to hurt each other, you're still throwing as hard and as accurately as you can.

I walk to the base of the cliff and recall the day Jimmy got himself halfway up undetected. Chumley was behind him, swarming at his heels, with me keeping the older kids busy with rocks thrown from my own pile on the beach. On this day the older kids were under the command of a boy with the nickname Chip. He got the nickname from a broken front tooth that his family had never fixed. The scion of the Eldredge clan, Chip was a victim of his ancestors' genetic heritage. Basically, he had no neck, like he was hit on the head with a carnival sledgehammer, not that I gave a damn. His appearance might have been the reason for his meanness, but that was no excuse. He was just mean is all. Chip liked to pick on the smaller, quieter kids and he had never been challenged until that day.

———————

Handhold by handhold, Jimmy makes his way up the exposed cliff-face with Chumley at his feet, dragging his extended girth along him. I remain on the beach, throwing rocks up the cliff. My actions cause Chip to show himself at the rim, red-faced and angry.

"We're not set up yet!" Chip hollers down.

"Vikings attack! That's what we do!" I shout back.

"Vikings were tall, not puny like you," Chip laughs. "Was your mother one of those pygmies they got in Africa?"

"Leave my mother out of it!" I protest, throwing a good-sized stone that lands harmlessly at Chip's feet, like I threw up a grape.

"Who taught you how to throw, Cal, your dad? Oh, that's right, he croaked. Couldn't swim, way I heard it. Shoulda been wearing one of 'em floaties they give to little kids. Might've saved his ass!"

Drawing back, I fire up another rock, only this one clears the rim and sails over the parade grounds. I hear it smash into one of the keepers' quarters' windows, many of which are already broken from previous conquests.

"Must have hit a nerve!" Chip laughs at his fellow castle guards. Looking up and down the beach, he asks, "Where are your punk friends? They sail off and leave you?"

"You'll be seeing them soon enough," I grumble.

"Surprise attack, hey?" asks Chip, looking behind him.

"Prepare to be outflanked, Fang Face!" I yell. As I do, Chumley loses his footing and slides down the cliff sending up a cloud of hazy, brown dust. Chip drops to his knees and peers over the raised rim.

"Why if it isn't Master Hallet coming to get us," laughs Chip. Turning to his fellow castle guards, he continues, "We have guests, boys! What say we give these Norsemen a proper English welcome!" I throw another rock and hit Chip on his right hip. Rubbing his hip, Chip points down at me and says, "I'll deal with you later, Forrest!" To his castle guards, he shouts, "Find me something big! This is going to be fun!"

Chumley starts back up the cliff as I run around replenishing my rock pile. In short order, Chip is handed a dirt bomb the size of a bowling ball. Lifting the loosely formed mass above his head, Chip hollers, "Wakey wakey! Eggs and bacy!" and lets the dirt bomb drop from his hands.

"Incoming!" I yell.

Pressed against the cliff-face, Jimmy avoids the dirt bomb, but Chumley isn't so lucky. The rock-infested clump explodes across his exposed chest and sends him plummeting down the cliff for a second time, landing on the hard-packed sand at the base with an audible thud.

"How'd that feel, Tonto?" bellows Chip, with his fellow castle guards collapsing in laughter around him.

I don't see the rock until it's too late. The pain is heavy and sharp. I collapse on my knees and pitch forward, pressing my throbbing cheek against the cool, wet sand, trying to muffle my cries.

"I can't miss!" says Chip, to the cheers of his guards. "Two down, one to go!" Turning his attention to the raised rim, Chip goes down all fours and peeks over the lip, encouraging, "Keep climbing, Jimmy. Few more feet and you'll be in range, and no amount of your rich daddy's money is goin' to save you this time."

"It's not worth it!" I yell up the cliff, holding my swollen jaw.

"Sure, it's worth it, Jimmy," Chip retorts. "Don't listen to Cal. He's a quitter, like his old man. But not you, Jimmy. You're no quitter!" Chip and his castle guards whip their hands over their heads and pummel Jimmy with rocks. Hugging the cliff, Jimmy takes the barrage and keeps climbing. I leave my dwindling rock pile behind and run to where Chumley sits upright on the beach, coughing up dirt.

"We need to create a diversion."

"A what?"

"Diversion. I need you to run a buttonhook so I can sneak up the backside."

"Out there?" Chumley asks, pointing to the strand of beach stretched out before us. "Are you kidding? I'll get plunked for sure."

"Jimmy's getting pummeled. It's our only chance."

"Why don't you run and I'll climb?"

"We already tried that."

"Right. Damn, I shoulda brought my football helmet."

I clap Chumley on his back, inadvertently causing another coughing fit, and run to the base of the cliff. Resigned to his fate, Chumley drops into a three-point stance and calls out, "Red 23! Red 23! Set! Hike!" and he is off the blocks and running. Cutting left and then to the right, he turns it on and heads for the boats. I take the opportunity and begin pulling myself up the backside of the cliff with the help of an exposed tree root, and I am halfway to the top when I hear one of the castle guards call out, "We got a runner!" I turn to watch Chumley finish his buttonhook, and he is almost to the cover of the boats when a flat-rock skips off the back of his head and pitches him face-first into the surf.

"Another winner!" shouts Chip from above the rim. "How'd that feel, fatass?"

I continue climbing undetected. Nearing the top, I slip over the raised rim and roll to the right and out of sight. I lie on my stomach behind a stand of red heather, watching Chip and his guards roll an enormous boulder up to the raised rim. Chip looks over the lip, saying, "I'll say this for ya', rich kid, you're one tough SOB. But guess what, I've got another rock, and this time it's all she wrote. Get ready to go beddy-bye!"

I leave my camouflaged post and approach Chip and his castle guards from behind. Quickly closing the distance, I push the guards off the cliff one by one. Standing face-to-face with a confused Chip, I ask him a simple question, "Can penguins fly?"

"How the hell should I know? I'm not a fucking penguin!"

As he says this, Jimmy comes over the raised rim and, wrapping his arms around Chip's waist, lifts Chip high into the air and tosses him backwards. I glance over the lip watching Chip fall, the loose rocks from his splayed fingers appearing to rise above him. Cupping my hands, I call down, "Are now! Better start flapping your wings!"

I stand with Jimmy on the rim, rubbing my swollen jaw that's probably broken. Jimmy, the back of his T-shirt in shreds and his neck and shoulders covered in angry welts, doesn't seem to notice; he just smiles at me. I smile back. Chumley joins us at the rim, rubbing his freshly beaned skull and grinning stupidly like his namesake, Chumley the Walrus.

Chip and his fellow castle guards peel one another from the hard-packed sand and return to their boats. Pushing the boats into the surf, they sail out through the Teeth, not wanting to retake the castle. The three of us stand on the rim. Taking one another by the hand, we raise our arms and shout in unison, "Valhalla! Valhalla! Valhalla! Vikings forever!"

Approaching the cliff face, I pull myself up on the same exposed tree root. I gain a foothold on the extended lip and roll my body over the raised rim. I stand facing the Monomoy Light Station, set behind overgrown parade grounds with its withered and paintless flagpole flying flagless as it has since the day I first sailed out here. The forty-foot cast iron tower has remained, surprisingly, but the sheets of hurricane-strength glass that once surrounded the light are gone as is the powerful light itself. Strange that I wasn't able to see the tower from the barrens.

Attached to the tower like a thumb is to a hand is the keeper's quarters. With its patches of missing shingles and windows long since punched black, the quarters resemble a sunbaked skull picked at by vultures more than it does a bunkhouse. Most of the outlying structures are gone, blown away by the wind, but there is another structure that has remained: the generator house.

Built entirely of Barnstable red brick, with no windows to let the weather in, the house sits off by itself as if orphaned. I go to the cast-iron door and check that it's locked, and it is, and I'm glad that it is. I'm not ready to revisit what happened inside. I leave it alone and continue walking to where the trail begins that will lead me down to the Powder Hole. It's the same pathway Tiger and I took on that windless, soulless night a year ago to the day, and we weren't alone.

THE POWDER HOLE

S tepping onto the trail, I focus on the ground under my feet and I can almost see the footprints we made that night, the two of us lifting our heavy burden over the dunes, struggling with it *here* and stopping to rest *there*. Before hitting the trail that night, I dug a ditch and filled it with the dead man's clothes: black hoodie, black T-shirt and jeans, black boots. The underwear I let the dead man keep, along with his socks. Dousing the pile with lighter fluid, I lit a match and set it all aflame. I sat down on the soft sand and watched the clothes burn while Tiger was inside the generator house doing the wet work: breaking teeth, clipping off fingertips, and gouging out any noticeable scar tissue. It was after he brought the body outside that I had him lay it out on a ream of sailcloth before taking over and double stitching the sail over the body, then tying the leftover cloth into a monkey's fist, as is sailor tradition.

Our trip to the Powder Hole took place without comment or stall, and I recall the moon being at its fullest, casting the surrounding dunescape in a sterile, fluorescent glow. Carrying the body between us, we came off a high dune and descended onto a lush moorland where creatures of various size peeked out at us from the bush, their bestial eyes flashing in the gloom. I knew not what they thought of our nighttime excursion and did not care, for I was past the point of sorrow. I was mooncussing.

I'm walking backwards, carrying the shoulders, with Tiger walking forward, carrying the feet, the body sagging between us like a cheap sheet of plywood, having not yet undergone rigor mortis. Struggling with the body, we come over a steep rise where a vast expanse of flat-calm water the color of coal is laid out below, the moonlight bleeding into as if it were a black hole set deep in the cosmos. Following the dimly lit pathway winding down the slope, we soon find ourselves carrying the body over a rock and shell-strewn shoreline. The air is especially foul here, stale and pungent. Not the fetid stench of low tide, but something else that can best be described as dead, and dead we are, only one of us deader than the other two.

After laying the body out on a spongy bed of tidal marl, I look down at my onetime friend and wish it were me sewn inside the sail-cloth. No more pain and heartache, just a peaceful descent into the abyss followed by the long-forgotten dream of some eternal reward. Except I'm lying to myself. I don't wish it was me stitched inside, and as far as my onetime friend is concerned, the dead don't get to wish, they only know that they are dead if they know anything.

I am alone with my thoughts when Tiger, hunting around the tall grass, comes out with a pair of shell-encrusted cinder blocks no doubt left behind from a long ago mooring. I watch him clear away clumps of sea grass and petrified barnacle, using only his ragged fingernails to scrape the blocks clean. I remain detached, not believing that we are actually doing this, that it's a dream, a nightmare that I will eventually wake up from. Only it's not a dream. It's real and I'm the cause of it. Me. Nobody else. And I'll have to live with that, like I'm doing now.

I watch Tiger take a coil of thickly woven rope from his duffel bag and wrap the body from head to toe. Threading the remaining line through the eyes of the cinder blocks, he secures the rope in a bowling knot and lifts the blocks. I take my cue and pick up the body. Dragging it into the water with Tiger following, we wade out as far as we can before swimming with the body to where I believe the middle of the Powder Hole to be. Then, without prayer or ceremony, Tiger lets go of the cinder blocks and I let go of the body, watching it sink in the murky black water before swimming back to shore.

Cutting across the dunes, I try retracing the path we took that night but seeing that it's day and not night, I don't have to try so hard. Mounting a high dune, I see again the Powder Hole laid out below, reflecting the sun like a frying pan caught on fire. I find it hard to imagine there was a town here once: Whitewash Village. Population 200. A tavern for sailors and a public schoolhouse #13 teaching students K-12 the three Rs. The people of the village dried and packed cod and mackerel, storing them in packing sheds perfumed with fish oil before shipping the dried meat by schooner to the fish piers of Boston and all the way to Manhattan. Once a deep, natural harbor, the Powder Hole has long since been sealed off from the Sound, what with the many hurricanes, nor'easters, blizzards, and such.

To walk its shoreline, as I am doing now, you'd think that you were walking on sand, only you're not, not really. What appears to be sand is, in actuality, the pulverized skeletons of thousands of dead fish, making the Powder Hole a truly Dead Sea and more than apt for what we were doing that night. I try recalling where Tiger and I waded in with the body but can now only remember the day of the killing, and not the night, for whatever reason. Any and all memories before or after, I draw a blank. I don't even remember hiking out here or why I'm here. I can't make sense of it.

Over the past year, I forced myself never to think of the actual killing and I've gotten pretty good at it. Only now I believe the time is right to remember what happened on that day and why. Once I see the actual body, I will have made the journey and life for me will go on, whether I get my money or not. I've always viewed what Tiger and I were doing, as far as the grow goes, as a means to an end. Basically, to get the town and Dale Hallet off Gramp's and my backs.

Tiger obviously had other plans for his share but he never mentioned them and I never asked. Doesn't take much to live a happy life and, looking back on it as I have on this trip, I realize that I didn't have it so bad. While hypnotic and chaotic at times, this journey I've taken to get to this spot, I feel has been good for me, not that I can remember any of it right now, only that it's been harsh and yet cleansing at the same time. Only to be truly cleansed, I must finally come to grips with what I did or didn't do, and for that, I must force myself to remember what happened on that fateful day while not leaving anything out. Not that I have a choice.

It was a day like any other July day on the Outer Cape, hot and humid with a 50 percent chance of a late afternoon thunderstorm. I'd been wet trimming since dawn, first cutting down the sturdy stalks with Mr. Rondike's razor-sharp machete, then bucking off the buds and hanging them to dry in the midday sun. The work is repetitive as it is rewarding and also tiring, but I don't mind, knowing it to be the first and last harvest of its kind. With Tiger out patrolling the surrounding wood and thus making himself a buffer to any nosey camper who might hear the commotion and want to investigate, I continued on unconcerned, hacking away and breaking a sweat. Though, to be truthful, to get to our grow site, said camper would have to be a hell of a woodsman.

I put the grow spot on the three acres we own that were farthest from the house, deeply wooded with no roads anywhere nearby and yet still within hose distance of our furthest and biggest kettle pond. I also put it there in the event the grow might be raided and I could claim ignorance. After all, how can one person, whether they own the land or not, be responsible for policing six-hundred-plus acres, most of which are situated deep within our wood? I could blame Dale and his rich Nantucket buddies who surveyed the land without Gramp's permission, and it would be a win-win.

I also made sure that it wouldn't be an easy trek through the wood with no trail leading in or out, and that we wouldn't use the same pathway twice when we came and went. Given my slight stature and that I grew up in this wood, I knew more Indian trails than Tiger ever knew existed, and there were some trails where Tiger had to go down on all fours to follow me.

I am nearly done. All that's left is to double-bag the leaves and buds and carry them out. The hardest part will be carrying the bags through the wood and into our barn, then stashing them in the bed of the IH, under a tarp brimming with freshly cut brush. The bags themselves, once filled, stand as tall as a trash can and weigh anywhere from thirty to sixty pounds. I expect the harvest to yield up to sixty bags, give or take.

Once loaded, Tiger is to then drive the IH, bucking and stalling, to New Hampshire, where he'll deliver the harvest to a fellow Nam bro of his who also happens to be the sergeant at arms for a local Hells Angels chapter. After the weighing and the paying, I'll have washed my hands of the matter, that is, until Tiger returns with the profits. My job was to plant and grow the seedlings, which I did, the harvest itself being more bountiful than Tiger and I could have possibly imagined. His job was to find a buyer and drive the truck, and hopefully, that's what he did.

Tiger had yet to tell me what his plans were for his share of the split, but I expected it to involve his daughter and her twin boys. If Gramp knew what we were up to, he never mentioned it, choosing to remain inside the house and not take his weekly strolls through the wood. Me, I'm not sure what I'll do with the money. I could hand it over to the bloodsucking town to pay off our debt, but how would I justify it? It's not like I have my own fishing boat and crew to wash the money. I get paid in cash and I'm so far off the grid that I don't exist, like most fishermen I know. And that's when I saw it: a large, shadowy figure looming within the wood.

I go about cutting down the remaining stalks. Could be a deer, only a deer wouldn't stray so close to camp. A deer would have heard me slashing away and run off. From the corner of my eye, I watch the figure skulking behind a vine-entangled pitch pine off to my right. I continue the work while furtively scanning the ravine. The figure moves from the pine to behind a black oak. I pretend not to notice. The figure appears to be that of a man, wearing a black hooded sweatshirt, black sweatpants, and black combat boots. I have no idea who the man is or what he's doing so deep in our wood, and I find it hard to believe that someone could get past Tiger, but there he is, hunched behind the oak, watching me.

I take a step back, pretending to admire my handiwork. I take another step back and hear a branch break, then another. Quickly I turn around to see the man dashing through the wood in the opposite direction, and it is then that I recognize the figure. Hanging my head, I drop the machete and give chase.

A strong wind whistles through the trees like a funeral dirge to carry me forward through the wood like a reaper of lost souls. Rather than chase the hooded figure, I head for the trailhead, knowing the grow to be surrounded by impenetrable bramble. Small branches snap and crack off to my right and I know that he's in the thick of it. Hurtling a moss-covered stump, I hike up and over a tall berm before sprinting down a natural depression to where the intruder comes into view, tangled in bramble and thrashing about.

Running low to the ground, I close the distance quickly and hit the man in the small of his back, bursting the both of us through the thicket and tumbling down the east-facing slope of the largest kettle pond. I grab hold of a thorny rosebush and stop my descent. The hooded intruder isn't so lucky as he continues down the slope, cart-wheeling the whole way before finally splashing into the pond.

I pick my way down the slope, watching the man favor his right hip as he lopes about the shallow water. Stepping onto the narrow beach, I wade into the pond and approach the intruder from behind. The man continues to struggle within his sodden sweatshirt. I take hold of his hood and drag him further into the pond. I can't see his face, but I do notice his bottom jaw and mouth working feverishly, trying to tell me something. Only I can't hear him, the thunderous beating of my heart muffling all sound.

Placing my left hand on top of the man's head, I push him under, with his two hands fighting against my one, but to no avail. A stream of air escapes his nostrils as I turn my arm into a steel bar, knowing that soon he will take his first breath. I imagine the man's pupils expanding, then dilating under the hood, and there is a moment of violent thrashing before the man's bottom jaw stretches wide, and he drinks it all in. Floating languidly within my grip, the man leaves the world with nothing left to hold him. A shadow falls over the action. I look up the slope and see Tiger standing on the western rim silhouetted against a bloodred sun. He has his M16 slung over his right shoulder with its barrel pointed down, shaking his head back and forth while he kicks aimlessly at the ground.

As my brain defogs, I seem to recall there being a defunct pier near where we scuttled the body that night, and as I look to my left, I see a row of wooden pilings marching into the tepid water like a company of drowning infantry. I align my body with the pier and wade into the marl. Sinking up to my chest, I swim out to where the pilings end, then, facing due east, I swim to the spot where I believe we sank the body. I tread water as I position myself over the spot. Taking a breath, I sink below the surface and sound, and I am at zero visibility with the water around me clouded with muck and marl like I'm swimming inside a liquefied sandbox.

My heartbeat pounds in my ears as I touch bottom and sweep my arms back and forth, hoping to clear my vision, but it's of no use, so I swim blindly onward. I am about to resurface when the knuckles on my right-hand brush against a coarse, flat object that I know to be a cinder block, given my days bringing up lost moorings. Plunging both hands into the swirling silt, I locate the cinder blocks and follow the cabled rope to the body, still tightly wrapped in sailcloth. The water mysteriously clears and I notice the sailcloth is punctured with holes, no doubt from the various creatures feeding from within.

Taking my slime knife from behind my belt, I begin the arduous underwater task of cutting through the intricate stitching covering the intruder's face and head. I watched my childhood chum die through a watery lens that day, and as I cut through the last of the stitching and pull back the sailcloth, the face is finally revealed, and it's a face only a mother would recognize, that mother being Junebug. The flesh appears translucent, with both cheekbones visible under the skin, along with wavy strands of chestnut hair having grown long and curly during its soggy interment. The eyes and tongue are missing, of course, no doubt eaten by the crabs and other shellfish that somehow survive here, and his nose has been picked at by something.

I expect to feel more emotion, but I don't. Afloat above the body, I leave the face exposed and cut further along the stitching so that more creatures can get at him, for as Gramp always says, "The most vicious creature in the sea is the lowly starfish. Into its belly we go, bones and all, as if we were never here but for the ship's log."

I step from the water peeling strands of eelgrass from my legs, waist, and chest before taking a seat on a knotty piece of driftwood to wring out my sopping, sandy hair. I look about my surroundings and try to imagine how it was before the wind and the waves took it all away, only I can't. Memories are for those who lived them, taking the truth of the times to their graves with the broken slabs of concrete poking out from the dunes their only postcards.

To ask for forgiveness now would be farcical. He'll never forgive me, so why bother? How was I to know that Chumley wasn't a cop at the time, that he'd gotten canned for writing too many parking tickets to the wrong people? What was he doing out there in the first place? I knew what he was doing; he was spying on my operation. Bringing in a bust like that, he knew, would put him right back in uniform. He went looking for it and he got what he deserved.

I do feel bad about Junebug's endless searching. Her "visions" sure didn't tell her anything. According to the one and only letter written by Gramp that actually reached me, he wrote that after Chumley went missing, Junebug showed up at our parlor door begging Gramp to get in touch with me, asking that I go to California after I was done fishing to look for "her Jonathan." Rumor was, according to the letter, that after getting canned, he skipped off to the Golden State to try out for the Raiders and hopefully make the team as a walk-on. It was a dream he'd shared with his onetime cop buddies. I never wrote

Gramp back because I couldn't. The return postage would have left me vulnerable should anyone be looking for me. I kept sending him his grocery money, only I did it through Tiger whom, up until that point, I trusted. I don't know if Gramp ever got the money, but he's alive, so he must have. Needless to say, I never went to Oakland.

Free and clear is how I see it, although I don't feel free and clear. More like pursued and hunted. Truth be told, it was a good piece of police work. Takes a Mooncusser to catch a Mooncusser and Chumley, though flawed, was a Mooncusser. I only wish he'd used his talents for going after the real criminals, like Jimmy's dad. They might call themselves politicians, prancing about town shaking hands and kissing babies, but when they're not cutting ribbons and playing in charitable golf tournaments, they're dining for free and strong-arming local business owners for kickbacks and campaign contributions.

At least Officer Repoza wasn't one to take a bribe unless it was a cold beer. Given the chance, he might have done some good for the town, but instead, he came after me. Everything I had worked for was at risk: the house, the land, Gramp's care, my freedom. I couldn't let him get away. I had to act and I did. Why should I be ashamed and blamed? I didn't come after him, he came after me and he paid the final price.

GENERATOR HOUSE

Slogging through the dunes, I come to the back of the keeper's quarters. From here, I can either drop into the barrens and head for my boat or continue on. I choose the latter. It's as good a place as any to hide the money. For all I know, there's nothing here, but if something is there, I'll have to use all my five senses, and maybe a sixth, to find it.

Stepping over a tall stand of coastal panic grass, I come to the kitchen door at the back of the quarters. I reach for the doorknob and jiggle it, knowing that it will be locked, and it is, only I know where Tiger hides a spare key. I lift the third shingle to the right of the knob, and a rust-coated key drops into my palm. Unlocking the door, I step into the kitchen, where I start a search of the place, first pulling out drawers and opening cabinets, then looking under the fridge and tapping on the walls.

I don't expect to find anything, and I don't, but for the petrified remains of a deer mouse and a handful of crud-encrusted flatware. The light station plays host to a troop of Boy Scouts in early June and apparently, there's no merit badge for washing dishes. I leave the kitchen and wander into the living quarters. It's no Grand Hall, with a low ceiling under which one can barely stand, along with threadbare chairs and a long, beach-wood table leaning crookedly in the corner, appearing to hold the whole place up.

The room's many south-facing windows have long since been punched out by rocks thrown by me and others over the years, but the paneless windows continue to let in sunlight, along with a flock of small, brown Harris's sparrows that dart and dive about, making a noisy nuisance of themselves. I bat away the birds until they settle on the sills and hush. I recall there being some sort of bathroom off to my right, more like a hole in the floor, along with bunk rooms upstairs, but whatever is hidden, if there is anything hidden, will be hidden here.

Skipping the oaken armoire, sitting heavily in the corner, I focus my attention instead on the pinewood floorboards. On hands and knees, I sweep away the loose rocks and drum my fingers on the wood, listening for a loose plank and in no time do I find a two-by-eight-inch with its penny nails missing at both ends. Using the blunt edge of my slime knife, I ease the board up and set it aside. Sinking my right arm into the narrow slit, I feel around the cold, damp sand. I continue until my splayed fingers land on a canvas satchel of some kind. I lift the satchel through the slit and place it on my lap. Unzipping the satchel, I take out Tiger's M16, minus its firing pin. I set rifle and satchel aside and reach again into the slit.

Sinking my right arm up to my armpit, I stretch out and pat the sand. After two or three sweeps, my fingers land on a squarish, metallic object. I drag the object across the sand inch by inch. Using my slime knife, I take its pointed tip and unscrew another plank, then put it aside. I carefully bring the box up to sight, only it's not a box, it's an ammo can painted Army green. I shake the can and hear what sounds like loose paper jostling inside that could be money.

Placing the can on the floorboards, I sit staring at it. The reason for my long absence at sea, the toil of the harvest, and the ultimate sacrifice it took, could all be inside. I'm reluctant to open it — having worked so hard for so long, I'm not sure that I can take another disappointment. I feel like a kid on Christmas morn holding a brightly wrapped present that's hissing from within. Bending forward, I release the side latches and crack open the lid. I see that it's not money inside but Tiger's personal papers: his honorary military discharge from the Army Rangers along with a copy of his birth certificate – Tiberius Forrest Watson, born Stillwater, Mississippi, January 19, 1954. I find his middle name a bit disconcerting. While I'm sure, there are many people spread about the globe with the surname of Forrest, though I'm not sure how many spell it with two r's instead of one. I've never met any, but that doesn't mean they're not out there.

Normally, a middle name is a name you get from an uncle or aunt or grandfather, etc. Or it's a religious name, but it can also be a surname from a previous generation. Is Tiger a relation from a previous generation? Perhaps he came from the loins of a long-lost uncle or cousin? Is that why Gramp let him camp in our wood and grow whatever he wanted to grow, legal or otherwise? Is this another secret Gramp's held back from me in a lifetime of secrets that I was never quite old enough or mature enough to ever hear, even today?

I toss aside Tiger's childhood photos of his Lizabeth, along with pictures of her now grown-up, towheaded sons. Instead, I focus on a black-and-white snapshot of a couple standing in front of a tarpapered shotgun shack. Tiger's Ma and Pa, I believe. I check them for any family resemblance and don't find any. Tossing the snapshot over my right shoulder, I dig deeper into the can and take out what looks to be a property title attached to a bill of sale. I look at the title and see the address to be 23 Shore Road, the one-time address of the Salem Witch, and according to the bill of sale, the address is now the home of one Tiger F Watson. And there at the bottom is Gramp's scribbled name followed by the date of purchase: August 20 of last year.

With my heart beating like a snare drum, I pick up the bill of sale and look at the sale price. $357,000. Cheap for around here, but not that cheap. I go over the numbers in my head and come to the conclusion that Tiger bought the house with my share of the profits while no doubt pocketing his share to spend on his daughter and her boys. I leaf through the paperwork, and it appears to be perfectly legal, with even the town clerk signing off on it. Only wouldn't they want to know where the money came from? Surely Tiger's meager ranger salary wouldn't cover it. And then I see a thick roll of US Treasury check stubs at the bottom of the ammo can.

I undo the heavy rubber band and scan the dates; they go back to when Tiger rotated out of the Army for the last time, some twenty years and counting. Digging deeper into the can, I find Tiger's bank statement from August of last year. I look at the deposits he made that month and see that they're all from his US Treasury checks that never expire until they are cashed, totaling $310K. I stare at the bank statement and then I get it. Tiger's been living on his summer grow money and stashing away his monthly military checks, or CRSC – Combat Related Special Compensation, for a rainy day. That day finally came when he bought the old girl's house from Gramp, and thereby washing clean both of our shares. Brilliant!

Gramp's had the money the whole time I've been away, but I wouldn't have known any of it because I was jumping from deck to deck, hiding. Why didn't he tell me that he or we owned the witch's house all these years? I know why because he wanted to keep me here, but I also see why he did it. I was, and probably still am, a young upstart and he was afraid that I'd sell the house out from under him to escape my bondage. He's right, I would have, but I would have paid off our back taxes in full before I ever touched a penny.

I only hope that Gramp gave the proceeds to the town and didn't buy the Chatham Squire. He should have trusted me. After all, it's me who's shipped out since I was a kid, risking my life to keep our collective chins above the waterline. Perhaps Gramp knew of our mooncussing but kept it to himself, keeping away from our grow, and was awaiting my return to tell me the good news. Either way, the weight I've been carrying, where it concerns our land, has finally been lifted from my shoulders. I feel my true age again. Not twenty-two, battered and beat down, but twenty-two, youthful and full of promise.

The world is again my oyster! At least with Tiger, the witch's house stays within the family, so to speak, and not the Chatham Historical Society. If they really were a historical society, they would have erected a statue of Captain Nehi on Gould Park long ago, only the town's so-called "upper crust" have always looked sideways at the Forrest Clan, so they can go screw themselves. My heart fills with mirth as I replace the documents, pictures, and check stubs. Tiger's rifle, minus its firing pin, I put back inside the canvas satchel and zip it closed. Placing both the can and the satchel back under the floor-boards, I then refit the planks as I found them and screw down the two-penny nails.

Once outside, I put the rusted key behind the third shingle to the left of the kitchen doorknob and head for the barrens and back to my boat. Passing the generator house, I notice that its cast-iron door is slightly ajar. How can that be? When I checked the door earlier, it was locked. Tiger has the only key on a chain that he keeps around his neck, so if some Boy Scouts get trapped inside, he'll be able to get them out. That's why he always keeps the door bolted and also to keep prying eyes from seeing the blood-soaked floorboards that might still be wet in spots. Perhaps a strong wind blew it open, only the heavy door opens inward and not outward, as it appears now.

"Hey, Tiger! Are you in there?" I call out. "It's Caleb. Got back this morn, at least, I think I did. Gramp told me about the sale. Let's you and me go to the Squire and pound some brews!"

Crickets is what I hear in return, literally from inside the structure. I go to the door. Using both hands and driving with my legs, I push it wider. With the sun shining straight down, as it has the day long, all I see is the doorframe with the interior remaining a mystery. I peer into the darkness and notice a flaming set of firelit eyes looking back at me from the pitch. A deep, throaty growl follows, forcing me to take a step back, and then another as the black wolf emerges from the abyss, its long, tapered ears flattened against its thick skull, snarling viciously with its elongated snout dripping rabid foam. I turn and take off at a dead run.

I race across the parade grounds with the wolf fast at my heels, nipping at my flailing ankles and calves. With my legs furiously pump-ing, I run for the raised rim and jump. Plunging down the cliff face, I land on my side on the hard-packed sand and groan. My body vibrates from impact as I lie in the fetal position expecting the wolf to be at my throat any second. And yet when I finally look up, I see not the black wolf but *Sea Gypsy*, dragged beyond the high tide mark, fully canvassed. I crawl to my boat and begin pushing her into the drawing surf, not knowing or caring how she got there.

Standing in the surf, I climb aboard at the stern and take up the mainsheet. The mains'l fills with an off-shore breeze as I kick the tiller to starboard and sail out between the Teeth. Chancing a backwards glance over my right shoulder, I look to the rim where the black wolf stands in stark relief against the forever-setting sun. Throwing back its bony head, the wolf lets out a long, mournful howl as a Blood Wolf Moon begins to form on the eastern horizon.

TOBY

I follow an underwater jetty that begins in the dunes and continues far out to sea in an orderly formation. I try a northerly tack, but the offshore wind is still too strong to come about, along with the outgoing tide that continues to draw well past its allotted hour. If I were a religious man, which I'm not, I might suspect the Timekeeper was tipping the world in an effort to thwart my retreat. A bump on the head doesn't explain these visions I've been having, nor does having drunk too much seawater or sailing under the hot sun the day long. What I'm experiencing goes deeper. These events are somehow real and happening in real time. The bite marks on my heels and calves are proof enough of that. I need to talk to someone, have them tell me that I have air in my lungs and blood coursing through my veins, and that I'm not crazy.

The wind and tide carry me further from land, and I feel the nausea coming back on. I am fearful of another attack. To retch again like that, especially on an empty stomach, might rupture the linings of my esophagus, and if that were to happen, all would be lost. I try stifling the nausea by recalling a more pleasant memory where I was more the reluctant hero and not a ghoul.

And for that, I am returned to the Big Race. I wasn't so much excited about the race as I was the chance to see Toby again. Only instead of being abovedecks, as Skipper Mack had hinted, he put me belowdecks, in "the sewer" as it was known, racing about the small hull attaching jib and spinnaker, then sending them skyward. I wasn't too upset about it, being that my favorite pastime was watching Toby leap crosswise over the hatch, her tanned and trim legs flashing in the sunlight as she traveled up the 110-foot mast to clear a halyard or straighten a jib.

On this particular day, we were set to go on a practice run against a boat and crew from the Netherlands on course B, two or so miles south of Point Loma. Heading out to the course, I was allowed to stand on deck and sing fight songs along with the crew, and I was belowdecks when the boats lined up. And it was there I remained, in the sewer, waiting for Dennis, the lead sail trimmer, to call down for a sail change. Truth be told, I felt at peace within the confines of the hull, listening to the boat thump against the oncoming rush of wave, and I was alone with my thoughts when the second horn blew, causing *Hard Charger* to abruptly change course, sending my forehead slamming against the fiberglass hull.

"Did we hit a whale?" Toby calls down, the twisted tendrils of her golden hair filling the open hatch.

"Only my brain," I answer, rubbing the lump rising on my brow.

"Are you okay?" she asks.

"Right as rain!" I reply, pulling myself up with the help of the sunken mast.

"Where's the spinnaker Dennis called for?" asks Toby. "It's blowing a doozy up here!"

"Coming right up!" I holler back, the bump on my head beating like it has a heart of its own. Toby shakes her golden locks from the hatch and disappears to shout orders at the crew. Taking a fresh spinnaker from its stowed compartment, I attach it to a halyard and send it topside. Mission accomplished, I take hold of the sunken mast and hug it, fearing another one-sided bout with the hull.

I am still hugging the sunken mast when shouting erupts abovedecks. Peeking my head over the hatch, I am greeted with a wave to the face and fierce winds whistling past my ears. Sweeping back my wet hair, I look at the crew hiking off the portside with their wind-burnt faces cocked skyward. I follow their gaze to see Toby, strapped inside a safety harness, swinging like a tether ball fifty feet up the mast.

"Little warning next time you haul in!" she shouts down.

"Always go up with one hand on the mast!" answers her father from the helm, spinning the Big Wheel to starboard and then to port.

"Nice bump ya' got there, fisherman," says Billy Boondocks, sitting at the base of the mast, working the coffee grinders — brutally turning the stainless-steel winches to trim the giant mains'l.

"Feels more like Mount Olympus," I say back, touching at the beating bump.

"Did my time in the sewer. Tight as hell down there. Why Mack hired you. Remember to keep your knees bent with your hands at your sides ready to shoot out."

"I'll remember."

"Oh. One more thing."

"What's that?"

"Puke on a clean white sail doesn't look good on camera. The TV boys don't like it, and neither do I when I bring them up. So, try not to get sick."

"I'll do my best."

Spotting my head poking above the hatch, Skipper Mack takes off one of his boat shoes and throws it at me, shouting, "Get the hell off my deck!" Ducking back below the hatch, I stumble about the sewer like a drunken sailor. I take Billy's advice and bend my knees, keeping my hands at my sides ready to shoot out. But before I can gain a solid footing, another wave slams into the hull with thunderous force that sends me skidding on my backside.

"Sleeping one off, are we?" asks Toby, her hair again filling the hatchway.

"Thought I'd meditate a while," I reply, with my hands linked across my chest.

"Dennis called down for a short jib. Didn't you hear him?"

"I heard him all right," I say, sitting up. "Short jib heading your way."

"Too late. I need you to get a gennaker ready."

"Righto!" I answer, pulling myself to my feet.

"You'll have to move a lot faster come race time."

"Will I?" I ask, stretching and cracking my sore back.

"If you want to sail *Hard Charger*, yeah!" commands Toby.

"You'll get your gennaker, now get the hell out of my sewer!" Toby disappears from the hatch to shout orders at Dennis.

Later that night, I lay battered and bruised atop a lumpy mattress inside my cheap hotel room. It had been a trying practice race and my body ached in places I'd long forgotten. Pressing a cold, wet cloth on my throbbing forehead, I figured I blew it, but grateful for the experience. Another day of restful bliss within this glorified crack den, then I'd be back on the road and hitching for home. My only regret is the girl. She barely said "boo" to me except to yell down the hatch whenever I sent up a backwards sail. After docking, skipper and crew went on to dinner, leaving me behind folding and stowing wet sailcloth, and I was topside when Toby finally stepped off the boat without a backwards glance in my direction.

Lying on the lumpy mattress, the more I think of her, the more upset I get, and I am about to curse her name when the door to my hotel room bursts open. Much to my chagrin, Toby walks in carrying a bucket of seaweed that she proceeds to dump over my head.

"I christen thee Sewer Man! Crew took a vote. You made it."

"Now where am I supposed to sleep?" I ask, pulling strands of wet seaweed from my head and shoulders.

"Not in this shithole, that's for sure," replies Toby. "A tight crew eats, sleeps, and shits together. You're moving in with us."

"With you?" I ask, raising my eyebrows while spitting out wet sand.

"No," says Toby, skirting the subject. "You'll bunk with Dennis. Pack your gear. I'll wait outside."

"No need. Gear's packed. Let's roll."

"I knew there was a reason I liked you," says Toby, playfully batting her eyelashes.

I am given a basement room in the "Big House" befitting my new stature and not much else, not even a bed. I don't remember falling asleep that night or if I slept at all. I do remember waking early the next morn and finding Toby naked, but for my T-shirt brushing her teeth over a large ceramic bowl.

"We've got to get you a proper mattress down here. My back's killing me," says Toby, arching her back and spitting out a mouthful of bluish toothpaste.

"Was it…fun?…Did we…"

"Listening to you snore? Best night eva'!"

"Where's Dennis?"

"I moved him in with Billy." Smiling wolfishly, I unzip my sleeping bag and motion for Toby, but she spits again and shakes her head.

"No time," she says, looking at her dive watch. "There's breakfast, the three-mile run, then we go to the boat."

"What are we, the Marines?"

"Something like that," she replies, tossing me my wet toothbrush.

We practice basic seamanship all week, with Toby leading the three-mile beach run each morning before going on to the boat, first swabbing the deck and righting the sails, then rehanging all the lines and retying the cleats, only tighter. Instruments are checked and rechecked; wind, weather, and wave heights are forecast. Even the temperature of the water was called for to see if we'd be running fast and light or slow and heavy that day. It was all a bit technical for someone who's always relied on the pull of mainsheet and vibration of tiller in hand. I go about my business as best as I know how, repacking the various sail packages more to my liking while trying to catch glimpses of Toby leaping crosswise over the hatch.

On this day, the race we are competing isn't practice, it's for real and going up against Dennis Conner's *Stars and Stripes,* no less. Leading an elite group of sailors, each a knowledgeable skipper in their own right, Conner was attempting his third quest to represent America in her defense of the Cup. Standing between Conner and his Cup quest is a ragtag crew of forget-me-nots with me chief amongst them. I liked our chances and wouldn't have wanted it any other way.

We pushed off the dock at 7 AM sharp and sang our way out to the course. Now, this was to be a serious contest, no start overs and no substitutions. If your mains'l tears after the starting horn sounds, it will be like you were never in the race. You'll be out. Same goes for skipper and crew. If anybody goes overboard, they better hope a spectator boat picks them up because nobody's slowing down. I remain in the pit, acting the true sewer man, lining up the halyards for their trips up the mast. I make sure I keep my knees bent and my hands out, having learned my lesson well. I haven't seen a solitary crew member since we reached the course, but I feel that I am where I should be, belowdecks, doing the unglamorous yet challenging grunt work while going mostly ignored.

Hard Charger measures seventy-five feet from transom to prow, with her belowdecks measuring fifty-six feet, meaning that when Dennis or Toby calls down for sail change, I usually have some running to do. Ensconced within the hull, I can sense the pull of the boat, whether she's tacking to port or to starboard, running in heavy weather, or skimming the surface and running light. Pressing my cheek against the sunken mast, I can sense which direction the wind is blowing, so most times, I'll have the right sail package pulled and hooked before the call comes down.

"How's it going?" asks Toby, leaning over the hatch.

"You tell me."

"We're still in it, so we might as well win it."

"Let's win it then. What do you need from me?"

"Nothing. You're doing great. I just wanted to look at you."

"Back at ya', Sweet Knees."

"Sweet knees?"

"That's all I see of you lately."

"Is that so bad?"

"Nope."

"Not to worry, Cal. You'll be seeing a lot of me." And with that, Toby extracts herself from the hatch to shout orders at the crew. I stay focused in the pit, bouncing on the balls of my feet like a prizefighter in his corner.

Hard Charger heels sharply to starboard. I take out a fresh jib and clip it to the halyard. When the call comes down, the jib is already on its way topside. I guessed right. The race continues with me letting the boat dictate which sail to pull, and it isn't long before Dennis stops calling down for sail changes. I sense that we are running a good thirty to thirty-five knots before the wind, but whatever is going on abovedecks, if we are leading or trailing, I haven't a clue.

I poke my head above the hatch and take a quick peek topside. I spot Toby huddled with Dennis at the base of the mast, checking the electronic displays for wind speed, boat speed, heading, and the like. Glancing furtively over my right shoulder, I see Skipper Mack spinning the Big Wheel, nicely exposing *Charger*'s belly while sailing her as straight as a snapped plum line. Facing forward, I find the horizon devoid of sail, and it is only when I look aft do I see *Stars and Stripes* pursuing from three boat-lengths back.

Turning the winches like a gorilla pedaling a tricycle with its hands, Billy Boondocks calls down to me, "We've got trim sails and a leg to go. Nice job in the sewer, fisherman. Conner must think we have wind radar. Soon as I see the clew, I crank it straight up. This one's in the bag!" I cringe, wishing Boondocks hadn't said that. To taunt Her now is to taunt Fate. She could still come over the sides and swamp us, or She could stop the wind all together. She has that kind of power.

Skipper Mack shouts my name. I flinch, expecting a boat shoe to come flying my way. Instead, he motions me to the helm. I climb on deck and crab-crawl my way to the helm. Looking about me, the sea appears rough in spots with exaggerated cat's paws building to both port and to starboard as Mack keeps the Big Wheel in play, expertly sailing between the paws and grabbing just enough wind to keep us from having to tack.

"What's the good word, Skipper?"

"Conner's nipping at our heels. He's faster on the calms, but if this wind holds and I can keep her upright, I should be able to out-point the bastard. Beats slapping around Cockle Cove in a dory, don't it?"

"I've never gone so fast under sail. She truly is a *hard charger*."

"That she is, m'boy! That she is!"

I look up the mast. "Mains'l looks heavy. Want me to send up another?"

Skipper Mack shakes his head, saying, "Change it now and Conner will try to close. A race like this, you take what you get, but I might call down for a change on the final leg, so have one ready to go."

"Will do, Skipper!" I say before crab-crawling my way back to the pit. I try waving to Toby, but she's still head-to-head with Dennis, so I slip over the hatch like a wet seal. My home is the sewer and that's where I plan to stay until the finishing horn blows. I take out a dry mains'l and hook it to a halyard waiting for the call.

The sound inside the hull is like a jet engine. I cup my left hand over my left ear and rest my right hand on the mast. I feel it bending in the strong wind, but it's not the mast that concerns me as it is the mains'l, wet and heavy with sea salt. Made entirely of carbon fiber, the mast is specifically designed to withstand high winds, but a mains'l laden with seawater can still tear if weighted down, and the wind hits it right, even though it's cut from Kevlar-sheeted nylon.

The sunken mast twists in my hands as *Hard Charger* tacks hard to a weather heading and, I would imagine, into the final leg of the race. I pound on the ceiling, trying to get Billy's attention, but the thundering seas drown out all sound. A sharp ping travels down the mast, followed by *Hard Charger* abruptly righting herself and measurably slowing. Angry shouting erupts abovedecks. I pop my head up in time to see the split mains'l carry down the mast and crash into the sea. Toby and crew race to the foredeck, where the giant sail has wrapped itself around the bowsprit. Climbing from the pit, I kneel next to Billy, who's stayed his post at the base of the mast. Tapping him on his beefy shoulder, I say, "I've got a new main hooked and ready." Billy shakes his head and points up the mast.

"No good, fisherman. Point clew's jammed at the swivel shackle. We're fried, dyed, and laid to the side."

"Can you get me up there?"

"That's Toby's job."

"Toby's busy. Can you get me up there or what?" Looking across the foredeck, to where Toby and crew struggle with the entangled sail, Billy turns to me, grinning, "Shoot the pole, fisherman! Better hold on 'cause I'm gonna get you up there in a hurry!"

Wrapping the spare halyard around my right forearm, I give Billy a thumbs-up. He begins cranking the stainless-steel winches like he's riding in the Tour de France heading into the Pyrenees. Feeling that my arm is about to be pulled from its socket, I lift from the deck and rocket up the mast at an accelerated rate. I signal down to Billy to drop me off at the upper spreaders, which he does.

Stepping onto the thin, T-shaped spreaders, I let go of the halyard and hug the mast. Pitching back and forth like I'm riding a pendulum, which in a way I am, I look forward and see that the waves have become taller and are now breaking across the bow, sending up great plumes of sea spray. I look down at the helm, where Skipper Mack spins the Big Wheel, struggling to put *Hard Charger* into the wind while Toby and crew gather the torn main and drag it from the sea. Looking aft, I see *Stars and Stripes* gaining on our port while *Hard Charger* sits befuddled in the water, basically at a dead stop.

I look up the mast to where the point clew is jammed below the masthead. Slipping my slime knife from behind my belt, I clamp it between my teeth and shimmy my way up the mast, pirate style. *Hard Charger* dips and rises with the swells, her every motion more exaggerated the higher I climb. Reaching the brass-capped masthead 110 feet above the deck, I take the slim knife from my teeth with the tension of my slippery thighs the only impediment from a long way down. I cut the torn clew from the swivel shackle and toss it seaward. Looking down the mast, I see Billy cranking the coffee grinder with Toby pounding on his back, yelling, "Go! Go! Go!"

A fresh mains'l shoots up the mast at a frightening speed, nearly breaking my hand when I reach down and grab it. "Damn, that hurt!" I shout to no one. Rubbing my sore hand, I hastily clip the new clew to the swivel shackle while the crew threads the giant sail along the twenty-foot boom. I am about to begin my descent when a buffeting wind fills the sail that sends sailor and mast plummeting toward the angry sea. I hold on at the masthead as *Hard Charger* heels on her beam-ends at an obscene angle. The wind continues to howl, pushing the mast further into the surf until I am dipped chest-high in the frigid Pacific, only to rise again with the bleached soles of my bare feet now running over the tops of the cresting waves.

Fearing another watery plunge, I pull myself up and lay laterally along the mast. Battered by the waves, I lose my grip and plunge toward the sea. Before hitting the water, I grab hold of the port stay wire as the mast begins to lift from the sea, running afoul of Conner's *Stars and Stripes* transom, with skipper and crew running away from my exposed backside.

The buffeting wind lags and the mast rises anew. Holding on to the stay wire, I swing my legs like a gymnast and let go. Tumbling through the air, I land on my back and carry down the sail like it's a waterslide. Nearing the bottom, my rear end bumps off the boom, causing my body to take flight toward the watery wrath, but for the good graces of Skipper Mack's outthrusted forearm. Taking me by my flying hips, Mack slings me on deck, where Billy Boondocks, of all people, catches me and places me on deck like he's putting down a vase from the Ming Dynasty. Toby takes over at the helm and in no time, she regains our position, but it's too late as *Stars and Stripes* cuts across our bow and deflates our sails. Realizing that I just lost the race, I scuttle across the deck and drop into the sewer. I stay there, not wanting to resurface and chance being clapped in irons and perhaps even keelhauled. If that happens, I'll welcome the punishment. I screwed up. I should have stayed in the pit. What was I thinking?

I busy myself by folding and stowing wet sailcloth. I feel the boat slowly gaining way. I go to the hatch and look up and see nothing but blue sky above and not Toby with her dirty blond tendrils dripping into the pit. She's given up on me, and why wouldn't she? I blew it. Surprisingly, I don't hear any chatter or screaming abovedecks. Resigned to my fate, I climb from the sewer, ready to take whatever verbal or physical drubbing I've earned. Crawling onto the deck, where Skipper Mack and crew circle me, I cringe slightly, only instead of being keelhauled, I am given a standing ovation.

"Damnedest bit of sail-work I've ever seen!" shouts Skipper Mack, slapping me on the back with his meaty mitt.

"Stunt you pulled was worth the price of admission! Way to go, fisherman!" brays Billy Boondocks. "Hope the camera boys caught it!"

"But we lost," I argue back. "And I'm the cause of it."

"What ya' did, my boy, was give *Hard Charger* a chance," says Skipper Mack. "I should have listened to ya' about the main. Either way, Conner would have won. He's too good a skipper and his boat's just too damn fast. He can keep the Cup and I'll keep the expression you about wiped from his face with your wet britches!"

The rest of the crew chuckle as they walk past me, shaking my hand and clapping me on the shoulder before returning to the business of sailing the boat. I walk over to Toby, who's held her post at the helm, spinning the Big Wheel. "Let's have it," I say. "At least you'll give it to me straight."

"Never do that again," she says, without looking at me, as crew and captain go about their business, pretending not to listen.

"You were busy and there wasn't time to argue. What can I say? I messed up."

"Damn right you messed up," admonishes Toby, continuing not to look at me.

"Won't happen again, obviously."

"Going up the mast without a safety harness? Are you out of your mind?" she asks in a cracked voice. Looking at me now, she continues, "You could have broken your neck, and no race is worth that."

"I'll make it up to you."

"Got that right — when we sail in, you're going to take me to dinner. Someplace nice with white tablecloths and heavy silverware and I'm going to order whatever I want, and so will you. We're going to drink expensive French wine, and you're going to pay for it and leave a big tip."

"For your information, *First Mate*," I reply defensively, "I always leave a big tip, and as far as taking you to dinner, that's what I was planning on doing anyway. Until now."

"Don't give up, son!" shouts Skipper Mack from the bow. "You've got her on the ropes! Keep punching!"

"She's hardheaded, this daughter of yours!" I shout back.

"Is there any other kind?" asks Skipper Mack. "And she's purdy to boot, but she's getting a little yella' 'round the gills and she wants herself a man and that man is you. Whether ya' like it or not."

"Can we not have this conversation in front of the crew?" asks Toby, continuing to sail the boat.

"Like we don't already know," comments Billy, smiling while waving Toby off.

"So, are you going to kiss her or what?" asks Dennis.

"Ah, nuts!" I say. Walking around the Big Wheel, I take Toby in my arms.

"What makes you think I want to kiss you after all that talk?"

"Because I want to kiss you."

Holding Toby by her shoulders, I easily lift her off her feet and into the air, then bring her close and kiss her tenderly on the mouth. She tries to resist at first but soon gives up and kisses me back, only much harder, to the delight of her cheering father and crew. Toby holds my face in her hands and looks me in the eyes.

"What you did was pretty amazing. Dangerous, but amazing."

"Sometimes you've just got to improvise," I reply.

"Will you…improvise…on me?" she asks, flashing her long lashes at me.

"Gladly," I answer and kiss Toby a second time. That's when Skipper Mack hip-bumps Toby from the helm and takes the wheel, grinning like the Cheshire Cat.

I rise and fall with the swells remembering the warmth of that day. I want to return to it, to bask again in the California sunshine. But I can't. There is only the present and the morrow if I am allowed to see tomorrow. "Every man's choices are his own, so own them," my father was fond of saying. I believe that I have owned them, only that was then and this is now. It's time I got up and got after it. I never wanted to be rich, not really. What's the point? You're still staring at the same walls, and so what if they're gilded?

A working farm comes to mind, as it always does when I'm feeling low, but farming would be the same as fishing: hard on the back and intellectually boring. I want something different for my life, something I can put my name to. An idea begins to take form in my foggy brain. In no way is it a novel idea, and it's one that I've considered from time to time, but now the time seems right. With the land's back taxes paid off, I feel it's time that I make a stand. In the not-too-distant past, I wanted to break away and travel the world, but now I feel I've traveled enough and it is here, with Toby, that I want to be.

I see myself turning the land into a park of sorts. A park without all the rules normally associated with parks. A park with no roads, only trails. Campers will have to hike into their rustic campsites and hike out, letting birdsong and not car horns play with their senses. I'll fix up the house and turn it into an inn that caters to outdoorsmen and women, along with writers, artisans, musicians, poets, and professors and such. A hostel if you will, and not one for the Richie Riches of the world. They've got the Chatham Bar Inn, after all. Hippies will be welcome along with the recluses amongst us, but on a pay-to-play basis. The land has always been a refugee outpost, so I might as well make it legit.

I'm in charge. This is my show, and what a show it will be! I'll turn our Grand Hall/Valhalla into an elegant dining room, serving our guests breakfast, lunch, and dinner. I'll have to remodel the kitchen into a commercial kitchen and get the beehive ovens working again. A few more trips at sea should do it, and I'll have Gramp tend to the saloon that I always envisioned in our front parlor. Why wouldn't he want the job when he can drink for free here rather than spend his money at the Chatham Squire, under my watchful gaze, of course. He'll still have his Chart Room off limits, only to those he doesn't invite inside, although I'm sure he'll let anyone in who asks as long as he can spin his tales of yore.

Once I get the house cleared out and cleaned up, I'll empty the barn and turn it into a nautical museum that Gramp can run, taking our guests on tours while they listen to him explain his nautical waste heap going back two hundred years or more. After that, I'll build a realistic general store and stock it with the best foodstuffs, using only products made by local Cape vendors like me, along with fishing poles, bait, and gear that actually work, not like the other crap where you're liable to spend your whole day fishing for a minnow.

I envision a bandstand featuring local bands, only bigger and better than the one at Gould Park. Might take a while, but once I get back and stay focused, I'll get it done, hopefully with the help of Toby, if she takes me back, only this time when I meet her on the docks in Woods Hole in a couple of weeks, I'll have a real ring to give her and not a "remembrance ring."

After getting that done and settled, I'll buy a charter boat and take those who pay me into the Realm and do some real sportfishing. Who better to charter out to the Grounds with than an actual born and bred "bogger," and not some summer resident with a bigger boat and nowhere to go, pretending to be a real skipper while not knowing what bait to use. As Monomoy recedes behind the stern, I am reminded that I'll have to find another route to the fishing grounds rather than using the bay where I'd have to pass the decommissioned light station twice a day, which I don't think I could handle, at least not right now.

ISLE OF NANOHO

I am joyful for the first time in a long time. No longer will I pine for the dead. There is only the living from here on. I am about to tack for shore and sail for home when the wind suddenly ceases, and "King Maushop's smoke" rolls in. My visibility goes from fifty yards to twenty, to ten, blanketing *Sea Gypsy* like a shroud. Time appears at a standstill as I take the shortened oar from the cuddy and begin paddling, not knowing if I am gaining or losing way. With the boom allayed to the mast, the mainsheet goes slack in my hand. I reach over the side and find that the sea itself is at a dead calm and unmoving.

Dipping into my seabag, I take out my handheld foghorn that I always have on board for times like this. Having no running lights, *Sea Gypsy* is rife for ramming. Being this far out is most dangerous because there could be anything steaming about: cruise ship, trawler, oil tanker, etc. The "smoke" begins to clear in spots, letting in rays of setting sunlight, and I soon find myself within an ever-expanding expanse of sea, like I'm sailing within the eye of a hurricane.

I put away the foghorn and take up the spyglass, focusing its crosshairs on a speck of land in the distance just below the lifting mist. The Nantucket Galls, no doubt, though I don't believe I've drifted that far. A Fata Morgana more likely, or what us fisherfolk call April's Mirage — a phenomenon where the summer humidity reflects off the cold ocean water and makes far-off land appear well within reach. Another one of Her dirty tricks to tempt wayward sailors to their doom.

Within the windless, waveless sea, *Sea Gypsy* carries toward the rising landmass as if pulled by a cable. From this distance, I make out tall trees on the isle, so tall that it can't be the Galls, where there's hardly enough topsoil to raise a shrub. I judge the trees to be at least sixty feet in height and ramrod straight, like the original timber felled long ago, and not the stunted, woody plants that we having growing on the Cape and Islands today. If the spec is truly an island, I have no name for it and it has no right to be there.

Pushing the tiller to port, I attempt to come about, but I'm kept in-stays with no wind to tack my way out. I see black smoke corkscrewing upwards from a fiery pit on the beach. I bring the spyglass back up and focus its crosshairs on a group of men congregating around the fire. They are of a swarthy complexion, tall and muscular, cloaked in loincloths with their eyebrows painted whalebone white. I notice an older man standing behind the tree line. Looking to be well over seven feet tall, the elder has an athletic build like he could run down a five-point buck. His tribal status is further enhanced by a necklace of bone, shell, and eagle feather draped across his broad chest, and his face is the only face painted in what appears to be dried animal blood. I believe the elder to be the tribe's king or sachem, perhaps even King Maushop himself and not the legend. One thing's for sure, the annual Wampanoag Powwow this is not. This tribe lives on the island.

Floating closer to shore, I watch a handful of braves scoop a wooden spade full of burning embers from the fire and lay it down in the center of a recently felled tree. Using the sharpened edges of their stone tools, they begin hoeing out the smoldering wood and sculpting, I would imagine, a dugout canoe, or what Uncle Joseph calls a '*mishoon*.' I focus the spyglass further inland and spot a well-ordered village nestled within the tall trees, the bark and branch dwellings covered in seal, deer, and I believe, river otter pelts. I know from Uncle Joseph's talks that these 'wetus' are only temporary and can be moved at a moment's notice. Sweeping the lens further along, I come upon a courtyard of sorts, where women and children sit on embroidered mats stringing together strands of clam, bead, and other forms of wampum.

I am about to lower the spyglass when a small boy stands up and scampers from the courtyard. Running between the sachem's long legs, the boy points at my boat and shouts, "Pawana! Pawana! Pawana!," pawana meaning whale. Plucking their spears from the beach, the braves race into the surf.

I glance about me, looking for a fluke or a hump to rise in the still water, but I don't see any, not even the placid footprints a whale leaves behind when it sounds. The braves withdraw from the surf and return to their fire, admonishing the boy as they pass. The sachem, however, continues to look out over the open water. Gripping a tall lance collared in eagle feathers, he steps onto the beach as the boy runs up to him, tugging on his elongated fingers and pointing directly at me, again yelling, "Pawana! Pawana! Pawana!"

I pray for a breath of wind to get me out of there, but my prayer goes unanswered. Instead, I stand in the cockpit and carry the boom to port. My actions cause the brass jaws on the boom to rattle against the mast. The sachem draws back, having apparently heard it. Lifting the lance, he balances it on his right shoulder. Any momentary fear the sachem had vanishes as he steps boldly into the surf and launches the spear. Lifting high into the air with amazing speed and arch, the lance appears to overshoot *Sea Gypsy* before taking a sudden downward trajectory. I throw my body into the cuddy and cover my head with my arms. A loud "thwack!" emanates from above. I look out to see the lance shivering above me, its keen, obsidian head buried deep within the base of the mast.

I chance a quick peek over the gunwale and see the sachem standing befuddled in the surf. Bending at the waist, he reaches down and scoops up a handful of sea that he then splashes on his face, wiping away the dried animal blood. Walking further into the surf, he extends his right arm with his elongated fingers splayed out. I jump on

274

deck and run to the bow. Holding on to the mainstay, I walk onto the pulpit and lean out over the water to match the sachem's gesture. He doesn't appear to see me. Standing in the surf, he looks past my boat, still keeping his arm in the air with his fingers splayed, as *Gypsy*'s mains'l fills, and I am taken from the island on freshening winds.

TEMPEST

Gathering the loose line at my feet, I coil it and go about checking the cleats and bolts, then take whatever else I have strewn about and stow it high in the cuddy but leave the lance stuck in the mast as a touchstone to my sanity or insanity. It's a light, puffy wind filling the mains'l, though strong enough to finally carry me north. Sitting atop the stern, I see that Chatham and the other towns stacked along the spit are blanketed behind a cloud bank of thick fog, and I can barely make out our dueling weathervanes turning listlessly above the mist. Taking a port tack, I haul in and head for home, the now stiff onshore wind stretching the mains'l and helping me along.

With this fresh wind comes a renewed sense of urgency. I need to get to dry land, and I need to get there fast. I need to get off Her and away from Her tricks. I don't care where I beach *Gypsy*, as the beach is all equal distance from where I sail. I take up the coiled rope and dip back inside the cuddy to pull out a short spinnaker. Hopping on deck, I walk up to the bow and tie off on the bow chuck, then thread the rope through the spinnaker clews and run it up the mast in front of the mains'l. Taking the payout, I lash it to the pulpit and return to the stern, where I sit on the bench seat admiring my handiwork. The sail looks sloppy as hell until a misplaced wind hits and carries the spinnaker over the water. Wrapping the mainsheet around my left forearm, I stand atop the stern and ride *Sea Gypsy* as if she were a chariot swung low by the heavens.

Right then, a bald eagle of great size soars over the masthead clutching in its talons the severed head of a fawn, still in her spots. The fleeting image drops me to my knees. I can't take it anymore. I feel that I'm going insane, even as everything seems to be going my way. Or is it? I've witnessed most of what the sea has to offer, but never have I seen a sight so grotesque. Only I know it to come from Second Mother, another one of Her tricks to keep me on the water and within Her realm, retching up my guts. I consider dropping the sails and kneeling in the cockpit, letting the wind and the waves take me in, but I'm too close to ending this ongoing nightmare, so I stand in the cockpit and take hold of the tiller.

The skies have darkened further and the first fat raindrop lands on my forehead, then another. She's outflanked me yet again, only now I have the barrier beach within sight. I sail for it and after landing *Sea Gypsy* safely ashore, I'll secure her in the high dunes and walk home, not caring how far or how much rain falls. I won't melt. Only I won't be walking, I'll be running.

I sail full before the wind, with my impromptu spinnaker stretched to its fullest, pulling at the pulpit like a double marker hooked through the gills. I'm surprised that there are no rollers rolling in, and yet the onshore wind has definitely kicked up, and in my favor. Another curious thing is that there are no clouds sliding in front of the rising Blood Wolf Moon, and yet the fat raindrops continue to fall. I've never experienced this kind of weather before unless it was a slanting rain that can come from a system as far as three miles out or more. Only this rain isn't slanting, it's dropping straight down, regardless of the wind, as if it were tears from heaven. And that's when it dawns on me, that I'm caught in a whirlpool and/or the beginnings of a waterspout, truly the worst of Her tricks.

A wall of roiling water encircles *Sea Gypsy*, spinning from east to west, and I sense Her many eyes seizing me up and judging my commitment. Enclosed within the fury, I yell up to the sky, "All I want is to wake up to the smell of bacon frying! Is that so much to ask? Stop judging me! I'm a murderer, just like you! There! I said it!"

A plume of sea spray breaks over the bow, followed by a flash of lightning that turns the sea to silver. Standing atop the stern, I kick the tiller to port and haul in the mainsheet. I look up at my wind-bent mast and realize that this time She's playing for keeps. Spinning round and round, *Sea Gypsy* joins with the whirlpool and is quickly sucked from the top-water. The mainsheet unravels from my forearm as I am lifted from my boat and set aswirl within the angry tempest. Spiraling downward, I am carried along the sandy bottom for what feels like an eternity. I try swimming out of the current, but I'm no match for Her furious strength. Clumps of seaweed brush against my body as I continue along the ever-deepening bottom, seemingly for miles. I relax and go with the wave in the event that it will eventually lose its momentum and release me. Only it does not, becoming a current of its own invention.

Another lightning flash strobes the water above and illuminates my surroundings. I drift over a sunken wreck sitting upright on the bottom. The ship looks familiar and as I float by, I see the words *Sea Pearl* painted slovenly along her port bow. Whatever light there is fades fast and turns the surrounding sea as black as the awful facts. And it is then that I see it, from a bird's-eye view, perhaps even that of the landless gull: *Sea Pearl* turning counterclockwise amid raging seas with her trailing net acting as an umbilical cord to strangle its infant host before pulling it under.

I am released by the current and left floating in an abysmal abyss as a glowing cloud of fluorescent plankton rises up from the depths, agitated by the storm, the tiny organisms streaming into and out of my nose, mouth, and throat. I take in water as I would take in breath and I feel that I am at last a true bonefish that I've always perceived myself to be, and it is only habit that propels me to the surface.

Afloat within the bioluminescence, I knock into a solid mass that causes my chin to sink into my chest. Pain reverberates throughout my body, and I sense that my neck is broken, but when I turn my head from side to side, I know that it's not. I spin around and see that it's a drowned fisherman I've struck. I take hold of the fisherman's rubberized bib overalls and stop my ascent, but the man's face eludes me, masked in a tangle of rust-colored topknot adrift in the water like the poisoned tendrils of a Portuguese man-o-war. I massage the fisherman's scalp seeking purchase, then, grabbing a fist full of topknot, I tilt back the man's head and it's as if I'm looking in a mirror. Neither mark nor blemish corrupts the image and I appear to be at peace for the first time in a long time.

A wave of deepest sorrow runs through my body. It's a sadness fueled by all the love in the world that goes unused. Love that's left unsaid, refused, ridiculed, and squandered. Love that's called everything else but its true name, which is LIFE. How can we be so dumb? How can we have taken this precious gift and not opened it? Why do we choose anything else but love? Perhaps I should ask myself that, only I might not want to hear my answer.

I am underwater and I am crying, not realizing that I am hugging the body, my body, adrift just below the surface. I don't want to let go. I want to stay with the body, help it along and get it aboard my boat where I can breathe the breath of life back into it. I take the fisherman by his collar and swim for the surface, and I am a mere half fathom from breaching the waterline when a dark shape rises from out of the depths and tugs at the body. And then there is blood, so much so that I have trouble seeing.

The fisherman bobs in my arms with bits of his ragged flesh and splintered bone drifting in the current. I feel another tug and when I look down, I see a reddening tide flowing from beneath the fisherman's legs, absent below the kneecaps. There is another tug and the fisherman is taken from me. "No!" I shout into the water whilst twisting around to watch the body, my body, plunge into the deep.

Somersaulting forward, I sink like a lead weight cast into a shallow pond. Extending my right arm, I take hold of the fisherman's outstretched hand and together we descend. Our progress to the bottom stops suddenly as the great hammerhead shows itself and begins to circle. It's the same one from earlier in the day, with my titanium-tipped spear still wedged within its bleeding gums. The shark continues circling, swimming closer and closer with each pass. I kick at the fish but to no effect. I try reaching for the shark's scythe-like tail and miss. Holding on to what's left of the drowned fisherman, I turn the body away and offer the shark my own flesh, which it does not take. Excited by all the blood in the water, the great hammerhead continues to circle, swimming faster and faster with each pass until I can't keep my eyes on it and let go of the fisherman.

An eruption occurs somewhere below, followed by a plume of disturbed water. Billions of tiny bubbles blur my vision. I sweep away the bubbles to see the blond dolphin rocketing past me and ramming its bottled nose into the hammerhead's exposed midsection, ejecting a bloody ball of meat, bone, and sinew from its mouth before spiraling off into the void.

Floating above the fray, I watch the dolphin try to nudge the body, my body, to the surface, but the fisherman turns onto his back instead, releasing a large amount of trapped gas from his bowels, then sinking toward the bottom, where sleek shadows glide in the blood-strewn depths. Amazingly, the dolphin stays with the fisherman, circling fiercely and chasing away the smaller sharks until there are too many, and it finally banks off and rockets into the gloom. I look down in ghastly horror as the body, my body, is torn apart in a flurry of quick attacks, disappearing into the murky depths bite by bite by bite.

INTO THE REALM

I break the surface gulping hot, oily air, so hot that it burns the back of my throat like I'm sucking on an exhaust pipe. I am afloat in thick, syrupy water with the humidity pressing against the sea like a giant rolling pin, flattening it. I look about the surrounding seascape that is devoid of any landmass. Neither are there any aircraft scraping across the sky. Nor are there boats steaming or sailing about but for my prized *Sea Gypsy* that I see sitting on the top-water like a fly caught on flypaper, miraculously upright after her backwards plunge into the whirlpool.

I swim to my boat, my arms and legs barely able to cleave through the sloppy seas that have the consistency of a can of Campbell's condensed soup. Nearing the bow, I reach for the pulpit and pull myself aboard, then step over the coaming rail and cross the cockpit, where I collapse on the bench seat at the stern. And it is there that I lie, squinting up at a bloodred sun shining down from above like a melting glob of flaming ore. By its position in the sky, time of year, and declination to the horizon, I should be well in sight of land, if not on top of it, and yet none exists, the sea a curving, dead-calm water-world of uninterrupted space.

Exhausted and dry-mouthed, I roll from the bench seat and into the cockpit, where I stretch out on the raised beams and hide in the cooling shadow of the mains'l, and it is only when I close my sun-puffy eyes that I sense the mains'l filling with a steady wind and propelling *Sea Gypsy* forward. I dream of her sailing across longitudes and latitudes, across time zones and timelines, across seas, oceans, lakes, rivers, glaciers, and straits without ever having to tack. I come awake for the briefest of moments and see the sky above bathed in colors resembling an artist's drop cloth, followed by uncharted star formations never before seen from our solar system dancing in the night sky, that and a waning, misshaped moon, only a moon much smaller than our own.

I come awake on the second day and there are trees taller than the tallest redwood, their lush boughs draped high above *Sea Gypsy*'s tell-tale windsock. I blink and the trees are no more, replaced by a raging-river coursing through a vast gorge lined by horizontal strata of multi-colored rock rising thousands of feet straight up. Blinking twice, and there are creatures of a variety as yet imagined trotting and swimming alongside *Sea Gypsy*. Though gigantic and possessing large, sharp teeth, I view these creatures as not necessarily terrifying but curious of me and my boat as I am of them.

I slip back into unconsciousness, and when I wake on the third day, there are persons of various tribes and stripes peering down at me from the gunwales: men, women, and children, their expressions ranging from sorrow to indifference to reserved judgment. Some are costumed in regal splendor and wearing heavy jewelry, while others are dressed in their fisherfolk fashions of their day, with still others having faces crusted in dirt and animal fat, appearing no more human but for the glint of intelligence in their eyes.

One by one, these lost kin of mine push *Sea Gypsy* onward as night turns to day and day becomes night. Weeks go by, then months, years. Decades become millennia and millennia turn into eons with eons morphing into epochs until time has no meaning and it is only the memory of time that I am left with.

Above me there are no stars, only deep planetary space and I am shivering. So cold are my surroundings that I feel my bones will crack. Icy snot forms over my nose and mouth, and I can hardly see out, the lashes of both eyelids smothered in a clinging frost, but it is the silence that affects me most, a silence so profound that it's deafening. My ears bleed from it.

What remains active is my mind, replaying each day of my short life in minute detail. Toby keeps me company on the better parts, and I want to stay with her, but it's not allowed. Then there's my father and our brief time together and for that, I am grateful, along with Gramp and his many teachings that continue to sound in my brain. I'm sorry that I had to leave him so vulnerable and alone. There just wasn't enough time and yet, as I look back, a thousand years can easily fit into a single day if used correctly.

That said, why was Gramp standing on our bluff today and why was he crying? If he was searching for his Flossy, he would have searched for her inside the house while mumbling to himself in her voice. Looking out across the bay and into the realm, he wasn't thinking of her, he was thinking of me. And Tiger, why would he abandon his cabin and take his dress uniform with him? He's all out of "fallen bros," at least that's what he told me the night I shipped out. He put on that dress uniform for me. Doing the math, on or around the day that *Sea Pearl* went to the bottom, it would have taken that many days in between July 4th for the Coast Guard to deem *Sea Pearl* "lost at sea" along with the crew manifest that must have included '*Yours Truly*'. Whatever tears were shed today were shed for me and me alone.

I am returned to the murder and to the emotions I felt: anger, betrayal, hate, but also kinship and a loss of love. I try recalling what it was Chumley was trying to say to me as I forced him under, only before I do the memory of a conversation I had with Junebug comes to the forefront of my dwindling mind. Growing up in the sandbox together, she and my father were like brother and sister, and it was Junebug who was at the docks the day he shipped out for the last time.

Harbormaster Jim Sherman was doing paperwork inside his Stage Harbor office the morning the *Debra Ann* was getting fitted and fueled for her trip to the Banks. Jim had his windows open, trying to catch a cross breeze in the sticky heat, when he heard Junebug and my father arguing on the gangplank.

"I watched Jack walking down the pier with his seabag slung over his shoulder, like he always does, only this time he had a woman following him. She was dressed kind of strange, like she was a fortune-teller or a belly dancer. Anyway, she caught up to Jack and they started arguing. She was telling him about a dream she had, a dream that had Jack inside his wheelhouse goin' over his charts when a ship steamed out'a the fog as 'high as the sky,' as she told it, and rammed his boat without warning. The woman pleaded with your dad to delay his trip, but Jack just smiled, saying to the woman, 'Watch over the boys,' then climbed aboard." Jim told me this one summer when I was working for him as a pier steward, shuttling skippers and their guests to their moored boats in the harbor. This was long after my father went missing, and I'm still not sure why he waited so long to tell me.

Having never paid much attention to Junebug's "visions," or the hereafter for that matter, I didn't know how to handle the information, and I still don't. Her dream seemed plausible enough. Happens all the time, which is why the job of being a commercial fisherman is so dangerous. "Heaved Under the Bow" is how we fisherfolk refer to it if indeed it happened that way. Not having an answer, I figured I'd go to the source, that source being Junebug.

Chumley was away at football camp, so I knew I'd be alone with Junebug, if she was home. Located at the end of a long and winding dirt road, the land wasn't so much unincorporated as it was uninhibited. To my knowledge the Wampanoag Nation has never claimed ownership and neither has the town. A no-man's-land is what it was like the town surveyors forgot to mark it on their grid. Approaching the house, I saw Junebug tending to her herb garden, and when I walked over, she turned and handed me a cold glass of lemonade like she knew I was coming.

"Here," says Junebug. "You must be thirsty after such a long walk."

"I am, thanks, Miss Repoza," I say, draining the glass. I don't ask for Chumley and she doesn't bring him up. Instead, she takes the empty glass from my hand and leads me into her garden, where I join her pulling up weeds. Tossing away fistfuls of the sandy roots, I confer with her about my conversation with the harbormaster. At first, she ignores me and goes about smudging her herbs with a smoldering bushel of sage. I am about to bring it up again when she finally speaks, only without looking at me.

"Jack was a good man. He was a friend to me and my Jonathan. While it is true that I have these visions you speak of, they are also followed by headaches that are so painful that I sometimes forget the vision. When Jack went missing, I was surprised and hurt like everyone else, and if I was at the pier the day he shipped out, I do not remember."

"How can you not remember?" I press.

"There are times, Caleb, that when I dream, I am actually sleep-walking, only not the kind of sleepwalking you see in the movies or on TV where a person goes around with their hands held out and their eyes closed, bumping into chairs. No. It is not like that at all. My grandmother had a different name for this. She called what I do 'Tsalagi,' meaning 'people who walk inside caves.' These caves are caves of the mind and they show scenes on their walls that may or may never happen. I could be driving Jonathan to school and be sleepwalking at the same time. Part of me is driving the car, using my blinkers and stopping at red lights, while another part of me is inside a cave. There are many caves, and it is easy to get lost. If I was at the pier that day, I must have been inside a cave because I do not remember. Sometimes not remembering is best."

"Couldn't you try to remember?" I ask.

Junebug shakes her head. "I will speak of this no further. If I had more to tell, I would, but I made a solemn promise to your father and I plan to keep it. I'll only say this about Jack: he's in a good place and he continues to watch over us, only he cannot prevent our troubles or solve our problems, though he would like to."

"Is he…disappointed in me?" I ask, with my head down.

"Never! Jack is proud of all of us, and he continues to be! And he is especially proud of you and my Jonathan! Now go home, Caleb, and don't forget to bring a bushel of your delicious strawberries the next time you visit." And with that, I was ushered from her herb garden with a playful kick to my backside.

I try again to make out what it was Chumley was trying to tell me on that fateful day, but however hard I concentrate, his pleas go unheard like an unplugged radio. He wasn't so much begging as he was trying to tell me something, something he thought was important for me to hear. Using my only advantage, which is time, I look back at his barely visible face under the hooded sweatshirt. Focusing on his working jaw, I take note of the placement and curvature of his lips and tongue that were visible that day. With millennia's repeating, the movements of his mouth begin to give me clues as to each word and their importance, our one-sided conversation repeating within my frozen brain as if on a continuous loop.

"...round house...why I'm...to tell...old girl...left it...don't worry...I'll blame...drifter...what are you doing?...Stop!... my mom and your...had an affair...Can't breathe!...Don't, Cal!...your dad is...I'm your brother!"

The rest of Chumley's confession, if it was a confession, I can't make out. Either he had taken in water, or I had pulled his hood over his head, but I've enough on my plate to take a bite. His argument that he was there that day to tell me about the witch's house being ours was his first mistake. He was there for one reason and one reason only, to bust me and get his job back. And his inference that he is or was my half-brother is comical. We couldn't have looked more different, and yet, when I think harder on it, he is or was a full year younger than me, and when my mother passed, days after giving birth to me, my father was so despondent that he wouldn't leave the house, according to Gramp. And so, to keep up with the bills, it was my grandfather who put on his sou'wester and shipped out on a tanker as a merchant marine.

He left his Flossy behind to look after my father and me, even putting me in the bed with her at night, fearful that I might turn onto my stomach and die in the crib. Of course, I don't remember any of this, only Gramp's retelling of it. And I was too young to recall if my father went out during this time, but if he did go out, it wouldn't have been to the Squire. It's likely enough that he would have visited Junebug. After all, they grew up together and were practically brother and sister. The word "practically" catches in my throat. Nobody is *practically* anything. You either *are*, or you're *not*, and they weren't. How much comforting Junebug gave my father and where it might have led, I'll never know because he's dead and Chumley's dead and, unless I'm dreaming all this, which I sincerely hope that I am, I'm dead also.

Gramp always said that Claire Burlingame was our ace in the hole, but I never knew what he meant by it and he never told me. Why all the secrets? I know why, to keep me in stays, so I wouldn't leave him. The old girl willing her house to our family would guarantee its upkeep for generations while our house fell into disrepair year after year. What spell had that crazy old hag cast over my family? Maybe she was a witch. If true, the hard decisions I've had to make over the years have been for naught. All of them doomed from their very point of conception. I failed to see the puppet master's strings that I should have cut long ago and taken the reins, only I didn't, and now I'm afloat in a boat heading for some eternal waterfall.

My heart hardens with this new knowledge of my misbegotten destiny, but in this endless, endless night, it is my own self-loathing that consumes me. I try to cry for my one-time friend, for my half brother, if he was my half brother, and if I am crying, I can't feel the tears as my cheeks are frozen. Remorse is what I'm feeling. Not for my dead friend, but for a life lost defending a patch of land that never belonged to anyone but to the earth itself. We are all ants building our castles in the sand only to watch the tide rush in and wash it all away. I remain stuck to the floorboards, shaking uncontrollably, with the starless night spinning above me like a wet, black pearl, endlessly, endlessly spinning.

My body aches and my joints are stiff as I come awake on what must be the seventh day. I find that my eyelids are heavy with frost and I have to use my fingers to force them open. Once I do, I see that the sun has returned. Not the glob of molten iron like before, but the natural sun using all of its natural warmth to unfreeze my frozen bones and melt the glacier that has become my topknot. Clearing away icicles dripping from my nose and mouth, I take a first, straining breath and find the air to be both salty and sweet with the sky above devoid of any cloud cover and the daytime temperature warm yet somewhat chilled.

I pull myself up by way of the mast and stand in the cockpit, stretching my tired and knotted torso. I twist my hips cracking the sorry bones in my back while shaking out my stiff joints. I look to the bow and see that I am again within the protective arm of the barrier beach, wondering how many times I made it this far and how many times I failed. Looking up the mast, I sight a familiar friend riding one-footed on the masthead. The landless gull has returned to its post and barks heartily down at me. I wave up at the big bird, careful to stay just south of its ruffled tail feathers. I'm not sure what the gull thinks of me, and I'm not about to ask it any questions. I'm just happy to see it.

Slapping the boom to port, I regain position at the stern and take the tiller in hand. Old-time band music drifts across the bay on fading winds as I sail for home and I am about to take a starboard tack when fireworks ignite in the daytime sky, exploding in multicolored, iridescent starbursts. I look to the gull, who barely takes notice of the twinkling embers as they flare and sputter about *Sea Gypsy*.

I was right, today is, without doubt, the Fourth of July, only I do not know what year it is or if I am truly awake. But I know this, my senses have never felt more acute. Coming about, I tack past Watch Hill, where a conspiracy of hunchbacked ravens caws at me from the wind-stunted pines. I caw back and it is then that I see her, Claire Burlingame, the Salem Witch, standing within the frame of one of her checkerboard windows staring aimlessly over the barrier beach under a shock of white hair. I've come too far to question what I'm seeing, so I wave up at the old hag and go about the business of sailing my boat. She doesn't wave back.

Passing the Tern Island Wildlife Sanctuary, fully flowered and without any cabins or telephone poles, I notice a band of Monomoyic Indian children fishing for minnows along the shoreline. "Pooneam! Netop kuwonukumish!" I shout, meaning, "Hello! I greet you in friendship!" though I haven't a clue how I know these words and their meaning. The children look at me in silence as I sail pass. "Wunnish!" I yell. "Go in peace!" and sail onward, ducking from rocks thrown at me by the children. "Kids will be kids," I mumble to myself and sail on.

Tacking and jibbing around Minister's Point, it appears that half the town has turned out on the descending banks to watch me sail by. How nice of them. Only they're not regular townspeople per se, but Methodists or "Baby Dunkers" — the women trailing long, black dresses cloaked in black bonnets with beaded veils, and the men wearing stovepipe hats and dressed in their best bibs and tuckers.

It's a curious gathering, to be sure, and one that I do not plan to attend, so I sail on. Watching the boat pass, the congregation wades into the water waving their nicked and tattered King James Bibles over their bowed heads while chanting in Latin, "Paster noster, qui es in caelis, sanctifcetur nomen tuum!" I place my hands over my ears to blot out the words for fear that I might know them, and I do. The Lord's Prayer. They've come to pray for me and chance drowning. "No thanks!" is what I say to them and haul in.

Tacking away from the Point, I set the bow chuck over the Horse Shore and sail for it. I am running along at a good clip when I pass what look to be recently erected oyster shanties set up on the out-washed plain, their stooped inhabitants weighted down in leather waders, pitching and hauling their newly woven nets against the incoming tide. I wave at them, but the oystermen are too busy working to lift their heads. Good for them!

Round Cove appears on my port. I point the bow into the wind and take up Gramp's spyglass, focusing its crosshairs on Community Beach, where I scan the sands for signs of life. The lens falls on a lanky teenage girl sitting at the tip of the jetty breakwater, reading a book and smoking a cigarette. The girl looks vaguely familiar. Watching me sail by, she closes her book and waves. It dawns on me that the girl I am looking at is Jen, only not the sexy siren of my dreams. More the pretty yet somewhat awkward teen she was the night she was taken from the world. I hop on deck and point to the bluff. Nodding, Jen rises, flicks her cigarette into the surf, and walks the length of the jetty, where a large white dog awaits her. Only it's not a dog, it's a wolf, a white wolf, perhaps the same white wolf I passed while hitching in Alaska, now keeping Jen company while she strolls the shimmering shores of Elysium.

I slap the boom to starboard and round the bluish dune at the point, and our decayed wharf comes into view, only no longer decayed. Tied off on its sturdy pilings is none other than my father's boat, the *Debra Ann*, afloat alongside a fully rigged whaling ship, with other vessels moored further offshore: a twin-masted schooner lying abeam a pirate flagship masquerading as a Danish merchant, but nowhere do I see a Viking longboat. I must have guessed wrong on that one. No matter, as it's good to be home if this is my home. I choose not to think too much on the subject and go with the flow.

Entering our small harbor under luffing sails, I pass beneath the arching bluff standing defiant and resilient against the wind and the waves as it always has since times eternal, with the house proper looming behind it, erect and noble as it was first raised. Off to my port, I catch sight of a wisp of a woman dressed in all white hurrying down the winding trail leading to our harbor beach. Hidden behind the laurel, the woman's delicate features remain a mystery to me but for her eyes that are cone-shaped, bright blue, and striking as my own.

My mother steps onto the wharf where stands my father, shaking a balled fist at me and fighting back a smile. I am glad to see him, glad to see them both, and yet I hold back from waving, believing that somehow the Timekeeper will pull the rug out from under my feet. Instead, I smile warmly as I edge ever closer to the wharf while keeping my wits about me.

Picking up a berthing line coiled at his feet, my father whips the heavy rope above his head and lets fly. I go to the bow and step out onto the pulpit. Holding on to the mainstay, I lean over the water and reach for the rope and miss. I watch the rope splash behind the stern and notice my father scowling as he reels in the line hand over fist. As he does this, the ship's bell tolls from atop the highest knoll and I know that my time is running out.

I contemplate diving over the side and swimming to shore, but for the hammer-shaped shadow circling below, and I don't want to go through that again. I look about the harbor for a bent dorsal fin and don't see one, the blond dolphin being part and parcel of another dimension, a dimension that lives and not one filled with the already dead and dying. A police siren wails in the distance. I ignore it. Right then the landless gull lifts from the masthead and soars again over the Eastham dunes and back out to sea.

I look to the mains'l and watch it fill with a buffeting, offshore wind, a wind that I know I can't defeat. My only chance is to grab the rope, so I stay my post and wait for my father. Whipping the now-wet rope above his head, he lets fly for a second time. It soars over the water in a continuous arch with the line uncoiling at his feet. I watch my mother raise her hands to cover her eyes as I drop into the cockpit and run to the stern. "Lessons learned are always the hardest," I hear Gramp say from somewhere inside my brain. Leaning over the barn door rudder, I stretch out my right arm with my fingers splayed, forever and ever grasping at the separating air, then…from out of a deep blue haze of time, I come awake on a patch of lumpy crabgrass, looking up at the worn tread of a tractor tire swaying above me like a clock weight.

Made in the USA
Middletown, DE
06 September 2022